by
KB Shaw

Cover Artist: Dug Nation

ISBN—978-0-692-96162-9

Library of Congress Control Number: 2017915416

Published by
iPulpFiction.com
Chandler AZ, USA

Thanks

When I was in the theater, I was taught that a good play isn't written—it's rewritten. That's certainly true of novels as well. I have found that a trusted group of readers is helpful in the process of rewrites. First and foremost among my group is Mary Moore, my editor and partner. Without her this book would not be what it is.

I also want to thank my daughter Christen Shaw-Morris, Harry, Janice, and Jill Shaw, Hugh and Nancy Starkey, and Raven Grimaldi for their insightful feedback.

PART ONE
THE
HISTORIAN'S
TALE

"We pledge our lives to the Service of Today
and the Building of Tomorrow."
—*The Code*

Terms

annum: an archaic way of measuring a person's age; 12 consecutive months (two thirds of a cycle)

cycle: the eighteen-month solar cycle from HighConjunction to High-Conjunction

HighConjunction: 1) the period when Neworld's two suns are perfectly aligned with SolMinor eclipsing SolMajor; the period is marked by crippling snowfalls; 2) the 10-sol celebration that occurs during this period, when families gather, seclude themselves indoors, feast, and exchange gifts, concluding with bonfires ignited by the re-emerging families

HighNoon: the time of day when SolMajor is at its zenith

kon: the indestructible spirit that inhabits all living beings

LowNoon: the time of day when SolMinor is at its zenith

miss: a term of direct address for a female who has borne a child for a male contract

missus: a term of direct address for a female with a contracted child

missy: a term of direct address for a female without children

RedNights: the middle of summer when SolMinor dominates the night sky

skreel: any number of small creatures, both insect and animal

sol: the time period from HighNoon to HighNoon

SolMajor: Neworld's larger, brighter, more distant sun; short form—SolMaj

SolMinor: Neworld's smaller, dimmer, nearer sun; short form—SolMin.

Dangerous

The treason of these papers is not just in the
actions they document, but in their very existence.

1.1.1

IT BEGAN with the spy in the tree.

It was a clear, crisp dawn in early spring. I was cleaning Headmaster Hunninger's office—a large, wood-paneled room on the second floor of the Mount, a boy's school near Agricitta. The air was stale and filled with drifting motes of dust, so I decided to open the balcony doors to let in a fresh breeze. The headmaster's balcony looked westward over the Mount's courtyard. SolMinor had been up for almost two hours and SolMajor was just rising. The giant chestnut tree that grew outside the courtyard's western wall was silhouetted against the indigo-hued sky. As I opened the doors I caught some movement among the black jumble of still-sparse leaves. It could have been nothing... or an animal... or a person. I couldn't be certain, but I suspected it was a spy.

To stop and stare would only let the spy know I saw him. So I looked but a moment, then went about my duties. I only needed a moment because of my secret talent.

Actually, I have two talents. The first is a knack for remembering everything I've seen or heard since my tenth cycle, when I was in my fifteenth annum. I kept this talent secret. Only the head of staff, Missy Howard, knew of my second talent—my ability to draw. Not only can I visualize any moment in my life from the last two cycles, I can also sketch every detail of that moment. I hoped these talents would be the key to my escape from the tedium of the Mount.

So, as I cleaned the office, I stole glances at the tree with the intention of doing some drawings. If my plans worked out, I would expose the spy in the tree.

Now I have nothing against spies. Young men like me, young men without families, are sometimes bought by one powerful franchise or guild family or another, and placed on a rival's house staff to spy. I was unsure of this spy's purpose, but the first sons from many franchise families boarded and studied at the Mount. So the spy in the tree was probably employed by a rival franchise school, one of the guilds, or a guild school—perhaps even the Council.

In fact, I often thought about becoming a guild spy myself. As a servant, I was as invisible to the students and most of the faculty as the spy in the tree. With my hidden talents and my access to all these privileged prigs, I could make a small fortune selling what I knew of their secrets, personal fears, and private perversions. Or maybe I could spy for a franchise family at a guild school. However, for all my bluster and bravado, my life at the Mount was all I knew and, although I desired change, I was afraid of leaving.

When I finished cleaning, I took one last look at the tree as I closed the balcony doors.

1.1.2

I WAS... I am... a no-contract foundling. In Neworld, reproductive contracts are handed down from parent to child. Each citizen is allowed to reproduce him- or herself. Apparently both of my parents had already used their contracts or, perhaps, I was outright abandoned. Either way, I didn't inherit a contract and I wasn't a citizen—I was a ward of the state.

The Council placed me at the Mount to be raised from infancy through my coming of age. Until my 18th annum, I would be in service to, and property of, the Mount. Except for a few day-trips to nearby Agricitta, I have lived my entire life within sight of the Mount's walls.

The Code requires that all males be "stemmed" in their tenth cycle, when they reached fifteen annums. Stemming can be reversed when a man enters a reproductive contract—a man with citizenship, that is.

Curiously, my stemming was the first event in my life that I remember in clear and precise detail. It seemed unnecessary since my contact with females was limited to some older women on the house staff. My visits to Agricitta were so supervised that I barely had a moment to look at the town girls.

At the time of the events in these papers, I was in my seventeenth annum. Two weeks after High Conjunction I'd be eighteen and a free man. A man with no rights, to be sure—but free, with at least the possibility of becoming a citizen and having the right to earn or buy a reproductive contract.

. . .

I EXITED the headmaster's office through the servant's panel and scurried like a skreel along the narrow serving passages that ran between the walls of the school. The serving staff were like *kons*— the students and faculty knew we were there, but we were seldom seen. We were all on a strict schedule that ensured rooms were empty when they needed servicing. The house staff was so proficient and the schedule so precise, we rarely ran into each other, much less one of the boys. Our only regular contact with students was when we served meals in the Great Hall, and our only time together was when we ate in the basement kitchen.

I decided I had time to do a few sketches before the breakfast service, so I ascended four flights to my room.

. . .

MISSY HOWARD was new to the Mount when she found me drawing in the dirt with a stick. She must have been just sixteen or seventeen annums at the time. I must have been five or six—it was before I got my memory talent, so I don't recall precisely. I do remember her long auburn hair, her friendly smile, and how she smelled of lavender. She was the one who told me stories of intrigue among the franchise and guild families, of rivalries and spies.

"Now, drawing is a talent you can trade on when you're older, Fallon," she said. "It's a talent that could buy you citizenship. It's a talent fit for a spy; so you best not let anyone know about it for now." Over the cycles she brought me paper and pencils and encouraged me to draw in secret.

. . .

ALTHOUGH nobody but Missy Howard ever came to my room, I kept my drawings and supplies hidden in a box under my bed. I slid it out, opened it, and rifled through its contents until I found several blank sheets of thin paper. Taking a pencil in hand, I closed my eyes, visualized the moment I first noticed movement in the tree, opened them, and began to draw quickly. I repeated the process for each glance I had taken.

My window faced east, toward the rising sol. I fastened the first drawing to the window with some tape and examined the dark patch that I thought was the spy. It was tight against the tree's trunk on the lowest level of branches. Then I positioned the second drawing over the first so I could compare the positions of the dark patch in each. It had moved to a higher branch and took on the appearance of a standing figure. The third drawing showed the figure crouching on a yet higher branch and, in the fourth, the figure was sitting with its—his—feet dangling.

I smiled with satisfaction. I had discovered a spy!

1.1.3

TWO WEEKS later I asked Missy Howard to my room with the intention of revealing my most secret talent. She was now about thirty annums and had risen to assistant head-of-staff, but her smile remained warm and she still smelled of lavender. I began by telling her about the spy as she was examining my layered drawings, which I had again taped in place against the window.

"How did you draw these?"

"From memory."

"And how long did you examine the tree for each drawing?"

"No more than a second each."

"Four images, from so short a time, from memory... How accurate are they?"

"Very."

She studied the progression of the form in the tree. "It's probably just a child playing."

"But he's been up there every day of the week for the past two weeks. A kid from town would be in school..."

"And you're *just* telling me now?"

"Like you said, Missy, it could have been a child playing."

She considered the possibilities for a moment. "So what if it is a spy? That's no business of ours, now, is it? Let the powers-that-be have their little intrigues. Don't mention the spy to Dean Ambrose. And don't make any more of these sketches, understand? It could be dangerous."

"The leaves are too thick to see anything now, anyway."

"You know exactly what I mean." She gave me a stern look. "I'll burn these," she said, rolling up my drawings and sliding them into a deep pocket. "And we won't talk of it again."

1.1.4

THE SECOND WEEK of 8th-month was hot and humid as it often is in the middle of RedNights. The franchisers were still on summer break and the faculty and most of the staff were home or off on holiday. I had retired to my room for the evening when I heard the clopping of hooves and the rattle of wheels on the drive. I arose from my bed and went to the window. SolMajor cast long shadows as it set in the west, while SolMinor radiated a reddish glow as it rose in the east. It was the headmaster's carriage, so I quickly dressed and hurried down to greet him at the front door.

Missy Howard, Dean Ambrose, and I reached the front hall at the same time.

"Do you know what this is about, Dean?" asked Missy Howard.

Even in this heat, Dean Ambrose was dressed in his usual black frock coat and starched white collar, with slick grey hair trimmed in the tonsure style of academics. He dabbed a handkerchief at the sweat beading on his brow, then adjusted the pince-nez low on his pointed nose. "I have no idea. The headmaster is supposed to be on holiday in Primacitta." He gestured for me to open the door.

The headmaster, a short, portly man with piggish features, rushed through and walked briskly toward the grand staircase. Ambrose and Missy Howard trailed in his wake. I closed the door and followed.

"Guests will arrive within the hour," said Hunninger as he swept up the staircase. "They will meet in the Great Hall and must not be disturbed."

"Who will greet them at the…" said Ambrose.

"I will. Alone. I want all of you in your rooms before they arrive. That means you too, Ambrose." He waved us away. "Be off now!"

1.1.5

I RETURNED to my room, snuffed the candle, then positioned myself far enough from the window so my face couldn't be seen from outside.

The first carriage arrived within the hour, the others shortly after. The main part of the Great Hall was on the first floor, which meant I couldn't hear anything that was about to happen. That was unacceptable.

Four servant panels opened into the Great Hall: two on the main floor and one on each balcony at the ends of the hall. I donned dark clothes before heading down the passages in my stocking feet. I knew those passages so well that I didn't need a candle to find my way to the west panel on the upper level.

The panel was in a dark recess between shelves, but I opened it slowly just to be safe. The gas lamps weren't lit, and the tall windows on the north wall to my left were shuttered. I could hear the scrape of chairs on the stone floor and whispers in the darkness. I got on my belly and crawled to the balustrade where I would have a clear view of what was going on.

Suddenly, a match was struck and a directional lamp lit, its beam directed toward the south hall doors. I was distracted by a glint of light directly across from me. I glanced up just in time to see Dean Ambrose drop into a crouch behind the east balcony's balustrade, then prostrate himself just as I had.

The hall doors swung open, illuminating three men. The two on the outside wore long, dark coats and wide-brimmed hats. One was thin and tall; the other was a bit shorter and stout. The third man, small in stature, was in grimy, sweat-soaked undergarments with a black bag over his head. His hands were bound in front of him. The Dark Men had the other firmly in their grip.

"Bring the prisoner forward," came a deep voice from the darkness behind the lamp.

Prisoner? I had never heard the word before.

As soon as the men stepped into the room, the doors slammed shut. The Dark Men dragged the prisoner to a spot barely a meter-and-a-half in front of the lamp and tore the bag from his head. I swallowed a gasp and instinctively edged back from the railing. His eyes were darkened, one swollen shut. His nose was pushed to the side and caked with dried blood. His lips were cracked and bloody. The Dark Men took up positions a half-step back.

"Are you Vernon McCreigh?" It was the deep voice I'd heard earlier.

The bloodied man stood silently, his head hanging, his eyes staring blankly at the floor.

"Are you Vernon McCreigh?" Deep Voice asked more forcibly—threateningly.

"And what if I am?" He coughed and blood dribbled down his chin.

"Tell us about the Movement."

No answer. I barely caught the command that came from the darkness—not a word, really, more of a grunt. The stout Dark Man, who stood slightly behind and to McCreigh's left, punched him in the kidney. The prisoner groaned and sank to his knees. The Dark Men stepped forward, hauled McCreigh to his feet, then resumed their positions.

"Just tell us what we want to know and you can go home. It's that easy."

McCreigh raised his head slightly and glowered toward the lamp as if he could clearly see the figures seated in the darkness beyond its glare.

"I know who you are," he croaked, straightening up as best he could.

"Who heads the Movement?"

"I know your secrets." There was hatred and defiance in McCreigh's voice.

Another grunted comment came from the darkness.

The stout Dark Man stepped forward and lashed out at McCreigh's head with his arm, striking a fearsome blow with his elbow. There was an audible *crack* as the man's skull jerked violently to the side. McCreigh's dead body hung limp in the air for a moment, then crumpled in a heap on the floor.

"Bloody Below!" said Deep Voice. "You were to intimidate the man, not execute him!"

"He was going to die before morning anyway," offered a thin, reedy second voice from the darkness.

"But this was to be an interrogation first… find out more about the Movement," came a third.

"What is done is done," said Deep Voice.

The lamp went out, plunging the Great Hall back into darkness. Chairs scraped against the floor, and I could hear movement.

"Take care of him," said Deep Voice.

"Disappear him?" I think it was one of the Dark Men.

"No. The body will send a message. Make it look like an accident. That will satisfy the citizens, yet the Movement will see it for what it is."

The hall doors opened and I could barely make out the silhouettes of three men exiting the room. The Dark Men followed, dragging McCreigh's body. The doors shut. The empty silence belied the violence that had filled the Great Hall just minutes before.

There was a noise across the way from me. Ambrose. I couldn't see him in the darkness, so I didn't even blink until I was sure that he was gone.

1.1.6

I COULDN'T sleep.

Who could after seeing what I had seen? So I sat at my desk, lit a candle, and started to draw. Lots of black, a pool of light, a battered man, a bloody head, a heap on the floor. I'd seen the necks of chickens being snapped and cows being slaughtered, but I'd never seen a dead person before—much less one being killed. I looked at the image of the heap on the floor. I had drawn it in detail—the slack expression on the beaten face, the loose way the arms and legs folded and splayed, the pool of piss in which it lay. Was this heap of skin and bone Vernon McCreigh, or just a hunk of dead meat? Was it his *kon* that had made him a man? Had it left his body to return to Below, only to rise through the Fount of Life and be reborn in another person? I was miserably hot, soaked in sweat, and I felt like vomiting.

There was a soft rap on the door and Missy Howard slid in, still dressed in her uniform. "The last carriage just left," she whispered.

I turned toward her, but I said nothing. Tiny beads of perspiration sparkled on her skin like jewels in the candle's flickering light.

She smiled. "I assume you made your way down to the hall."

I gathered my drawings, got up, walked to my bed, and spread them out in sequence. I inclined my head to indicate she should have a look.

She came and stood beside me. As she followed the line of sketches, her face darkened. Her hand clasped mine. Tears streamed down her cheeks. "What... why... who..."

"They, the Dark Men, called the man a prisoner. What is that?"

"Did they say who he was?"

"They asked him if his name was Vernon McCreigh. Do you know him?"

She shook her head.

"What's a prisoner?"

"Oh, uh... it's not a word found in the *1900*. It's not taught in school. The Council knows many words not in the *1900*... words that are only used in private."

"But what does it mean?"

"You know what a captive is?"

"Yes, like a bird in a cage."

She nodded. "A prisoner is a captive who is accused of doing something very bad. Someone who is awaiting punishment."

I had never heard of such a thing. If you do something wrong, you are reprimanded, fined, or sanctioned immediately, according to the Code.

"Did he say anything? McCreigh, I mean."

"Only, 'I know who you are. I know your secrets.'"

Missy Howard scooped up the drawings, rolled them into a tube, and wagged them at me like a teacher lecturing a troublesome student. But her tone was fearful—pleading. "The Dark Men, as you call them, can't catch you with drawings like these. Understand? Promise me you won't draw these images again... ever... promise... PROMISE!" She was shaking me by the shoulders.

"I promise."

She put her arms around me, lay her head against my chest, and began to sob.

1.1.7

EIGHTH-MONTH dragged on. It was the time of cycle, three weeks before the faculty and staff came back for the new school term, when I was on my own in the Mount. Headmaster Hunninger had left the morning after the incident. Missy Howard had gone to Primacitta to visit family. Ambrose usually stayed to boss me around, but even he was gone.

My habits were so ingrained that I still performed my duties according to schedule, and I even did extra work tending to the summer garden.

There were two major benefits to this time of the cycle. First, I was allowed to eat whatever I wanted because the old food stocks would be replaced by the time the students arrived. Second, I would spend some of the hot, lonely nights soaking in cool water in the luxury of the faculty bath. Of course, the student showers were marginally better than the small stall in the staff's washroom, but the faculty bath was much finer and stocked with a variety of aromatic salts.

I had been on my own for eight days. SolMajor had set and SolMinor was just rising when I returned to my room after an evening's work in the garden. I was soaked in sweat and covered in grime. A cool bath sounded good so I shed my dirty clothes and made my way to the faculty bath. I didn't use the passages. There was something liberating about walking the halls of the Mount bare-naked.

Just as I cracked open the bath door I heard a splash. Through the narrow opening I saw Missy Howard step out of the copper claw-foot tub and reach for a towel. My bodily response was immediate and beyond my control. I backed down the hall as quickly and quietly as I could, but I bumped into a console table that sat against the hallway wall, making its contents rattle.

"Fallon?"

I turned and ran—frightened, embarrassed, and aroused. I ran to the student showers and stood under a cold stream, watching as the garden grime rinsed away, but my arousal didn't.

I recalled what the kindly white-haired doctor had told me after my procedure: "Being stemmed doesn't mean you don't function anymore, only that you can't reproduce. You'll still get aroused. It's normal. Understand? It's okay to... uh... handle the situation. You know what I mean? In fact, it's encouraged for anyone without a contract."

So I handled the situation, dried off, then returned to my room through the passages, slipped on clean sleeping shorts, and crawled into bed. I tossed and turned for an hour before getting up, lighting a candle, and beginning to draw. It was a series of sketches of Missy Howard as she stepped from the tub. My body was reacting again.

There was a soft rap on the door and I heard Missy Howard, draped in a cotton robe, slip into the room.

"You all right?"

I was overwhelmed with conflicting emotions. Without turning toward her, I took my drawings and tossed them on the bed. I inclined my head, indicating that she could look at them if she wanted. I heard her move closer, pick up the sheets of paper, and shuffle through them.

"I returned early," she said. "I didn't want you to be alone after what you experienced. I saw you in the courtyard and de-cided to clean up before inviting you to have dinner with me in the kitchen. I didn't mean…"

She stood behind me and draped her arm over my shoulder, placing her hand over my heart. She kissed me on the top of my head. She seemed small—delicate.

"You've grown into such a lovely young man."

She pulled me up from my chair. When I turned toward her, it was as if I were seeing her for the first time. She had always been larger than life to me—an authority figure with a deep knowledge of the life and politics on Neworld. Now, I towered over her by a full head.

She rose up on her toes, wrapped her arms around my neck, and we kissed. She smelled of lavender. She stepped back and slipped the robe from her shoulders, then stood there, unashamed, letting me take in every detail of her body.

She came to me… slid her hands down my hips… my shorts fell to the floor.

"My given name is Jenna," she said as she took hold of me and pulled me into bed. She led me, guided me, taught me. It was a wondrous night… as were the days and nights that followed.

OF COURSE, I had read the medical books in the Mount's meager library and the Council's *Guide to Contract Etiquette*. I'd even purloined a copy of *Coupling for a Successful Contract*, which contained simple yet evocative drawings illustrating various methods to ensure conception. All the literature said coupling was a necessary activity that ensured the survival of Neworld.

However, my reading hadn't prepared me for the host of conflicting feelings that coupling with Jenna had stirred in me: raw passion, tenderness, the desire to please and to be pleased, and an intimacy I had never imagined. I wanted to spend every minute of every day with her. I dreaded the start of the new term and the thought of her giving anyone else her attention.

I feared this feeling of possessiveness because *Contract Etiquette* clearly warns about developing attachments: "The two parties must honor the end of the contract, or early termination if one party withdraws." But that didn't matter to me. Jenna and I were different—special. We weren't coupling to fulfill a contract. Neither were we "ensuring the survival of Neworld." We had formed an emotional bond. The title "missy" meant Jenna still had her contract. We would be together forever. I would earn my citizenship, and we could contract to have a child. The future seemed so clear.

Then Dean Ambrose returned unexpectedly and began giving orders. That night, when Jenna came to my room, I took her into my arms.

She put her hands against my chest and pushed us apart. "We can't continue."

"Why not?"

"Everyone will be coming back in a few days. And there's something about Ambrose…"

"What?"

"I don't know… something. Things are about to change."

I took her in my arms again. "Yes, they are. I'm about to become a free man. Then we can…"

She looked saddened. "No… we can't."

I let go and stepped back.

She became stern, acting like an adult putting a child in his place. I was overwhelmed with feelings of both shame and anger.

"You don't know what's happening," she said. Jenna got to her knees, reached under my bed, and dragged out my drawing box.

"We must get rid of these before anyone else returns." She lifted the box onto the bed and opened the lid.

"My drawings?"

"And your pencils, erasers, all of it." She swept everything on my desktop into the box, then replaced the lid.

"Why?"

"Because I say so. No one can find them in your room."

She took the box and started for the door.

"Your talents are too…"

"Too what?"

"Dangerous."

"Dangerous? For whom?"

"For you. For me. For every living being on Neworld."

x~1.1

1.2

From Here to There

1.2.1

I WAS sweeping dead leaves in the Mount's courtyard when I next spotted the spy in the chestnut tree.

I had first noticed the spy back in the spring. Now, eleven months had passed and the dark nights and paralyzing snows of HighConjunction were fast approaching. The air was crisp and tinged with the acrid smell of the fields that had been flash-burned after the harvest.

The Mount is located a few kilometers upslope, or west, of Agricitta on the North Grade, a vast area of undulating hills north of the Riftwater River, which bisects Neworld from west to east. The North Grade is dotted with small farms and groves of fruit and nut trees but it's mostly open fields of grain. From its vantage point atop a large hill, the Mount looks over expansive fields of wheat and oats.

The openness of the plains allows for strong seasonal winds in the last three months of the cycle. The winds, a hard frost, and the setting sols conspired to reveal the spy. The chestnut tree, dappled in shades of russet and dark yellow, had begun to shed leaves. SolMinor, in steady pursuit of its big brother, was just touching SolMajor as they descended directly behind the chestnut. Silhouetted amongst the thinning branches was the still form of the boy.

I was considering whether or not to finally tell Headmaster Hunninger about the spy when someone entered the courtyard behind me.

"Fallon, what the B are you thinking?"

I turned to face Dean Ambrose. The pink flush of his thin face stood out starkly from his black wool frock coat. He stood stiffly, clutching a sheaf of yellowed papers in one hand, and scowled over the wire-rimmed pince-nez perched low on his nose.

Missy Howard was at his side, attired in her usual grey ankle-length dress and white cotton smock, with her hair pulled back severely. We hadn't been together in months. I hid my feelings, but I was still hurt and angry over the way she had broken things off. She gave me a stern look. Something was wrong. Were those my drawings in Ambrose's hand?

The dean was awaiting my reply. I've described my two secret talents but I may have a third, if you can call it a talent—I'm an excellent liar. Ambrose was a bit shorter than I am, so I had to look down to make eye contact. I've found that good, solid eye contact is best when lying. Most people think you can't look them straight in the eye and lie. They're wrong.

"Sir?" My voice was calm and innocent.

"I am asking you, Fallon, what are you thinking?"

"I'm thinking of sweeping the courtyard, sir, just as Missy Howard instructed. Well, mostly that, sir. You see, as I was sweeping, I glanced up at the tree—the chestnut over the wall. I think there's…"

"No, not what are you thinking of… not… not what are you thinking of right now… I mean…" The vein on his left temple stood out and pulsed as his face passed from pink to crimson. He raised his hand as if to strike me, as he often had when I was younger and shorter, but he only wagged the papers at me accusingly. "I mean, what are you thinking by having these?"

I resisted shooting a look at Missy Howard.

"That would depend upon what those are, sir."

"Don't wiseass me, boy. If you weren't a ward of this institution, you'd be wandering the uplands, I dare say. So don't… don't wiseass me."

I struggled to keep my composure, telling myself that I'd be a free man in a little more than a month. I wanted to shout it in his face. My insides were gnarled and the pounding of my heart had fallen into rhythm with the dean's pulsing vein.

"But sir, my reply was neither wise nor asinine. I haven't a shade what it is you're flailing about in front of you. So how can I answer?"

It was Ambrose who broke eye contact first, looking to Missy Howard for support, then back at me. "I know you know perfectly well what I have," he blustered.

"You *know* I know? How can you know what I know?" I took a step back and pulled my best expression of fearful realization. "Can you read my mind now?"

I had gone too far.

"F-F-Fallon!" He wagged the roll of papers in the direction of the courtyard door. "Come with me. I'm taking you to the head-master. He'll want an explanation. If you wiseass him, ward or no ward, you'll be out on the street by the setting of SolMaj."

I decided not to tell the dean about the spy. Why should I tell him, or anyone, about the boy in the tree now?

The dean and Missy Howard started toward the Mount. I hes-itated, turned, and made eye contact with the boy in the tree, com-municating my situation with a grin and a shrug. To my great surprise, the spy leaned out of the shadows and lifted the brim of his hat in a friendly greeting or, perhaps, a farewell.

I gasped when a mane of shaggy, copper-colored hair fell about the spy's shoulders. The spy was a girl, maybe a cycle my junior. Her hair fairly glowed in the soft reddish light of SolMinor. It is an image that is vibrant in my mind to this day.

1.2.2

IF THE revelation of the spy was a surprise, what awaited me in the headmaster's office was a complete shock.

As soon as we entered the ornate confines of the entrance hall, the dean pushed me toward the grand staircase. Teachers and students, none of whom I could call friend, stopped and watched as I was marched up the wide stairs. The hall echoed with the buzz of whispered comments and the hiss of gas lamps. The sound reminded me of a hive of angry bees.

The stairs split at a landing under a large stained-glass window depicting the Fount of Life soaring into a bright blue sky. The double doors of the headmaster's office were directly at the top of the left-hand flight. As we approached, Ambrose propelled me forward. Stumbling, I slammed against the doors and clutched the large brass handles for support, but my momentum drove them down, releasing the latching mechanism.

As I fell, I heard the crash of the doors striking the walls—and the cursing of Dean Ambrose. I glimpsed Headmaster Hunninger in the gap between two high-backed chairs that sat in front of his desk. The expression on his face was that of one who had been caught with his hand in the mince pie and he anxiously slid a leather pouch from the desktop. Then my chin struck the hard wood floor, sending a lightning bolt of pain through my skull. My eyes tried to focus on the expanse of floorboards that lay before them.

"Dean Ambrose," came Hunninger's voice, "what is the meaning of this... this intrusion?"

"It's Fallon, sir. Missy Howard found these in his room." I heard the dean slam the papers onto the desk. "They're pages from some Solarist propaganda!"

Not the drawing! What the B is Missy Howard doing by claiming she found those—What did they call them? Solarist papers?—in my room?

I raised my head enough to see the dean standing in the gap between the two chairs.

"And how could Solarist propaganda get within the walls of the Mount?" It was a woman's voice.

The dean was as startled as I. He turned to his right and looked at the chair from which the voice had emanated.

"I apologize, Headmaster," said Ambrose. "I did not realize you had a guest."

"A very distinguished guest, Ambrose. Missus Mara Grier from Primacitta."

Grier? I knew the name held rank in Primacitta, the oldest and largest citta on Neworld, as well as in Agricitta, near which the Mount was located. Built on the very edge of the east rim of the Basin, Primacitta was several sols from Agricitta. I wondered what important business would cause her to come so far.

"I beg your pardon, Madam." Dean Ambrose bowed awkwardly to the guest and timidly backed away from the desk until he was behind my range of vision.

When I gathered myself into a kneeling position, I saw the woman. She was elderly, maybe forty cycles or so—sixty-some annums—and stern-looking. She turned and looked down at me through dark eyes set into an alabaster face. Judging by her attire and bearing, she was a powerful citta dweller—a *very* powerful citta dweller. You'd expect the face of such a person to be pale, but something about her looks did not fit. Her silver hair was unusually short, almost mannish in its cut, and her face was etched and weathered by the elements as if she were an agrarian from the fields.

The woman turned back to face the headmaster. "May I look at that propagandist drivel?" All I could see was a tight, beaded sleeve of her black satin dress and her slender hand gesturing toward the sheaf of papers on the desk. Another detail didn't fit. Her nails were trimmed short like those of a manual laborer.

The headmaster handed the sheaf to the lady. She clucked as she leafed through the papers and said, "This is the very boy about whom we spoke, is it not?"

"Yes, Missus. This is the boy you want. This is Fallon." The headmaster half-stood, then leaned forward across his desk. "Get up, boy! Show Missus Grier what a healthy, strapping young man you are."

As I struggled to my feet, he resumed his seat and spoke past me. "You are excused, Ambrose."

"Well… um… of course, sir."

"And close the doors behind you."

"Yes, sir."

When the doors clicked shut, the headmaster leaned back in his chair. He smiled broadly at the lady. "If you approve, he's yours."

"I'm what?"

"Quiet, Fallon. Let Missus Grier have a look at you."

"Have a look at me? I don't understand. I'll have my freedom…"

"Not after having these vile documents in your room, you won't." The woman set the papers on the desk as she rose from her chair. She was almost my height, held there by the rigid confines of her corseted dress and beaded choker over a high lace collar. She had all the intimidating trappings and superior manners of a person of position. Yet there was something in her level gaze, not a threatening something, but something reassuring, that silenced my protests.

Missus Grier made quite a show of examining me. I use the word "show" because that's what it seemed to be.

"He's almost reached manhood," offered the headmaster, sounding like a salesman of used carriages. "He'll be eighteen in a few weeks."

She felt my arms and shoulders.

"Strong as an ox."

She examined my teeth.

"He may be troublesome at times," said Hunninger. "But I assure you he is a hard worker. Stemmed, of course. So that won't be an issue."

Finally, she inspected my mop of brown hair.

"And we've taught him the basics, of course. Reading, writing, a bit of calculating."

Yes, the Mount did teach me the basics. However, I had to *steal* the rest of my education—another thing that I kept secret, thinking it would make me more valuable as a spy. I'd listen to lectures from behind panels, read the texts, and even take the term-end exams, surreptitiously slipping them into the grading stacks under the name of A. Newman—a surname unknown on the world. It drove the faculty crazy over the cycles whenever the nonexistent student ranked with, and sometimes topped, the high-honor students. I relished the overheard discussions of the faculty and students as they contemplated who A. Newman was. Of course, I had the advantage of "taking" only the classes I was interested in. Although I hadn't taken an exam in two school terms, the debate as to A. Newman's identity raged on.

The woman retrieved the sheaf of papers from the desk. "And what about these, young man? How did this Solarist twaddle come to be found within the walls of the Mount?"

I thought about telling the truth—I hadn't a shade where they came from and didn't even know what *Solarist* meant. But let's face it, the dean was right. I am a wiseass, if only to bullies like the dean and fools like the headmaster. Missus Grier was neither a bully nor a fool. There was no way I could wiseass this woman. Yet, something in her eyes challenged me, almost playfully, to lay it on. So, without an *uh* or *um*, and with unyielding eye contact, I replied.

"I found them, ma'am."

"Where?" the headmaster roared.

Missus Grier's face lit up with the headmaster's reaction and seemed to say, "Go on, boy."

I shifted my focus to Hunninger. "Behind the bushes along the west wall, sir."

The headmaster grunted like a rutting pig.

"By Below, I swear it's the truth! It was shortly after visitation day. Perhaps some family sneaked them in."

"I assure you our families are some of the finest in Neworld," he said to Missus Grier. "Our students will be heads of franchise boards and government officials. I doubt…"

"That is of little consequence," said the woman, dismissing the headmaster with a demeaning gesture. "What matters, young man, is what you think of this propaganda. Do you believe any of this nonsense? Do you believe Neworld is not the center of the universe? Do you believe there are humans on other worlds? That we are their descendants?"

How could I believe it? I had never heard such ideas before. "No, ma'am. I don't believe it."

"Good boy," said the headmaster. His fist hammered the desktop. "Praise be Below, you are not a lost *kon*."

"I do not believe it, ma'am," I continued. "But I have no reason to think it's twaddle either. At least no more reason than to believe or disbelieve what we all learn about Below and the Fount of Life. I have seen proof of neither."

The headmaster sprang to his feet and leaned forward, supporting his weight on the knuckles of his clenched hands.

"Faith does not require proof, Fallon. With proof, you lose faith. And when you lose faith, you have lost your *kon*."

Missus Grier turned to the headmaster. "You are right, sir. The boy will have to be taught the difference between proof and faith. On my honor, I will make that my prime responsibility."

"He is acceptable, Missus?"

He addressed her as Missus. That was valuable information.

"Quite acceptable, sir." She paused, gave me a fleeting glance, then said, "And the price? Was the sum sufficient?"

Images flashed through my mind: the leather pouch, the head-master's pudgy hands, the guilty look on his face. I had just been sold like an animal. I should have been upset. By Below, I should have been outraged! But I wasn't.

The headmaster's face turned scarlet. He stared down at the desk as he spoke. "We will miss you, Fallon." I guess he couldn't look me in the eye and lie. "Get your things from your room and meet Missus Grier in the front hall."

The woman turned to leave. "Young man, do you have valu-ables or something you need in your room?"

I did not tell her of my prized box of sketches that had been confiscated by Missy Howard some months earlier. The images were all clear in my mind and I could sketch them again at any time. "Just my clothes, Missus, and a few grooming items."

"Those I can replace." The headmaster couldn't see the kind-ness in her dark eyes as she spoke. I turned, opened the doors and, with a grand bow, gestured the lady through. I followed at her heels like a gosling after a goose.

I did not shut the doors behind me.

1.2.3

MISSUS GRIER said nothing as she led the way down the stairs and through the hall. As we approached the front entrance, I raced ahead to open the heavy door.

"Thank you, Fallon."

"Most welcome, ma'am," I said, following her out.

Even though I had been sold into servitude, the sound of the Mount's doors being shut behind us was not the sound of expul-sion, but of release, if not freedom.

SolMajor had set and SolMinor was just peeking above the horizon. Gas lamps illuminated the wide stone steps and the gravel drive where an elegant black coach waited. It was drawn by four powerfully built horses—two white in the lead and two black behind. Their lustrous coats gleamed under the combined glow of the gas lamps and the soft reddish light of SolMinor. The coachman was a burly fellow who looked uncomfortable in his livery uniform. He was almost my height and had neatly cut hair, greying at the temples. Even though his skin was the hue of creamed coffee, his complexion still seemed pale and weathered like Missus Grier's. He opened the carriage door as we neared.

"Everything satisfactory, Missus?" the man asked in a rich baritone voice.

"Yes, Bedford. Please pardon me if I defer your introduction to young Fallon here until later. I want to leave this disgusting place as soon as possible."

I offered Missus Grier a hand up. As I followed her into the coach, Bedford said, "Pleased to meet you, Fallon."

"Thank you, sir. The feeling is mutual."

Bedford closed the door, then the carriage jostled about as he climbed up onto the driver's perch. I positioned myself in the seat opposite the lady, facing the rear of the carriage. With a shake of the reins, we were off. But we didn't get far before we slowed to a stop. I looked anxiously out the window. We were just outside the Mount's walls, at the intersection of the drive and the road to Agricitta. Why were we stopping? Had Missus Grier changed her mind? Was she going to send me back?

I practically jumped out of my boots when the left side door flung open and the carriage shook as someone clambered aboard. It was the copper-haired spy. She pulled the door shut and plopped herself down next to me. A broad smile and sparkling green eyes enhanced her freckled face. She stuck out her hand and said, "Hello, Fallon."

I shook her hand.

Her grip was firm. "Name's Aidan. That means *fire*. I think it's because of my hair."

"You are overwhelming the boy with your enthusiasm, Addie."

"Yes, Grandmother."

I looked quizzically at the lady.

She smiled. "You are right not to believe something without proof, Fallon. I owe you an explanation."

Here it came. The revelation. She was not who she pretended to be. She was probably some impostor, or possibly a spy herself, come to recruit me. I had often fantasized about this moment—about becoming a spy. But now I wasn't so sure.

"My name is Mara Grier. This is my granddaughter, Addie. I am mostly as I appear. I am the matriarch of a powerful family from Primacitta. At least, what's left of it."

My mind finally put things together. Grier. Primacitta. Powerful family.

"The franchise Griers?" It was an inappropriate question for someone in my position, but there it was, blurted out and hanging in the air. The founding families of Primacitta held most of the basic franchises on Neworld. The Grier family held the corn franchise.

"You know your history then, do you?"

"Histories are forbidden, Missus," I said, looking her straight in the eyes. Then I gave her a small smile and continued, "But I've had the benefit of a *franchiser's* education."

The Missus raised an eyebrow at this remark. "So your years at the Mount weren't wasted. Very good, young man. Very good. We've been looking for a person like you for some time. It was a family friend who suggested you."

"Suggested me? Who?"

"Missy Howard."

"Jenna? When?"

The lady raised an eyebrow at my familiar reference to Missy Howard.

"Oh, several cycles ago, when you were a boy."

I tried not to register my surprise. Franchise family or no, I felt uneasy at having been under this woman's scrutiny, having been spied on, manipulated for so many cycles. Was Missy Howard only using me?

"Missy How... Jenna... regards your powers of observation highly and..." Missus Grier withdrew the Solarist propaganda papers from her sleeve, leaned over to place them in a storage pouch on the carriage wall, and then withdrew something else from the pouch. "She gave me these."

She handed me an item I recognized immediately. It was an assortment of papers bound between two pasteboards and a small cloth purse containing pencils. The papers were some of my sketches.

Anger tinged my voice. "Missy Howard took those from me months ago. How did you..."

"We needed to see your ability firsthand. She gave the drawings to Addie, and Addie brought them to me—except the last series from that dreadful night. Jenna brought those herself."

"I've lived with Jenna's contract father since early in the spring. He has the orchard down the road from the Mount," said Addie. "I've been watching you from the tree."

"I knew you were there."

"Did not." She opened the portfolio and withdrew a sketch. It was the fourth tree drawing. She pointed to the black figure on the branch with two legs hanging. "That's not me. Could be a boy, could be a cat, but it's not me."

"Well, maybe not you, exactly, but I knew *someone* was there."

"You sketched the likenesses of every faculty member," said Missus Grier, "from memory?"

"Yes, ma'am."

"And these?" She had separated out the full-length sketches of Missy Howard stepping out of the tub.

I looked from the sketches to Missus Grier, then to Aidan, my face flushed with embarrassment.

"There's no shame in these, Fallon, no reason to be embarrassed. They are proof of your great talent. She is a beautiful woman, is she not?"

"I just drew what I saw."

"Here's something I'll wager you didn't know. Bedford was the first to realize…"

"Below! Your driver saw these too?"

"Bedford's not my driver. He put these in this order, aligned them, and fastened them in this way." Missus Grier laid the pasteboard portfolio on her lap and set the stack of sketches on the pasteboard. Missy Howard was wrapped in a towel and looked out of the drawing as if startled. Missus Grier lifted the top pages, literally exposing Missy Howard as she was just starting to step out of the tub. Then she let one page fall after the other, and the pictures moved! It was like watching Missy Howard come to life.

"You'll draw me one day," said Aidan.

"Aidan!"

"You know I'm not as young as I look, Grandmother. Jenna told me I couldn't do better if he were my first. I might want to contract with him…"

"Enough, young lady."

Overwhelmed with it all, I closed my eyes and slumped back in my seat. I sorted through the images in my mind, trying to make sense of the swirl of events. Was I being maneuvered and manipulated like a piece in some grand game? For certain, I had been observed, tested, and purchased. The social position of Missus Grier and her use of deception clarified my status.

"What do you want of me?" I said in resignation. "Am I to become a spy for the corn franchise?"

Missus Grier laughed. "No, nothing as petty as that. You're not going to be a spy." Her tone became serious. "Fallon, we need someone with your power of observation and drawing ability, someone who does not believe one thing or another, someone who wants to believe something and is seeking proof so he can believe."

She paused, considering the weight of her next words. "We need someone without a family."

"Whatever it is you want me to do... it's dangerous then?" It was more an affirmation to myself than a question.

She nodded.

I felt like I had no control over my life. I needed to grasp for some meaning or purpose I could call my own. "And what's in it for me? Will I get my freedom?"

"You're free now."

"Then again, what do I get from this—if I survive, that is."

"Survive or not, you'll have the proof you need to believe or not believe."

"To believe or not believe what?"

"In *kons*, in the Fount of Life, in Neworld."

1.2.4

MISSUS GRIER spared no expense on our trek down-country. In Agricitta, I was fitted with new clothing from boots to bowler— and not the stiff, black wool, servant formals with waistcoats and starched collars. Instead of a waistcoat, I wore a green and brown woolen sweater over a white cotton shirt with the new-style collar that folds back over the sweater. A soft brown tweed coat, dark brown slacks, shiny black dress boots, and a black bowler completed my traveling clothes.

We took the Plains River Road east toward Primacitta. The road was the major east-west overland thoroughfare through the North Grade. Because Neworld is sloped from the northwest to the southeast, the entire trip was downslope. I had never been any farther away from the Mount than Agricitta. None of the books I'd read or lectures I'd listened to had prepared me for my journey.

The road was busy, packed with people trying to get to wherever they planned to ride out the coming HighConjunction with its crippling snows. The people of Neworld needed to be off the roads and snug in their homes within the next five days. I was amazed that Missus Grier had made the trip all the way to the Mount with so little time to travel.

The sights along our route fascinated me. Starting about a kilometer outside each town, the road was lined with tall, overarching elm trees that must have offered welcomed shade to travelers during RedNights. However, barren of leaves, their gnarled and twisted branches reached across the road like menacing arms. Beyond the one-kilometer limit, it was open road. To the left were the plains with their smattering of farms and trees; to the right, the river flowed toward Primacitta. I had seen steamboats and barges moored in Agricitta, but I had never seen them churning their way up and down the river. They too would be moored and river travel stopped within a day or two. The North Grade stretched well beyond the far bank of the river, all the way down to the Riftwater. South of the Riftwater lay the South Grade, which was pretty much a twin of the North, but its open prairies were used to raise livestock of all sorts.

No words of great consequence passed among us in the carriage that need be reported here. We talked about mundane things like the harvest and the approaching HighConjunction. Although, looking back, I can see that was by design. After all, my ignorance was my major asset.

I regularly looked out the window and observed the countryside. The air was hazy with smoke from the field flashing, and it was like viewing the world through sleepy eyes. In places, thin layers of smoke skimmed the surface of the river like wisps of fog. After a period of observation, I would take out my portfolio and pencils and begin to sketch the images stored in my mind—the agrarians harvesting the last of the crops before the crippling snows; the people of the small towns gathering wood for the Post-Conjunction pyres; Addie asleep, lying with her head resting on Missus Grier's shoulder…

We stayed three nights in small inns that catered to the upper class. All were located on the riverbank where they could host land and water travelers alike. I had expected to share quarters with Bedford in the stables, as would be the custom with male servants during a journey. However, we had private rooms in the inn both nights. We also ate in the inn's dining area and had access to not only the inn's shower rooms, but also their private baths. All three nights I lounged in hot, soapy water. The amenities of the trip helped brighten my spirits.

While I was soaking in the tub that third night, the bath door creaked open and a nightgowned Aidan slipped in, holding a silencing finger to her mouth.

"What the B, Addie?"

She shut the door, came to the side of the tub, leaned over, putting her hand on my chest for support, and kissed me on the cheek.

"You're a foundling, so you don't have a contract, do you?" She crouched next to the tub.

"What's it to you?"

"I know I don't look it, but I'm of age." She rubbed her hand on my chest. "I haven't been with a man yet."

"So?"

"Jenna talked about you."

"Yeah, what'd she say?"

"She said I couldn't find a better man to be my first. And with you being stemmed, I wouldn't be risking my contract."

I didn't know how to respond. I'd been manipulated, bought, and talked about as if I were some object. I felt like I was being used, but my body didn't care.

Aidan's hand slid slowly under the water. "Jenna says everything still… Oh, my!"

She was leaning in to give me another kiss when there was a sharp rap on the door. Aidan withdrew quickly to the wall next to the door, a hand over her mouth stifling a laugh.

"Turn in early tonight, Fallon." It was Bedford. "We leave before light. It's a long push home tomorrow."

Aidan put her ear to the door and listened as Bedford retreated. She looked at me expectantly. "Well, what are you waiting for?"

"You go."

"I can't be seen leaving the bath with you in here. What would Grandmother think? You need to go first and see if the hallway's clear."

"Hand me the towel, then."

She smiled and shook her head.

"Come on…"

"Don't be embarrassed. Let me see."

"No… Please hand me a towel."

She relented.

"Okay, now turn around."

She complied.

I quickly dried off, put on my robe, and tapped her on the shoulder. "I'll tell you if the hall is clear." I stepped into the hall, looked both ways and listened for footsteps, then poked my head into the bath to give her the all-clear.

"I know you sit up late to draw what you've seen each day." She opened her gown for only a second before slipping past me. "Draw that," she said, dragging her hand across the front of my robe as she passed.

She wasn't the child she appeared to be.

1.2.5

IT WAS nearly a double dawn with both sols rising within a half-hour of each other.

"Show us your drawings of the trip," Aidan said coyly.

"If you please," I said to Missus Grier.

She smiled. "Yes, I'd like that."

I handed her the portfolio. "The ones from this trip are on top."

Missus Grier studied each drawing before handing it to Aidan.

"Of course, I only draw things of interest." I shot a look at Aidan, who mocked a pout.

"I adore your sketches of the workers in the fields. And you capture the different characters within the pubs." Her mouth formed a worrisome frown as she asked Aidan to hand back some of the earlier drawings.

"Did you notice?" I said, as Missus Grier held two drawings side by side.

"Notice what?" Aidan slid closer to her grandmother to examine the sketches. Missus Grier shifted the drawings so they could both see. "I don't..."

Missus Grier handed Aidan one of the drawings and pointed with her free hand to a couple of places on each.

Aidan suddenly drew a startled breath.

"May I?" I retrieved the remainder of the portfolio, sifted through a few pages and withdrew a single page with two detailed portraits. I handed it to the ladies.

"These two men were at all three of the inns."

"It could be coincidence, I suppose," Missus Grier offered unconvincingly.

"Could be," I agreed. "But two things bother me. First, the way they skulk in the background with their hats pulled low. Second, I've seen them before."

"Where?" Missus Grier's tone was insistent.

"At the Mount. It was…" I began to dig deeper into my portfolio, looking for my sketches of the prisoner.

"Don't bother. You won't find the drawings you're looking for. They're much too dangerous to carry around the countryside. Jenna told us everything."

"They're the Dark Men." I pointed to the stouter of the two. "He's the one who killed McCreigh."

"Wessler… Earnst Wessler," said Missus Grier. "A paid agent of the Council. This other must be a cohort. Were they there by chance, or were they following…?" She fell into silence.

Aidan and I exchanged concerned looks.

$$x \sim 1.2$$

1.3

Through the Mist

1.3.1

IT WAS HighNoon when we reached the outer district of Primacitta, a sprawling metropolis built around the Riftwater Delta. The delta is formed by two rivers, the Riftwater and the Plains, which converge eight kilometers east of the Rim Falls. The delta widens to almost two kilometers, terminating in the Riftwater Falls—the most spectacular of all the Rim falls.

Primacitta is a sprawling metropolis of more than 250,000 people. The citta, despite its location on the far eastern edge of Neworld, is the hub of commerce among the settlements as well as the seat of government and heart of the financial system. Its outer boundary is roughly a semicircle, with the Rim as its eastern terminus. Capitol Island dominates the center of the delta. Bridges connect it to the franchise district to the north and the guild district to the south.

Each district is set back from the edge of the Rim by a strip of forested wilderness about a kilometer-and-a-half deep. This area has no parks, paths, or scenic lookouts that would allow one to survey the vast, foreboding, and forbidden Basin that lies below. A grassy, lightly wooded promenade serves as a buffer between the wilderness and the citta.

The eastern terraces of Capitol Island look out over the Rim Falls and offer a view of the white mists of the vast Basin and, in the distance, the roiling fountain of vaporous *kons* that jet more than two kilometers into the sky. This is the sacred Fount of Life, said to be the source of life on Neworld.

· · ·

IT TOOK US more than an hour to traverse the citta to the RimEdge section of the franchise district, the oldest part of the citta and the closest to the Rim. This is where the elite live.

A high stone arch marked the entrance to the Grier estate. Bedford directed the horses through the arch and up the long, curving gravel drive. The surrounding trees and lush vegetation were so thick that I could not glimpse the manor from the entrance. When we finally rounded a bend and broke into open lawn, I was taken by surprise. I expected the Grier manor house to be a grand, impressive stone structure. However, it was modest in both size and architecture. It was a rambling, asymmetrical, two-story affair with a many-gabled roof and vine-covered walls constructed of heavy timbers, brick, and stucco. The building looked more like an agrarian cottage than the manor of a franchise family.

After the ladies had exited the carriage, I helped Bedford pull down the luggage.

"Now that we're safely home," he said, "let me properly introduce myself. I'm James Bedford. Some call me Jim, but most call me Bedford." He extended his hand. "Welcome to the team."

Team?

Several men came from the house and carried the luggage inside. We followed, climbing the steps to the front entrance and entering the foyer. A half-dozen or so people were milling about in the foyer. They smiled warmly when they saw Bedford but when they noticed me, their manners changed. Some quickly looked away, as if the sight of me repulsed them; others looked down at the floor like scolded children. No matter their reaction, they all scurried away into adjacent rooms, purposefully closing doors behind them.

As the last man slipped through a door to what appeared to be a library, I was able to glimpse two things that struck me. The first was the most beautiful woman I had ever seen. She had shoulder-length, raven hair that framed a flawless face, a shade lighter than

Bedford's but with the same deep-brown eyes. She was almost my height and had a shapely, yet athletic, body. I only saw her for a second, but her image was burned into my mind.

The second thing that struck me was a large map hanging on the far wall of the room. I instantly recognized the outline of Neworld: the lowlands that covered the eastern part and the insurmountable two-kilometer-high Rift that defined the western boundary of Neworld and prevented exploration of the mountainous area beyond. Seeing the map from this distance, the outline of Neworld reminded me of the bottom of a shoe, with the Rift and the unknown lands beyond being the heel and Neworld being the sole.

The vast Basin surrounded Neworld, serving as a buffer between the world and the void beyond. I had seen similar maps, but there was something odd about this one. Several lines of different colors extended eastward—*beyond* the Rim into the Basin. The longest of these lines snaked its way to the Fount of Life!

Who were these people? I was suspicious of their secretive ways and uncertain of their purpose, so I thought it best not to ask about what I had seen. Instead, I asked, "Why is everyone avoiding me?"

"It's the protocol, lad," said Bedford.

"What's a protocol?"

"A procedure. A process."

"A process to do what?"

"I can tell you this much. You're going to be asked to do something, to go someplace no one has ever gone, make observations, and report what you find."

"I still don't see why people can't talk to me."

"That's because all of us know what we expect you to find—what we hope you will find. We need an impartial observer. Do you get what I mean?"

"When I come back… *if* I come back… you don't want me to report things that I think you *want* to hear or see."

"Exactly, lad. The less you know—the lower your expectations—the more reliable your report. At least that's the way the thinking goes."

He put his two large hands on my shoulders. "And don't go fretting about coming back. You aren't going to die or any such thing. It's a hair-raising venture we're about, to be sure, but you're in good hands, lad—the best."

With that, he turned and strode toward the rear of the house. "We must hurry now. We must be ready to go by this evening."

1.3.2

I WAS shown to a small, windowless room in the north wing of the manor and asked to wait. It was sparkling clean and contained only a chair and a small table with a washbasin, a cloth, and towel. A simple mirror and some wooden pegs graced the walls.

"Shed your clothes—all of 'em—and leave 'em on the pegs. This'll be your last chance to wash for a bit," said Bedford as he left the room, closing the door behind him.

I barely had time to take off my shirt when I heard a commotion in the hall. I put my ear to the door.

"They're at the front gate." The unfamiliar voice sounded urgent. "They're threatening to break it down."

"Have you initiated procedures?" It was Bedford.

"Yes. Everything's being secured in the quarters."

"Good work, Percy. You need to buy us some time."

"We will, Jim. Good luck."

There was a knock. The door cracked open and Bedford's hand appeared, holding a set of johnnies—long winter underwear.

"Don't dally, lad," said Bedford. "Plans have changed. Put these on and meet me in the next room."

"I'll be right there." I quickly stripped and slipped into the johnnies. They weren't baggy like normal johnnies. They were made of a loose-weave cotton that fit me like a second skin. I squatted, stretched, twisted, and bent. No matter what, the skivvies moved with me. Impressed, I went to meet Bedford.

"I've never seen a weave like this, sir."

"That's because it's not woven. It's knitted. But there's no time for small talk now." He threw me four calf-length wool socks, a knit shirt with a long, tubular collar that could be rolled down or extended to cover the entire neck, and a pair of tan canvas pants.

"These should fit you fine. Now mind you, put on one set of socks, then the pants. Tighten the straps on the pant legs, and then put the second pair of socks over the pants."

When I put the pants on, I discovered they had a wide band of material at the waist that was folded down like a shirt collar over a wide leather belt. I didn't know if this flap was functional or some sort of strange citta fashion.

As if he had read my mind, Bedford said, "Tighten your belt and fold the waist flap back down for now, like I have. See?"

I pulled a puzzled face.

"It'll make sense in a bit, lad. Now hurry. Just cinch your pant legs and pull those outer socks on." He was sitting on a bench, lacing up a pair of boots. "Then come over here and find a pair of boots that fit comfortably."

Oddly enough, the workmanlike leather boots were only ankle high.

I gave Bedford another look. As he was about to respond, I said in my best attempt at a baritone voice, "It'll make sense in a bit, lad."

Bedford laughed. "C'mon, and you'll see. The others are probably waiting in the cellars."

The hallway was filled with men and women scurrying about with boxes and arms full of documents. Their activity seemed to be urged on by a loud thumping coming from the front of the house.

Bedford led me quickly through the house, across the entrance hall where several men were bracing the front door against the incessant pounding by those demanding access. Bedford broke into a trot, leading me to a heavy door in the kitchen. It was constructed of solid timbers and straps of iron.

He retrieved a cast iron key from his pants pocket and unlocked the door. With a clank of tumblers falling into place, the door swung open without a sound. Beyond was a winding, wood-paneled stairwell illuminated by a single gas lamp. Bedford closed and latched the door behind us. The clank of the lock struck a note of dread within me.

I looked Bedford in the eyes. "The cellars seem a strange place to start a journey."

He looked back. "You surely speak the truth there, lad. I can understand your fears..."

"I'm not afraid..." I said sharply.

"Your concerns, then. Is that all right? Concerns?"

I nodded sheepishly.

"I assure you that you have not fallen in with a den of thieves, if that is your concern. We are honorable people with honorable intentions." As he spoke, he never broke eye contact. I hoped he was not like me in that respect.

"Do you believe me, Fallon? 'Cause if you don't, I'll unlock this door right now and you're free to leave."

My brain told me I should trust him and Missus Grier too, but my pounding heart wasn't so sure. "No, I'm fine. I mean, yes, I believe you."

"Well then? Lead on, lad." He clapped me on the shoulder. "The stairs aren't wide enough for me to get around you. There's no place to go but down. Step lively now."

Down! My heart still raced. I found it hard to breathe. I hated the tomb-like cellars at the Mount. They were dank and depressing, filled with skreel, bugs, and the detritus of life at the school.

This cellar wasn't damp or musty; gas lamps lit it brightly, and there was no evidence of vermin. It had the feeling of active use, not neglect. There was an area to store fruits and vegetables, grains, and cured meats.

I felt a sudden wave of foolishness. Here I was, nearly eighteen annums, almost an adult, and I was acting like a child. My heart began to slow. I took a deep breath.

"No one else is here yet."

Bedford shot me a curious smile as we entered the curing room and wound our way between rows of hanging carcasses. At the far end of the room was a metal butcher's table that drained into a bloodstained grate in the floor. A rack holding an assortment of knives, saws, and cleavers was mounted above the table. Bedford stepped across the bloody grate and reached for a cleaver that was deeply embedded in a support timber.

The memory of Vernon McCreigh's dead body struck fear into my heart. My pulse accelerated and my chest tightened. I quickly flashed through the most recent images in my mind, cataloging every carcass we had passed: six pigs, twelve sides of beef, two lambs, no humans. That was a bit of a relief, but I considered my options just the same. I could lunge for the table, grab a knife or cleaver to defend myself, or I could run—but to where? The only exit from the cellar was locked.

1.3.3

THERE I stood—on the bloodstained cellar floor, surrounded by the hanging carcasses of slaughtered animals—while a man I didn't really know reached for a butcher's cleaver embedded in a timber. I couldn't breathe as Bedford's fingers closed upon the cleaver's handle. I had always imagined a life of adventure outside the walls of the Mount, but I never imagined it would be this short.

Instead of pulling the cleaver out, Bedford pressed down on the handle and the wall beyond the grate swung away, revealing a small alcove.

Seeing the look of consternation on my face, Bedford laughed. "Aye, it's a bit disconcerting, I admit. Quite by design, I must say. But it ends here. From this point on, your journey will go from macabre to amazing." Bedford gave the cleaver a sharp tug and a twist and it dislodged from the beam. He stepped into the hidden passage and motioned me to follow. "I think you'll find we're the last to arrive."

As I approached, I realized the area was a landing at the top of some winding stairs carved out of the native rock. The stairwell, which appeared to be hewn from the stone in a natural crevice, was pitched in blackness but I could hear faint sounds echoing up from below. Voices?

Bedford moved to a black metal box mounted on the wall and began to crank its protruding handle vigorously. The mechanism made a low groan that grew steadily to a shrill whir as he cranked it with increasing speed. In a moment, the stairs were washed in a soft, yellow-green glow. I saw that a set of cords ran from the box to a series of glowing disks attached to the walls of the stairwell at intervals.

Bedford hung the cleaver on a hook by the sliding panel. Its weight pulled the hook downward, and the panel glided shut.

"Come along then, lad," said Bedford. He tapped one of the glowing disks as he passed. "Phosphorescent lamps. The static box sends a charge through connecting wires, causing the lamps to glow for a period of time. The brightness and duration depend upon how fast and how long you crank the box."

We must have gone down more than 200 steps before we entered a sizeable cavern, which seemed to be a warehouse. Only a small area at the bottom of the stairs was illuminated. The lamps in this place were large and were mounted on stands, each with its own static box.

Missus Grier and two men were there, all attired in the same manner as Bedford and I.

"You have the replacement static box for run 12?" asked Missus Grier.

"Plus a spare and some lamps if we find any other outages," said one of the men. The second man was lashing down a pack on the first man's back.

"Ah, Fallon!" said Missus Grier when she noticed our arrival. "Sean. Tobey. This is our new team member, Fallon."

When the two men turned to greet me, I saw they were a bit older than me—nineteen or twenty annums. One was shorter than me—under two meters. He was lean, with close-cropped hair and a scraggly black beard. The laugh lines next to his dark eyes betrayed a mischievous nature. The other man was half-a-head taller than me, clean-shaven, with blue eyes and long, light-brown hair pulled back in a ponytail. Both were muscular and sported noses that had been broken at some point—probably in a fight or two.

"Good to have you on board, Fallon," said the tall one. "I'm Tobey. Tobey Andrews."

"And I'm Sean Halloran… We're twins."

"Twins?"

"Not identical, of course, but twins just the same," said Sean.

"Your drawings are quite astounding, you know," said Tobey. "Jenna says you can sketch with great detail from memory. Is that true?"

"You know Missy Howard?"

They laughed and spoke in unison, "She's our sister."

"Your sister?" This was awkward.

"She has a different contract mother, but the same birth father," said Tobey.

"So, about your sketching, is it true?" asked Sean.

"You, uh, haven't seen my drawings?" I glanced toward Missus Grier.

With a bemused expression she said, "They have not seen *all* of your work—just examples of flora and fauna sketches."

"So, can you sketch accurately from memory?"

"Yes," I said with an air of relief. "Yes, I can."

"Then he'll be able to continue giving us data after he returns," said Sean.

"Excellent," said Tobey as he clapped me on the back. "It's great to have you on the team."

There it was again—*team.*

"Give Fallon his pack, and let's get moving," said Bedford from somewhere in the darkness.

I heard the whir of a static box being cranked and saw a pathway of lights that led out of the cavern. Missus Grier and Bedford disappeared into the lighted shaft. The twins helped me strap a large canvas pack on my back, and then we went in pursuit of Bedford and Missus Grier.

"Where are we going?"

"Down," said Tobey, who led the way.

"And out," said his brother.

"Is it also part of the protocol that I shouldn't know where we are going?"

"Not at all. We're headed down almost two kilometers," said Tobey.

"And out into the Basin," said Sean, who took up the rear. "It's not that we don't want to talk with you, Fallon, but we can't tell you much more than that. It'll take us the better part of five days to reach our destination. On the way, you're going to see things very few people have seen. If you are as observant as Missy says, your mind will be on overload. I should think you'll be aching to get out your sketch pad to record what you've seen."

"As you will discover," said Tobey, "that will be impossible during each day's march. However, you'll get a chance when we rest at a waystation."

As we descended, Tobey made it clear that he was leading the way because he was the elder of the two (by ten minutes) and holder of their father's contract.

"Now be careful here," Sean said. "It gets quite steep and some parts are damp and slippery from seepage."

Some time later I heard the whir of another static box being cranked as we caught up with Missus Grier and Bedford. The next section of tunnel lit up and we were off again with hardly a pause. This process was repeated perhaps another dozen times before the shaft finally leveled out.

We entered a fair-sized chamber that was illuminated as part of the last run of lights. One end was filled in with a stone block wall and fitted with a heavy metal door.

"Packs off, and suit up, gentlemen," said Missus Grier.

After we removed our packs, the twins pointed to shelves where the rest of our clothing was neatly arranged. I did as they did: First, I slipped a pair of knee-high rubberized boots over the leather boots. Next, I folded the waist flap up and unrolled the collar on the knit shirt, covering my neck. One of the twins handed me a double-breasted canvas jacket. It was fastened with two rows of brass buttons and tapered neatly at the waist, where it cinched tightly around the waist flap, just above the belt. The collar was tall, stiff. It overlapped and buttoned shut to completely protect the throat.

Protect? Against what? I had a pretty good idea when I saw the bowl-shaped helmets. Each helmet had a gauze drape that enshrouded the head and tightened around the shirt and jacket collar with a drawstring.

"Bugs?" I asked.

"Big bugs," replied Tobey. "Be sure the netting is cinched snugly over your collar."

"Now put on some gloves and tighten your sleeves over them like this. See?" said Sean.

"Lamps on," said Bedford.

On the peak of each helmet was what I had come to recognize as a static box. Its crank was on top, and a lamp was mounted on the front.

"Like this, lad. Hold your helmet down like so, then rotate the crank about twenty to twenty-five times. The faster you can crank, the stronger the light. Yes, that's it. Now when we open the door, hurry on through, you hear? We don't want to leave it open too long."

Sean was by the door, cranking a static box. I heard a hiss behind me and turned to see Tobey using some sort of device to fill the chamber with a light mist.

"It's bug killer," said Tobey. "The mist will kill the fliers and cling to all the surfaces to kill any crawlers that might sneak in. Get ready, Fallon. We'll need to move quickly now. And try to hold your breath as we make the passage."

"Done," said Sean as he finished cranking.

Sean stepped back and yanked the door open. Bedford was the first one through, then Missus Grier, me, and Tobey, who immediately started to mist the tight corridor we had entered. Sean followed quickly, securing the door behind him.

Tobey set down the misting device and said, "Done."

The corridor reeked of the bug spray. I held my breath, but that didn't stop my eyes from stinging. Another block wall and metal door, which Sean called a hatch, stood before us. Bedford was spinning a wheel that moved locking bolts from their closed position. The wheel stopped turning with a loud clank. Bedford grasped the heavy handle, pushed down, and pushed forward. The door opened with a groan and we made a quick exit.

"Welcome to the Basin, Fallon," said Missus Grier.

1.3.4

I STEPPED into a deep grey world with a boggy stench and an atmosphere as thick as the heaviest fog I had ever encountered. It was alive with swarms of buzzing insects, some of which emitted slow pulses of colored light. The ground felt spongy underfoot. It appeared to be a thick layer of soggy mulch, although no leafy plants were visible to account for it.

"Above you is more than a kilometer of mist—clouds really," said Missus Grier, loud enough to be heard over the incessant hums, cricks, croaks, and buzzes. "It is next to impossible to tell day from night down here. Yet there are gargantuan trees that reach almost to the top of the mist. They have wide, flat canopies and thrive on the moist soil, the nutrients provided by their own rotting leaves, and the little sunlight they can gather. Also, as you can see, there is an abundance of life down here, most of which is harmless."

The word "most" stuck in my mind.

"Usually, the Basin is comfortably warm," she continued. "However, with the approaching convergence, it will cool down rapidly. By the time we reach our destination, this fog will begin to condense into rain and the settling will occur. As Sean told you earlier, to observe the protocol, we'll travel mostly in silence. When your task is finished, we'll answer any and all questions you might have. Look, listen, and make mental notes. You can record your thoughts during our rest periods, if you wish."

"I'll take the lead," said Bedford. "Fall in behind me, lad."

We followed a string of lamps mounted on posts a little over a meter tall. The cable connecting the lamps served as a guideline. Sean explained that the number of lamps in each string had a limit, so the illumination was broken into runs. Each run began and ended at a large post that held two static boxes—one for each direction of lights. At the end of every fourth run was a waystation.

We hiked at a brisk pace. Our lights only penetrated fifteen-or-so meters, but I scanned the area around me constantly in an effort to record as much as I could in my mind. It was the flying bugs that demanded my attention first. They were everywhere. Some were the size of a mote of dust and seemed to drift in the thick atmosphere. Others flew on gauzy wings that spanned the width of my outstretched hand. Then there were knots of illuminated bugs that seemed to rise from the ground in swirling clouds whenever they were disturbed.

"We call them luminaires," said Bedford, as if he could read my thoughts. "Because they often clump together, you might think they're all one type of insect, but they're not. Each color is a different species—a female of the species, to be more accurate. They pulse to attract a mate. Unfortunately for them, they attract more than mates. Watch closely the next time we rouse a cluster. There!"

A many-colored cloud rose from the damp ground.

"You see?"

"Yes. The bigger bugs swooped in. They eat the luminaires?"

"That's the way of life down here in the Basin."

A bit farther on, we passed through a range of rock formations that formed undulating mounds some three meters high. They looked more like large cauliflowers than rocks. From the rocks rose several small swarms of luminaires, which, as I expected, attracted the larger flying bugs. Bedford halted the group so I could observe. To my astonishment, any predator that swooped and snatched its prey was drawn slowly down into the folds of the cauliflower rocks.

"Look closely," Missus Grier said.

"What the B?" I realized that the glowing dots were not luminaires at all, but tiny illuminations on the tips of slender tendrils. "The rocks... They're alive."

"What you see as rocks are the outer shells of a colony of living creatures we call fauxlites," Bedford said before motioning me to move on.

The second run of lights skirted the mammoth trunk of a tree that took more than four minutes to pass. The bark was like that of trees on the surface of Neworld, but the scale of its craggy surface was staggering. A person could comfortably fit into the crevices formed by the splitting bark. Someone could easily scale the tree by traversing the network of crevices. Is that how Missus Grier knew about their height and wide canopies? I wondered if Addie had ever scaled their heights.

We wended our way through, over, and under a system of roots that were often as thick as a man is tall. At one point, we were assaulted by a vile smell. Nestled in the fork of a root was a massive, gnarled object that I recognized immediately. It was a fungus—and if what I knew about fungi on the surface held true in this alien world, it was not the edible kind. Globs of some sort of jelly-like substance clung to portions of the fungus. Various colored luminaires hovered around the gelatinous globs.

Bedford raised a hand. "Let's stop again for a minute, for the lad's sake."

I was about to gag. "I'm quite all right, sir. Let's move on."

Sean rested a hand on my shoulder and inhaled deeply. "The smell isn't too much for you, is it, Fallon?"

"No, of course not." I inhaled deeply to prove I was as much a man as he. Half a breath was enough to make me double over and dry-wretch.

"That was rather brutal of you, brother o' mine," said Tobey.

"You are incorrigible, Sean," said Missus Grier as she rubbed my back soothingly. "Are you all right, Fallon?"

"Yes, ma'am. I don't need a break. Really."

"I didn't say we should stop to give you a break, lad. I said we should stop for your sake. You should see this." Bedford gestured toward the fungus. "It is a rare sight."

"He's right," said Missus Grier, sounding as if she had just grasped what Bedford meant. "It is something you should document. We have written accounts, of course, but no visual record. Can you stand the odor a while longer?"

I straightened myself out, hand pressed firmly against my stomach. "Yes, ma'am." I tried not to groan or sound whiney, but I don't think I succeeded.

Tobey pushed Sean toward me. "Go on, you skreel, apologize."

"I... I'm sorry, Fallon." His repentant expression was not at all convincing. "I wouldn't have done it if I didn't like you." The corners of his mouth twitched, then broadened into a smile. "Honest." He held his hand up in the sign of peace.

I couldn't help myself. As I returned the gesture, I began to laugh. The twins joined in.

Sean stepped close, wrapped his arms around me, and said quietly, "Sorry, little brother. Truly, I am."

Little brother! I didn't know if it was just a figure of speech but I didn't care. That was the first time in my life anyone had treated me like family.

"So get on with it, then. See what you need to see so we can get out of this wretched place," said Tobey.

Missus Grier pointed at a particular puddle of dark goo that rested in a bowl of the fungus. "There's an entire cycle of life to be observed here. See that darker material? That's the remains of two or more adult creatures. Too bad there isn't a live adult for you to see. When they are ready to mate, the adults are attracted to the scent of the conjugal plant."

"The giant fungus?"

"That is correct. Oh, you are a lucky charm, young man. Look, over there."

A translucent organism floated through the mist. It looked like a fancy gelatin mold of unique design, with a multitude of fine tentacles dangling and writhing beneath. The tips of the tentacles pulsed in the same colors as the luminaires, snagging any unsuspecting insect that came to prey. I was beginning to see some of the patterns of life in the Basin. The creature looked too heavy to float. Yet it was deadly graceful as its tentacles danced through the air, selecting this bug, then that, just like the fauxlites.

"As far as we can tell, there is not a male and female of the species," said Bedford. "But when two or more adults come into contact over a conjugal plant, they embrace each other."

"It's the embrace of death," said Sean.

"And life," said Missus Grier. "As their tentacles intertwine, they sting each other to death, just as they sting the insects they snare. They fall to the conjugal plant below and decay into the dark, syrupy material I first showed you. The pool nourishes both the fungus, countless luminaires, and the ten or more embryonic creatures contained within it."

"Those clear globules are juvenile creatures," said Bedford. "The fungus eats more than half of the infant creatures. The ones that survive form tentacles and begin to consume the luminaires that are attracted to the sweet decay and, eventually, they develop tendrils and begin to snare the larger insects. As the insects are digested, the creature fills with gas and expands. Eventually, the buoyancy of the gas is more than the weight of the creature, and it rises from the fungus to hunt in the mist until it returns to begin the cycle anew."

"And all this is possible because the poor creature doesn't have an arse and can't fart," said Sean.

"Well then," said Tobey, "you're in no danger of floating away on the breeze, are you? 'Cuz you're the biggest arse I know."

1.3.5

SEAN WAS in the lead when I heard the gurgle of running water ahead. A sound and some movement to my left drew my attention. I strained to see what it was and listened intently. A few paces farther, I heard another sound, more clearly this time. It sounded like a heavy bag of grain, or sand, or something of the sort, being tossed onto the boggy soil. I looked toward the source of the sound. The mist thinned for a few seconds and I glimpsed a pale-skinned, toad-like creature, about the size of a watermelon. Its protruding black eyes were as large as a grown man's hand.

I focused my attention on the stream as it came into view. Farther downstream, another toad creature leaped, escaping from our probing lights. When Sean's foot neared the surface of the stream, the water erupted with a flare of sparks as if a log was tossed on a dying fire.

I came up short. "What the…?"

Tobey walked into me, almost knocking me over.

Sean, who was nearly to the other side of the stream, stopped and turned. "Everything's new to you, isn't it, little brother? Those were just lightning fish. Like minnows, only they flash light when they're spooked." He turned to resume his lead, still explaining. "As you've seen, without light down here, many animals, even plants… Ahch! Damn!" Sean froze.

"Careful now, Fallon, watch your step," cautioned Missus Grier as we gathered around Sean.

Tobey examined the area around his brother carefully before he stepped onto the bank and sank to his knees in front of Sean. "Did it get you?"

"Nah. But I can feel a barb pressing on the inside of my leg."

It looked to me as if Sean's foot was wrapped in several of the decaying leaves from the basin floor.

Bedford knelt behind Sean. "You take those two, and I'll take these. Okay?" Tobey nodded. "Gently now," Bedford cautioned as he and Tobey slowly slid their hands between Sean's boot and the clinging leaves. We don't want to hurt it."

"Hurt *it?* That's my leg it's got hold of."

"Shut up and hold still, brother."

"On three then?" said Bedford when their hands were in position. One… Two… Three."

With more effort than I would have expected, the two managed to pry the leaves away from Sean's boot. As soon as Sean was able to lift his foot, the leaves folded back, becoming indistinguishable from the rest of the debris that littered the basin floor.

Sean stepped back. "No harm done." His tone was tinged with both relief and apology.

"That was a beginner's mistake," chided Bedford. "You'll fall in behind Fallon when we resume. Tobey, you'll take the lead. Come here, lad." Bedford motioned for me to kneel beside him. Missus Grier was close at my back. "Can you see it?"

I looked at the spot where Sean's foot had been. All I saw was a clutter of… Wait. There it was, a diamond pattern, about three quarters of a meter long by a half-meter wide, that didn't quite match the surrounding ground. "Yes, I do. What is it? A plant of some sort?"

"No, Fallon," said Missus Grier from over my shoulder. "It's an animal common near water in this part of the Basin. We call it a toadsnare."

"You mean it preys on those giant toads I've seen?"

"Yes, lad," Bedford said. "That's exactly what it does. Look closely at the four points of the diamond. See those barbs? If a toad crosses paths with one of these buggers, the toadsnare snaps shut like a trap, piercing the beastie with four venomous barbs and killing it within minutes."

"It could have killed Sean?"

"No, but it would've made him very ill for several days. So be careful, lad. We can't afford to have you laid up. Time is of the essence. Lead on, Tobey. We must be on our way without further delay."

1.3.6

AT THE end of every fourth run of lights was a waystation from the outside. The station looked like a naturally occurring mound covered in the same damp mulch as everything else on the Basin floor. A stone arch, which encased a metal hatch similar to the one at the entrance to the Basin, jutted out from the mound. We passed the first station without pause. Bedford had retaken the lead by the time we reached the second station. "We'll stop here, but only long enough to eat, drink, and relieve ourselves. We're on a schedule."

Once inside, I could see that the station was a sturdy dome built of poured concrete or a similar material. The station was eight or nine meters in diameter—large enough for a party of six to bed down comfortably. It was equipped with a bug mister, its own illumination system, a source of fresh water, a fireplace, a rough plank table with benches and stools, and a privy.

I followed the lead of the others, who removed only their gloves and helmets to eat and drink. No one went through the commotion that would have been required to visit the privy. We left the station in the same way we had first entered the Basin, only this time Sean let me do the fogging.

At the end of run 11, Sean needed to replace the run 12 static box before we could move on.

We stopped for the night—although I cannot swear it was night in the world above—at the fourth waystation. We ate together at the table and listened to the twins' banter about the approaching HighConjunction celebration.

"Do you think it's snowing up home?" said Sean.

"Not for another day or two, I think," said Tobey.

"This is the first HighCon that we won't be with the family."

"Yeah, I'll sorely miss being trapped indoors with the folks for a month," said Tobey.

"We were lucky, you see," said Sean. "Ma wasn't the first to contract Pa."

"He was a bit in demand, you might say," said Tobey with a wink.

"And Ma had contracted out to a guild man when she was young," Sean continued. "When they first got together, Pa hadn't planned to use his contract. But having twins forces the issue a bit, doesn't it? Then he surprised everyone by accepting his responsibilities… merging households…"

"And they've been together ever since," said Tobey. "They even saved up and purchased a second contract for Mom. We have six other brothers and sisters, one way or another."

"All of Pa's kids come to spend HighConjunction with us."

"Cooped up together for two weeks."

"But the presents!"

"And the food."

"Mince pie and candied yams."

"Hot mulled cider and crusted apples."

"Aye, the crunchy shell suspended over the hot, moist spiced apples…"

Crusted apples? How could they talk about crusted apples after everything we had seen today? But this world wasn't new to them, was it? And that damned protocol probably prevented them from talking about what was really on their minds—the project they had brought me for. *Bought* me for, to be more accurate. A dark mood descended upon me.

"Excuse me," I said tersely as I pushed myself back from the table and retired to a cot as far away from the others as possible. Why should I be angry? I wasn't a slave, a servant, or even a spy. I had had more adventure in the last few days than in the entire rest of my life. I closed my eyes and tried to catalogue all the unusual images: giant trees, bizarre rock formations, massive fungi, exotic toad-like creatures with pale, translucent skin and bulging black eyes the size of saucers.

Floating in the mist before me, snagging insects, was a gelatinous, tentacled organism. Such a strange sight. I was so mesmerized by its movements, I didn't notice it was getting closer. Too close. I sensed that it wasn't just drifting, but moving with malevolent intent. It was bigger than I had thought. I was about to call the twins for help when a menacing tentacle as large as a man's arm shot out toward me, its sticky surface grasping my shoulder. I twisted away and swatted fiercely at my shoulder.

Tobey yanked his hand away and jumped back from my cot. "Fallon. Calm down! It's me."

I pulled myself into a sitting position. I could feel my heart racing and the sweat running down my face.

"You okay?"

I took a deep breath and exhaled slowly. "Yeah. Sure. I must have dozed off."

"Dozed off?" Tobey snorted. "It's been seven hours. Time to get moving."

As we advanced ever eastward, I noticed a steadily building breeze. Each day, we covered less ground as the wind steadily increased. The temperature dropped and the mist turned to rain.

The ninth station lay in ruins, crushed long ago by a massive fallen branch. A tunnel was cut through the branch where it had blocked the path.

On the fourth day I became aware that the mulch floor of the Basin forest had given way to bedrock and the bugs had disappeared, as well as all other signs of life. We were now laboring across a desolate, windswept landscape. When we stopped at a waystation to lunch, we tucked the gauze netting inside our helmets and stowed our gloves in our packs.

"We're almost there, lad," said Bedford. "At least, if you're going by distance. There's only one station left between here and the base. We'll spend the night there. But the rain and the wind are going to fight us. They'll fight us hard. It will take most of tomorrow to make the last push."

"Is this the dangerous part you warned me about?"

Bedford's eyes gleamed. "Nah. This is the fun part. It's the lightning leg."

. . .

WHEN WE were about halfway to the last station, I heard the distant report of thunder. By the time we reached the dome, great sections of the sky were painted with broad strokes of brilliant blue/white light.

The fifth day was a real pisser.

I was startled to wakefulness by a loud hissing sound and sharp clap of thunder.

"That was close," Sean called out with glee. "And it sounded like it struck the ground."

Bedford and Missus Grier were already sitting at the table, having breakfast.

"Come join us, lads," said Bedford.

When we were all seated, Bedford began, "Since you lads have never been down here during a settling before, this is as new to you as it is to Fallon. So listen up, you hear? With the settling underway, the lightning will be more intense than usual. As the atmosphere condenses, the likelihood of ground strikes increases."

"Brilliant!" said Sean. "No pun intended."

"Speak for yourself, brother. I never liked this leg, even when the lightning just lit up the sky."

"Although there are no bugs buzzing about, I want you to pull your collars up as high as they will go—cover your mouth if you can—wear your netting down, and gloves on." He pointed to four lengths of rope lying on the table. Each was about a meter-and-a-half long with broad metal clips on the ends.

"The wind will be brutal. We need to take special precautions. So, when you're all dressed, you each need to take a rope and secure one end to your belt, near the buckle. Got it? Then you'll attach the other end to the back of the belt of the person in front of you. Sean, you take up the rear. I'll lead from here. If you need to, use the lighting cable to help pull yourself along."

When we were ready to leave, Bedford listened at the door, trying to get a sense of the ebb and flow of the howling winds. I saw his mouth moving slightly as he silently counted the seconds.

"Ready? After this next one, then." He grasped the latch as the wailing wind reached its peak. "Four... Three... Two... Step lively now!"

Bedford swung the door open. Immediately, the weather assaulted us in full force. Bedford went directly for the static box. As he cranked furiously, Sean secured the station door. The wind whipped the drops of rain so viciously, I felt as if I were being pelted with small stones. The netting blunted the force of the rain against my face, but it held the deflected water within its weave, obscuring almost all vision. At times, the only thing I could see was the blurred yellow-green glow of the next lamp refracted through the embedded moisture. I only let go of the guideline when we reached a lamppost. Otherwise, I just slid my hand along, gripping tightly to pull myself forward or steady myself.

The wind was stronger than any I had experienced on the surface, but that was not what made it treacherous. It was the swirling. It seemed to hit us from all sides. As we trudged on, I was able to get a sense of the cycle of the wind as it shifted from front, to right, to back, to left, to front again. Even this sensibility of pattern could not prepare me for the sudden malicious intensity of this gust or that. Front or back, I was partially protected by the nearness of

Sean and Tobey, but a particularly brutal side attack would send our entire line reeling.

We walked for hours and covered very little distance. My left arm was sore and my hand numb from the effort of following the guideline. My shoulders sagged and I forged on mechanically, my eyes half closed. I was so fatigued I could not even escape into the images in my mind. I wanted to lie down, curl up, and go to sleep.

Then, all of a sudden, we were sheltered from the wind. My body stiffened. My mind became alert. The rain still came down heavily, but it was no longer whipped into a frenzy by the wind. I dared to un-cinch my netting and pull it back so I could see my surroundings more clearly. On either side of us rose high walls of rock. "Walls" is not the correct word, because it implies structure. These were more like long piles of loose rubble that rose three meters high. The ground began to slope down. Ahead was the gaping mouth of a tunnel.

"We're here, Fallon," said Missus Grier. "Another short trip underground to reach the base, and then I can explain what you are to do."

1.3.7

LIGHTNING cracked and sizzled overhead. Rainwater cascaded in sheets along the path that sloped toward the tunnel entrance.

"Down there?" I said somewhat stupidly to no one in particular.

Tobey came alongside me and draped a beefy arm over my shoulder. He kicked at a stream of water. "Just go with the flow, boyo."

"At least we'll be out of the bloody rain," said Sean.

The short trip underground that Missus Grier had promised was almost twice as long as our passage from the surface of Neworld to the Basin. We went down about the same distance, but

63

the tunnel, excavated out of solid bedrock, was straight and not as severely sloped. The floor was rounded, so water running down from the Basin was channeled to either side, giving us a dry path to tread. Once in the full shelter of the tunnel, we were able to stow our helmets, gloves, jackets, and outer boots, making this part of our trek much more comfortable.

Revitalized by a walking lunch and the anticipation of what lay ahead, I had a chance to reflect upon the journey. Every image I brought into focus challenged what I knew, or thought I knew, about Neworld. At first, I dwelled upon the strange nature of the hidden world that was the Basin. My mind slowly settled on images of man's intrusion: the long network of lights, the waystations, and now this tunnel. Who did all this? How long did it take? Why? A shiver ran up my spine, not of fear or cold, but of realization. I was part of something big—something grand—something that spoke to the greatness and importance of man.

All these wondrous visions could not compete with that of the raven-haired woman. I needed to draw.

We arrived at a short stretch of level ground that ended at a rise of wooden steps. The steps bridged a shallow chasm into which the runoff water flowed. At the top of the steps was a door constructed of stout timber and metal strapping.

"Welcome to Observation Base, lad," said Bedford. He pushed open the door and led us into a short, dark hallway. Unlike the tunnel, the floor here was smooth—polished. Light fell across the floor some twenty meters down the hall. A thunderous jumble of noises reverberated down the passage. I tried to sift through the sounds in my mind. The low grinding of a grain mill? The high whir of a static box? The metallic clanking of a chain being pulled through a pulley? The rhythmic beat of a massive clockwork? People shouting?

We traversed the hall and approached the opening through which the light fell.

"We call this room the command deck," said Bedford as we entered a large, circular room nearly fifty meters in diameter.

Like the tunnel and the hall, this was not a natural cavern. It was sculpted from the bedrock. The walls were rough-hewn stone, while the floors were as smooth and polished as those in the Mount. The command deck was composed of three concentric galleries overlooking a central pit. Gleaming metal railings ringed each gallery.

At fifteen meters, the top gallery was the deepest. It fronted a series of rooms that were framed out in finely crafted wood that again reminded me of the dark wood panels and moldings in the Mount. Some rooms, which I assumed served as offices, had large glass windows. The others were most likely living quarters. The wide floor between the rooms and railings held equipment bays, material bins, and storage areas.

The middle gallery was two meters below where I stood. It contained specialized work areas. Fourteen men and women were working at their stations.

"Another dozen are off-shift," said Missus Grier. "They've been working day and night preparing for your arrival."

Transfixed, I descended two levels and walked to the rail of the inner gallery. It was only two meters deep and had just one function: to give an unobstructed view of the pit.

The pit was about eight meters in diameter. A disk constructed of heavy timbers strapped with metal was lowering slowly, as if it were a lid being set on a pot. My gaze followed the cables from which the disk was hung. They led to a pulley system rigged to a sturdy trolley that moved along tracks twelve meters above the pit floor. The whole affair was operated by a gear mechanism mounted on the floor of the upper gallery, directly across from me. The mechanism ground to a halt as the disk settled into place. The command deck became silent except for the voices of workers.

"Hatch secure?" called a man stationed by the gear controls located on the level below the mechanism.

"Hatch secure," confirmed a woman on the opposite side of the pit.

"Operation terminated. Discharging power," came a voice from somewhere unseen.

Missus Grier joined me at the rail.

"What's it all for?" I asked. "When... how... why did you build all this?"

"All your questions will be answered in due time." She pointed to the pit. "That is the portal to your final destination. And that," she motioned upward, "is your transportation."

High above the trolley tracks was a grid of walkways suspended from the ceiling. The walkways enclosed what I can best describe as a giant clockwork. It was a complex system of gears, ratchets, and coils of spring steel. Suspended directly over the pit was a metal sphere big enough to hold a man—big enough to hold me. Its surface was not solid, but rather a metal mesh supported by a tubular internal framework. Distributed across the surface were rectangular openings inset with what appeared to be glass. Bulging canvas bags were lashed to the circumference of the sphere. Attached to its bottom was a very large version of a focused static lamp.

"So, you want to lower me in that contraption, into what I can only assume is another hole in the ground, to have a look around and draw pictures of what I see."

"That's about right," she said. "However, that is not just another hole in the ground. Do you have any idea where you are?"

"In the Basin somewhere..." Images flashed through my head. One came into sharp focus: the map I had glimpsed in the manor house.

"East of Primacitta…" I concentrated on the lines that snaked out from Primacitta into the Basin. They led to a vague swirling pattern. My mouth gaped at the realization.

"The Fount of Life." My voice quavered. "You want to lower me into the Fount of Life."

The Fount rose from the Below. It was the source of life and the place where the vaporous *kons* returned upon death. It was not a place for the living.

x~1.3

1.4

The Descent

1.4.1

MISSUS GRIER took my hand in hers and spoke in a motherly manner. "Fallon, our protocol could only protect you from being tainted with our ideas and expectations. Now you must try to rid yourself of the teachings you received since you were a child. Do you understand?"

I didn't... I couldn't answer.

"I know what's going through your mind. But remember what you said to me at the Mount? About needing proof? Do you remember, Fallon?"

I nodded.

"You will discover the truth. You'll bring the truth back to Neworld."

"But won't I... the Fount... Below... Won't I die?"

"No!" She grasped me by the shoulders. "I fear I must break the protocol to counter the effects of your conditioning. I'll tell you this much about our beliefs. We think there is nothing at all supernatural about the Below or the Fount. It is a natural feature of Neworld. Your *kon* will not be pulled from you as you descend."

"But you told me yourself that I might not return."

"Because I'm a truthful woman, Fallon. You might be injured or possibly become lost or even die. That is true. But the reason is not what you imagine. The reason is all this." She made a sweeping gesture across the room. "This machinery is untested. Something can go wrong. If it does, it will be our fault, not the result of some supernatural act. Make this descent. Your observations and sketches will reveal the truth to us all."

I was ashamed of my fear, yet I could not muster my resolve.

When I did not reply, Missus Grier looked at me sympathetically. "Come. Let me show you to your room." She led me toward the upper gallery.

"If our calculations are correct, the settling will not be complete for another two days. Then we will have about a day and a half in which we can safely make the descent. Ah, here we are. Unpack and relax. Take time to sketch what you've seen so far and think about what I'm asking you to do. But don't feel pressured. All will not be lost if you decline. If you don't go, Sean or Tobey will make the descent. They don't have your powers of unbiased observation or your drawing skills, but they can bring us back the basic data we need. Feel free to walk about and explore. Someone will get you when dinner is served."

I unpacked and changed into fresh clothing. Then I sat in a daze—for how long I'm not sure. My brain couldn't process everything; therefore I couldn't focus on anything. I needed to empty my mind so I began to sketch. As the images flowed from me, my thinking cleared. My enthusiasm grew with each completed sketch.

I was working on a drawing of Ravenhair when there was a knock at the door. It was Tobey. "Dinner's set, Fallon. Come on and I'll show you to the mess."

I secreted Ravenhair's sketch under my pillow, then shuffled the rest of my drawings into a stack and took them with me to the mess. It was a spacious room that served as both a kitchen and dining hall with two long, wooden tables.

"Over here, lad," called Bedford, motioning to an empty space on the bench opposite. "I saved a seat for you."

Missus Grier was sitting at the head of the table. As I took my seat, I tossed the stack of sketches where both she and Bedford could see them. Missus Grier picked up the papers and began to leaf through them. She examined one, then passed it to Bedford. He passed it to the next person and so on.

I ate as casually as I could while this process went on. I observed the looks exchanged among the people at the table and the smile on Missus Grier's face. When all the sketches had made it around the table, I said, "I'll do it. I'll make the descent. I think this is what I'm meant to do."

"I think you're right, lad," said Bedford. "This *is* what you're meant to do. Now here's the plan."

1.4.2

I DISCOVERED that the team's calculations were not precise. This was the biggest threat to my safety. They were certain of the sequence of events to come, but not of their exact timing.

First would be the settling. This started when the Conjunction neared and the temperatures dropped. I had seen signs of it when the Basin mist started to condense into rain. The cold air squeezed the moisture from the atmosphere. On the surface of Neworld, this resulted in a heavy blanket of snow that brought normal daily life to a halt for a month or more. Down in the Basin, the snow turned back to rain. Finally, the skies over all of Neworld cleared. If people disregarded the Code and ventured from their snowbound homes to trek to the edge of the Rim, they would see it for what it really was—an alien world waiting to be explored.

On the second night of HighConjunction, which was the darkest, coldest night of our calendar, even the column of mist rising from the Fount would settle and the winds it created would die. The following solrise would begin to warm the Basin and revitalize the Fount. I would have about ten hours to descend, make my observations, and return.

After dinner, Sean and Tobey took me to the sphere for an orientation. Once up in the walkway, I could see the two massive spools of cable that would be my lifeline. The twins explained that suspending the sphere from two cables would prevent it from spinning.

"Do you know how far down I'll be going?"

"We could never get an exact reading because of the winds the Fount normally generates," said Sean. "Those spools up there each have 3.7 kilometers of cable. We estimate the depth of the Below to be about 3.4 kilometers. We won't lower you past 3.2."

Tobey guided me to a control panel. Just beyond hung the sphere. "The cables are marked in units of a tenth of a kilometer. We'll lower you to 2.8, then wait for your signal."

"Signal?"

"Yeah," said Sean, tapping one of two small phosphorescent lights on the console. "In the sphere you'll find two static boxes. One is marked ASCEND and the other DESCEND. Three swift turns on the DESCEND box will signal us to lower you another tenth of a kilometer. If you crank the ASCEND box, there's no stopping until you're home."

"And how do I go down and come back up?"

Sean took a piece of paper from the console, crumpled it, and tossed it over the railing. "You quite literally fall down."

"But it's a controlled fall. About an hour and a half for the initial descent," said Tobey, indicating a series of sizeable metal levers. "And those spring coils assure your return. As you fall, they tighten. To come back up, warn us with your signal. Then start releasing the balance bags—those canvas bags filled with scrap iron. The more bags you release, the faster you'll rise."

Sean opened the mesh door to the sphere. "There's only room for one in there. Climb on in. The shape and open structure are meant to reduce the weight and minimize any effect winds might have on it."

There was a mesh floor about a quarter of the way up the sphere. Below it was a static box, its crank protruding through the floor.

"That little box over there, with the cushy padded seat, is where you'll sit on the descent. To get your bearings, when you sit there, you're facing east. Got it?"

I nodded and pointed vaguely in the direction. "East."

Tobey grinned. "And the seat is hinged. Go on, open it."

I did as he instructed and discovered a chamber pot.

Sean laughed. "Can't have you shitein' or pissin' in the Fount of Life, can we?"

I closed the seat and shifted my attention to the static box crank. "This must power the bottom light," I said.

"Yes, the searchlight," said Tobey.

I pointed to two wheels mounted to either side of a glass-covered portal near the floor opposite the seat. "What are these for?"

"They allow you to direct the searchlight. The floor will be covered with a padded mat for the trip. Many of your observations will be done kneeling and peering out that or one of the other floor ports. Crank it up and try it out."

It took at least thirty stiff cranks to get the beam of light to full intensity. Within a few minutes, I understood how the wheels directed the beam of light.

For the next day and a half I learned all I could about my task. I requested two modifications to the sphere—the addition of two waterproof pouches for art supplies and finished drawings, and direction markings etched into the sphere's vertical supports to help me reference the relative positions of anything I might observe.

"With your memory, why take your sketching tools?" asked Bedford. "Take more time for your observations and draw when you return."

"I need to sketch while I'm down there—just in case. You know… if something happens to me, you'll get to see at least part of what I saw."

1.4.3

A RAP on the door of my quarters roused me from a fitful sleep filled with strange creatures, dark pits, green eyes, freckles, and soft, flowing raven hair.

"It's time, lad," said Bedford. "Report to the mess. Bring your gloves and helmet."

When I opened the door to my room, I noticed that the big gears across the pit were slowly turning. The portal was almost completely open. I walked down to the railing of the inner ring to get my first look at the Below. I don't know what I expected, but I was disappointed to discover I could only see the craggy walls of the hole that opened onto the Below. Well, at least there were no wandering *kons* floating up. I shrugged and made my way to the mess.

Everyone welcomed me warmly. Some greeted me with the open-palm sign of peace. Others shook my hand and wished me luck. Then the leader of the descent team, Brian Randall, briefly reviewed procedures with me and assured me of a safe ride. After greeting me, the descent team left to man their positions and make final preparations. Only Missus Grier and Bedford sat with me as I ate a hearty meal.

"You'll have a basket with an ample supply of water, bread, and cheese with you," said Missus Grier, "so you won't go hungry or thirsty."

"Your sketching materials are stowed and ready," said Bedford, putting a hand upon my shoulder. "This is the moment of truth, lad, and you're its courier."

I felt the weight of my responsibility in that hand. Tears began to well up in my eyes. "I'll do my best, sir."

Missus Grier rubbed my back with a gentle hand. "Don't be frightened, Fallon. Everything will go smoothly. I'm sure of it."

I smiled at the lady. "I'm not frightened in the least, ma'am. I'm overwhelmed with joy. My life, even if it ends today, will mean something. How can I thank…"

She cut me off. "None of that, young man. Our thanks to you is as great, so we need not mention it at all. But I will say this: I envy you. I've dreamed of this moment since I was a young woman. Except, in my dreams I was the descender. I was the explorer."

Bedford accompanied me to the sphere, where he secured the netting around my high-collared shirt. "Wear this and the gloves as a precaution. If bugs are, as I suspect, not a problem, feel free to strip down to comfortable clothing. No matter what, you'll need to shed the gloves to do your sketching."

I stepped into the sphere and took my seat.

Bedford closed the hatch and latched it. "Remember to check the skies. They should be clearly visible above you. At the first sign of light, you start your ascent, do you hear me, lad? I want you back here before the Fount starts to recycle."

"I will be."

He patted the side of the sphere, almost affectionately, then withdrew his hand and gave me the open-palm sign. As I returned the gesture, I heard the winch disengage and felt the sphere begin to move. I quickly decided that sitting was not the position I wanted to be in. I knelt on the floor and looked out one of the lower viewports. The base was awash with light. Many of the team stood by the railing encircling the portal, watching my gradual descent. The pit looked like a gaping mouth, ready to swallow me. Its rock-walled throat was a one-way path to the dark bowels of Neworld.

The walls soon surrounded me, the reflected light from the base diminished, and the black disk beneath me grew steadily. Abruptly, the pit wall ended and there was nothing. I simply cannot convey the utter blackness of the void. Even on the darkest night of HighConjunction with neither sol in the sky, there is still starlight. Enclosed in a darkened room, you can still sense the walls and furniture about you. Here, I was looking into nothingness. My mind had naught to fill the void. All I had to ground my mind was the vibration of the sphere and an ever-deepening thrum that seemed to resonate from the suspension cables.

I could feel the rate of descent increasing. I got to my feet and looked up through the top port. The launch bay was no more than a small wafer of light, then a solitary star in a pitch-black sky, then nothing at all.

I returned to the floor and started to crank the static box. Fifty, fifty-five, sixty turns as fast as I could. I dropped to the viewport with the control wheels and guided the light in what should have been a complete arc. Nothing. Shite. The light had failed. The mission would be a total failure.

Then I noticed it. A brief streak of light, like a shooting star. I stared patiently. Minutes went by. Nothing. Had I imagined the flash? There was a "plink" on one of the upper viewports. I cranked my helmet light so I could investigate. The greenish-yellow beam revealed beads of water scattered across the viewport. I switched off my helmet light, returned to the light controls, and gazed down again. My patience was rewarded when I saw another shooting star. Only I knew it wasn't a shooting star. It was a drop of water falling though the beam of my searchlight. The light was working, but the air was so clear that I could not detect its beam.

I got up and settled myself back into the seat. There would be nothing to see until I reached the first stopping point at 2.8 kilometers.

Nothing to see? I began to reflect on what I had been taught since childhood and what Missus Grier and the others could only hint at. I was in the Below, where our *kons* return when we die and are renewed through the Fount. That was the point of the pledge. We worked hard to serve today and build a better tomorrow to which our regenerated *kons* would return. We would enjoy the rewards of our hard work in this life… in the next.

I cranked the helmet light to full-power once more, swept it about the sphere, and made note of how calm and clear the air was about me. The Fount was a turbulent column of water upon which *kons* could ascend to the world. But there was no Fount now. Were no children being born in all of Neworld? If any were, were they born without a *kon*?

With the Fount "settled" and the atmosphere clear, what should I see dangling beneath the lowest reaches of Neworld? Shouldn't I see stars in every direction, except straight up? I switched off the searchlight, rose, and proceeded to look out every viewport. No stars were visible below or to the east, south, west, or north. As Bedford had predicted, I did see a ragged patch of stars above, stretching off to the east. I sat down again, removed my helmet, and pondered what the lack of stars below and around me meant. I was at a loss.

Little by little, I became aware of a deep, rumbling noise rising from below. I decided to return to the floor port and give the light another try. I was half up from my seat when the sphere jolted to a halt. My knees buckled beneath me and I crashed gracelessly to the floor. Thank Below, it was padded.

2.8 kilometers. I excitedly cranked the static box at least fifty times to be sure I had maximum brightness. I scanned the Below in every direction. Nothingness. I got to my feet, gave the DESCEND light three swift cranks, and quickly took my seat. I'd learned my lesson. I would remain seated until the next stop.

2.9 kilometers. I repeated the process with the same results. The only difference was the level of the distant roar, which steadily increased as I descended.

3.0 kilometers. Nothing.

3.1 kilometers. When pointed straight down, the beam glinted off something. It was like the reflection of SolMin off the pond in the Mount's courtyard. Was there water below me? I sent the signal to descend.

3.2 kilometers. Yes! There was water as far as the beam could reach. Then I noticed the distinct reflections of a wake. Something was moving below the surface. I swung the light in the direction of the wake. There was a sudden roiling of the water, and then all was calm. Was this a pool of restless *kons*? I needed to be closer. I sent another signal and resumed my seat. The sphere did not descend. I had forgotten that 3.2 kilometers was the planned limit. I rose and cranked the signal again, paused, and gave another three cranks.

Resigned to the fact that this was as close as I was going to get, I retrieved my drawing materials and sat cross-legged on the padded floor. The wake wasn't much to draw, but at least it gave me something to do.

To my surprise, the sphere started to descend. But it only went down maybe another hundred meters. The team must have discussed what to do and decided to let me request lower depths, but in smaller increments. Five more times I was lowered closer to the surface of this great body of water. At the last stop I was able to see the creatures, great and small, that populated this mysterious world.

Something bird-like flew through the beam of light, skimming the surface of the water over what must have been a school of fish. It didn't have feathers or distinct wings, or even a head. Its smooth, greyish body was roughly triangular in shape, with a wide end being its front and the opposite point being its rear. As I studied it, I could see it had a definite, elongated body and two bony arms that attached where the head should have been. The triangular shape was the result of skin that stretched from the tail point to the end of the arms. From above, I could not see any claws or talons, but it dragged a long appendage in the water behind it. When it snagged a fish, the tail coiled forward, bringing the fish to the flying creature. In an instant, the fish was gone, and the tail uncoiled to troll the water once more.

Two more of these skimmers appeared. I can only guess that they were attracted by the success of the first. They each caught a fish.

A fourth skimmer glided toward the school. Its tail had just contacted the surface when the water erupted in a frenzied froth. A nightmarish creature leaped out of the water, devouring the entire school of fish and the fourth skimmer with them. From my vantage point, it appeared to be all mouth and teeth. The shocking display of violence left me breathless, my heart pounding. How high could that thing jump? Was there something even larger and more vicious lurking just beneath the surface? I considered the wisdom of having them raise me a few meters. I was going to crank the ASCEND box but I remembered what the twins had told me. Once I signaled to come up, there would be no stopping until I was back at the base.

I took several deep breaths and exhaled slowly to calm myself, then concentrated on my sketches. A large animal's back arching above the surface... I became so immersed in my drawing, I was barely aware of the passing time. A long, suckered tentacle reaching toward the lamp at the bottom of the sphere... I didn't stop to eat or drink. A spider-like creature that was able to stride on the surface and spear small fish with any of its needle-sharp legs...

After a considerable length of time, I remembered that I had not cranked the searchlight since my first stop at 2.8 kilometers. I charged it to full power, then returned to my scanning of the Below. I hadn't realized how dim it had gotten. The light now penetrated much farther, revealing an even greater surprise—a shoreline directly east of my position. There was an island in the Below! It was rocky, wet, and barren, from what I could see, but it was land.

I was sketching a span of shoreline when I noticed a faint glow in the far distance, about level with the sphere. How long had I been down here, anyway? I had not once checked the sky above to see if dawn was approaching. I looked up and saw the rough-edged disk of stars in the blackness above. I turned my attention back to the distant smudge of light. It was interesting, but how could I sketch something as indistinct as that?

What could it be? Another sphere? My own reflection, somehow? It seemed to lie far beyond the island, which meant that the source of the light must be very large. The smudge gradually grew brighter until a shaft of light slashed through, slanting in my direction. I was facing east. The shaft of light must have been the combined rays of the sols. The rugged outline of the island was highlighted in the distant light. As the sols rose, the shaft receded from me, leaving the island in silhouette. I sketched furiously, not noticing the sharp-edged shaft dissolving into a milky blur—or the gentle breeze wafting through the sphere.

I glanced through the top viewport and saw that the disk of stars was dissolving into a pinkish glow. It was solrise. I should have started my ascent. I shot to my feet, stowed my ream of sketches, and cranked the ASCEND box vigorously. I was barely seated when the sphere started to rise, but I found myself drawn back to my viewing position on the floor, stunned by something amazing. I rubbed my eyes to make sure they were clear. The light from above cast a glow on the Below. The size of the island and the vast hole in the Basin above me—the mouth of the Fount—were revealed. By my estimation, both were the same size and shape.

But that is not what stunned me. An immense object—or was it a structure?—rested on a plateau some distance from the shore.

The complexity of its construction was staggering, so I hurried to retrieve pencil and paper. I had to hold the fluttering paper in place to draw. I was able to sketch for only a few minutes before a wall of mist obliterated my view of the object and, finally, the entire island.

The wind picked up and the sphere began to sway. I stuffed that last and most important sketch into the pouch, sat down, and braced myself. As I rose at an agonizingly slow rate, I thought about all that I had seen: the large body of water with its creatures, the island, the distant shaft of light, and the hole in the Basin above me. The Fount was definitely a hole in the floor of the Basin, not the boundary between the world and the heavens. From its sides poured a half-dozen waterfalls of proportions too large to do justice with words. Their torrents plummeted thunderously to depths of the Below.

What was that other source of light, then? Another hole? But why did it appear so much lower than the Fount?

The wind began to whistle through the mesh. The sphere started to swing in ever-increasing arcs like the pendulum of a clock. Why wasn't the sphere rising faster? The constant motion set my stomach churning and my head spinning. I braced my hands against the structural ribs on either side of the seat and looked longingly out the top viewport. I was still at least two-and-a-half kilometers from the underside of the Basin.

The cables groaned. The rising sphere shuddered to a stop. I sat, stricken with fear, as the sphere continued to sway precariously in the wind. A terrifying screech descended from above as if being transmitted down the length of the cables. It grew louder and nearer until the entire sphere resonated with sound. The vibration rattled me to the core and I was forced to put my hands over my ears.

Suddenly, the sphere plummeted, lifting me from my seat before it came to a bone-jarring halt. The iron-laden balance bags banged against the mesh. My body crumpled to the floor.

A cable must have snapped or the winch must have broken. I was flat on my back, staring upward. I could see that both cables were secure. So it was the winch…

"Bloody B!" The problem hit me like a ton of scrap iron. I struggled to my feet. My legs felt limp. My vision was swirling. I tried to focus as my fingers fumbled over the knot. At least it was a neat bow. I yanked on one rope, the bow released, and the ballast bag fell away.

The sphere did not rise. The twins had instructed me to release the bags so the weight would remain evenly distributed around the sphere, so I clawed my way to the far side and let loose another bag.

No upward motion.

I discharged a third bag, then a fourth and a fifth. The cables groaned as they had before the fall. I feared the coming screech as I rapidly released another bag and another. The groaning lessened. Two more bags plunged to the Below. I felt the sphere begin to rise. I didn't sit down until all the bags had been set free.

I looked out one of the eye-level viewports toward the far blur of light that lay somewhere beyond the island. Then I looked up through the upper viewport at the far reaches of the massive hole in the Basin. I could see the thickness of the bedrock glowing in the rosy light of dawn.

That's when it struck me why the distant light was so low. I shifted my view between the two viewports. If the upper port represented the Fount, and the lower, more distant, port represented the far light… It was the exact same relationship as the two viewports! The source of the far light was another hole in the Basin, and the Basin was curved, just like my sphere. I was riding in a sphere, within a sphere.

The atmosphere thickened with mist. The Fount became just a bright patch in a thick fog. The motion of the sphere was so violent that I lowered myself to the floor, unfastened two sides of the padded matting and wrapped it around me. I closed my eyes, hoping to ride out the ascent in this manner, but my head swirled even more. I felt the bile rise in my throat and I struggled to kneel before the seat. I lifted the lid and emptied the sparse contents of my stomach into the chamber pot. The sphere lurched unexpectedly, causing me to fall forward and strike my neck against the lip of the seat. I gasped for air as I tried to push myself back. The last thing I remembered was the seat crashing down on my skull.

1.4.4

WHEN I awoke in my quarters, the twins were sitting at my bedside. I felt the lump on the top of my head before trying to sit up. "I made it back, then?" I said, with a weak smile on my lips. "How long have I been out?"

"Since we don't know when you took the knock on the head, we can't say for sure," said Tobey.

"But you've been back for less than an hour," said Sean. "Whenever you're feeling up to it, Missus Grier and Bedford would like to have a word with you."

"I'm ready now," I said as I started to pull back the covers.

Sean and Tobey got up to leave the room. "Stay put, Fallon," said Sean. "They'll come to you."

Missus Grier and Bedford arrived before I could reposition myself into a comfortable sitting position. Missus Grier smiled brightly at me.

Bedford gave me a concerned look. "How're you feeling, then, lad?"

"A bit sore and queasy."

"You should have come up sooner, you know."

"Yes, sir. I know." My eyes welled with tears of shame. "And I forgot to undo the ballast bags…"

"But you made it back, lad. You made it back."

"And that's all that matters, Fallon," said Missus Grier. "You must stay in bed until this evening, but I'm certain you'll be fine."

She handed me the stack of my drawings. "Do you feel up to talking to us about your descent?"

I took a moment to shuffle through the sketches, arranging them roughly in chronological order, then started my account. They were infinitely patient with my narration and frequently asked questions about what I had drawn and if I could produce more drawings when I felt better.

When I came to the sequence when the distant shaft of light appeared, I explained my idea of the sphere within a sphere.

"Quite well thought out, young man," said the Missus. "Your Headmaster Hunninger wouldn't have reasoned half so well."

When I reached the last sketch, the two exchanged a look I couldn't decipher.

"How clearly did you see this object, Fallon?" It was Bedford speaking now.

"Very clearly. I didn't have time to sketch all the detail before the mist rolled in. But, given time, I can render it more accurately."

"And its condition, lad? Did it look like a wreck? Was it corroded? In disrepair?" There was an air of excitement in his voice.

I closed my eyes and pictured the object. "No sir. It seemed shiny and new. Yes, shiny. I don't think that shows in my sketch, but it was mostly made of metal, I think. But it wasn't rusted like you'd expect."

"That's good, Fallon—very good indeed," said Bedford.

Missus Grier took my hand in hers. "As I told you earlier, I envy you. You've delivered not only the truth about the Below, but the truth about our whole world. You'll be remembered in our histories until the end of time."

"But…" I hesitated.

"But what?" said Missus Grier.

"Do you still have to follow protocol? Or can you now tell me what you expected to find Below?"

Bedford laughed, "No lad. There is no more protocol to follow."

"We didn't know what you would find, Fallon," said Missus Grier. "We did expect to find water down there, but we had no idea that it would be home to the creatures you've drawn. We believed—and I think you've proved—that the world is a sphere."

"We believe there is much more to the world than our little island," said Bedford.

"An island?"

"Yes, Fallon, an island," said Bedford. "You see, we think the Basin was once the floor of a giant body of water, an ocean, that separated our island from the rest of the world. We believe that this land is no more than a shell."

"I don't understand."

"Have you ever had a crusted apple, lad?"

I nodded.

"Good. You know how the apple cooks and falls away from the crust when it's baked?"

"Yes, sir."

"Well," continued Bedford, "that's what we think happened when this world was formed. The warm insides cooled into a ball slightly smaller than the crust upon which we live. At some point, massive parts of the Basin caved in and the ocean water drained to the surface of the inner globe."

"I think I understand. Like I figured—a sphere within a sphere."

"Exactly," said Missus Grier.

"But what about the object on the island? Can you explain that?"

"I could only guess what it is," said Missus Grier. "However, I think you can explain it."

"Me?"

"Yes, you." She handed me the drawing of the structure and a pencil. "Let's test how good your eye for detail actually is."

She placed her finger on a part of the sketch that indicated a relatively flat area. It had a row of dark rectangles running its width that were underscored with some squiggles. "Can you focus on this area of the structure? Concentrate, Fallon."

I closed my eyes and focused. "The dark areas are smooth and glossy. Like glass." I opened my eyes and began to sketch the details. "Yes. Like a row of windows. See? Like this."

"And beneath these windows, lad. What are those squiggles?"

I closed my eyes again. I was puzzled and disturbed by what I saw. A tremor shot through me as I opened my eyes in astonishment.

"What is it, Fallon?" said Missus Grier.

"Writing."

"Writing?"

"Yes. I saw it clearly."

She smiled at my words. "And what did this writing say?"

I penciled in the letters: IE *NEWORLD*.

$$x \sim 1.4$$

1.5
Consequences

1.5.1

TEARS STREAKED Missus Grier's pale face and her voice quavered. "The craft itself, Bedford! In pristine condition after all
these centuries."

"I wonder if it can still fly," said Bedford.

"Fly? What are you talking about?" I asked.

"Remember this?" Missus Grier handed me some yellowed
papers.

"Uh… It's the Solarist propaganda Dean Ambrose claimed I
had."

"Yes, papers like the ones Missy Howard gave him so he'd
bring you to the Headmaster… and to me. Look it over as I explain.

"Those papers refer to a very important book that I have in
my possession. The book claims to be the log of a craft that could
fly among the stars. It was called the *Interstellar Explorer Neworld*."

"IE *Neworld*," I said, tapping my finger on the drawing.

"Yes. It came from another world called Earth and bore more
than 5,000 people. It also brought the embryonic sources for almost all the plants and animals found on our island. The animals
and plants down here in the Basin are the true natives of
Neworld."

"Your discovery proves that the book is not a fiction," said
Bedford. "It's not the product of some overwrought imagination.
It is, in fact, the partial record of an incredible voyage and the
beginning of life on Neworld."

"Have you ever thought it odd that we count a person's age by annums and not cycles?" asked the Missus. "And why is an annum only two-thirds of a cycle—twelve months instead of eighteen?"

"To be honest, I just accepted what I was taught," I replied. "But now, everything I know may be a lie."

"I wouldn't call it a lie," said Bedford. "It's more of a fiction."

"Ha!"

"So you appreciate the irony, lad."

"To the *Service of Today* and the *Building of Tomorrow*," I mused.

"A world without history," said Missus Grier, "can't question its past."

"And the Council hides all this from us?"

Bedford hesitated, as if searching for the answer. "We don't think the Council knows the whole truth. Of course, they understand that the beliefs built around the Fount, *kons, and the* Below are fiction—the Council chambers look directly down the delta, for B's sake. They have a clear view of the Basin, and the entire Council spends HighConjunction there."

"However," said Missus Grier, "we believe that the original settlers kept their secrets so well that the full truth has been forgotten."

"Then why kill McCreigh? Why were we followed from the Mount? Who was beating on your door?"

"Fear of the unknown," replied Bedford. "Knowledge is power, lad. You understand? The Council feels threatened by any challenge to the belief system they foster and the Code they enforce."

Missus Grier looked troubled. "And they are afraid of what we might know," she added.

"You asked how all this got built... by whom... for what reason. The truth is, I discovered it—*re*discovered it, I should say—when I was a young girl. It's a story I will tell, for the record, at some time. We didn't build the tunnels that lead down from

Neworld, the waystations, or this facility. We don't have the tools. The people who had the ability to build a ship to the stars did this."

"But why?"

"Perhaps to give us a path home—if we want it," said Missus Grier. "It's like they created a puzzle—a *series* of puzzles—that we have to solve to earn the knowledge."

"Your work is done then, Missus," I said. "You've found your truths."

Missus Grier shook her head. "No, Fallon, our work is just beginning. There are so many questions to be answered. What lands lie beyond the Basin? Are there other people on this world? How do we journey to these lands? What about exploring the world Below? Exploring the IE *Neworld*? Getting it to fly?"

Bedford grasped my arm. "What about returning to the stars?"

1.5.2

BEDFORD and Missus Grier seemed preoccupied. After announcing that we would all head back to Neworld as soon as possible, they conferred in one of the small offices while the rest of us worked feverishly to stow the equipment and secure the Observation Base.

"They're concerned about those back home," Tobey told me as we manhandled the sphere into its dock.

"Was it men from the Council beating at the door?"

"Give a little slack, Sean," said Tobey. "More… That's it, boyo." He wiped his brow and motioned for me to hand him a fastening strap. "Sure enough, it was what you call the Dark Men."

"If they don't know about all of this, why is the Council so concerned?"

"They see the Movement as a threat to the Code—a threat to their beliefs," said Sean.

"To their authority—their power," said Tobey.

"Aidan… The people back home… They're all right, aren't they?"

"We don't know, lad." It was Bedford's deep voice. "We need to get topside to find out. You lads done here?"

"One last strap," said Sean.

"Good. So head to the mess when you're done, get some food, and suit up. We're all heading home—the entire Observation Base crew. The waystations are too small to handle the lot of us so we'll be leaving in three groups. I want the three of you with Missus Grier and me in the first group. We leave within the hour."

We were fed, attired, and waiting by the Observation Base door before Missus Grier, Bedford, and the others arrived. We attached the short links of rope that would tie us together for the Lighting Run and were on our way.

I was astonished by the sight that lay before me when we emerged from the mouth of the entrance tunnel. There was no lightning and the wind was brisk at our backs, but not as strong as before. It was comfortable and clear. Clear! I could see the wind-swept rocky surface, studded with scrubby plant life that slanted away from the incessant wind.

I heard a muffled sort of roaring behind us. I turned and my gaze was drawn skyward as I tried to comprehend the enormity of the towering column of moisture soaring into the heavens. The upper region of the Fount plumed toward Neworld, where it would drop crippling snow for the next month or so.

"You'll trip and fall if you don't watch where you're going," said Tobey, who anchored the tail end of our human chain.

I pointed; he turned to look. "Bugger me!" He stopped dead in his tracks, sending a jolt up the line that almost brought the whole procession to our knees.

"What the bloody B, Tobey?" boomed Bedford from the front.

By this time everyone was gazing in wonderment at the Fount.

"It's only water vapor, not the *kons* of men," said Missus Grier, "but its precious moisture truly brings life to Neworld."

"But it's topside for us, which is this-a-way," said Bedford with a grand sweep of his arm. "We'll make good time with the wind to our backs."

A dark wall rose from the Basin floor about two kilometers ahead and its size and substance were revealed as we advanced. By the time we reached the first waystation, the trees dominated our view. Soon we were in the forest. It had been a mysterious challenge to the mind when glimpsed through the dark mists, but now it was simply spectacular. The leafy canopy of yellow-green and amber didn't start for maybe a hundred meters above our heads, but the broad leaves, which were as long as two men are tall, were so thick that we soon needed to crank the light runs and our helmet lamps to make our way.

We entered waystations only to sleep, preferring to take our rest periods and lunches out in the open.

The crew took their lead from Missus Grier and Bedford, who were quiet and concerned.

As we trekked on, I began to think about Neworld—about what would spur 5,000 people to bring countless plants and animals to this distant place. Were they forced to flee? That didn't seem right. It would take a lot of time and resources to prepare for such an epic venture. So was it a choice? Then why Neworld? Why this particular island rising from the bed of a vanished ocean? Why the Code and the stories about the Fount?

My thoughts drifted back to the plants and animals. With a world as astounding as this, why would they bring so many types of plants and animals? To make Neworld more like home, probably. Which types are from Earth, and which are native? Did the settlers kill off entire species of native life to make room for the new ones they brought?

Then, what would be the consequences of this new truth? Would it—*should* it—change Neworld? What good would it do? We're happy living the way we live, aren't we? We're healthy, housed, and well fed. Everyone has something to do, a place to be. What possible good could come of this new knowledge?

1.5.3

WITH THE WINDS to our back, we made better time on our return trip. The temperature dropped as we neared the base of Neworld. Snow didn't sift through the canopy of leaves, but there was frost on the ground and the locking wheel on the metal hatch was stiff. It took both Sean and Tobey to get it open. There didn't seem to be any bugs around, but the twins followed protocol and sprayed the antechamber before opening the inner door.

Tobey led the way as Sean hustled us in before securing the outer hatch, spraying again, then securing the inner door.

The others seemed to know what to do, so I just tried to not get in the way and to mimic what they did. Missus Grier was keeping us focused on stowing the gear. Out of the corner of my eye I noticed Bedford and the twins steal away and head up the stairs. I quickly shed my boots and outer garments, hoisted my pack over my shoulder, and took off after them.

I could hear them talking some distance ahead of me. I couldn't make out the words, but by their tone of voice, I knew it wasn't idle conversation.

When I reached the warehouse level, it was dark. I heard a faint tapping sound, then the whir of the static lights across the way, and I saw the three men silhouetted against the green glow of the lamps. I started to run. They turned, and squinted into the darkness as they heard my footfalls.

"It's me," I called.

"Fallon, you needn't have…" started Bedford.

"Maybe not, but I'm here just the same."

Bedford considered me a moment and was about to speak when I said, "Do you hear that?"

We all listened.

"No," said Bedford. "What is it you hear?"

"An echo, maybe, from below." I cocked my ear. "There it is again."

"I heard it too, that time," said Sean. "It was faint, but it wasn't an echo from the stairwell."

Again.

"That direction." Tobey pointed to the left side of the darkened cavern.

"You sure, Tobey?" snapped Bedford. "From over there?"

"Positive."

"Okay, you and Sean hurry up to the door. Look around, but don't try opening it before you come back and report to me. Be off with you now."

Bedford began to crank one of the large stand lights. "Fallon, crank up a few more, then follow me." He raced to the far end of warehouse, which became illuminated as he cranked up a light.

The tapping was louder.

"Help me with this," he said as I approached.

We put our backs to a shelf that stood against the wall. It creaked and groaned as we slid it across the stone floor. Behind it was a tunnel that dead-ended about two meters in. It was large enough for two grown men standing abreast to walk through comfortably. The tapping reverberated in the tunnel.

"Find me a hammer or a metal rod or something. Then crank a couple more lights on this end."

Not more than a few paces away was a tool bay with sledgehammers, pickaxes, and any manner of stone-working tools. I grabbed a small hand tool with a hammerhead on one side and a pick-claw on the other. I gave it to Bedford, then dragged a couple of stand lights closer to the tunnel and cranked them to maximum brightness.

Bedford waited for a pause in the tapping before striking the end wall of the tunnel three times. Immediately, three taps replied.

Two taps—two taps in reply.

Tobey and Sean came racing across the cavern.

"It's warm up there," said Sean. "The door's almost too hot to touch."

"We think there's been a fire," said Tobey. "Those Dark bastards either broke in and took everyone…"

"…or they burned the house down around them," said Sean.

"This is not the time to speculate, lads. It's time to bust rock." Bedford held up his hammer. "Fallon, did you find anything larger than this?"

"This way!" I said to the twins.

In seconds we were armed.

"We only have less than a meter to penetrate," said Bedford.

He and Sean took the first turn at the wall. I retrieved a couple of shovels so Tobey and I could remove the rubble. The pick work was tiresome so we took short shifts. Progress was slow, but it was progress.

Tobey and I were in the tunnel when Missus Grier and the others arrived from downstairs. They were approaching when Tobey's strike sounded hollow, then mine broke through. We stopped, took a step back, and stared at the rough circle of gaslight that shone through. The joyous noise of clapping and cheering met our ears. I turned toward Bedford with a broad smile, which faded when I saw Missus Grier weeping on his shoulder.

Tobey put his mouth to the hole and called out, "Stay clear. We're coming through."

Ten minutes later, we'd opened the wall almost to the size of the short tunnel. Addie stood in the front row of a group of about thirty people who waited on the other side. They were dressed as if for an early fall day, with sweaters or layered clothing.

When Tobey and I stepped through, Addie rushed forward, gave me a big hug and a kiss, and then ran to her grandmother in the cavern behind me, sobbing with joy.

Ravenhair stepped through the throng.

My heart pounded as she approached.

She reached out her arms in welcome.

I smiled.

Then she embraced Bedford, who had come through the opening.

"Lenore," said Bedford.

"Dad," said Ravenhair.

1.5.4

OVER THE next several days, we talked to everyone who had been in the house when we left. This is the story they told:

The molding around the front door was beginning to splinter, and the wall to crack, under the relentless pounding. But the sturdy door held.

Lenore Bedford put on her housemistress smock and made one final sweep around the great room to make sure nothing was left behind. She picked up some papers from a table and tucked them into her smock pocket.

"Go now," she said to the two men with their back to the door. "You know what to do."

As soon as she was alone, she called, "Stop that. Stop that right now. You're breaking the door."

The pounding continued.

"I dare not approach the door, much less open it with you pounding so."

Silence.

"Are you done, then?"

"Open the door," came a man's shout.

Lenore stepped to the door and slid open the small eyehole. Four men in black coats and slouch hats stood shivering in the cold. It had begun to snow.

"Quiet now. The Missus has come home quite ill. I've been tending her and just got her settled when you started your banging."

"Open up."

"Shouldn't you be home with family? The HighConjunction is nearly here, and the snow has begun to fall. We're tending the ill, and preparing to shutter-up for the season, as you should be."

"Open... the... door!"

"On whose authority?"

"The Council's."

"For what purpose?"

"A search. Open!"

Lenore shut the eyehole and unlatched, unbolted, and unlocked the door. As she opened it, the Dark Men flooded in after the one who had done the talking. The last man through shut the door behind him.

"Identify yourself," said the stout man.

"This is our house. You first."

The man glared.

Lenore remained silent.

"The name is Wessler. Earnst Wessler. I've come on Council business. And you are?"

"Lenore Bedford."

"Miss... Missy...?"

"That is of no importance since I would never contract with a man so... of your age."

"And why are you here?"

"I run the household. My father is the butler, carriage driver, butcher... You get the idea. We have just a small staff—we're understaffed actually. That's how Missus Grier got sick. A friend told us about a boy at the Mount. That's why she made a hasty trip before the snows to... How do I say this delicately? Acquire some cheap help."

Wessler looked dubious. He reached into his coat and withdrew a folded sheet of paper. He shook it open and held it out for Lenore to see. "Orders from the Council to search the house and grounds."

"Search? For what?"

"Solarist materials."

"We have no... No, wait... Missus Grier gave me this to dispose of." She pulled the papers from her smock and handed them to the Dark Man. "She got them at the Mount. From Headmaster Hunninger, I believe. I haven't had time to burn them."

Wessler skimmed the pages. "Yes, these should be burned... and the Solarists with them."

"Well, that seems to clear that up. You have what you came for, so good day to you, gentlemen."

As she began to open the door, Wessler kicked it shut. "Search the place," he said to the men. "Account for everyone here!" He turned on Lenore. "I want to see Missus Grier."

"I told you, she's ill in bed."

"Now!"

She led Wessler toward the back of the house. Two of the men were tearing the great room apart as they passed. Lenore was certain nothing would be found.

"They're making a mess!"

"You'll have all HighConjunction to put it right."

Missus Grier's rooms took up the south rear corner of the sprawling house. The bedroom was dark, with the winter shutters closed both inside and out and the heavy drapes drawn. Their footsteps and the clang of heating pipes were the only noises in these back hallways.

"Try not to disturb the Missus," said Lenore as she opened the bedroom door.

There was a faint hiss from the radiator. The room was warm and misty from steam. The light from the fireplace made the foggy room glow and pulsate.

"Lenore?" came a weak voice from the bed.

"Yes, it's me, Missus. And a man from the Council."

Coughing, she said, "Oh, please keep him a safe distance. I don't want to be the cause of someone else spending the HighConjunction sick in bed."

The Dark Man took one step into the room.

"You just returned from a trip, Missus Grier."

"Yes…"

"Where did you go?"

"To the Mount… to buy myself a servant boy."

"Was that the only reason for your trip?"

"Yes. Ask that little pig Hunninger if you doubt me." She coughed heavily.

"And on your return trip, did you make any stops?"

"Three. We spent the nights at a few inns. One was called the Ramshead, I believe, and another was the Glynnsforde… Glynndale… [cough] Glynn-something…"

Wessler, apparently satisfied, held up a hand to stop her. He stepped from the room and motioned Lenore to follow. She joined him in the hall and closed the bedroom door.

. . .

AIDAN waited five minutes before getting out of bed and removing her grandmother's bedclothes. She "reconstructed" her grandmother's form with a couple of extra blankets and pillows, crept to the door, and cracked it open to see if the way was clear.

She slipped into the hallway, quietly closing the bedroom door behind her. Then she padded softly down the hall a few meters, where she pulled back a tapestry, opened a servant's passage, and disappeared.

. . .

WESSLER AND LENORE ran into another of the Dark Men as she was leading him through the labyrinth of guest rooms and the servants' quarters, which were filled with smells from the kitchen.

When the trio arrived in the kitchen area, they found two cooks busy with their holiday preparations. Aidan was there too, sitting on a stool with her arm curled around a large mixing bowl, working a wooden spoon. She looked surprised when she saw the two men.

"Search this area," said Wessler to his companion. "The others will work their way back here." He pulled out a stool next to Aidan and sat down. He looked at her intently.

"Lenore, who is this rude man?"

"He's from the Council."

Another look of surprise.

"Have we met?" said Wessler.

"I don't think so. I'd remember you."

"Are you sure? *I'm* sure. It was recently."

"It couldn't have been. I was on a trip upland with my grandmother. We only just got home today." She turned to Lenore. "How's she doing?"

"I looked in on her just a bit ago. The room is warm and she seems to be resting comfortably, Miss."

Wessler looked between the two women before settling on Lenore. "These old manors—" He was interrupted by the arrival of the other Dark Men. He held up a finger, halting them in their tracks. "As I was saying, these old manor houses were built with servant passages, weren't they?"

"Yes," answered Lenore without hesitation. "Let me show you…"

"Show them," he said waving his hand vaguely in the direction of the men who had just entered. To them he said: "Be thorough."

Lenore opened a panel next to the larder door. "This is the passage to the dining room. If you'll follow me…"

When the men were gone, Wessler reached out and touched Aidan on the shoulder, as if he were picking a piece of lint, then he brushed the back of his hand against her copper hair as he withdrew it. "Why don't you show me to the cellars?"

Aidan turned to the cook, a sturdy looking woman of about fifty, and tipped the bowl in her direction. "Is this stirred enough to leave it, Effie?"

"'Tis, Miss. But let me show the man to the basement. I need to check on them men doin' the butcherin' anyways."

"She'll show me around," said the Dark Man flatly.

"But I'll be comin' along just the same, if you don't mind."

"I do mind."

The cook finished cutting a potato, set down her knife, wiped her hands, and started toward the cellar door. "It's this way, now." She pulled a cast-iron key from her apron and unlocked the heavy cellar door. "Are ya comin' or aren't ya?"

Wessler stood up angrily, almost knocking over the stool. With a jerk of his head, he told Aidan to follow the cook's lead.

Immediately, the Dark Man knew that it would take a larger crew to search the dimly lit cellars thoroughly.

"Are there any servant passages down here?"

The cook scoffed. "These *are* servant passages. Other than curious children explorin', who else would come down here besides us?"

She led Wessler into the curing room and through the hanging carcasses. An older man and a young lad were standing at the butcher's table with their backs toward the visitors. A single gas lamp on the back wall lit the butcher's table casting the men as silhouettes.

"No, no," chided the man. "Put your whole shoulder into it, like this." He raised a cleaver over his head and brought it down in a violent manner.

"Uh-hem..." said the cook to get the men's attention.

The two turned toward the noise. The stocky older man had dark skin and close-cropped hair graying at the temples. He was wearing a white butchers coat and leather apron. The younger man was dressed the same, his apron and face smeared with blood.

"Mister Bedford, this man is from the Council. He's having a look around."

"Uh? The Council? Looking around?" He wiped both hands on his apron and extended one in greeting.

Wessler made no move to reciprocate. "Bedford, the house-mistress's father?"

"Yes."

"And this is...?"

"Fallon. A new boy we got from the Mount."

The Dark Man studied them both for a moment before turning on his heels and saying to the cook, "Take me back upstairs."

Aidan followed as far as the cellar stairs, then headed back to the curing room.

"Do you think they bought it?" asked the young man, wiping the blood from his face.

"Hope so," said the older man as he hung his apron on a peg and unbuttoned his butcher's coat, revealing layers of sweaters that made him look heavier than he was.

* * *

WESSLER MARCHED straight to the front hall, calling for his men as he went. Lenore followed close on his heels. The Dark Men converged on the hall at almost the same time.

"Find anything?"

The men indicated they had nothing to report. Wessler grunted. "What's the count?"

"I found two male servants," said one.

"One beefy, the other lean?"

"That's them."

"The twins," said Wessler.

"And we questioned a maid," said another man.

"That's three. With the two in the cellar, the cooks, the old lady and her granddaughter, and the housemistress, that makes ten. Does that check out with the number of occupied rooms?"

"We counted the Missus and the Miss, and seven servant's beds. That's nine."

"Who's the extra…"

"The new boy, Fallon," said Lenore. "He brought nothing with him from the Mount. We haven't given him a room yet."

Wessler gave her another stern look before opening the door. "Did their names match the list?"

"Yes, sir. Except for the boy. He wasn't listed."

Wessler led his men into the cold. The snow was already ankle deep.

"Nobody comes or goes…" he was saying as Lenore closed and secured the door. She pressed her ear against the wood.

"Seal the doors, windows, any way out of this place. The snow will be halfway to the eaves in a few days, but I don't want them to be able to tunnel their way out."

• • •

THE DARK MEN must have planned their actions from the start, for they had what they needed with them. Lenore and the eight others followed the hammering sounds from room to room as the Dark Men boarded up the house.

Lenore had no illusions that anyone would be leaving the house anytime soon. It troubled her, but she found solace in the fact that the Dark Men had not discovered the two passages on the basement level—one leading to the massive living and working quarters and the other, even more secret, passage that led to the Basin. Only a select few knew exactly where this passage was. Lenore was the only person still topside who knew.

She gathered the staff in the kitchen. "I don't think it's safe to stay up here. Percy," she said to the man who had impersonated her father, "go down to the quarters and organize the men into parties. Gather every scrap of food and any supplies we have in the house and take them to the quarters. Addie, you need to go along... and send the women to me. Effie, you and Anne gather all your kitchen stuff together. Tom and Harvey, pack it up and haul it downstairs. The rest of us will collect blankets, towels, bedding, clothes... anything... everything we might need for a long stay."

The opening to the underground living quarters was not as hidden or secure as the door to Below. It was behind a shelf in the granary in the south cellar. The shelf was on a track that slid back from the granary wall into the anteroom of the quarters. The controlling winch could only be operated from the quarters' anteroom. However, a small trap door—just big enough for a small person to crawl through—was hidden inside a crate on the bottom shelf. The crate was filled with bags of flour.

Without the flour in his hair to make it appear gray, Percy Williams looked his true age, 27 annums. He and Aidan quickly removed the sacks. Then Aidan leaned into the crate, popped open the trap, and crawled through. Before Percy had the last sack back into the crate, the shelf was moving. The granary echoed with the click, click, click of the winch.

Slowly, the quarters' anteroom was revealed. Aidan had already crossed the wide chamber and was descending the long ramp down to the quarters. There were almost thirty people waiting in the quarters. It was an enormous area carved from and into a naturally occurring cavern, much like the warehouse level of the

Basin passage. The quarters could easily house more than three hundred, if need be, and not seem cramped. It was laid out like a small, self-contained village and even had an independent gas system for lighting, heating, and cooking. The only way in or out was through the granary.

The team worked quickly and efficiently. They had practiced for exactly this sort of event. Everyone was exhausted by the time they had amassed and stowed everything they could bring down.

Lenore gathered the team in the anteroom. "We're all going to be here for quite some time. At least until Missus Grier and the others return. Maybe… probably… longer. Percy, organize a small patrol to take turns topside, watching the house."

"Yes, Miss."

"I've lost track of time," she continued. "We all need to get some rest."

. . .

A WEEK went by without incident. HighConjunction had come and gone. Whatever was supposed to happen at Observation Base had happened by now, and it was the main topic of conversation among the team. On the surface, the people of Neworld were still celebrating the long holiday. In a few weeks they would, as tradition dictated, open their front doors and dig their way out. Many people would clear the snow from the top of their bonfire piles, douse the logs with lighting fluid, and set the pyre ablaze, eventually melting away a large circle of snow, emulating the return of SolMajor, and celebrating the coming of planting season.

It was the middle of the night, if one could tell. Lenore and Addie were taking the patrol. The gaslights in the hallways were lit so the patrol could see and hot water still flowed through the iron radiators so the patrols would not freeze. But the fireplaces were dark and the flus closed to hold out the cold.

Lenore was in the great room when she heard what sounded like running water. She saw a stream of liquid flowing across the floor. Her first thought was that a hot water pipe had burst, but the smell dispelled that notion in a hurry. It was lighting fluid—countless liters of fluid—coming from where? She followed the flow back to the fireplace. The Dark Men were pouring lighting fluid down the chimney!

She raced from the great room to the dining room. A stream flowed down the hall and she didn't need to look in.

"Addie! Addie!" There was no answer.

Fluid streamed from every room that had a fireplace.

"Addie!" Lenore rushed to the rear of the house—where she thought Addie might be. She found her asleep on her grandmother's bed. The floor was soaked in fluid. The bottoms of the draperies and bedclothes sopped it up.

"Addie!"

Aidan sat up, startled. She was disoriented and partly overcome by the fumes. Lenore grabbed her and dragged her from the bed. Aidan slipped on the wet wood floor, and her clothing became drenched. "What..."

"No time for questions. Come with me. Now!"

The two slogged through the stream to the kitchen. Fluid was coming out of the stove vent and the hearth.

A horrifying, deep *whoosh* reverberated from the front of the house and the walls shook. A bluish light came from the hall as the fire spread across the sheen of fluid that covered every floor.

"They must have ignited it in the great room," said Lenore.

Aidan still did not fully comprehend what was happening, but she realized the danger. "If the gas lines rupture, the whole house will go up."

Lenore yanked open the cellar door. The fluid was flowing down the stairs. She closed the door and descended to the cellars. The fluid had not yet spread far. Maybe there was hope.

They sprinted to the granary. The shelf was in its open position. Lenore called for help and several people responded.

"They've set the house ablaze! Start closing the entrance."

Aidan was fully aware now and flew into action, running down the hall some distance and closing every door she could as she came back.

"Good thinking, Addie," said Lenore when Aidan returned. Lenore slammed the granary door shut. Then they all retreated into the anteroom and watched anxiously as the shelf was cranked closed.

"This is still too dangerous," said Lenore. "Everyone down to the quarters!"

They withdrew to the quarters and waited. A slight trembling and a shower of dust and rock confirmed their fears.

All were silent. They were fearful and demoralized but eventually their discipline and training brought them together to discuss the options. None looked good. Even if there were a clear way out, the Council would be watching. They had to stay put. The Council would think ten people had died in the fire—they had their names on a list. But they were unaware of the existence of the others who had been concealed in the quarters.

Lenore went to the office Missus Grier maintained in the quarters. She removed a drawer from a cabinet on one wall, reached into the opening, felt around, found what she was told would be there, and removed a small envelope.

She withdrew a yellowed card that had a strange symbol on it. When she flipped it over and read what was printed on the other side, a trace of a smile formed on her face—the first in many days.

She found a hammer in a tool bay, and then sought out Percy Williams.

"Come with me."

"Where to?"

"We need to search the walls near the bottom of the ramp for this marking." It was two intersecting ovals with a dot in the center of the overlapping area.

More than an hour later Percy shouted, "Over here! I've got it."

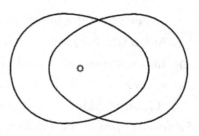

Lenore ran to Percy's location. She held the card next to the image carved into the stone. She raised the hammer and struck the image three times. Clink. Clink. Clink. She waited about thirty seconds, then tapped again. Percy gave her a questioning look. She handed him the card. "Read what's on the other side."

Percy's eyes widened as he read. "I'll organize the men. We won't stop until we get a response."

For more than two days they tapped three times every half-minute or so. Morale was low and the man on duty almost didn't hear the first faint response.

Doubtfully, he replied with three taps.

Two taps.

Emotions flowed. He struck the wall forcefully two times. Then tears welled up in his eyes and he yelled, "They're here!"

$$x \sim 1.5$$

1.6

Historian

1.6.1

THE DESCENT and our discoveries were not important that day, or night—we'd lost track of time. It was a time of shock, grief, confusion, and uncertainty.

Several hours after our arrival, Missus Grier pulled Bedford, Lenore, and a few other people away for a meeting.

I didn't know where I was, I had no place to go, and I had nothing to do so I wandered aimlessly through a series of structures Bedford had called *the Commons*. I was emotionally drained and physically exhausted. My brain conjured no images. I leaned my back against a wall someplace and slid to the floor. My chin sank to my chest...

"Fallon."

It was a woman's voice in my dream.

"Fallon."

A hand on my shoulder roused me.

"Fallon," said Lenore softly. "The Missus wants to see you. Gently now..."

Gently? She saw my puzzlement and pointed down as she put her finger to her lips. "Shh..."

Addie was asleep, her head in my lap, my left hand resting in her hair. I looked sheepishly at Lenore.

Addie stirred and said sleepily, "I'm awake." She sat up, yawned, then kissed me on the cheek.

Addie and Lenore exchanged looks.

"I'll take him," said Addie.

A warm flush swept across my face.

Lenore shrugged, turned, and strode purposefully away.

As I watched Lenore leave, Addie got to her feet and reached out her hands. "C'mon."

I took her hands, letting her help me to my feet.

"Grandmother sent me to help you find a room, but you looked so comfortable, I decided to lie down beside you."

Very few people were moving about. The gaslights were either extinguished or turned low.

"This is it," said Aidan after just a short walk. "I'll wait for you and show you to the pods when you come out."

. . .

MISSUS GRIER looked worn when I entered her office. She sat behind a desk and motioned me to take a seat.

"Fallon, you've done everything we've asked of you and more," she said. "Now it looks like you'll be stuck with us for some time longer. I hope you'll accept my apology."

"I'm not sorry, ma'am."

There was a spark of happiness in her eyes. "Do you mean that?"

"Yes, ma'am. I do. I feel like I didn't start to live my life until that day you bought me."

I smiled.

"Bought you, indeed." She perked up at the memory. "That swine, Hunninger." She sighed deeply as weariness washed over her again. "Seems like ages, though it's been less than two weeks. I am so grateful that you are now part of the family."

Family.

"I shan't keep you long," she continued. "I have a favor to ask, then you can go back to your room. Addie did get you settled, didn't she?"

"Uh… Yes, thanks," I lied.

"Good. I must tell you that your abilities are already talked about and respected. Several different department heads have requested your services…"

"I'll gladly do whatever you ask."

"That's good to know, but my position gives me some authority so I want to make my request first. Now, as you're aware, a lot has happened since you've come to us. Neworld might be about to change for the better, or possibly worse. We can't be sure. Will we be benefactors to our world, or its betrayers? Only future generations will be able to tell, and to do that, they will need a record of what we discover and what we do. We need a historian. Will you be the first historian of Neworld, Fallon?"

I was stunned. "Historian? I'm not sure I know what that means, exactly."

"Nor do we, but we have documents, here in this complex, that will help you figure it out. We'll work through it together."

She sat patiently as I considered what she was asking of me. Historian? How long would it take? How many weeks, months, cycles? Every yesterday is history, isn't it? It would take the rest of my life.

"I'll try," was my answer.

"I can't ask for more. Your first task will be to talk to everyone who was left in the house when we went away to the Observation Base. Take the time you need, then write it up and present it to me."

I nodded.

"We've sent everyone else to bed, so off with you. Sleep as long as you need to. We're not going anyplace. When you are fully rested, just ask anyone for anything and they will help."

1.6.2

ADDIE had two handheld static lights cranked up and turned on when I came out of Missus Grier's office.

"There are a dozen dormitory pods that branch off from the community area. Do you have a preference?"

"My room at the Mount was in the attic, so it was secluded and quiet. I liked that. I could use some time by myself. Someplace I can write and draw without interruptions."

"That'll be easy. Most of the pods are empty because this place is beyond huge, and the team is pretty close-knit so they stay in two adjacent pods. First, we need to get your bedding."

She led me confidently through the darkened Commons. It dominated the center of the quarters' main cavern. It was laid out like a small village with streets and an open courtyard at the center. The two- and three-story buildings were constructed of stone blocks and bricks, with wood doors and trim, and glass windows. The architecture was similar to that above ground. We reached a shop-like façade that had "Dry Goods" painted on the window. Addie opened the door and shone the light on shelves stacked with clothes, bedrolls, blankets, sheets, and pillows.

"Everywhere down here stays about this temperature all cycle 'round. So take what you think you need," she said while leading me through the large shop. "Sweaters are nice, or you can layer clothes. When they're dirty, drop them at the laundry and come back here for a clean set. You'll definitely need bedding…"

I lugged the bedroll (Addie insisted I needed the wide one), a blanket, and some sheets. Addie carried two pillows, several towels, and some washcloths. I began to appreciate the size of the quarters, and just how secluded I'd be, as we made our way to Pod G. Each pod was a rectangular area carved into the rock at the end of a short tunnel. The pod tunnel had broad double doors at both ends, giving the pod its own privacy.

When we entered the pod, Addie balanced the pillows on my load, went to the front wall, and cranked a static box a few turns. A series of overhead lights began to glow softly, just enough to illuminate the pod. It was laid out with the same sensibility as the Commons. A spacious open area in the middle held an informal meeting area and several long tables with benches. Everything was covered with layers of dust. Ten rooms were partitioned off on each of the left, right, and rear walls—much like the offices and rooms in the Observation Base. Their fronts were crafted brickwork that gave each room a distinctive look. The rooms were large enough for a door and one or two windows. I didn't see any "facilities" so I reminded myself to look for a bedpan the next day.

"Whaddya think?"

"Even in my tired state, I'm impressed."

She closed the tunnel doors, took the pillows, and went to a room with a window on each side of the door.

I followed.

"Is this okay?"

"Anything will do."

This time she balanced everything but a towel on my load. She was inside and cranking another static lamp before I crossed the threshold.

This wasn't a room. It was more like a small cottage. The front area had a sitting space and a small dining/kitchen area with cupboards and a sink. Everything inside was dust-covered too.

"Does the water run?"

"Not sure. I was just about to find out." She crossed to the sink and turned a handle. There was a hissing sound, then a gurgle, then a flow of greyish, stinking water.

"This pod hasn't been used for as long as I can remember."

The water soon cleared and smelled fresh. Addie set to work, cleaning the tabletop with a wet towel. It was blackened almost immediately and had to be rinsed several times before the job was done.

"There," she said, again taking her share of the supplies. "You can set your load down now."

"We have some more cleaning to do before you can get to bed."

She rummaged under the sink and found a metal bucket, which she filled with water. "Well, why are you just standing there? Come get the bucket."

She took the wet towel and grabbed another dry one before heading toward the door in the back wall, which stood ajar. She pushed it open with her shoulder. Another whir of a static box.

I followed.

The back half consisted of a good-sized bedroom with a private bath and privy to one side. It didn't have a tub, only a shower, but it was an unimaginable luxury.

Together we cleaned the raised stone platform that served as a bed. When we ran clean water in the shower and privy, I was surprised to find that the sinks and showers had both hot and cold water. We retrieved the bedding from the dining table and made up the bed.

Our tasks completed, she put her hands on my shoulders, stood on her toes, and kissed me on the lips. I watched as she turned and headed for the front door. The light in the front room blinked out, but I didn't hear the door. Addie came back into the bedroom. She was naked. She was a grown woman—a beautiful woman. She snapped off the bedroom light and moved into the room, where she was silhouetted by the fading glow from the bath light.

"It's been a hot, dirty day. We should clean up." She stepped into the shower and turned on the water. Her copper hair turned dark with moisture and clung to her face and body.

I followed.

That night was not the same as with Jenna. Aidan was sweet, tender. It was her first time.

1.6.3

I AWOKE with Addie's head on my chest, her arm around me. I ran my hand through her hair. It felt good. It felt secure. It felt right.

She stirred, kissed me on the chest, and then fell back asleep. With no windows, the room was perpetually dark. My eyes drifted shut.

I don't know what time of day it was when Addie shifted her hand and roused me. She kissed me on the lips and positioned herself on top of me.

"I almost died that night in the fire," she said as she moved her hips slowly, bent down, and kissed me again. "I was half-overcome with fumes, and terrified... not of dying, but of the chance that I might never see you again... and never be with you."

Another kiss.

"Thank you for not turning me away."

"I'm glad I didn't." I raised myself up and kissed her upon the face and body.

She began to cry.

"What's wrong? What have I done?"

"Nothing. Everything is right." She increased the rhythm of her movement. I responded in kind. "At this moment, everything is perfect."

It was perfect.

• • •

"WHAT WILL your grandma say?" I asked as we lay there exhausted.

"We're both of age..." she said.

"Both of age?"

"Yes, I believe the day the house burned was your birthday."

"My birthday!" The day I was looking forward to all my life, my eighteenth annum, had come and gone and I hadn't given it a thought.

"Fallon, you're of age… You're free!" She showered me with kisses, then whispered playfully in my ear: "Plus, you're stemmed, so I don't have to worry about my contract."

"What contract?" I asked.

"You know."

"You do realize that you're technically dead, don't you? We're both dead."

"Dead." She sat up. "Bloody B! My contract reverts to the Council to be auctioned off."

"Consider my position: I barely existed in the eyes of the Council, and now I'm dead. I died on my bloody eighteenth birthday." I fell silent and still as a corpse.

She put her hand over my heart and said, "Oh, no!" She moved it down my body, probing, then stroking. "I think you *are* dead. You're getting stiff."

We laughed.

"You know, your grandma…"

"You're thinking of Grandmother, now?"

"I'm talented. I can do two things at once."

She withdrew her hand.

"What about Grandmother?"

"She asked me to be the historian."

"A historian?"

"*The* Historian. The first historian of Neworld."

1.6.4

ADDIE AND I sat at the kitchen table and talked. We decided to keep our relationship secret for a while. Addie would make her way back to the Commons first and I would appear a discreet time later. Before she left, I performed my first act as historian by having her tell me her version of what happened in the house after Bedford and I had left. She was buoyant when recounting how she had played her grandmother—"We fooled that Council skreel!"—and broke down when recounting the horror of the fire. We hugged and kissed. I soothed her. She made me feel needed.

Finally, she got up to leave. She told me how to find the mess hall, which opened on the Commons courtyard, and reminded me to bring the hand lamp so I could find my way back.

We hugged and kissed in the doorway. I couldn't let her go.

She pushed me away, laughing. "Tonight... tonight. You have work to do, Historian." And she was off.

She was right, of course. There was a lot I needed to do. I needed to get my new rooms cleaned and supplied. I needed to familiarize myself with the quarters. I needed to stock up on writing and drawing materials. I needed to find clothing beyond what I had on my back.

I needed to find out how to be a bloody historian.

• • •

JUDGING BY the fare offered in the mess, it must have been lunch.

After I got my food, I found Tobey and a woman sitting at a table, with Sean seated across from them.

"Mind some company?" I said.

"Not at all, boyo," said Sean. "Have a seat. We're just discussing a problem."

"And what is that?"

"Being dead," said Tobey. "Me and Mary... Oh, Fallon, this is Mary Jo Wilkinson. Mary Jo this is..."

"*The* Fallon?" She rose. "Pleased to meet you."

"The pleasure is all mine."

Mary Jo was several annums older than the twins. Her blond hair fell softly on her shoulders and her demeanor seemed more serious than that of her companions.

Tobey pulled her back down and gave her a look before turning back to me. "We entered into contract some months ago. Open-ended, you know. Either of us could use our contract to claim the child."

"I'm to have first right, of course," said Mary Jo.

I was aware of the Code. I nodded my understanding.

"But now he's dead, he doesn't have a contract..."

"Hmm. Wow. I mean, you can still contract him to father a child, can't you?"

There was an awkward silence.

"There's more to it than that," said Sean. "Tell him, brother."

"I'm the eldest son and heir," said Tobey.

"But he's dead, leaving me the heir," said Sean.

"You're dead, too, brother. But no matter how you slice it, I'm a man without property."

It was a difficult situation.

"Having never had property myself, I can't say that I fully understand your problem, but I studied the Code at the Mount and I appreciate all the implications. Is there a magistrate on the team?"

The twins laughed at the thought.

"We aren't quite part of the system," said Tobey. "The Council would like to see us all dead."

"Yet you worry about the details of contract code," I said. "I think we all have a lot of *kon*-searching to do. Are we for the Code—for the Council—or not?"

1.6.5

LENORE AND AIDAN were approaching the mess area as I was leaving.

116

"Good day," said Lenore brightly.

"Hello," said Aidan. "Did you find a place all right?"

"Yeah, I'm over that-a-way someplace. Pod G, I think. Thanks for showing me where the bedding was."

Lenore looked between Aidan and me before saying: "The Missus told me that you accepted the position of historian. Good... that's good. I'm supposed to help you. Get you set up. Show you around. Answer questions. That sort of thing."

I nodded. "Thanks."

"Aidan and I are just about to have a bite. Care to join us?"

"No thanks, I just ate with the twins."

"Then let's get together when I'm done here," said Lenore.

"Fine. I need to find supplies for my room. Meet you in about an hour?"

"And how will you tell when an hour's passed?" said Lenore.

"Uh... um..."

"Better pick yourself up a watch, first thing," she said coolly. "One hour." She looked at a small watch pinned to her blouse. "It's 1:08 now. We'll meet by Missus Grier's office. Remember where that is?"

"Yes, ma'am."

She entered the mess. Aidan raised her eyebrows and flashed me a half grin before following Lenore to lunch.

Lenore didn't seem to care for me too much. I admit that I'd had fantasies about her after that brief glimpse in the house. I drew her. I never drew Addie. I felt guilty, somehow, as if I had done something wrong—as if I'd betrayed Addie. I rubbed my temple. So many thoughts, images, sounds, and smells—all within the last two weeks. My heart was racing. I was awash with conflicting feelings. For nearly eighteen annums I'd been secluded in the Mount. I was better educated than most people in Neworld, but I wasn't prepared to be among them socially.

I took a deep breath and calmed myself down.

BEFORE I PUT the new watch in my pocket, I checked the time: 1:15.

To my relief, I found there were small carts that could be used to transport personal supplies. I made my round of the shops, stacked up the cart, and ran it back to my pod. I was running late, so I just left it in the pod's common area. I figured it was safe.

2:00. As I was sprinting back to the Commons I realized that I had been groggy the night before and really didn't remember where Missus Grier's office was.

2:05. I practically accosted the first person I met, a small woman with dark hair. "Where's Missus Grier's office?"

The startled woman pointed and I took off running. "Thanks," I yelled.

2:07. I arrived before Lenore. I had time to catch my breath and straighten myself out.

2:08.

2:10.

2:30.

3:14. "Come with me." Lenore passed by without breaking stride. I quickly caught up and fell into step.

"I understand that you've met Mary Jo Wilkinson."

"Yes, at the mess."

"She'll be your assistant. She's an excellent administrator. She'll arrange your interviews, transcribe your work, organize your files, and procure whatever you may need in supplies of reference materials."

"Sounds good."

"You'll have an office in the library, which is right over here."

Mary Jo was already at a desk when we arrived. Seven people were sitting at a table. They rose as one when we entered. I nodded in their direction. They sat. *Peculiar.*

Lenore led me into an office. Mary Jo followed us, closing the door behind her. With the blinds drawn, we had privacy.

"As Missus Grier told you, your first task is to document the events at the house. I am your first interview. The others who stayed in the house are waiting in the library." Lenore took a seat in front of the small table that served as a desk. Mary Jo sat off to one side with a pad and a pencil.

I rubbed my temple again and took a deep breath. I pulled out the chair behind the table and assumed the position of historian.

"Where should I start?" said Lenore.

Mary Jo poised her pencil.

I asked Lenore, "What's she doing?"

Mary Jo replied. "I'll make a record of everything that anyone tells you."

"Why?"

"So. You don't forget."

"I won't forget."

Lenore scoffed.

I turned on her. I had had enough. "Okay, I'll tell you where to start…" and I launched into a detailed description of her actions from the day I had first glimpsed her through the map room door. I was even able to recall some conversation, which I hadn't before.

"So, what happened next?" I asked, spitting out each word angrily.

Lenore was impassive. "Mary, you may leave." She waited until we were alone before she looked at me warmly and said, "Impressive."

She pulled her chair closer and put her elbows on the table.

"Sorry if I've been cool to you. 'Most beautiful woman,' you said."

I blushed. Had I really said that? I needed to learn to filter my raw memories before telling them to others.

She put her hands atop mine. I felt uncomfortably warm. Her foot brushed mine.

"So you desire me?"

"No. Uh… I just think you're beautiful."

I could tell her foot was bare when it traveled up my leg, to my inner thigh. I had no control over my physical response. She moved her foot slowly across my groin.

She looked at me seductively. "It feels like you desire me."

"That… that's just a physical reaction. I can't control it."

She increased the pressure and rhythm. "Don't try."

She began to massage my hands. I flung her hands aside. "I admit I thought about you. But I have feelings for someone else."

Her face hardened. Her foot stopped moving but she held it in place.

"Aidan?"

"Yes…"

She curled her toes and increased the pressure. I groaned. She shoved her foot hard enough to send the chair, which didn't have wheels, skidding back.

"What the B?!" I was doubled over in pain.

"I care for Aidan, very much… She's like a sister. If you ever cause her any pain…" She let the threat hang in the air before asking: "Does Missus Grier know?"

"No—not yet."

Lenore pushed her chair back and assumed a cool demeanor. She gave me a curt smile and then began to recite her story for the record: "I glimpsed you as well before the door closed…"

Her accounting was clear and concise, and it meshed with Aidan's.

1.6.6

THE NEXT few hours flew by. The interviews told me a lot about people's perceptions of events. The accounts all differed, but told basically the same story. I considered if I should expand my interviews to those who had retreated to the quarters with the files, maps, and papers as we were leaving. I ran the numbers in my mind—there were a lot more people here than I saw in the house that first day. I decided that this was a question for another time.

Now that I had the information, how should I present it? I was only familiar with the textbooks at the Mount. We didn't have histories—The *Service of Today* and the *Building of Tomorrow* and all that malarkey.

I stepped into the library and looked at the shelves of paper files. I saw only a few books and those were the same texts you could find anywhere.

Mary Jo greeted me: "Can I help you, sir?"

I had never been called sir before. It made me uncomfortable.

"Just call me Fallon, please."

"Yes, s… Fallon."

"Do you prefer Mary or Mary Jo?"

"To be truthful, I prefer Jo."

"Well, Jo, do you have any ideas on how to write a history?"

She gestured toward the shelves. "These are all reports of one sort or another that we have compiled over the cycles. I guess they qualify as histories, of a sort."

I sighed. "I'll start looking them over tomorrow. Walk you to the mess?"

When we reached the Commons' center, it was abuzz with activity. Tobey must have been watching for Jo, for he materialized out of the crowd, a broad smile on his face.

"Mary! Fallon! The second group from the Observation Base has arrived. Randall and the rest should be here tomorrow."

Our numbers were swelling. I wondered how long we could last down here.

"Come along. Sean's holding us a table and we already brought food from the mess." He took Jo's hand and pulled her toward the crowd before addressing me. "You coming?"

"No, I need to find the Missus. Have you seen her anywhere?"

"She's in the mess with Aidan and Lenore."

Great.

Lenore saw me as soon as I entered and excused herself before I arrived at the table. She passed me without a word or a glance.

"May I have a moment, Missus Grier?"

"Please, have a seat."

I took a position opposite Aidan and her grandmother.

"I don't know how to say this any way but straight up, and I apologize to Addie if I upset her."

I could see Aidan tense up and frown.

I swear, my heart was going to explode.

"I have feelings for your granddaughter, ma'am."

That got Missus Grier's attention. She looked at Addie, who was looking intently at me.

I'm in the soup now.

"Do you share these feelings, Addie?"

Her body relaxed and she smiled. "Yes, Grandmother."

"Are you asking my permission to…"

Aidan came around the table and sat next to me. "We have already been together, Grandmother." She put her hand on mine.

Missus Grier remained silent. She examined the two of us as if, together, we were something new—some*one* new.

"You're of age, Addie, and so is Fallon. Neither of you has a contract, but given Fallon's situation, what does it matter?" She smiled and set both of her hands atop ours. "I was young once. You have my blessing. Surely we all deserve a little happiness, don't we? Now, young man, get yourself some food. We'll talk as you eat."

"Thank you, Missus."

I told her about the interviews, my uncertainty on how to proceed, and my plan to look at the library reports in the morning.

"We are putting a lot of trust in you, Fallon. And in you, Aidan, if you want to be his partner in this endeavor.

"Any objections, Fallon?"

"None ma'am."

"Be forewarned. It can strain—or shall I say *test*—a relationship to both live and work together."

"Be it as it may," I replied.

"Then it's settled. What do you think of Miss Wilkinson? She's an excellent transcriber and we have found her most trustworthy. Can the two of you work with her as well?"

We both said we could.

"Great. Be in the library by eight. If you haven't done it already, Fallon, requisition an alarm clock."

"I'll take mine," said Aidan.

I made the rounds, welcoming the members of the Observation Team. The twins raised their eyebrows when they saw Addie with me. I shot them a look before either could make some wise remark.

"Jo," I said, "we need to be in the library at eight."

"Who's Jo?" asked Tobey, who was confused when Mary replied, "See you at eight."

"Jo?" asked Tobey.

"Yes. I prefer it."

"You didn't tell me."

"*You* didn't think to ask."

Sean sat there grinning. "Shoulda been in the contract, maybe," he said, trying to further stir up the beehive.

Jo boxed his ears. Tobey, in an effort to regain Jo's favor, followed suit.

We slipped away early, making a stop at Addie's pod to pick up her belongings. She had a small, one-room unit in Pod A. We gathered her things on a table in the meeting area. Then I searched for a cart, remembering I had another one waiting for me, laden with supplies.

As I was loading the cart, Addie went next door and knocked. Lenore opened the door. I couldn't hear what they said, but Addie was animated and happy. Lenore's smile seemed forced, but she hugged Addie and appeared to wish her well. When Addie walked back to me, Lenore's smile faded. She shut the door.

1.6.7

THE THREE of us were in the library by 7:30. Missus Grier and Bedford arrived a little before 8:00. They seemed pleased that we were already waiting.

Bedford closed the library door and locked it. This was something I had never seen done in the quarters. The shops all stood open for anyone at any time. Something was up.

"Bring two more chairs into the office, will ya, lad?"

Before he sat down, Bedford also locked the office door and made sure there were no gaps in the curtains.

"This is a critical moment for the Movement and for Neworld," said Missus Grier. "Aidan and Miss Wilkinson know much more about the Movement than you, Fallon, but you have critical new information that only the Observation Team knows. We have kept our secrets compartmentalized, in case one of us was captured by the Council and questioned by those Fallon aptly called the Dark Men."

"For instance, Aidan and most of the crew here in the quarters knew about the mission in the Basin," said Bedford. "But only a handful knew how we got there. Even fewer knew the details of the mission. No one except Mara and I knew about the emergency connecting tunnel between the quarters and the passages to Below. All Lenore knew was where, in case of such an emergency, to find the envelope telling her where to tap. The people who built all of this appear to have been excellent planners."

"The point is," said Missus Grier, "Only Bedford and I know our most guarded secrets. That is about to change. The three of you are going to become the guardians of the knowledge and assist us in bringing it to light."

A weight had descended upon our shoulders as surely as I had descended into the Below.

Addie clutched my hand.

"So, lad and lasses, here's what we're thinking: Fallon is the historian—our first. Aidan, you're the researcher. Whatever Fallon wants or needs to know, you'll help him find the answers. Jo, you are the recorder, the archivist. And you'll find it to be an astonishing archive."

"Fallon and Addie have already accepted their positions," said the Missus. "What about you, Jo?"

Jo looked at me and Addie, then Bedford, then Missus Grier as she considered the offer. "Yes, ma'am. I'm honored to accept."

Missus Grier clapped her hands together. "I'm so happy. I've been waiting many cycles for this moment."

Bedford stood. "Congratulations." We all rose and he shook our hands. "This is a historic day. A most historic day."

x~1.6

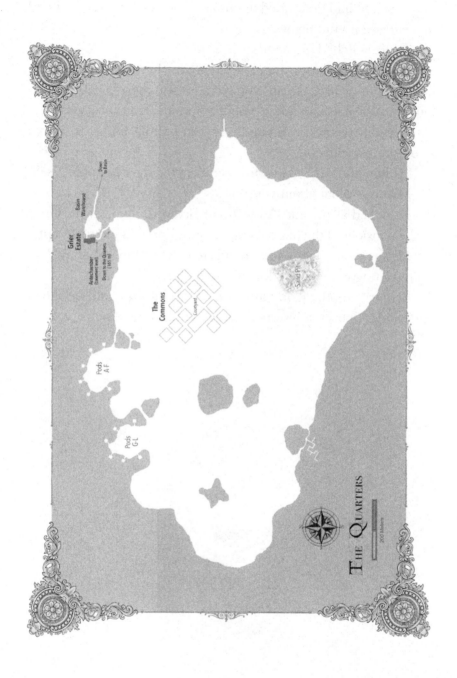

The Quarters

200 Meters

Grier Estate

Basin Warehouse

Down to Basin

Antechamber (basement level)

Down to the Quarters (165 ft)

The Commons

Courtyard

Pods A-F

Pods G-L

Sand Pit

Revelation

1.7.1

"NOW, for our first order of business." Missus Grier led us from the office into the library proper.

Bedford drew a long cardboard tube from one of the shelves. He removed some rolled papers and spread them out on the table.

"Maps of the quarters," Jo informed me. She was obviously experienced in such matters. She retrieved four small, polished stones from another shelf and placed them on the four corners of the map.

"Gather 'round, lad and lasses. As you know, we are trapped down here. The only way out was here—through the granary entrance. We've suffered a partial collapse of the antechamber."

He pulled another map from the bottom of the pile and positioned it over the first. It was a map of the Grier estate, but because it was semi-transparent, we could see the outlines of the quarters and cellars beneath it.

"You can see that the antechamber was not directly under the house. It was to the south of the cellars, with the quarters extending off to the south and east from there. For security reasons, the Basin chambers are unmapped. They'd be here, east of the house, and north of the quarters."

"We are fairly certain that the cellars are in worse shape than the antechamber," said Missus Grier. There was a tinge of anger mixed with the sadness in her voice. "Perhaps even a total collapse."

She sighed and mustered a smile. "But there is hope."

"We can dig our way out, can't we?" asked Addie.

"We could," said Missus Grier. "But we're sure the Council is watching, so it's best to bide our time. We have stockpiles down here that can last a group of our size two, maybe three, months. And we have this..." She withdrew a card from a pocket and handed it to me. "Do you know what this is?"

I recognized it instantly and passed it to Addie, who shared it with Jo. "It's the symbol that marked the connecting tunnel to the upper Basin chamber," I said.

"My daughter and Percy Williams..." said Bedford. "Have you met Percy, lad?"

"Yes, sir. Yesterday, when I conducted my interviews."

"Well, he and Lenore had a thought. What if there were other such tunnels? So Percy organized crews to search the walls for other occurrences of this symbol."

Jo asked, "Did they find any?"

"No," said Missus Grier. "Not this symbol."

Bedford tapped a spot on the map. "First, this is the location of the tunnel we opened between the Basin warehouse and the quarters. Since we've only installed gaslights in the antechamber, the Commons, and the few work areas we've reclaimed, most of the quarters remain in darkness. Consequently, we never paid much attention to these tunnels." He tapped two other places. "Besides, they appeared to be dead ends. This tunnel leads east, almost to the Rim, by our calculations, and this one heads south about fifty meters."

The usually calm Missus interrupted him, her eagerness betraying her excitement. "They dead-end in bedrock and each has a unique symbol etched in the center."

I tapped a fourth spot on the map—another secluded dead end. "And this?" I asked.

"Good eye, lad. That is the most secret of secrets known only to the Missus and me."

"And now you," added Missus Grier. "There are too many people about during the day for a group our size to slip off into the darkness unnoticed. Fallon and Addie, you have unwittingly chosen an ideally secluded place to live—the perfect location for a clandestine rendezvous. Take an early lunch. Make a show of your youthful passion and everyone will understand your absence this afternoon."

Jo looked at us and smiled.

"Can you find Pod G, Jo?" asked Bedford, pointing to its location.

"Yes, sir."

"In the dark? No lights?"

"Yes, sir."

"Fine, that's settled," concluded Missus Grier. "We'll meet a little after noon."

. . .

AT LUNCH we started playing our roles. Addie and I came out as an "off-contract" couple while Jo was felled by one of her headaches—a real, if occasional, condition she suffered. After a quick meal interrupted by pecks on the cheek, handholding, and general mooning about, Addie and I made our wink-and-a-nod excuses to sneak off.

We were waiting at the mouth of the pod tunnel when Jo arrived a few minutes before noon, clothed all in black. She was a smart woman. Missus Grier and Bedford dissolved out of the blackness ten minutes later.

Bedford carried the tube with the maps. "Follow us."

"In a few days we won't have to sneak off like this," said Missus Grier.

I'm sure that all three of us struggled to remember the path we took. I wasn't sure that even my memory would be sufficient to help me find my way in total darkness. We meandered down a maze of passages, each of us dragging one hand along the wall to keep us on course.

"It'll take you a few trips to remember how to get here in the dark," said Bedford.

A hundred meters down one tunnel we came to a dead end. I heard the sound of rocks being moved, then the scrape of metal on metal. A small door opened on the wall about chest high, exposing a series of lights laid out in a grid. They were marked:

$$1 \quad 2 \quad 3$$
$$4 \quad 5 \quad 6$$
$$7 \quad 8 \quad 9$$
$$\# \quad 0 \quad *$$

They were like nothing I'd ever seen before—and bright enough to illuminate our faces.

"Watch this," said the Missus. "In spite of the fact that it took James and me countless hours over a number of cycles to discover, you won't need Fallon's abilities to remember this."

She pressed the lights in a series: 12345#. In a manner similar to the granary entrance, the stone wall slid away from us. We entered a small, darkened area. We heard the wall slide shut, and then the room was filled with light as bright and as white as the light of SolMaj. The walls were smooth and polished to a sheen.

I looked around and couldn't find any gas lamps. Bedford pointed to the ceiling and we all looked up. The entire ceiling was emitting light.

"This," said Missus Grier, pointing to a glass plate embedded in the stone wall, "turns it on and off, with a touch of a finger."

"I've seen plates just like that all over the Commons and in the pods," said Jo. "They don't do anything."

"We know," said Bedford without elaboration. He motioned toward a metal hatch on the left wall. "You've seen one of these before, lad. Go ahead, open it."

I stepped forward and readied myself to put my back into turning the locking wheel. I was amazed at how easily it turned—I could have done it with one hand.

"This hatch," said Missus Grier, "is as old as the IE *Neworld*."

I understood the implication but Addie and Jo were puzzled by the reference.

"As historian," she continued, "and more importantly, as the descender, you will have the privilege of explaining to your team."

There was a hiss as the hatch opened.

"The temperature, air pressure, and humidity in this area has been precisely controlled ever since the room was created," said Bedford.

The room lit up upon our entrance. There was a polished glass table in the center of an expansive area. Under the table were ten metal stools. Lighted glass cases lined three walls from floor to ceiling. We browsed along the walls, wondering at the artifacts, books, and unknown items the cases contained.

"What are these?" Addie was shuffling through papers she found on the table. "They're Fallon's drawings, aren't they?"

"Yes, they are," said the Missus.

Jo moved beside her, to see for herself. "Oh my… How horrible, all those rows of gaping teeth."

"Are these real?" asked Aidan. "Did you see all this in the Basin?"

I went to the table and sorted the drawings into two groups. "Those," I said, "were in the Basin."

I gave Missus Grier a questioning look.

She nodded her assent.

"And those were in the Below."

They both gasped at the words.

"That was the lad's mission, don't you see? To show us what's in the Below."

"And what did you find?" asked Jo.

I separated the images of the IE *Neworld* from the other drawings. "This."

"Pull up a stool," said Missus Grier as she sat down at the table. "The boy has a story to tell."

1.7.2

BEDFORD broke the silence that filled the room when I finished recounting my descent into the Below. "Now that's history, lad. Full of life. Personal."

"But how do I put it to paper? What form does a history take?"

"As Bedford said earlier, these people, the Builders, were excellent planners," said the Missus. They anticipated the very situation that exists today. Each item here seems to have been selected for a reason—it has a purpose. You will find that the items are subtly grouped," she said, pointing to the top shelf on the left-hand wall, "and arranged progressively starting from there. They made it easy for us: the cases are numbered. The first set contains books—very old books that they, in their wisdom, thought to bring with them on their long journey through the stars and to preserve for us. You will find examples of histories, texts, fictions, diaries, and journals."

"I find the histories stiff—lifeless," said Bedford. "Pay attention to the journals and diaries. You've never read anything like them. It's like living the person's life. Start by reading those—the journals and diaries. They'll help you find your voice as historian and start the three of you thinking about the challenges we're now facing."

"You will learn of countries and cultures, of language and art, and of religion and war. I've studied the items of this room for many cycles," said Missus Grier. "Now is the time to document the story they tell. It's up to you to tell that story to the people of Neworld."

Bedford moved to the other end of the table and laid out the maps. "This room is unique… at least we thought so until yesterday. It is powered by an energy the planners called *electricity*. We installed gaslights in the small section of the quarters that is currently lit. We assume that the entire quarters used to be lit in the same manner as this room.

"We also found what might be controls on the walls all over the Commons, shop areas, and dormitory pods. But we never found the source of the electricity or figured out how to turn it on."

Missus Grier pointed to the southern tunnel. "The symbol on this wall looks like a bolt of lightning."

We all exchanged excited looks.

"And the symbol on this wall," she continued, "is two birds."

"Could it be a way out?" asked Aidan.

"We think so," said Bedford, a gleam in his eye.

A thought came to me. "Are there numbered light grids like here?"

"No, lad, we'll need to break out the sledgehammers."

"Now to decide. Which way do we go first?" asked the Missus.

"We have enough workers," said Aidan. "Can't we go both ways at the same time?

"This is *history*, granddaughter. The historian cannot be in two places at once.

"Out, then," said Jo.

"Yes, out," agreed Aidan.

They turned to me. I did not reply immediately.

"It's HighConjunction," I said finally. "Where would we go? Neworld is snowbound for another month-and-a-half, at least. And the Council could be watching wherever it leads. It may only lead back down to the Basin, and we already have a way to get there."

I paused to think.

"Go on, Fallon," said Missus Grier.

"We have supplies, and you said we should bide our time." I faced Addie and Jo. "I say we go south."

They nodded.

"We agree," said Bedford. "Jo, head back to the Commons. Round up Lenore, Percy, and the twins. If the last of the Observation Team has returned, grab Randall too. Fallon and Aidan, you return to your pod and then make your way back from there." He pulled a watch from his pocket. "The Missus and I will meet you in the library at 3:00."

1.7.3

WHEN LENORE found that I was part of the meeting, she greeted me as if nothing had happened. And I, her.

Bedford laid out the maps and explained the situation for the benefit of the twins and a tired and overwhelmed Brian Randall, the group's chief engineer. He swore them to secrecy, then told them of the archive room and explained what he and the Missus had learned about electricity.

Bedford laid out a plan to meet at the south tunnel at midnight. "Bring hand lamps," he said. "Tobey, you and Sean grab two sledgehammers. Randall, bring whatever tools you think might be needed." He scratched his head and continued, "The tunnel is a good distance away but it's straight into the wall. No twists or turns. The pods are on the other side of the Commons and it'll be after lights-out, but someone might hear the pounding."

"If they do, they do," said Missus Grier. "We're going to end this secrecy soon anyway. If our hand is forced early, so be it."

· · ·

SEAN AND TOBEY stood with hammers in hand as the rest of us directed our lights at the lightning bolt symbol on the wall. The tunnel practically echoed with the sound of our collective heartbeats.

On Missus Grier's nod, they raised their tools. Tobey took the first swing. The hammer met so little resistance, it slipped from his hand and disappeared through the hole it had made. We heard it clatter to the floor beyond the wall.

"What the B?" said Tobey, looking back at us.

Sean secured his grip and swung, inflicting a gaping wound from chest height down to the floor. He leaned forward. "Someone, hand me a light."

I was closest so I handed him mine. He directed it at the edge of the wound.

Tobey crouched, scooped up some rubble, and sifted it through his fingers. He rose and held his hand out for us to see. "Mortar," he said, "or something like it, made to look like bedrock."

"Not more than thirty centimeters thick," said Sean. He peered through the gouge. "I can see a set of small lights on a wall about three meters in."

Missus Grier took Bedford's hand and squeezed it. Addie gasped. Jo embraced Tobey, then playfully boxed him on the ears.

"Stand back," said Tobey. He turned and gave the wall a swift kick, and then another. He quickly opened a hole big enough to walk through.

Sean scraped the sharp edges off the opening with the hammer handle, then stepped back and, with a sweeping gesture, said, "I believe the honor is yours, Missus Grier."

The Missus stepped forward and ran her fingers over the grid of lights, almost caressing them. When we had all gathered in the chamber, she said, "Could it be, James? Could it be the same?"

"Aye, I would be willing to wager that it is. The planners would test you with one, but reward you after that. They did the same thing with the symbols on the wall. They gave us the first symbol, but not the others. The first wall was difficult to breach, now this…"

Missus Grier's finger hesitated, hovering above the light numbered 1. She pressed in the sequence. A section of the wall slowly slid open. She stepped through and touched the inside wall. The room lit up, revealing another hatch.

Our excitement was palpable as Bedford turned the locking wheel. There was no hiss this time. No lights came on as we entered. We all shone our lights over the walls, revealing a long room about four meters wide with another hatch at the far end. Our hatch was close to the right-hand wall, which held a static box. Percy cranked it to full power and we turned our lamps off.

Our small band drifted toward the far hatch, examining the room as we went. The left wall reminded me of the room that led out into the Basin. It had tool bays, shelves of gear, and benches to sit on. Nearer the far hatch, heavy coats with hoods hung on the wall. They had the look of our winter coats but the feel of our rain-gear.

"May I?" asked Lenore as we reached the second hatch.

"Of course, my dear," said Missus Grier.

Lenore struggled a bit to turn the wheel. It was not as pristine as the others. There was a bit of a "pop" when it unsealed, and it kicked inward, almost knocking her off her feet. I caught her.

We were immediately assaulted by a blast of cold, damp air.

Tobey put his shoulder to the door and Sean cranked the wheel as soon as it was closed.

"Seems this gear is here for a reason," said Randall as he began sorting through the shelves. We all followed his lead.

It was going on 2:00 in the morning when we finally reopened the outer hatch. The passageway ahead of us was dark, but it was equipped with static lights strung in runs like those down in the Basin. A low sound echoed down the tunnel. We walked for more than two hours, the sound getting louder with each step. The noise was deafening when we reached a stairway leading down. We descended single file—Bedford in the lead, me second, and the twins in the rear. It felt familiar, almost reassuring.

The steps brought us to a long, railed gallery that overlooked a vast, dark cavern. The roaring sound was unmistakable to everyone but me.

"Rim Falls," said Addie, her voice filled with awe.

Jo switched on her hand lamp and leaned over the railing to look down. Suddenly, the railing tore loose from the wall and gave way. Jo began falling into the void. Tobey's hand shot out, reaching for her. It slid down her body as she fell forward—down her back, down her leg, as he tried desperately to gain purchase. His fingers contacted the top of one of her boots. Just as she was about to slip away, his fingers clutched her ankle. Her weight pulled him to the gallery floor as her body slammed against the wall. Sean and Lenore reacted quickly but it was too late. Jo's foot slipped from the boot and she was gone.

"Jo-o-o-o!!" bellowed Tobey. He began to sob.

The rest of us stood in stunned silence. It had happened so quickly.

"Stand back from the railing!" said Bedford. "We can't lose another!"

"Tobey," said Lenore, rubbing his back, "You did what you could."

"Come, now, brother."

A feminine voice called out, "Tobey… Tobey… Tobey!"

"Jo?" said Tobey.

"Tobey, it's only about two meters down," answered Jo. "I'm a bit bruised but otherwise I'm fine." She moved away from the gallery wall and waved her light in our direction. "There must be a way down…"

As we carefully made our way along the gallery in search of a way down, banks of illuminated panels came to life overhead, exposing the most fantastic machines I had ever seen. Eight giant metal wheels resembling the water wheels that power Neworld's mills and factories were lined up at the mouth of the cavern. They rose fifty meters above our heads and gleamed in the light. One extended into the crashing water of the Rim Falls and turned as smoothly as it must have when the planners first built it. The other seven were retracted—pulled back from the powerful waters. All were connected to mammoth engines of some sort. The one paired with the moving wheel thrummed.

We located a stairway and soon found ourselves on the main floor. Tobey took Jo in his arms and kissed the scrapes on her face. Jo's fall may have triggered the lights somehow, but there were bigger things to think upon.

We wandered among the machines, gawking, enthralled, and indifferent to the cold. The engines were three stories tall and girdled with walkways. I accompanied Missus Grier, Bedford, and Randall on a survey of the engine that was working. The other team members looked for anything that might tell us how this all worked.

Randall laid a hand on the engine and felt the power of the machine. He trembled with the excitement of this discovery and the possibilities it presented.

The twins were waving for us to come down and follow them. They pointed to a large window in the back wall, high above the cavern floor.

They guided us to a door in the back wall. It was made of flat metal with no handles or locks. Tobey grinned as he pushed a round button beside the door, causing it to split in two and slide open, revealing a small room.

"C'mon," said Sean. Fallon and Tobey stepped in.

There were three more buttons next to the door inside the little room. Sean pushed the top button and the door slid shut. A moment later our knees almost buckled under us.

"What the B," cursed Bedford, as he kept Missus Grier from falling.

Randall beamed. "It's moving! It's moving upward quite rapidly."

"Bedford, this is an elevator," said Missus Grier, a hand to her mouth. She looked lively and youthful. "Just like in the books."

We glided to a stop and the door opened into a shallow room. It was lit only by the cavern lights, which shone through a four-meter-long window that looked out over the machines. The women stood at the window in awe. The cavern lights made the falls look like a shimmering silver curtain.

Centered on the window was a waist-high, sloping console with eight large, rectangular glass plates embedded in its surface. Four plates were positioned to each side of a now-familiar number pad.

Directly below the number pad was a small plate similar to the light switches. Randall touched it. No lights turned on or off.

He then tapped the sequence into the number pad. The eight large panels and the small plate flickered to life. We all gathered behind Randall as he examined what appeared to be colorful control diagrams for each of the eight machines. The small plate displayed a picture of four white buttons, each at the top of a vertical line. The words OVERHEAD LIGHTS were at the top of the display.

"Let's see what these do," said Randall. He tapped one of the buttons, then the next, and the next, and the next. He tapped them in different orders. No response.

Addie stepped forward, set the fingers of her right hand over the four buttons and dragged her fingers slowly down the screen.

The cavern lights dimmed and the curtain of water became transparent. We were looking east over an endless expanse of snow-covered treetops. The sky had begun to glow red as SolMin rose, with part of SolMaj exposed along the trailing edge. In the distance, the Fount was ablaze with sol light.

I stood next to Addie and took her hand in mine.

It was the dawn of a new day.

It was the start of a new cycle.

It was the day Neworld changed forever.

$$x \sim 1.7$$

1.8

Decisions

1.8.1

AN UNFAMILIAR female voice broke the silence as we gazed across the cavern at the spectacular solrise.

"Welcome to the power plant."

And then we saw the impossible—an attractive woman, no more than 40 centimeters tall, standing on the console. She was dressed in a trim, khaki uniform and wore her blond hair pulled back in a ponytail. We stood there, dumbfounded.

"Welcome to *what?*" asked Randall, finally breaking the silence.

"The power plant. The electrical generator facility."

No one spoke.

"Let me introduce myself. I'm the engineering avatar, Chief Anika Byström of TerraForma, a fully licensed colonization services corporation. It has been 284 Earth years, 7 months, 29 days, and 13 hours since this panel was last activated. That means we've been gone for a very long time and you are most likely descendants of the colonists who followed us here to C-39d. Congratulations for finding your way to this facility."

"What's an *Earth year?*" asked Randall.

"It is equivalent to three-quarters of your solar cycle," said Chief Byström.

"An annum…" said Jo. "A cycle is eighteen months. An annum is twelve months—three-quarters of a cycle."

"So when counting our age in annums, we're counting in Earth years," said Addie.

"Correct," said the chief. "Three thousand, four hundred sixteen months have elapsed, or one hundred eighty-nine point seven solar cycles, local time."

Missus Grier asked, "How did we come to be here?"

"The Neworld Foundation on Planet Earth contracted TerraForma to prepare this landmass for colonization and to support the habitation process for five Earth years. Because the physical and social engineering plans called for a colony with limited technology, we had to conceal the advanced technology and machinery we used to prepare this continent, designated Neworld, for habitation. The natural system of caves beneath this landmass offered a base of operations that would be unobserved by the colonists when they arrived and during our five-year service contract.

"Captain Maczynski and our corporate liaison, Vincent Grier, used the house we constructed above ground as their headquarters while they interacted with the colonial council. The TerraForma Corporation makes no judgments on anything other than physical sustainability. However, Captain Maczynski ran simulations of possible social development scenarios and expressed concern for the welfare of later generations. He and Mr. Grier devised a plan to leave behind what you have found so you could evaluate your situation and have the option to reintroduce technology into your society. We can't be sure what you have discovered so far, so I am not authorized to tell you more than how these generators work and which systems they power.

"Do you understand?" she concluded.

We were stunned. Again, we just stood there dumbly, staring at the image of the miniature woman.

"By your expressions, I suspect that holographic avatars are not part of your experience. Am I correct?"

It was Lenore who spoke. "No, they aren't." Lenore's face instantly appeared on the screen to the right of the number buttons.

"And what is your name, Miss?"

"Lenore. Lenore Bedford."

"Lanor Bedford" displayed below her image.

"Lanor Bedford," said Chief Byström.

"Lenore... L-e-n-o-r-e."

"Ah!" said the avatar with a trace of a smile. "An echo murmured back the word, 'Lenore!'—Merely this and nothing more."

The display corrected to "Lenore Bedford."

"Please introduce yourselves, one by one."

"Aidan Brennan," said Addie. "A-i-d-a..."

Brennan? I had assumed her last name was Grier, like the Missus. To me she was simply Addie, but how thoughtless of me not to ask her parental name. Then again, she never offered the information, either. In deference to my being raised as a one-name ward of the state?

It was amazing how quickly we took to talking with this imitation person. Chief Byström promptly reasoned that Bedford was Lenore's father and that the Missus was a descendant of the corporate liaison, Vincent Grier. She learned to identify us both visually and audibly.

"Will one of you be my primary interface?"

"We don't understand the question," I said.

"Will one of you be the person I will work with most often?"

"That would be me," said Randall. "And my engineering team."

"I look forward to meeting them. How should I address you? Brian? Mr. Randall?"

"Just call me Randall... No..." With a playful smile he said, "Call me Brian."

"And you can call me Anika."

Addie and I looked at each other with raised eyebrows. Was Randall flirting with this image?

Bedford pulled out his watch. "It's nearly 6:00. Say, two hours to return to the quarters, gather a crew, and..."

"I don't want to waste time going back," said Randall. "Leave Tobey or Sean with me in case I need help."

"I'll stay," offered Sean. "I'll begin by exploring that other floor the elevator opens onto."

"Good," said Bedford. "Tobey will discreetly gather your team and bring them back."

Randall thought a moment and then said, "Folks'll know something's up if my whole crew goes missing."

"Are you living in the base?" asked Anika.

"Yes," answered the Missus. "The estate has been destroyed and more than sixty of us are trapped in the quarters—the base."

"I will learn your terminology from Brian and adjust. You are the only ones in your group who know of this place?"

"That's correct," said Bedford.

"It is your decision whether or not to activate more systems," said Anika. "But if you do, you won't be able to keep this a secret."

"She's right, you know," agreed Addie.

"We have a lot of decisions to make," I said. "And they shouldn't be made rashly or all at once. But we can't hide this discovery. It can—it will—affect our everyday lives."

Bedford put his hand on my shoulder and said, "Right you are, lad. We shouldn't keep this secret." He then turned to the others and said, "Agreed?"

The decision was unanimous.

6:01 a.m. appeared on the screen at Anika's feet.

"Please set your watches to the time displayed," she said. "I need only Brian to remain here for now. The rest of you can return to the quarters. What do you call the village square?"

"The Commons courtyard," answered Jo.

"Gather your people in the Commons courtyard at noon."

1.8.2

I'M SURE that everyone's mind was filled with the same questions that overwhelmed mine, but the trip back through the tunnels was spent in silent reflection.

When we reached the mouth of the tunnel, it was a quarter past eight. We flicked off our static lamps and peered through the darkness toward the gas-lit Commons.

"I'm weary," said the Missus. "Let's bypass the Commons and return to our quarters to rest. We'll meet in the square at 11:30. Gather everyone with you as you come."

When Addie and I reached our pod, I inspected the walls of our cottage. I found a glass plate inside the door of each room, right next to the static box cranks.

Addie kissed me. "I've always known they were there, but I never gave them a thought. They didn't seem to do anything." She yawned and led me to the bedroom, where we collapsed on the bed. I twisted to set the alarm clock and when I rolled back to face her, Addie was asleep. I followed.

● ● ●

IT SEEMED like I hadn't even had time to dream when the alarm went off. I was hugging Addie, who was facing away from me. I pulled up her hair and kissed her on the back of the neck. Even though she tasted of salty sweat, it made me feel good.

Addie didn't stir, so I retrieved the clanging clock, then reached over her and set it on her side of the bed.

"Yeah, yeah, yeah!" she griped as she fumbled with the alarm.

"C'mon Addie. Let's get out of these stinking clothes," I said. I sat on the edge of the bed and cranked my static lamp. "Race you to the shower."

She got out of bed and crossed to the bathroom, leaving a trail of dirty clothes as she went. "No racing." She cranked the bathroom's static lamp, then turned the shower on. "Going to join me?"

It wasn't a passionate, coupling shower like our first night together. This may seem strange, but I think it was more intimate
than coupling. I just enjoyed the ritual of it, the touching, and the
soapy kisses.

Clean hair and fresh clothes rejuvenated us. We were out of
our pod by 11:15. Tobey and Jo or Lenore would get the people
in their areas to the Commons. Addie and I made the rounds of
the more remote shop areas to round up anyone who might be
working. We pulled seven people from three different shops, and
they all pressed us for information.

"What's going on?"

"Why's everyone required?"

"Something bad happened?"

We disguised *the* truth with *a* truth: "We're not sure what's going to happen. All we know for certain is that we're all to be in the
courtyard at noon."

It's interesting how groups form within groups. I had seen it at
the Mount: factions within the faculty and cliques among the students. As we entered the square, we encountered the entire Observation Base engineering team chattering amongst themselves.

"Have you seen Randall?" asked a young woman.

"He should be here," said Jerry Franz. "Did anyone check his
pod?"

"It's not like him to be late for a meeting," said the woman.
"I'll run back to the pods…"

"No, no," I said. "Don't go. It's almost quarter till noon."

"He's helping Bedford and Grandma with the meeting,"
added Addie. We extended our arms and shepherded them back
into the square.

One corner of the square was dominated by a large, flat rock
with two steps carved into one side. Missus Grier and Bedford
stepped up onto the rock and everyone grew quiet.

Someone tapped me on the shoulder. I turned and saw that it was Jo. "Come with me." She took Aidan's hand and Aidan took mine as Jo led us through the crowd to the rock.

Missus Grier began to speak: "As you are well aware, we are joined by the belief that our descendants came to Neworld from another world. For most of you, this belief comes from a few pages of writing known as the Solarist papers. Others have access to more information."

She gestured for me to mount the platform.

"You all now know about the descent team and they have told you the truth about the Basin—about the abundant plant and animal life—the true natives of Neworld. But we have additional details of the descent and I want to share that information with you today. You all know Fallon, I'm sure. And you know he was the descender. He has also been appointed the first historian of Neworld. Listen to his telling of the descent."

Bedford was looking at his watch. As I passed by, he whispered, "You have ten minutes, lad. Tell it like you did the other night."

The only sound in the quarters was my voice as I began my tale. I heard gasps when I told of the toothy monster and the suckered tentacle, sounds of concern when the sphere wouldn't rise, sighs of relief when I discovered my mistake, and laughter when the chamber-pot bench lid slammed on my head. Then I saw stunned faces when I read the letters I had recorded on my drawing—IE *NEWORLD*.

Bedford came forward and announced: "And, just last night, we made another major discovery."

As if on cue, the cavern was filled with a buzzing sound and a flicker of light. The buzzing faded into nothingness and the Commons became lit with a crisp white light as bright as a summer high noon. The crowd looked around in amazement. One woman held out her arms and began to twirl. The people around her began to laugh and clap. The woman raised her head and started to cry out in joy, but the cry caught in her throat. She stopped twirling and pointed upward. "Look!"

The gaslights and static lamps had never penetrated the dark heights of the cavern. Now, the source of the light was revealed high overhead—a massive dome that looked like a blue summer sky with white clouds drifting by. It emitted light like the ceiling in the archive vault and the panels in the generator room, but it displayed a lifelike, moving sky complete with a single, yellow-white sol directly overhead. It wasn't either of our sols.

Bedford clapped his hands and called out, "If I can have your attention please." He was not heard over the excited murmurings of the crowd. He tried again, with no effect. Tobey, the bigger of the twins, took notice, put his fingers to his mouth, and gave a shrill, penetrating whistle that got everyone's attention.

Bedford nodded his appreciation. "Thank you, lad," he said before addressing the assemblage. "I'm as amazed as all of you."

He raised his arms skyward. "This is beyond belief. There is so much we don't know about our own world. But we do know that the people who built the quarters were not the people who settled Neworld. They were the Builders, workers from another world who prepared the land topside for colonization. They were people just like us. They did not stay on Neworld, but they left us a trail of clues to their existence—the first of which was discovered by Missus Grier as a young girl. They left us a precious archive of writings and artifacts. Fallon and his team will examine them first, and then disseminate the information. The Builders also left us a new source of power they called *electricity*. It's the power that makes this light. We just discovered the source of this power last night. Engineering Chief Anika Byström is teaching us—"

"Who?" came a voice from the crowd.

"Anika Byström. She's one of the Builders—"

"A Builder?"

"Still alive?"

The crowd went wild with speculation.

"Quiet! Quiet!" boomed Bedford. "Everyone calm down."

He nodded to Tobey, who obliged with another whistle.

"Is there a living Builder?" asked a woman after the crowd quieted down.

"No," answered Missus Grier.

A man started to protest. "But Bedford said—"

"I'm at a loss for words," admitted Bedford. "She's... She's a..."

Suddenly, Anika's image appeared overhead, replacing the midday sky. The collective gasp was palpable.

"Welcome, people of Neworld. I am a projection of Anika Byström—an image. The physical incarnation of me is long dead by now. I have her knowledge and her memories, but I am not alive as you perceive life. You might say I am a ghost—a *kon*—in the machine. I am here to serve you."

The Commons was silent as Anika's image faded into blue skies and white clouds.

Bedford scanned the crowd. "Sean? Where are you, lad?"

Sean called out from the middle of the crowd. "Here, sir."

"Good. Make your way up front here. And I want Randall's engineering team to join you. Get yourselves organized and supplied with food, tools, whatever you need..."

Randall's voice came out of nowhere. "I can give you a complete list of what we need." The sky dissolved into an image of Randall in the control room. "Anika has taught me the basics of the system. She calls this *video*. It's two-way, so I can also see and hear you. The power of this is staggering. We have so much to learn.

"Sean, I'll talk to you and my crew at the engineering bay. Now, Bedford, if you can have everyone spread out over the Commons, the pods, and the workstations, we can begin to test the extent of this system, see if anything's broken. Be patient, though. This will be slow-going until my crew arrives."

"Thank you, Randall," said Bedford. "Sean will have your people to you in a couple of hours."

Randall's image dissolved and the sky reappeared.

Bedford addressed the crowd again. "Work it out among yourselves. Just make sure that we have a body in every area we use, and stay at your stations until Randall or his crew releases you. Percy, can you shut down these gaslights? Thanks. Now, off with you all. We'll meet back here after supper at 9:00.

1.8.3

ADDIE AND I headed back to our pod. From a distance, we could tell that light was spilling from the pod's entrance tunnel. Energized by the new discoveries, we ran to the pod and stopped just inside the meeting room. The ceiling was domed like that of the Commons, but on a smaller scale, and it displayed the same sky, only the sol was no longer straight overhead. I checked my pocket watch: 12:41.

Addie drew my attention to a small glass plate next to the static box. The plate was dark. Addie gave it a tap and it lit up like the light controller at the generating station. It had two sliding buttons: one vertical and one horizontal. A third button was marked CALL. She moved the vertical control down and up again. As expected, the sky above dimmed and brightened.

The horizontal button was set in the middle of a slider bar. When Addie slid it slowly to the left, the clouds and sol disappeared and the dome cycled through the whole range of colors. Back to center, and the sky showed the sol had moved a bit more. When she dragged it to the right, the roof displayed a dazzling number of stationary and moving patterns. She moved it back to center. There was something hopeful and reassuring about the clear blue sky.

She looked at the CALL button and gave me a questioning look. I knew exactly what it meant.

"Sure. Press it."

She touched the button and a long list of locations appeared. We couldn't tell where all the places were, since they had names we weren't familiar with.

"Suddenly, the sound of soft bells came from the control plate. The screen went dark and white letters appeared that said, "Incoming call." At the bottom of the screen were two new buttons: ACCEPT and DECLINE. Addie tapped ACCEPT.

Randall's face appeared, accompanied by his voice. "Oh, it's you. I just saw that this location had become active. It's called 'Dorm B' and I wasn't sure where that was."

"It's our pod," I answered.

"I should've known it would be you. Can you step back just a bit, so I can see you both? That's better. I've already talked with Sean at the engineering bay, Missus Grier at her quarters, and Bedford in the archive. Everything working at your location?"

"The meeting area has a sky ceiling like the Commons," said Aidan. "We were just playing with the controls. It's pretty incredible."

"We haven't been in our cottage yet," I said.

"Let me know if you have any trouble. I'll be here in the control room until my crew arrives. It's listed as 'Gen Control' in the directory. Exciting times!" The screen went dark.

"This is too much," I said, rubbing my temples.

Addie gave me a hug. I put my arms around her and kissed the top of her head. "I'm glad you've been with me through all of this. I wish you could have been at the Observation Base for the descent too."

She looked up at me. "You weren't sure you liked me, yet."

"I thought of you as a little girl."

"I showed you that I wasn't… At the inn… Remember?"

I tapped my temple. "You know I can't."

She punched me on the arm playfully, then we kissed. It was tender and passionate at the same time.

We walked hand-in-hand to our cottage. We didn't spend a lot of time playing with the room lights. The plate just inside the entrance was simple, with only the vertical slider to dim the ceiling and a CALL button.

The bedroom light let us control both brightness and color. We set it to give the dim, reddish warmth of RedNights. Addie's hair glowed like embers in the light. We took our time undressing each other before falling into bed. Images of Missy Howard surfaced in my mind—memories of her stepping from the tub, her naked body glistening in the gaslight, of the first night we coupled—my first time. Her body was more mature than Addie's, her breasts fuller. I shook my head, trying to clear the images. It felt wrong to be having these images as Addie straddled me. My feelings for Addie were different than those I had for Jenna—less impulsive, but no less passionate. We shared more than the physical act of coupling. I stopped Addie's rhythmic motions and rolled her over to the side.

"What is it?"

"Nothing," I lied, not looking her in the eyes.

She laid her head on my chest and moved her hand down my body. I grabbed her wrist and stopped her. She pulled away and propped herself on her elbow.

"Did I do something wrong?" she asked.

I couldn't look at her.

"Tell me."

"No, you didn't." I rolled to face her, kissed her on the breast, and said, "You're wonderful. We've been in the middle a lot of astounding discoveries…"

"We have."

"Yet, you are the most astonishing discovery of my life." I kissed her again.

"Then what's wrong?"

"It's me… I betrayed you."

"How? How could you have betrayed me?"

"Just now… I… I… You know how my mind works."

"Yes."

"Well… When you were on top of me, my mind…"

"Your mind what?"

"I saw images of Jenna."

"Jenna?"

"Naked. As she was getting out of the tub… When we coupled…"

"I saw your drawings," she reminded me. "So I can appreciate what you saw in your mind. She's beautiful."

"And so are you. I shouldn't be thinking of her. I'm with you."

"I know she was your first. I know you will always have images of her in your mind. She and I talked about you. About your relationship."

My anger toward Jenna was pricked. I started to say something, but Addie put her fingers over my lips.

"Women talk about things like that. I'm sure men do too."

"She used me. I was just something she wanted to control."

Addie sat up and gave me a little shove. "She didn't! You know that. She was taken with you."

"Then why did she…?"

"Because she knew you'd be leaving. It tore her to pieces, having to give you up like that."

"Really?"

"She told me she'd have considered using her contract with you if things weren't the way they are. I wanted you because you're stemmed, and Jenna said that you'd be a good first."

"Someone to practice with?"

She hesitated before answering. "Yes, practice. Both Jenna and Grandma have told me that if a woman is to get favorable terms in a contract, she must be experienced, and desired. That's the way of the world."

"The way of the world," I repeated.

Addie lay on her back and considered the soft glow of the ceiling lights. "But the world seems to be changing—for you, for me, for everyone."

"It does," I said.

"If this were the old world, I'd want to contract with you, if you were able. And I'd hope that you'd want to contract with me. And we would live together forever like Tobey and Sean's parents."

"I would, you know. I would contract with you... live with you... raise our children in one household."

She leaned into me and we kissed.

"Trouble is, I'm stemmed, we're both dead, and your contract has reverted to the Council."

"That leaves us with only one thing we can do."

"What's that?"

She climbed on top of me again and said, "Practice, practice, practice."

1.8.4

WHEN WE headed back to the Commons for supper, we saw pools of light scattered around the cavern in places we knew to be workstations and bays.

Addie grabbed my arm. "Stop a second... Do you feel that?"

"It's a breeze," I said.

"A warm breeze," she added. "And the air smells fresher."

"A wisp of pine?"

She smiled and nodded. She took my hand and we strolled leisurely to the Commons.

When we arrived, the sol was close to setting. We found Jo and Tobey sitting in the courtyard, looking at the sky and talking.

Tobey saw us approaching and said, "You know which direction the sol is set..."

"West," I said, verifying it with my mental image of the map of the quarters I'd seen.

"That's right, Boyo. Like our sols."

"But it's neither of our sols," offered Jo.

"And the sky isn't the same blue as our sky," said Addie.

"No," affirmed Jo. "It's more vibrant."

"Then whose sol is it?" asked Tobey.

I didn't have to think about it. I instinctively knew the answer: "It's the Builders' sol. They were a long way from home for who knows how long. Neworld wasn't going to be their home, so they made this place in their own image."

Addie squeezed my hand. "Earth," she said solemnly.

The four of us gazed at the setting sol. "Earth," said Tobey and Jo as one.

"Home," I said, and sighed at the thought.

After a moment's silence, Tobey said, "Not to be insensitive to such profundity..."

Jo interrupted. "Profundity? That's the longest word I've ever heard you utter."

"Just because I was a pugilist doesn't mean I'm not educated."

"I didn't know I was coupling with a pedagogical pugilist," teased Jo.

"A what?" he said.

Jo laughed. "Never mind."

"Anyway," continued Tobey, "We were hoping to catch you on your way to supper."

"Heading there now," said Addie, taking Jo's hand and leading us to the mess. She leaned close to Jo and said, "I know what pedagogical means, but what's a pugilist?"

"A boxer. A prizefighter. Tobey was a champion, you know."

"Really?"

"When I saw him fight... It was in Ellsworth."

"That's on the South Grade, isn't it?" said Addie.

Jo nodded. "At the mouth of Finger Lake. I was the reading and writing teacher there. It's a small town with no social life and few contract prospects for a woman my age, if you know what I mean. When I heard about the fight, I thought I owed it to myself to go. I'd never seen a prizefight before."

Jo glanced back at Tobey, then leaned in to Addie and spoke more softly. "I was attracted to him the moment he entered the room. His muscles... His bare chest... Long story short, I mustered the courage to talk to him after the match, and we... You know... I contracted him within the week! That was almost two cycles ago. We're almost out of contract and we haven't... I haven't..."

"What are you ladies talking about?" asked Tobey.

"Nothing," answered Jo.

The mess was crowded, so I offered to scout out a table and hold it while the others got our dinners. The ceiling light was set to a level only slightly brighter than the gaslights. The best thing about these lights was that they didn't sputter and flicker. Would the Grier manor still be standing if its lights had been powered by electricity instead of fueled by gas? No, it still would have burned, but perhaps the basement wouldn't have collapsed if there hadn't been an explosion. Maybe it would have left us a way out.

I tried to be unobtrusive as I waited by a table where three people were just finishing. I noticed that many had shed their sweaters and that everyone was talking about the lights and speculating about the sky ceilings.

Thankfully, the diners vacated the table just before Addie, Jo, and Tobey arrived. As soon as they sat down, I went to the serving line. The meal was a special celebration: tender, seasoned beef tied around sliced hard-boiled eggs and cooked in a tomato sauce, fresh baked bread, and a bean soup. On my way back to the table I passed Tobey, already heading for seconds.

After I sat down, Aidan put her hand on mine. I leaned in and kissed her on the cheek. Two tables away, Lenore sat glaring at us—at me. I couldn't understand why she didn't like me. No, it was more than that. She openly *dis*liked me. I wanted to march over to her table and have it out with her. But not now, not with all these people around, not on such a happy day as this.

We sat and ate and discussed everything that had happened. We didn't notice that the square outside the mess had slowly grown dark until there was a commotion and people close to the windows got up and started to leave. I checked my watch to see if we were late for the meeting, but it was only half past seven.

The people outside were excited and pointing to the ceiling. We followed the stream of people to the square and looked up into a starry sky unlike any we had ever seen. Something large, round, and silvery was rising in the east. It wasn't a minor sol, but something completely different. Its light was dim, yet crisp and cool.

Missus Grier and Bedford ascended the stone platform and the crowd quieted down.

"It's early," started the Missus, "but that remarkable object rising in the night sky has drawn everyone to the square so we might as well begin. Can you hear me in the generator room?"

"Yes, ma'am," came Randall's voice. "We're all watching from here."

Missus Grier nodded and continued. "You are probably wondering what that is up there—that silvery white disk. That is a moon or, more specifically, the Earth's moon. That was the Earth's sol we saw earlier today. The Builders called it the *sun*.

Earth is the place of our origin—our home world, if you will. That is a fact now, not just 'Solarist propaganda' as the Council would like you to believe."

The crowd cheered and clapped.

Bedford spoke next. "You may have noticed a slight breeze and a freshness to the air. That is all thanks to the crew in the generating station."

More applause.

"As we talked about before," he went on, "we can survive down here for many months if need be. Our discovery of the electrical generators will make it a more comfortable stay. It also will affect the decisions we have to make. Do we focus our efforts on finding a way topside, or bide our time down here and learn all there is to learn from this place?"

He and the Missus let the people talk amongst themselves.

I called out from the edge of the square: "May I say something, ma'am?"

"Please," she answered.

"I'm new among you, and I may be more overwhelmed than anybody here. Yes, overwhelmed with images, and thoughts, and ideas that tell me that our whole world is a lie."

"It *is* a lie," shouted someone.

A debate erupted among faceless voices from the crowd:

"Where do any of us have to go, anyway?" asked a woman.

"Right, the Council could be up above right now, digging through the ruins," said a man.

"We're bottled up in here, trapped like sheep waiting for slaughter..." shouted a second man.

"I heard that the generator room opens to the outside. Can't we get out from there?" said a third.

"There is no direct exit," came Randall's voice in answer to the last person's question, "and it would be dangerous to traverse the face of the Rim under the falls."

"Even if we got out now, the Council could track us through the snow and hunt us down like skreel," said an agitated young woman.

An average-looking man in his 50s stepped to the front of the crowd, then turned and shouted, "The Council can go couple with themselves! If we all make a break for it, they can't hunt us all down."

"You tell 'em, Frank," cried a young woman from the middle of the courtyard. "We should fan out and spread the truth. The people will rally to our side."

"Don't be naïve," said Jo. "The people of Neworld are content. Look at it from their point of view—*we're* the dissidents here, the minority, the blasphemers."

"The truth will out!" shouted another woman.

I pressed my original point. "See how unsettling this knowledge is—and you are the Movement! You *hoped* this all was true. But ask yourself seriously, what's going to happen to Neworld if we leave here, scatter to the four corners of the land, and dump our knowledge on the people all at once?"

A white-haired woman spoke from the back of the crowd. "I agree, we have to decide what to do with this knowledge before we leave."

"But we need to have all the facts before we make that decision," said a man near the platform.

"Can I make a motion? That's how it works, isn't it? Someone makes a motion, then we vote." It was the white-haired woman.

"Go ahead, Lizbeth," said Bedford.

"I move we postpone the decision to dig our way out of here for three months… until after the thaw. We have enough supplies to last that long, don't we?"

"Yes," answered Bedford. "If we ration."

"Good," said Lizbeth. "We can use those three months to learn what we can and discuss the consequences of our work."

"It's been moved that we sit tight down here in the quarters for three months. Is there a second?" asked Bedford.

"Second," came Randall's voice.

"Okay, lads and lassies, all those in favor, say 'aye.'"

There was a chorus of "ayes."

"Those not in favor, say 'nay.'"

The chorus of "nays" was equally loud.

"What about the other tunnel?" It was Percy.

Grumbling and confusion spread through the assemblage.

"What other tunnel?" asked the muscular man in the front.

Percy looked sheepishly at Missus Grier, who seemed to take no notice, and at Bedford, who glared at him.

The Missus motioned the crowd to quiet.

"There is a second dead-end tunnel that we think leads to another hidden passage," she said.

The crowd became unruly again.

"Is it a way out?"

"Why didn't you tell us?"

"No more secrets!"

She silenced them again, took the time to scan the entire team, and then spoke calmly: "We believed that the passage we did open would benefit all of us more right now and would provide us time to find a way out."

"I have a suggestion, ma'am," said Tobey. "Let Sean and me take a team to knock down the other wall and see what's on the other side. Exit or no exit, at least we'd know. Then we take our time, like Lizbeth said, to decide what to do."

"Second," yelled someone.

"No motion was made," boomed Bedford.

"Close enough…" said someone.

The square erupted with laughter.

"All in favor say 'aye,'" shouted the man in the front.

Unanimously, the crowd cried "aye" and began cheering and clapping.

Missus Grier leaned toward a scowling Bedford and whispered, "I think this is what the Builders called *democracy*."

He thought a moment, a smile slowly forming. He nodded and joined Missus Grier in the applause.

"Now, enjoy this beautiful night," said Missus Grier after the celebration quieted down. "Let's take a two-sol holiday before getting to work. The sol after tomorrow, we will have our HighConjunction feast here in the square. It's long overdue. Then we'll ration."

x~1.8

1.9

Options

1.9.1

"'LIKE SHEEP waiting for slaughter.' That's what the man said." I was in the meeting area of Pod G with Addie, Jo, and the twins. We were discussing some of the comments made during the night's meeting. "*Slaughter!* It's unthinkable that the Council would do such a thing. I wouldn't believe it if I hadn't seen them kill a man."

"You what?!" said Sean.

"Your sister, Jenna, never told you?"

"Told us what?" asked Tobey.

"About last summer, during RedNights."

They shook their heads.

"The Mount was empty except for Jenna, Dean Ambrose, and me. The headmaster returned unexpectedly and told us that important people were going to meet in the Great Room that night. He sent us to our rooms and told us to stay there."

I fell silent and sighed deeply as I recalled the events of that night.

"Go on," prodded Sean.

"I sneaked onto the upper level that rings the Great Hall. I noticed that Ambrose was there too, in the shadows directly across from my hiding place. He was spying, just like me. He never said anything afterward, so I don't think he saw me. I heard voices in the darkness below. Then a beamed lantern was lit and two Dark Men—the Council's thugs—dragged a third man into the room. They called him their *prisoner*. One of the Dark Men was Wessler."

Tobey asked: "The guy who burned down the manor?"

I nodded and Sean let out a low whistle.

"The men in the shadows asked the prisoner, McCreigh—"

"McCreigh?" asked Tobey. "Vernon McCreigh? A smallish fellow?"

"Yeah… You knew him?"

"He's an innkeeper in Plainsworth. I fought there a couple of times. Nice guy… Wait… *knew* him?"

I nodded. "They questioned him about the Movement. He refused to tell them anything so, on command of one of the men in the shadows, the larger Dark Man—not Wessler, slammed McCreigh in the head. I heard his neck snap. He crumpled to the floor, dead."

"Those skreel!" said Sean.

"I've heard stories about the Council," said Jo.

"What kind of stories?" asked Addie.

"Of disappearances… of accidents that weren't accidents…"

"'Disappear him?' That's exactly what Wessler asked," I said. "And one of the men replied, 'No. The body will send a message. Make it look like an accident. That'll satisfy the citizens, yet the Movement will see it for what it is.'"

Jo gasped. "So the stories are true?"

Tobey put his arm around her and held her close.

We sat in silent contemplation for several minutes. Then I made a decision. "We're a team, aren't we?" I said to Addie and Jo. "We've been tasked with documenting the history of Neworld, haven't we?"

"Of course," said Addie. "What are you trying to say?"

"We all have an important decision—all of us who are trapped down here like sheep. What should we do with our discoveries if—when—we get topside," I continued. "*Everyone* should have all the information about the Council's actions. I propose that we interview all the people here and document their stories about incidents such as disappearances or unusual accidents."

The others agreed about the importance of this undertaking.

"But we should wait until the festivities are over," suggested Jo. "Let's let everyone have a couple days of happiness."

"She's right," said Addie.

"We'll begin in two days then. The two of you will be busy in the archive…"

"The two of *us*!" said Addie. "And where'll you be?"

"I'll be with Tobey and Sean, breaking down the wall."

"I want to be there…" Aidan started to protest.

"And I want to begin my work on the archive, but the Missus wants me to witness, firsthand, the breaking down of the wall."

"We have too many tasks," said Jo. "They're going to overwhelm us."

"I agree. So who do we get to collect the stories from the people?" I said. "Any suggestions?"

"Lenore," said Aidan without pause.

I didn't respond and Aidan took offense.

"What's wrong with Lenore?" she asked.

"She… I… Um…"

"What?"

"The truth is, she doesn't seem to like me much."

"I don't think she dislikes you." Addie's reply didn't sound confident.

"I've seen the nasty looks she gives Fallon," said Sean—always happy to stir up an argument.

Addie withered at the nods of agreement from Tobey and Jo.

"She's been cool to me lately too. But I don't think she dislikes you, Fallon. She's… She's just… jealous, I think."

"Jealous," I mocked.

"Yes, jealous of you—"

"Of me? For what? Because I was given access to the archive and she wasn't?"

"No—well, maybe some—but mostly for you being with me."

I was dumbfounded. "She wanted me for herself?"

"OOOOH!" squealed Aidan.

"Men are that way," consoled Jo. "They all think every woman wants to contract with them." She glared at Tobey and Sean.

"What?" they protested as one.

Aidan chewed her lip, then said, "Lenore wants me... misses me, I should say. She's like my older sister. We've been inseparable ever since I came to live with Grandmother. That is, until last spring when I went to Agricitta to spy on the Mount. In spite of the circumstances, she was happy that we were together down here. Then you showed up and..."

"Again, I feel like I've done something wrong," I said.

"You haven't," said Addie. "I haven't. She hasn't. Anyway, I know she'd do a thorough job of gathering the stories."

"She would," said Jo.

"I know," I admitted.

1.9.2

THE SKY over the Commons was cloudless when Addie and I arrived for breakfast the next morning. People were dressed as if it were an early summer day. The mood in the mess was bright and cheery. We didn't see Lenore, so we went back to the courtyard and sat down, hoping to catch her on her way in.

Sean showed up a few minutes later, then Jo and Tobey.

"That was a good talk last night," said Jo.

"The first of many," I said. "We're going to have a lot to discuss about our findings in the archive."

Aidan's eyes lit up and a grin formed on her face. "Why don't you move to our pod?"

"That's a great idea," I said.

Jo turned to Tobey. "Would you mind?"

"No problem," he answered.

For once, Sean sat quietly, no mischief in his eyes.

"I slapped him on the shoulder and said, "You too, boyo.""

He smiled and said, "Lots o' room to spread out. You'll hardly know I'm there."

"Yeah, right," said Tobey, returning the smile.

We chatted excitedly about the new arrangements and I almost missed Lenore entering the mess. I shot up from the table and hurried toward her, grabbed her arm, and said, "Lenore."

She turned, saw it was me, and jerked her arm away, giving me that look I'd grown accustomed to. I could tell that Lenore saw Addie in the courtyard behind me and I could imagine the look on Addie's face because Lenore's expression softened suddenly, if artificially. She said, "Good morning."

"It is a good morning," I replied cheerily. She wasn't going to get the best of me today. Plus, I sincerely wanted to try to understand her feelings. "May we join you for breakfast?" I motioned to the gang at the table.

Lenore hesitated, but she finally forced a smile. "Certainly."

As breakfast progressed, Lenore began to relax. The more we shared, the more she became involved.

"To put it bluntly, this historian job is becoming an enormous chore," I said. "I can't read every word of every text in the archive or witness every event. I will have to count on all of you to carry some of the burden. We need to seek out sources for the histories we don't have."

"I don't understand," said Sean.

"We don't know the Council's side," I said.

"Grandfather might…" started Aidan before being cut off by Sean.

"Like that matters," he spat.

"But it does," said Lenore in support of our argument. "The Council is at the heart of our society and therefore at the heart of our history on this world."

"Who made the decision to burn us out?" asked Jo. "Why do they do what they do?"

"Histories and fictions," I mumbled.

"What did you say?" asked Aidan.

"The Code bans histories and fictions—both written and oral," I answered. "We're told, almost from birth, to never look back, but to pledge our lives 'to the *Service of Today* and the *Building of Tomorrow*.' When a student at the Mount tries to argue that the Council's statistical records are, in fact, histories, he's told: "Records such as births, deaths, and financial transactions are necessary for today's legal and commercial purposes. Production, weather, and crop yield records are essential for future planning."

"So?" said Tobey.

"Histories and fictions! The Council considers histories and fictions to be the same—lies. We have to prove them wrong. We must verify the stories we gather before we can call them history. If we can't verify something, it's just a story. It's just a fiction."

Lenore gave me a serious look. "What was your recounting of the assault on the manor—history or fiction?"

I had to ponder the question some time before I answered. "History. Everyone I interviewed was an eyewitness. They told me only what they themselves saw. In their entirety, all the interviews corroborated each other."

I considered my next question carefully before speaking it aloud. "Lenore, Addie, Jo—was there any attempt by you or others to coordinate your statements before talking with me?"

"No," answered Addie emphatically, followed by the others.

"Then yes, it was a history," I said, satisfied with my conclusion.

"That's the standard we all must abide by," said Jo.

I turned to Lenore. "Will you consider taking charge of compiling a history of the abuses of the Council?"

"I'd be honored. Your account of the assault on the manor will be the first entry and it will serve as a guide on how to present the stories I gather."

"I'm sorry we can't give you access to the archive. For the time being, only Addie, Jo, and I are allowed. But you are invited to join us in Pod G, if you like. Jo and the twins are moving over today."

She grinned broadly and held back tears.

"Welcome to the team," said Jo. The twins echoed the welcome.

Lenore put her hand on Addie's. "Thank you," she said. She reached across Addie with her free hand, lifted my hand, and set it atop hers. Then she tilted her head to the others and they offered their hands in a sign of unity.

"To history," she said.

"To truth," said Jo.

"May they both be the same," I said.

1.9.3

WE SPENT the rest of the day helping our friends make the move to Pod G. In fact, we discovered that many people were spreading out among the pods, now that we had electricity.

Again, I was struck by the concept of groups-within-groups. Although we were all part of the Movement and shared a common goal, people sorted themselves in various ways—friendship, working groups, even by age.

Interestingly, the people uniting in one pod were those who had voiced the desire to get topside, fan out across the land, and spread word of our findings without delay. Frank Bianchi, who seemed to lead the group, never missed a chance to share his feelings about leaving the quarters as soon as possible.

That evening, as Addie and I relaxed at a table in the square, Bianchi strode toward us. He had thin lips and a receding hairline. His body was tense and erect. I stood as he approached.

"We've never met," he said, extending his right hand. "I'm…"

"Francis Bianchi," I said, taking his hand and shaking it.

"Yes, call me Frank. May I talk with you?"

"Of course," said Addie, with her most charming smile.

The best Bianchi could muster was a weak smile. "Thanks," he said, as he pulled out a chair and sat. He didn't speak at first—just sat there, head bowed, drumming the fingers of his left hand nervously.

I broke the tense silence. "Are you here to convince me we need to break out and spread the word of our discoveries?"

"No, I figure you heard what I had to say about that the other night."

"I did," I said. "And I can't say that I disagree. But…"

"Yeah, 'but.'" He lifted his head and looked me in the eyes. "The reason I'm here is my son."

"I didn't know you had a son," said Aidan. "Which one is he?"

"He's not here, Miss. They took him. They took my son."

"Who are *they*?" I asked.

"The Council. I heard you wanted our stories about people who disappeared."

"Oh, of course. Lenore Bedford will be talking to everyone…"

"I want to tell *you*, the historian, personally. I want you to know why *I* feel the way I do about the people's right to know." There was a deep sadness in his eyes.

"Go on," I said.

"I'm not a Solarist. My son, Danny, was… *is*. He's a good boy, an annum or two older than you, I think. We're guildsmen. Wheelrights by trade. We lived in a small town on the plains. In the middle of nowhere—you know, don't you? You came from up Agricitta way, didn't you?"

I nodded.

"We're farther east. Like I said, in the middle of nowhere.

"Danny's a bright kid. Makes up stories to tell me and his friends—stories to scare us or make us laugh. I told him to be careful—you know, the Code and all. But we lived in the middle of nowhere, understand? Everyone loved his stories.

"Well, summer before last, Danny came back from guild school to serve his apprenticeship with me. He had these Solarist writings he got from a friend at school and they caught his fancy. Danny showed me the papers and I read them. I thought they were just more of Danny's stories. He said, 'No, Dad. This is real. It's history.'

"I warned him about histories—about the trouble it would cause if the Council caught him with the papers. But he said, 'Histories just tell the truth about the past. Why should that cause trouble?' I took the papers from him just the same. He didn't speak to me for a week and I couldn't bear it, so I gave the papers back. 'But hide them,' I said.

"One fifthnight during RedNights, we went for supper at the village inn. Like always, most of the village was there—whole families—for food, and the men for the ale."

I interrupted to ask, "What's ale?"

"What's ale?! Ale's a golden drink made from grain. Against the Code, you know. It makes you feel good—so it has to be against the Code, don't it? Gruber, the innkeeper, brews it in his basement. Only serves it on fifthnight. We live out in the middle of nowhere. What harm could come of it?

"So some of the boys pulled up a stool in front of the hearth and asked Danny for a story. He got up on the stool and said, "No story tonight, fellas." Everyone in the room called out for stories.

"No stories," he says, "But I have a history to tell." And he told them what the papers said—with some additions of his own. You understand—my boy has a great imagination."

"Sounds like a delightful person," said Aidan.

"Thanks, Miss. He is." He paused and looked down again, his fingers drumming the table.

With a sigh, Bianchi resumed his tale. "What we didn't see was the stranger who came in with his black coat and hat. It's the middle of RedNights, and he's wearing a long coat!

"Danny was almost to the end of his history when a whistle blew. We all turned toward the sound and saw Blackcoat..."

Addie leaned close to me and whispered, "A Dark Man?"

I nodded as I listened to Frank Bianchi's story.

"The door opened and a dozen men in green jackets with short clubs in their hands rushed in. Blackcoat kept blasting on the whistle and the thugs started swinging at anyone and everyone. The inn was in chaos. Screaming. Crying. Bloodied men, women, and children trying to get away."

Aidan gasped and clutched my hand.

"The whistle stopped and then the beating stopped. The only sound was the moans and whimpers from the wounded. Blackcoat walked to the middle of the room and shouted, 'You are in violation of the Code. Serving an illegal substance and gathering for the purpose of treason.' ·

"My Danny pulled himself up from the floor. Blood flowed from his head and down his swollen cheek. He stood up to the men and said, 'What treason?'

"Blackcoat signaled to one of his men and the skreel struck Danny in the gut with his club." Frank was fighting back tears. "Danny double... doubled over and... and that thug landed a blow on the... the back of my son's head. Danny fell limp to the floor.

"'The spreading of Solarist lies,' says Blackcoat. 'That's what treason.'

"The thugs dragged Danny from the inn and that's... that's the... the... last I ever saw him."

Bianchi collected himself before going on. "But that's not the end of it. They tied up ol' Gruber and took the rest of us outside under the glow of RedNights. They had horses waiting, and a wagon that looked like a cage. Then they set the inn ablaze. 'Gruber,' I cried, and started to run to the inn, but they beat me to the ground. I heard the old man screaming and the villagers, my friends, keening.

"'It was an accident,' said Blackcoat. 'You understand? An accident caused by the illegal activities of the innkeeper. Any of you say any different, and we'll come back and your houses will burn.'

"The thugs took us away, one by one, and warned us again before sending us home. Come morning, all the boys around Danny's age were gone. Tracks showed the horses had headed upland and we could see their dust on the horizon.

"I couldn't stand by and watch the villagers trying to rebuild their lives. Before my bruises healed, I headed to Agricitta to find out more about Solarists. A man named Howard saw my condition and took me in. I didn't tell him my story—I never told anyone for fear of what would happen to my friends back home. Mister Howard never asked, either. A good man, he is. He and his daughter, Jenna, were part of the Movement."

I was surprised. "Jenna Howard?"

"D'you know her? Yes, of course you do. She's head of house at the Mount, isn't she?"

"She's a... friend," I said.

"And mine," added Aidan.

"Well, they're the reason I came to be here with the Missus. And Danny's the reason I need to go topside—to spread the word. Someone has to stop the Council and I have to save Danny if he's still alive. You see how vicious these people are, don't you? My village... the manor. Someone's gotta stop them."

• • •

THE NEXT DAY was a whirl of joy, celebration, and speculation about what might lie ahead. Randall and all of his engineering team returned for the HighConjunction feast.

After dinner, he pulled the twins and me aside. "When are you opening the wall?"

"We're going to head over to the tunnel about 8:00 in the morning," said Sean.

"Why? You coming with us?" asked Tobey.

"Anika suggested that I might be of some use to you," said Randall.

"Did she say why?" I asked.

"No. She's pretty cagey like that," said Randall. "Even with my crew and me, she never tells us what to do. She just guides us with questions and nudges us to figure things out for ourselves. When I asked her about the Builders and the reasons people from Earth settled here, she said that was your job, Fallon. That seems to be the way the Builders have set this all up. We have to earn their knowledge—demonstrate that we're worthy of it."

"The Missus and Bedford said the same thing," I mused.

Sean said, "If you're coming, be at Pod G a little before 8:00. We'll leave quietly from there. No need to attract a crowd."

• • •

JO AND ADDIE had made an early start of it at the archive and Lenore was still asleep, so it was just Randall, the twins, and me in the pod at 8:00 the next morning.

Sean produced a pickax he had retrieved the night before. "We can probably kick the wall down if it's as flimsy as the other," he said. Then he added with a grin, "But this will do nicely if it's not."

The tunnel was at the far, eastern end of the quarters, which meant we wouldn't have to go anywhere near the Commons and attract attention. That end of the cavern was still dark, so we carried static lamps to help us find our way. During the long walk we speculated on what the bird-like symbols might mean, what we'd find behind the wall, and why Anika suggested that Randall be with us.

The cavern narrowed, then broadened into a second large room, which—I knew from the map I had seen—was not as large as the main cavern. But it was large enough that our lights couldn't reach the ceiling or even the walls around us. The floor felt smooth and level.

In spite of the map, I was expecting a tunnel like the one that led to the generator station. But this one was wide and tall—wider than the streets I had seen when I arrived in Primacitta.

We had been walking down the tunnel for a couple of minutes when Sean observed, "We must be almost to the Rim."

A moment later, Tobey—big, prizefighter Tobey, who was in the lead—yelped like a startled child afraid of a monster in the dark. His lamp and pickax fell loudly to the floor.

"What the B, brother?" said Sean after running into Tobey's back.

"I saw something... ahead... in the dark..."

We heard movement somewhere down the tunnel. Whatever it was sounded large. Quickly, Tobey retrieved his pickax, as the rest of us cranked our lamps furiously to get full power. We huddled together and directed our beams down the tunnel.

Suddenly, Jo's voice emerged from the shadowy part of the tunnel ahead. "What took you so long?" Behind her were Addie and Lenore. Beyond them was what must have been most of the Movement, all waiting in the dark to surprise us.

"Maybe this will help you see more clearly," came Bedford's jovial baritone voice as the tunnel's ceiling became illuminated. It was a strictly utilitarian white light. "Step to it, lads," said Bedford, to a smattering of laughter. "Everyone is waiting."

The crowd parted so we could walk to the sealed end of the tunnel. As they stepped aside, I noticed that the well-worn floor had markings: sets of lines—yellow, white, solid, and dashed—that ran its length. This tunnel had a purpose when the Builders were still here. Would it be of any use to us now?

Missus Grier stood at the wall, pointing to the bird symbol. "These birds have inspired flights of fancy for all of us in the last couple of days. They give us hope of escape, of freedom. But be prepared if it is just another dead end. Don't let it dash your hopes." She stepped aside and said, "Tobey, bring this wall down."

He stepped up. In a high arcing swing, the pointed end of the pickax tore a line through the faux wall from two-and-a-half meters up, all the way down to the floor. He moved a meter to the right and cut another line. "Everyone, step back," he said before ramming the space between the lines with the head of the ax. He jumped backward as the thin wall came crashing down.

The vast room beyond was bathed in light. It seemed empty. It was a hundred meters to the far wall, where we saw a huge sliding door. The door, similar to a barn door, was made of the same gleaming metal we saw in the generator room. It was forty meters wide and twenty meters high.

"You should enter first, Fallon," said Bedford. "Look around and commit it to memory before any of us disturb it with our presence."

I cautiously stepped through the hole and walked twenty meters into the room before slowly turning counterclockwise to take in what I saw.

The big door looked as if it opened in the center, like the elevator door, with the two halves sliding on tracks inside the room. I saw a hatch to the left of where that side of the door would rest when opened. A *hatch*!

The north wall had another sliding door, about half the size of the entrance tunnel, and several regular doors, including one that looked to be an elevator. Three levels of windows indicated several floors of rooms. A balcony ran the entire length of the third level. What appeared to be four control consoles were positioned along it.

The west wall was lined with areas that were portioned off like stalls in a stable—five stalls to the right of the entrance tunnel and three to the left. But there were no horses here. In the stalls were machines. Each had wheels and the variety of designs made me think they were meant to carry things like our wagons and carriages do. Each stall contained tool and parts bays and panels with display screens.

Sean was taking a turn widening the tunnel entrance. I glanced down the stalls, nodded at the assembled crowd, and continued turning south.

The south wall had two large, empty stalls with retractable coils of a large-diameter hose mounted on the wall. Obviously, something bigger than the other machines should have been in each stall. I hadn't a shade what they might have been.

I waved for the team to enter.

"Please," said Bedford, "move to the center of the room, lads and lasses. Gather up in your teams; I may come to you and make assignments. Do not touch anything unless you are asked to."

Randall walked toward me, holding up his hand and calling, "Engineering, form up." He didn't have to say anything to me. His expression conveyed everything—*Where are we needed?*

I pointed to the displays in the stalls and the consoles on the balcony.

Without missing a beat, he assessed the situation and gave orders to his people, sending one to each stall and leading the rest to the elevator.

"Where's the mechanical team?" called Bedford.

"Over here," came a woman's voice.

He found the team and moments later they were dispersing to the stalls to help inspect the machines.

My little team had gathered around me and was surveying the surroundings. Bedford and the Missus came over. "Williams!" Bedford shouted. "You here?"

"Here I am," answered Percy as he made his way through the assembled groups.

Bedford stood between Lenore and Percy and put a hand on each of their shoulders. "The credit for this discovery—and for the generator station—goes to you two," he said. "Take one of Randall's team from a stall and go see what's beyond that sliding door in the north wall."

I was watching Lenore and Percy leave when my attention was drawn upward—lights came on at the third level. Randall appeared on the balcony. He and his teamed congregated around the closest console. As the display lit up, their faces became illuminated and showed great excitement. They were too far away to hear, but I could tell Randall was speaking to the display. To Anika?

EERRT! EERRT! A harsh sound filled the room and amber lights flashed along the east wall.

"Aviary door is opening," came an authoritative male voice.

EERRT! EERRT!

"Aviary door is opening."

EERRT! EERRT!

"Aviary door is opening."

The alerts fell silent and the amber lights faded to red.

We all watched with great anticipation.

There was a low rumble and the large metal door parted, sliding left and right. As one, we drifted nearer, forming a long line so each of us had an unobstructed view. Aidan stood in front of me. I put my arms around her. There was no waterfall this time, but the opening door revealed another double solrise over the Basin. A flood of cold air rushed into the room.

A thrill ran through the crowd, with exclamations ranging from "oohs" and "aahs" to "Escape!" and "Freedom!"

"Stay back," ordered Bedford. "That's almost a two-kilometer drop off the edge." He signaled Randall and the doors began to close.

"That hatch over there must lead out," said Tobey. "How about if we check out the rooms in the north wall? If this place is like the generator station, I'll wager they have a stash of cold weather gear."

"I'm with you, brother," said Sean. "

Missus Grier nodded and said, "Be careful."

Tobey asked me, "You coming, little brother?"

"You couldn't keep me away."

As we left, Addie and Jo started to follow.

"Addie," said Missus Grier. "You and Jo are finished here for now. Head over to the archive and start your work."

Addie reverted to her little girl pout, but Missus Grier was immune.

"As you have often pointed out, Addie, you're a grown woman. That doesn't work on me anymore." She gave her granddaughter a stern gaze until Aidan relented, taking Jo's hand and heading toward the entrance tunnel.

"Listen now," called Bedford, clapping his hands to get everyone's attention. "If you haven't been assigned a task, head back to the Commons. We'll assemble in the courtyard after dinner to share what we discover."

1.9.4

LENORE, Percy, and Melissa Chawla from engineering had no trouble opening the sliding door in the north wall. It was controlled by a wall plate next to the door. The door opened onto a corridor that was twenty-five meters long and terminated in a second door. This door, controlled by a plate on the side wall, slid along the inside of the next room. The room, which was already lit when they entered, was two stories tall and extremely wide. They couldn't see to the far end. The floor space was filled with row upon row of metal tanks 3 meters wide and 150 centimeters high.

Suspended two-and-a-half meters above each edge of a tank was a clear trough. A grid of light panels and flexible tubing filled the space between the troughs.

Melissa turned to inspect the wall behind them and found what she had hoped to see: a small door and two levels of windows looking over the tanks. "Follow me," she said. "I think we'll find some answers in here."

As soon as they opened the door, a strong current of air blew down from the ceiling, apparently being sucked into a metal grid at their feet. They were in a small room that had another door on the opposite wall. Melissa opened it and they entered a pleasantly cool stairwell. "Upstairs should be a control room," she said

And it was. A wall of windows overlooked the tanks below and the troughs above.

Melissa stepped up to the control console that was configured like the one in the generator control room, keyed in the code, and watched as all the displays came to life. She expected to see Anika.

• • •

TOBEY'S assumptions proved true. The first floor of rooms contained offices, what appeared to be a small mess hall, and a dressing area with a door that opened a few feet from the hatch.

"Is it...?" asked Sean.

"Yeah, it's in the right place," I said. "Beyond this wall is the Basin."

"And a way topside..." said Tobey, adding, "Maybe."

We donned the appropriate gear, cranked open the hatch, and swung it inward.

. . .

"HELLO, I'm lead hydroponics technician Archie Maxwell. Welcome to the hydroponics farm." A section of the screen flickered and Melissa's image appeared at the avatar's feet. The words "Engineering Mate Chawla" appeared onscreen. A second image appeared, and the name "Lenore Bedford." A pause followed, then Archie asked: "Who might you be, sir?"

"Um. Uh. Williams," he stammered, looking at his companions. "Percy Williams."

His image appeared on the screen, labeled "Percy Williams."

Archie seemed satisfied. "Welcome to you all," he said. "Who will I be working with most?"

"Me for now," replied Melissa.

"Pardon for me saying, but you are an engineer. Is there an agriculturalist in your party? A farmer?"

"Yes, we have several," said Lenore. "Why?"

"I beg your pardon. Are you not familiar with hydroponics?"

Lenore looked at Melissa and Percy to see if they understood, but they only returned questioning looks. "No, we aren't," she answered.

"I understand. Perhaps Engineering Mate Chawla will suffice."

. . .

THE TWINS and I pulled up our hoods and cinched them tight as the cold wind whistled through the hatch. Tobey moved his bulk through the opening first. I took up the rear. It was with some difficulty that we closed the hatch behind us.

We found ourselves in a long gallery—a notch in the face of the Rim, actually. It was cramped: a little over two meters in height, so low that Tobey's head nearly scraped the stone overhang. It wasn't wide enough for two men to walk side by side.

When the Builders carved this gallery, they left a stone railing that was slightly less than chest-high and a meter thick. There was no way you could be blown over the edge or slip and fall to your death. The gallery extended southward to the large door, where it terminated with a railing.

Sean pointed a gloved hand and we followed him north. About forty meters on, he stopped and looked over the rail.

"Nice view?" I yelled over the noise of the gusting wind.

"Not bad if you like clouds," he said, hoisting himself over the railing, then rolling onto his back. "Hold onto my legs, will you?"

Tobey and I each took a leg. "Lift me a bit more, I want to have a look up."

A minute later, he told us to bring him in.

"How far down are we?" he shouted.

"I'm not sure, brother," said Tobey.

"A hundred sixty-five meters," I said. "It was marked on the map."

Sean shook his head. "I thought maybe I could climb out of here, but there's no way. If it was a shorter distance, maybe, but the Rim face is straight up, damp, and the wind is a killer."

* * *

"TO PUT it simply," said the avatar named Archie, "this is a self-maintained farm. Is there something that is in short supply that you would like? Wheat? Corn?"

"We're well stocked with grains," said Percy.

"Maybe something more perishable, then. Tomatoes?"

"Ha!" scoffed Percy. "It's the dead of winter."

"That doesn't matter here. How many of you are there?"

"About sixty," said Lenore.

"Please observe the tank directly below you."

All the lights in the hydroponics farm faded to black—except those above the first four meters of the tank below them and its two troughs. A mechanism laid a film along the bottom of one trough, followed by a thick layer of spongy material. Then the trough began to fill with water.

"The material at the bottom of the trough contains viable tomato seeds," said the avatar. "And the next layer holds the nutrient-rich liquid that will result in mature plants within two weeks. The tanks are used mostly for large-scale crops like grains and fauna like grasses, trees, bushes, etc."

"Trees and bushes?" asked Lenore.

"This land mass was designed to Earth specifications. It was first purged of problematic native vegetation, vermin, and insects. Any significant native life forms were relocated."

"Native life forms," said Melissa Chawla. "Like what?"

"It was our task to re-vegetate the surface with selected species of Earth plants, crops, and the varieties of insects need to ensure propagation. There was a large grazing animal that would have competed with your Earth livestock and damaged your crops. We used the birds to sedate entire herds and relocate them."

"To where?" prodded Melissa.

"Elsewhere," said Archie matter-of-factly. He continued, "Very little of the vegetation on Neworld is native."

"What about the Rim Forest?" asked Lenore.

"They were introduced by us and strategically planted as a buffer between the Rim and the planned city."

* * *

WE TRAVELED silently along the gallery for several kilometers. I wondered about the purpose of the gallery. Maybe it was just a place the Builders could go to get some fresh air—somewhere a couple could stroll under the stars. That didn't seem likely, given the fact that two people would have to flatten themselves against the wall and railing to pass each other.

We approached what seemed to be a tunnel, but proved to be a section of the gallery that was closed in by a thick wall of ice. Some light filtered through the ice, creating weird, disorienting patterns along the gallery. The gallery wall and floor were slick with ice. We had to tread carefully, but at least the ice wall held back the wind and it became quieter as we went deeper into the ersatz tunnel.

"A waterfall," said Tobey, who was now in the lead. "Look!"

Our way was blocked by a curtain of ice.

I said, "Looks like this part of the gallery caved in."

"End of the line," said Sean.

"Hold on there, brother," said Tobey. "I can almost see through this sheet of ice." He turned his back to the ice, reached out to us, and said, "Take my arms."

We steadied him and he thrust a foot backward. THUNK. Another kick. CRACK. With the third kick the ice gave way, revealing a three-and-a-half meter crevice separating us from the continuing gallery.

The gallery terminated another ten meters beyond the crevice.

At the end of the gallery was an ice-encrusted hatch.

$$x \sim 1.9$$

1.10
Love and War

1.10.1

WE WERE pleased to find Lenore, Percy, Randall, and the entire engineering team in the facility's small mess hall when we returned from our exploration of the gallery.

They were so excited about their own discoveries, no one thought to ask what we had found. There was chatter of an underground farm that could feed us all indefinitely… and wagons and carriages that didn't need horses. The carriages ran on electricity and were being 'charged' as we spoke.

"The Builders called this facility the *aviary*," said Randall. "Barnes, the Builders' guide for this area, couldn't—or wouldn't—say what the two large bays are for. One more bit of knowledge we need to earn somehow."

The room erupted with speculation and debate.

Sean tried several times, without success, to break into the conversation. Frustrated, he climbed atop a table and declared, "We found a way topside."

The room fell silent. Sean savored being the focus of attention and dramatically milked the moment before telling our story.

"But it's just a hatch," said one of the engineering team. "You can't be sure it goes topside."

"Where else would it go?" Sean countered.

"Another facility," suggested Percy.

"All of the Builders' facilities have been linked by interior tunnels," said Sean. "The gallery doesn't make sense as a passage to another part of the quarters; it's narrow, it's a long distance to the end, and it's dangerous."

"If it is a way out," said Percy, "it's also a way in."

Tobey rose and said, "Yes, I was thinking about that on the walk back. I was a fighter, you know. I always wanted my opponent directly in front of me. Like you said, some folks are afraid that if we find a way topside, the Council could find their way down and kill us, neat and clean—out of sight. But if this is a way out for us, it would be a terrible way in for the Council. They'd have to walk single file for several kilometers. They could never use brute force on us. Besides, we could easily block their way at any place of our choosing."

Lenore rose. "All of this is important, but it's getting late and we should report to the Missus before dinner. It's a long walk, so we'd better head back."

"Who said we have to walk?" said one of the engineers. "We have electric wagons! Follow me."

As the group started to leave, Randall grasped my arm so I would hang back. When we were alone, he tilted his head, indicating that I should follow him. He led me through a maze of corridors.

"This complex is extensive. Like the generator stations, it has sleeping quarters, its own mess, offices, supply rooms, and this."

He stopped in front of a metal door—not a hatch, but more secure than the other doors in the facility. Next to the door was a keypad with a glass plate that had the outline of an outstretched right hand on it. The sign above the plate had a word we did not know: ARMORY.

"I think this is why Anika wanted me to come with you—not to simply open the aviary door for you."

"Why do you say that?" I asked.

"Because she had me place my right hand on one of the displays at the generator station and took an image of it—a palm print she called it. Just me—no one else on the team. But she did ask if you'd be coming back, so I figure she wants your print as well."

"I don't quite understand."

"She said that palm prints are unique to each person. It's a way to verify I am who I say I am."

"To what end?"

"If my assumptions are correct, this pad opens this door."

"Okay."

"It obviously uses a palm print to open. I'm the only person I know who has had his print logged, therefore I'm the only person who can open this door."

"Have you?" I asked.

"Have I?"

"Opened the door."

"No. I wanted you here when I did. You and nobody else."

"Well, let's have a look," I said.

I didn't realize until the door slid open that I had been holding my breath as Randall pressed his hand to the plate. I exhaled as the room beyond was revealed. It was essentially a windowless, four-meter cube with black metal objects hanging on the left, back, and right walls. To either side of the door was a metal cabinet with doors and drawers of various sizes. A glass-top table like the one in the archive and a half-dozen stools filled the center of the room.

I opened several drawers and found boxes of brass cylinders with copper or lead tips on one end. I gave Randall a questioning look but he replied with a shrug.

"I don't like the looks of this place," I said. "We'd better not touch anything."

"I concur," said Randall. "Now that we have found it, perhaps Anika is allowed to explain. Can you come to the generator station with me tomorrow?"

I shook my head. "I really need to get to work at the archive. See what she'll tell you, then contact me at my pod tomorrow night."

THE OTHERS were gone when Randall and I returned to the aviary, so Randall led me to a small machine that had four seats: two in the front and two in the back, plus a small bin for carrying things at the rear. We sat in the front. There was a wheel in front of Randall and some pedals on the floor. When Randall placed his hands on the wheel, a display lit up in front of him and a female voice said: "Automatic shuttle to Town Center or manual?"

"Uh, automatic," replied Randall. "That sounds safer."

"Town Center?" I said.

"Must be what we call the Commons," said Randall.

With barely a sound, the machine began to move, first heading out onto the aviary floor, then looping back toward the tunnel and picking up speed. I clutched the seat, my knuckles white. We were traveling much faster than Missus Grier's four-horse carriage. When I turned to ask Randall if he could slow the contraption down, I saw an expression of pure joy on his face. I told myself I was being a foolish boy again—filled with fears and doubts like when the Missus took me from the Mount to her manor.

Randall turned to me, beaming. I tried to relax but could only return a tentative smile. He laughed. I released my grip on the seat and raised my hands to show him I had no fears. We left the lighted tunnel and sped into the darkness of the quarters, headed for the small dot of light at the other end. I lowered my hands and clutched the seat.

"No one needs to know," I muttered in the darkness.

"It's our secret," said Randall.

1.10.2

"WHERE DID you get off to, little brother?" asked Tobey as Randall and I entered the courtyard.

"We started talking, and before we knew it, we were alone." I quickly changed the subject, "So, what'd you think of the electric carts?"

"Exciting," said Sean. "I want to get my hands on one of those small ones. I bet they can really move."

"They can," I said. "Randall and I rode one back."

"We loved it," said Randall, shooting me a look.

"Missus Grier asked that we come to the library as soon as the two of you returned," said Tobey.

"I want a minute to see Addie," I said. "Is she around?"

"Already with the Missus," he replied.

Missus Grier, Bedford, Aidan, Jo, Lenore, Melissa, and Percy were seated at the library table when we arrived.

Bedford was saying, "And it can provide us with food indefinitely?"

"That's what Archie Maxwell says," said Lenore.

"We'll have a crop of tomatoes in a couple of weeks," said Melissa. "I know we're not sure how long we're going to be down here, but I think we should consider getting some crops started, to be on the safe side. If Brian can spare me and someone else from the generator station, I'm sure we can handle the hydroponics production."

"Pick whoever you want," said Randall.

"Percy, find Lizbeth Hendel. She's been supervising our stores," said Bedford. "Ask her and the cooks to coordinate with Melissa, will you?"

"If you don't mind, I'd like to go right now and start things rolling," said Melissa.

"Heading back to the aviary tonight?" asked Randall, knowing Melissa shared his unbridled enthusiasm for new challenges.

"Probably... most likely... Yes, I am."

"Take the small cart Fallon and I came in. It's fast," Randall said with a wink as she and Percy left the library.

"Have a seat, lads," said Bedford.

I took the chair next to Addie, which I suspect she had kept open for me. Sean slyly took the spot next to Jo, but Tobey showed great restraint by not taking his brother by the collar and dragging him to another chair.

Missus Grier turned her attention to me. "Lenore and Percy haven't told us of your findings, Fallon. They only said that you explored outside."

"I'll defer to the twins, if you don't mind, Missus. I only tagged along as a historian."

Sean said, "You tell it, brother."

Tobey succinctly recounted our excursion along the gallery. When he finished, Missus Grier asked, "And you think the hatch leads to a way out?"

The twins and I expressed our agreement on that point.

"Well then," said Bedford, "How do we bridge the crevice?"

We hadn't noticed him taking paper and pencil from the center of the table, but Randall was already sketching a plan when he spoke. "I have some ideas about that. We make a track something like the one on a kitchen drawer, and we bolt these to the gallery wall and railings... This isn't to scale—we'll need to take measurements... Then we construct a metal walkway that rides in the tracks, like this... It's maybe twice as long as the crevice is wide... See... And then we just slide it over when we want to cross, and pull it back when we don't... That should keep out any of the Council's Dark Men..."

Watching Randall draw his rough plan made me yearn to sketch. I'd been so caught up in events, I couldn't remember the last time I had drawn. It couldn't have been... yes, after my descent to the Below. Time was a jumble. How long ago was that? A month? Maybe more.

"That'll do the trick, boyo," said Sean. "But add a roof. We'll be going through a waterfall when it warms up."

"Randall, will you and the twins manage the project?" asked Bedford.

"I should be getting back to Anik… to the generators," said Randall.

"Oh, Brian needs to get back to Anika," taunted Sean.

Randall's cheeks flushed.

"Let it be, brother," said Tobey.

"They can spare me for the week or so the construction will take," said Randall, giving Sean an unyielding look.

"Good," said Missus Grier, rising from her seat. "We have a lot to share with the people tonight. If there's nothing else, I suggest we adjourn and go have dinner."

Everyone rose except Randall. "There's one more thing…" he began. All eyes were on him.

He was going to mention the armory. Something in my gut told me to keep its existence a secret so I shot Randall a warning look. Luckily, he caught my meaning. "Uh, Fallon and I have business to attend to before I start work on the bridge. I need to take him to the generator station with me tonight."

"Well, get something to eat before you go," said the Missus.

. . .

"WHAT IS the *armory?*" asked Randall.

We were in the control room of the generator station, talking to Anika.

"Why do you ask?" she asked.

"Don't be sly with us," said Randall. "We found a room at the aviary—the one that requires the palm print to enter.

"You didn't mention it to anyone. Did you?"

"Just Fallon, as I expect you wanted."

"Yes, the historian," she said approvingly.

"What is it?" I asked.

"You'll understand as you begin to explore the archive. You're going to learn a lot of words not found in your dictionary, words like *war, murder, execution, weapons…*"

I struggled to comprehend what she was talking about.

"When you start reading the histories, you will discover that people could be cruel, and they constantly fought and killed each other."

"Why?" I asked.

"For lots of reasons," said Anika, her voice tinged with sadness. "And for no reason at all."

"The founders of your world believed that people are inherently good—not bad. They thought that things like war and murder are learned and not a part of what they called 'human nature' so they purged your society of the concepts. In all these year, have you never had a war?"

I shrugged my shoulders, not knowing how to answer.

"Groups of people fighting each other," she said, trying to clarify the concept. "What you found in the armory are weapons—guns. We humans seem to take them with us wherever we go. For protection, we tell ourselves—to kill things that threaten us. But, too often, we've turned them on ourselves. Your founders rejected them and that's why you have no words for wars or murder…"

"But I've seen someone murdered," I said. "Vernon McCreigh… at the Mount."

"That is most troubling, Fallon," said Anika. "Murder is murder, even when there is no name for it. Perhaps you should consider the possibility that humans are *not* basically good. Maybe *goodness* is the learned trait drilled into you by generations of conditioning and your precious Code. Maybe people are bad—evil—by nature."

1.10.3

"I'M WORRIED," I said to Addie as we lay in bed. Her head was resting on my chest and I was running my fingers through her hair.

"About what?"

"The hatch." I didn't mention the armory, which was troubling me even more.

"The hatch? It gives us hope."

"It's dividing us, don't you see? There's a small group that wants to go out now, without a plan. They seem to be the same people who want to 'spread the truth to all of Neworld.'"

Addie lifted her head so she could look up at me. "And you don't?"

"I don't think I do." She didn't know it, but the armory was a part of my truth now. My truth allows me to have weapons—guns. It allows me to go out and kill people. Is that a good truth? Am I better for it? If I could un-know it, I would.

Addie drifted into a peaceful slumber, but my troubled thoughts held sleep at bay. I was careful not to wake her as I slipped from bed, gently closing the bedroom door behind me, and padded toward the kitchen. I raised the kitchen light about halfway, then sat at the table where I had gathered drawing materials. I hadn't let my memories out in this way since we came back from the Observation Base. My hand started moving, almost of its own accord. I began with an image of Addie standing naked in the washroom that first night we spent together and ended hours later with an image of the armory and its walls of death-delivering machines.

I stared at the paper, scowling. It made me angry for some reason—perhaps at the thought that humans could be so vile. Or maybe it was because I found myself curious about the guns—how they were made... how they worked. Could I ever use a weapon against another human being?

I slashed at the drawing with my pencil, defacing it with a hash work of black lines. I pressed so hard, the pencil snapped in two. I picked up the paper, crumpled it into a ball, and hurled it at the front door, where it fell to the floor. I rose, retrieved the crumpled ball, and took it to the kitchen counter. I set out a bowl and began to tear the paper into the tiniest pieces I could, letting them fall into the bowl. I then took the bowl to the privy, deposited its contents, and flushed.

Aidan stirred. "Fallon?"

"Yes."

"You okay?"

"Yes."

"What're you doing?

Trying to un-know, I thought to myself. But to Addie I said, "Nothing. Just had to go. Sorry to wake you."

I set the bowl in the washroom sink and joined Addie in bed, snuggling tightly against her and wrapping my arm around her. I closed my eyes and washed away the visions of the armory with memories of Addie, recalling her cheerful face, every curve of her body, and how she felt and smelled. I fell asleep with the warm thoughts of how much she meant to me.

● ● ●

IN THE MORNING, Addie and I hurried to the mess for a quick breakfast.

"Where's Jo?" I asked Tobey, who was sitting with Sean in the square.

"Don't know," he said. "She got up in the night and said she had something to do. Haven't seen her since."

"What are the two of you up to?" I asked.

"Waiting for Randall," answered Sean. "We're going to take him down to the gallery to get some measurements."

I nodded and we continued on to breakfast.

When Addie and I returned to the courtyard after eating, Randall was sitting with the twins. He waved me over. "Fallon, can you come with me to the aviary? I won't keep you long."

A few minutes later, nine of us were rolling through the darkness on a large electric wagon. Four members of the engineering team had met us at the wagon, which had two seats in the front and four cushioned benches in back. Each bench could comfortably seat three people. I sat in the front with Randall, at his request. Addie and the twins sat behind us. As we traveled, Randall showed me how to operate the machine "so you can use one of the small carts to get about."

"Sounds good to me," I said. *Bloody B!* I thought. *First thing I'm going to do is show Addie how to operate the contraption.*

When we arrived at the aviary, Randall steered the wagon into a stall and stopped it over a metal plate on the floor. "Don't know if you noticed these plates before," he said. "There are several on each side of the Commons, by the mouth of the generator station tunnel, and by the pods. I never knew what they were before now. They give the machines the power to run. My team will work with the Builders' deck chief and learn more today."

"Deck chief?" I asked.

"Like Anika... an avatar, you know... says to just call him Chief," said Randall. As we entered the office complex, he said, "Sean. Tobey. I'll meet you in the dressing room. I need a few minutes with Fallon, alone."

Addie gave Randall a questioning look.

"Sorry, Aidan," he said. "Perhaps you can have Melissa show you around the hydroponics facility."

I gave Addie a peck on the cheek. "I'll meet you there and then we can go meet Jo."

"Okay," she said grudgingly. "Don't be long."

● ● ●

RANDALL took me up to the level with the control consoles. "I didn't have a good night last night," he admitted. "My mind was racing."

"Same here," I said.

"Well, I got to thinking: these guides the Builders left behind to help us must be connected to one another. Melissa said the bloke in hydroponics knew who she and Lenore were, right?"

He keyed in the code and the console lit up.

"How can I help you, Mr. Randall?" said the deck chief.

"I want to talk to Anika, Chief."

The deck chief hesitated, then nodded. The outline of a right hand appeared on the display screen. "Palm ID, please, sir."

Randall pressed his hand against the plate.

"Scanning," said the chief.

A green glow appeared around Randall's hand, then faded.

The deck chief disappeared and a smiling Anika faded into view. "Good morning, Brian."

"Good morning," he replied brightly.

"Good morning, Fallon."

"Is it?" I replied.

"Are you troubled by what I told you about the armory?" she asked.

"Of course I am. It contains machines designed to kill."

"Or, as I said, to defend." She said it without inflection, just as a dry statement of fact.

After a few moments of silence, Randall said, "Well, I brought Fallon because, quite frankly, I don't want to be responsible for that awful room." He gave me an apologetic look.

"Understood," said Anika, "You no longer have access, Brian. And you, Fallon? Do you want access to the armory?"

I understood Randall's reluctance to accept responsibility for the room and its contents, but Anika's words stuck in my head. *Or to defend.* I thought. *Defend!*

I sighed and said, "Yes… I'll accept the responsibility, at least for now. We can seal it for good later if we want, can't we?"

"Of course," said Anika. "Place your hand on the display."

The hand outline appeared. I didn't hesitate to place my hand on the screen.

"Scanning."

As my print was being scanned I asked, "What can you tell us about the gallery that runs outside, along the Basin wall?"

"Sorry, Fallon. Neither I nor my colleagues have knowledge of places external to the quarters. We will help you understand and use the facilities you have found."

"Are there other facilities in the quarters we have not found?" I asked.

"No. However, you do not understand fully what you have found. We are here to serve, but you will find that much of the responsibility lies with you, Addie, and Miss Wilkinson."

1.10.4

JO WAS sitting at the table reading a small, leather-bound volume when Aidan and I arrived at the archive. Two other books lay on the glass top.

"I've been here all night," said Jo, wiping her eyes. "I couldn't get to sleep."

"Seems to be going around," I said.

Aidan walked over to Jo and picked up the books, one by one. *The Journal of Captain Maczynski... Tale of Two Cities.* You read these?"

"Uh-huh. I'm a fast reader. I think that's why the Missus put me on the team."

"Why are you crying?" I asked.

She slid the book she had been reading across the table to me. I read its title: *The Most Excellent and Lamentable Tragedy of Romeo and Juliet.*

"I can't pretend that I understood all the words," Jo said. "But it's about love."

"Love," said Aidan. "What's that?"

"I can't explain it. It's a strong feeling for another person that seems to be more than physical attraction. The writer says, 'Love is heavy and light, bright and dark, hot and cold, sick and healthy, asleep and awake—it's everything except what it is!'"

I said, "Seems confusing."

"It is. This boy, Romeo, and this girl, Juliet, feel love for each other and want to couple, but their families forbid it. They would… They would rather die than live apart." Jo started to sob. "'Under love's heavy burden do I sink.'"

I could almost understand those feelings. I felt a void within me when I was not with Addie—a void that was only filled in her presence. It was more than the physical act of coupling. Coupling could be contracted; this feeling I had for Addie could not.

Aidan put her arm around Jo to comfort her.

I sat and began to thumb through the book. I had trouble understanding what it was at first. It was mostly people speaking to each other or to themselves in a strange pattern of speech. Then Romeo said something that struck me: 'O teach me how I should forget to think!'"

Forget to think. If only I could erase the images in my mind—images of McCreigh's dead body and the armory with its dreadful machines.

I set the book down and placed my hands on the tabletop. There was a green glow beneath my right hand. An avatar of an older man appeared. He seemed to be a person of authority.

"Welcome, Fallon. Miss Wilkinson. Miss Brennan. I am Captain Bohdan Maczynski. How can I help you?"

• • •

CAPTAIN MACZYNSKI became our guide, our interpreter, our teacher. Conversing with the captain was unlike talking to Anika or the other facility guides. He could reason, argue, cajole, offer advice, and even crack a joke. It was as if he were a living person.

For the next two weeks Jo, Addie, Bedford, the Missus, and I practically lived in the archive. We learned the language of the

Builders and made plans to bring this knowledge to the Movement. Missus Grier and Bedford had read the books in the archive, but now they gained a new understanding of them.

We could place an artifact on the table and detailed diagrams and information about it would be displayed. We could discuss the books we read and get the captain's thoughts about our own situation. He explained the reason for leaving the trail of breadcrumbs for us to follow. He even referred us to the tale of Hansel and Gretel to explain the phrase "trail of breadcrumbs." He confirmed that the gallery hatch led to the surface just north of the Little Silver River, which was beyond the border of Primacitta's original plans.

Jo, in particular, became enthralled with the concepts of love, romance, and chivalry. Bedford couldn't get enough information about technology, while Missus Grier's interests tended toward social structure and government. Addie reveled in the fictions—not only the physical books the captain had placed in the archive, but also the electronic volumes available. I was captivated by the images and history of art in its many forms. We all loved music—most of it, anyway. We each had our own favorite forms.

Everything we saw or read spoke to the beauty of humanity.

* * *

ONE EVENING I was alone in the archive watching videos that the captain had not shown to any of us up to this point. It depicted the darker side of life on Earth. It was about a man who waged war on Earth and had millions of people killed in the name of racial purity. He ruled through intimidation and by playing on people's fears. I was appalled by the cruelty of our ancestors.

The captain took form on the table in front of me. "It only takes one person, one insane person, to oppress a nation or cause a war. The first man to use a piece of wood as a club probably ruled his clan and terrorized his neighbors. When someone learned to make a shield and throw a spear, the club became obsolete. Then came swords, bows and arrows, armor, guns, and on and on *ad infinitum*."

"We don't have…"

He cut me off. "You've read Lenore's reports on the prison camp and the killings, haven't you? "

"Yes."

"Do you doubt that the Council is behind them?"

"No."

"And why are they committing these atrocities?"

"Because they fear what we know. They fear you."

"That's hogwash, Fallon, and I think you know it."

I nodded.

"They may fear what your little group is up to," said the captain. "But that's not reason enough for what's going on. Something's happening behind the scenes. You need to find out what it is."

"When we get topside, we'll find out."

"I know that you want to go topside and, when you do, I fear you'll be in danger. Go to the armory and activate the table display there. The bridge will be ready in less than a week, so we don't have much time to teach you how to defend yourself."

• • •

WE HAD many thought-provoking conversations in the archive. While the captain revealed the horrors of crime, murder, and war only to me, the information he gave the others was enough to suggest not everything was good and beautiful on Earth. Even the disturbing deaths of the young lovers in Jo's favorite story suggested a darkness in humanity.

One afternoon, Missus Grier said to the captain, "It seems clear that your world was one of light and dark. Your stories, art, and music can be beautiful and inspiring—or angry and unsettling. It seems that your people could turn anything good into something hateful."

"You're correct, Missus. That is why, while I can't fully support the Neworld Foundation's intentions, I can sympathize with them. I'm a representative of the TerraForma Corporation. My job was to build out this landmass to our client's specifications, not to pass judgment. However, I believe that the Neworld Foundation denied human nature. They were committed to creating a world without disease, hate, war, hunger, sexual deviance, or the complications of romantic love.

"Others had similar ideas—read up on Karl Marx—and were doomed by not understanding the baseness of human nature. It was this concern that prompted me to leave my trail of breadcrumbs, just in case their little experiment went sour. Was the Neworld Foundation successful? On the surface the answer would seem to be 'yes.' You have prospered for all these years.

"Your explanation of reproductive contracts may have helped to control population growth, yet the practice seems cold and emotionless to me. Moreover, the idea of contracting or paying for sex was once considered immoral. It was called prostitution. But that is just a point of view. In my time, most people were tolerant of other lifestyles, of marriage between members of the same sex."

Addie was aghast. "I thought marriage was for reproduction. How could two men or two…"

"Marriage is not primarily about making babies, Aidan," said the captain. "It's not even really about love. People fall in and out of love without being married, and they have children too. Marriage is about social standing, legal rights, and responsibilities."

"Marriage is a contract," said Jo. "Only it binds the couples to terms set by their government or religion, and they are bound forever."

"There is divorce," reminded the captain.

"Don't get me started," said Jo testily. "Our contracts have terms and limits set by the couple—nobody else. When it's done, it's done."

"Where's love in all of this?" asked the captain.

"It's there—we just don't have a name for it."

"Where?"

"I love Tobey," said Jo. There was a tenderness in her voice—and a sense of realization. "I can see love in Addie's and Fallon's eyes and can hear it in their voices. Sean and Tobey's parents stayed together after their contract and they keep a common household. That's more than obligation. I say it's love. Missus Grier loves Neworld. If she didn't, she wouldn't struggle with the thought that all this knowledge will hurt the people more than help them."

The archive fell silent.

It was Bedford who finally spoke, tactfully changing the direction of the conversation. "The gallery bridge will be ready to deploy tomorrow. So, what would you do, Captain?"

"This is not my world."

"You can't get away with that," snapped Missus Grier. "We wouldn't be in this quandary if it hadn't been for *your* 'breadcrumbs.' If you hadn't 'sown the seeds of our discontent,' I would have grown up blissfully ignorant of your world. Neworld works, for the most part."

"The most part," said the captain. "What part doesn't work?"

"The Council," I said. "It kills people or makes them disappear. We've told you about the manor. And the stories Lenore has collected suggest that there is a forced labor camp upland. Some think it's on the largest Rift Lake island."

"So fix the Council," said the captain. "Why does it kill? What is it after?"

"Us!" said Addie.

"It fears the knowledge you have given us," said Bedford.

"I see two options," said the captain. "You could share this place with the Council and let them decide what to do with it."

"And the other option?" I asked.

"You can leave Neworld."

1.10.5

THAT EVENING before dinner, our core group met in the library. Missus Grier and Bedford laid out the two plans we had discussed earlier.

"Leave?!" said Lenore. "This is our home. This is where we live."

"This is where we died," said Addie. "Remember."

"I hate to admit it," said Tobey, "but it does seem that we may hurt Neworld more than we help it by staying. Our existence, our knowledge, is what the Council fears. Remove us and you remove the reason for the Council to kill."

"Where would we go if we left?" asked Sean. "Could we make a life in the Basin?"

Randall said, "It would be hard, but not impossible."

"If the stories about the people held captive upland are true, we'd be abandoning them," said Lenore.

"I know there are seven councilors—three representing the franchisers and four representing the guildsmen and workers," I said. "Do we know who they are?"

"No one knows their identities except the chancellor—and themselves, of course," Bedford explained. "The thinking is that their anonymity shields them from political influence, serving as the public face of the Council. The chancellor's heir assumes the position upon the chancellor's death or 70th birthday. He secretly convenes the Council on Capitol Island, where he meets with each councilor separately. It's a two-round process. In the first round, the chancellor presents the issues and collects the councilors' thoughts and arguments. In the second round, the arguments are presented to each councilor and his or her vote is logged. In the case of a tie, the chancellor casts the deciding vote."

"So, who's the chancellor?" I asked.

"Angus Brennan," said Missus Grier.

I looked at Addie. "Your father?"

She looked down at the table. "No," she said. "My grandfather."

"My late son had contracted with his daughter," offered Missus Grier.

"How did your son die?" I inquired.

"He became ill during harvest five cycles ago."

"Then your mother's next in line to become chancellor." I pondered the implications then asked Addie, "And where's your mother?"

Addie was on the verge of tears. "After father's death, she was quite shaken. She sent me to live with Grandmother."

"You haven't seen or heard from her since?"

"No. Not a word."

I shot a look at Lenore. "Accidents and disappearances."

Missus Grier gasped. Her eyes reddened and she began to cry. Bedford put a comforting hand on her shoulder.

I wondered, could this all boil down to bad blood between families, as in Romeo and Juliet?

"I should talk to the chancellor," I said.

"We'll go with you," said Sean.

"The captain and I have discussed this idea over the last week. It has to be me—alone. The fewer to go topside, the better, and no one knows me in Primacitta. I can nose around without raising suspicion. The captain's given me some insights in how to handle myself while I'm topside and how to negotiate with the Council."

"The lad is right," said Bedford. "The snows are melting and the chancellor will soon be receiving petitioners at the post-Conjunction court. There's a barrister by the name of Franklin who is one of us. I'll give you papers of introduction…"

* * *

EVERYONE was gathered in the courtyard.

"… and Fallon will petition the chancellor," concluded Bedford. "He'll offer to give the Council the generator station and the hydroponics farm as new franchises in exchange for our freedom."

"Can we trust the Council? We should leave tonight, all of us." Frank Bianchi, leader of the right-to-know faction was speaking. "We should get topside while it's dark and make a run for it."

The people around him began to shout: "Topside tonight!" "Spread the truth." "We want out!" "You can't keep us here."

"What if the Council is watching?" called a woman.

"We'd be caught," yelled someone else. "We've all heard the stories that Lenore has collected."

"That's why it's foolish for Fallon to go alone. If he's caught, it's all over. But they can't catch us *all*," argued Bianchi. "It only takes one. Just one of us needs to get away and spread the word."

His supporters became vocal again. Then those on the other side of the argument shouted back. The situation was getting out of hand.

Finally, Bedford signaled Tobey to whistle and the crowd settled down.

"Just give us one more week," pleaded Bedford. "One week for Fallon to carry out his mission." He focused his gaze on Bianchi and said, "Then anyone who wants to leave can leave."

Bianchi polled his faction and grudgingly nodded agreement.

As the meeting disbanded, Bedford pulled Percy and me to one side. "We'd better play it safe. Gather some men you can trust," he said to Percy. "Set up a guard at the mouth of the aviary entrance tunnel."

After Percy left, Bedford leaned close to me and whispered, "I suggest that you leave before dawn instead of tomorrow night as planned.

. . .

"I WANT to come along," said Addie as soon as we were together in bed. "Perhaps I could reason with Grandfather."

"I considered that, but I have a feeling in my stomach it wouldn't be safe for you. Best I go alone." I kissed her on the forehead and said, "What can you tell me about him?"

"Honestly, I have no memories of the man, or even my father, for that matter. And my images of Mother are fading—even in my dreams."

We didn't make love that night. Instead, we fell asleep in a comforting embrace.

. . .

THE EVENING before, we had gathered clothing appropriate for the weather topside this time of the cycle. Lenore had taken the cart and made a midnight run to the mess. She had a special treat waiting for us in the pod's meeting room: hot coffee and a bowl of fresh strawberries, newly harvested from the hydroponics farm.

I savored the berries while looking up at the half-moon setting in our ceiling display. *How could we keep this from the people of Neworld? How could we keep electricity and light and hydroponics and our world's history a secret?*

Randall arrived, and it was time to go. I kissed Aidan goodbye, and the twins and I drove off to the aviary. We didn't speak. We sensed that, once again, our world was about to change—and maybe not for the better. *Or to defend* popped into my mind.

When we reached the mouth of the tunnel, Percy's men had four people, three men and a woman, sitting on the floor with their backs to the wall. They were all dressed as I was—ready to go topside.

"They tried to sneak in," said Percy.

"Hold them here until midday," I said. "Then send them back to the Commons."

We parked the cart and went to the office complex. When we were almost to the dressing room, I made an excuse that I had left my gloves in the cart.

"I'll be back before you're suited up," I said.

I jogged down the corridors and made my way to the armory, placed my hand against the plate, and entered. I had surreptitiously studied the weapons with the captain over the last two weeks and knew what I was looking for—a pistol. I scanned the walls for the one I wanted, the one the captain had taught me to use. I found it, ejected the magazine, and searched for the proper ammunition. I filled the magazine, snapped it into the pistol, made sure the safety was on, and tucked the pistol into my waistband.

The others were just pulling up their hoods when I got back. We breached the hatch, then headed north along the gallery. The sky was clear and star-filled. I almost missed the sight of the moon in the night sky. I wondered what Earth was like. Our studies had shown that the people of Earth were self-destructive, so I wondered if it had survived its attempts to kill itself.

SolMinor was beginning to rise by the time we reached the crevice. The bridge was a marvel of metal tubing, wheels, tracks, pulleys, and ropes. With the bridge retracted, we were fully twelve meters back from the crevice. Randall pulled me into a meter-deep nook his team had carved into the wall of the gallery at the end of the bridge structure. "Stand in here and let the twins do their job."

Sean advanced to the end of the bridgework. He took the longer rope and handed it to Tobey behind him, then grasped the other one in his own hands. They both turned away from the hatch with the ropes trailing over their shoulders. Tobey was now in the lead. They wrapped the loose ends around their waists and Tobey shouted, "Pull!"

They strained into the ropes and took a step forward. The bridgework creaked. Sean gave it a backward kick. The bridge shuddered and began to move down the gallery. With every step, the bridge extended farther across the crevice. Tobey passed the nook, followed by Sean. I was now free to advance to the end of the bridgework and push. With the three of us applying pressure, it moved quickly and was soon resting on the far ledge.

The bridge wasn't tall enough for me to cross standing up, so I crawled. Water from the melting ice drummed on its thin metal roof. The bridge was solid and the crossing swift. I stood on the other side, turned back, and gave the twins and Randall a thumbs-up. They returned the gesture.

The hatch was free of ice, but somewhat corroded. I had to work hard to get the wheel to turn.

"Do you need help?" yelled Tobey.

I shook my head and leaned into the wheel. There was a grating sound and the wheel started to move. I worked it loose and spun it into open position, then swung the door open.

I pointed to the door and called back, "You might want to oil this thing when I'm gone." They laughed.

I stepped inside and noticed a static box at the foot of a metal ladder. I cranked the lights to full power and closed the door behind me.

x~10

Topside

1.11.1

I WAS looking straight up a musty-smelling, 165-meter-high tube only big enough around to spread my elbows 20 or 25 centimeters to each side. As I moved, I heard something crunch beneath my feet. I looked down and found the floor of the tube littered with the fine skeletons of skreel. I took a deep breath, grabbed a rung, and started to climb.

Time alone to think isn't a good thing when all you think about is what could go wrong.

What if the topside hatch won't open?

What if I can't find Franklin, the barrister, or I get caught?

What would the Council do to me? Kill me? Disappear me upland?

What if I get to the chancellor and he refuses to present our proposal to the Council?

What if they do accept? Will they honor our agreement?

What if…

SNAP! SCREECH!

One side of the metal rung I had grabbed broke and twisted downward. My feet were secure, but I lost my grip and started to fall backward. My spine slammed against the tube wall, sending a sharp pain through my body. My backside slid down the tube until I was wedged in a crouching position. When I pushed with my legs, it only drove me into the wall.

What if I die here?

I reached out, trying to grab a rung, but my fingers only grazed the surface. I thrust forward on the second try, but I still couldn't gain purchase.

If only my arms were a few centimeters longer.

I remained wedged for some time before I struck upon the idea of trying to use my shoulder blades to crawl my back up the wall… That didn't work.

I need a hook. A hook. What can I use as a…

I finally paid attention to the pain in my gut. I took off my gloves, shoved them in a coat pocket, then struggled to open the coat enough to retrieve the pistol, which was in my waistband—jammed between my leg and my stomach. Squirming and twisting, I worked it free. I held the pistol by the barrel, hoping to hook the handle over a rung. I reached out and found myself staring down the barrel of a loaded pistol. I didn't need experience with guns to know that was not a good thing. Very carefully, I pulled the gun back, ejected the magazine, and secured it in a buttoned shirt pocket.

Had I put a bullet in the chamber like the manual said?

I pulled back the slide and a casing ejected, striking the wall and clattering down the tube. I closed my eyes, hoping it wouldn't go off. I'm not sure how closing my eyes would protect me, but the brain isn't always logical when one's life is at stake.

I heard the bullet strike the floor and rattle around a bit before settling down.

Whew. I took a deep breath before reaching out again. I had to hook the pistol at the center of the rung to have enough depth to fit the grip between the rung and the tube wall. Once the gun was centered behind the rung, I shifted it toward the edge so it snugged tightly in place. I was then able to use the barrel as a handle of sorts and push myself up enough so I could bend forward and grab the next rung with my free hand. As soon as I had a secure grip again, I moved my feet down two rungs so I could stand comfortably and assess my situation.

The static lights were growing dim. Soon I would be in total darkness. I figured I had another twenty meters to climb, so I had to move quickly. I unwedged the pistol and tucked it into my coat pocket, retrieved my gloves, and began to climb.

When I came to the broken rung, I pulled on the remains that had swiveled downward. It seemed secure enough to support me as I stretched for the next rung up. I tested that rung before moving upward. It was a balance between safety and speed.

Finally, I saw a cavern above me and my intensity surged. Five rungs to go... four... three... two... one... I pulled myself over the lip of the tube. Then I lay panting on the wet, uneven stone surface. In the dim light I saw the topside static box mounted on the wall of the small cave. I crawled to it, got up on my knees, and cranked the lights. I sat with my back against the damp wall and rested.

I missed Addie.

I was glad she was safe in the quarters.

After a brief rest, I got to my feet and searched for a hatch. There was none—only a small burrow halfway up the wall, big enough for me to belly-crawl through. A trace of water trickled through it.

I had no choice, so I shimmied in and moved forward and slightly upward, inch by inch. Luckily, the burrow didn't get any narrower and it was only five or six meters long. My coat and pants were soaked by the time I emerged at floor level in a larger cave. A few thin rays of light filtered through a tangle of branches and bare vines that covered its mouth. A chilly breeze flowed in, which meant the cave was ventilated.

I went to the mouth and peered out. The cave opened onto the bank of a small river—the Little Silver, Captain Maczynski had said. The trees of the Rim Forest grew thickly all around. I knew that I must be mere meters from the edge of the Rim and at least two kilometers from the eastern limits of Primacitta. I forced my way through the bramble and looked up at the sky. It had clouded over and threatened to snow or possibly rain. It would do no good to be found coming out of the Rim Forest, which is forbidden to enter, so I decided to hole up in the cave until nightfall.

Snow covered the ground in shallow patches. I might have to meander a bit, but I wouldn't have to worry about leaving an easily followed trail through the snow. Then it struck me: How would I find my way back? I had only one option: follow the river on my return.

I searched the floor and found what I was hoping for: evidence of a firepit. Then I set about finding wood. I would get warm, dry off, sleep a bit if I could, and set out after dark.

1.11.2

THERE WAS a light dusting of snow on the forest floor when I woke. That was bad news since it meant that I would leave an easily discernible trail through the pine forest. I was still able to find bare patches here and there and detoured through them whenever possible.

It was after midnight when I reached the edge of the Rim Forest. I crouched down in the undergrowth some ten meters from the edge. As expected, there were no buildings nearby. I had studied a map of Primacitta before I left the quarters so I knew I would probably exit the forest near the north promenade. In the old citta, the wealthy family manors backed up to the forest. In the newer areas, a long, open park area—the promenade—served as an additional buffer between the city and the Rim. Just beyond would be a commercial district comprised of franchise warehouses, offices, and distribution centers.

I faced a problem: several inches of snow still blanketed the open expanse of the park and there was very little cover to shield me from prying eyes. In a few weeks the snow would be gone.

Retreating several meters into the forest, I decided to angle back toward the Little Silver so I could use it to traverse the promenade without being seen or leaving tracks.

The river was narrow, shallow, and free of ice. Its steep banks would provide cover if I crouched. If I walked along the very edge of the water, only the soles of my boots would get wet.

I proceeded upstream, stopping briefly at the edge of the forest. I listened for movement. All was quiet. I moved slowly into the park, halting every couple of minutes to listen. There was a footbridge ahead. I stopped. Listened. Footsteps! I dashed for cover under the bridge.

A patrol?

The steps drew nearer. Instead of crossing the bridge, they were coming down the riverbank. I skulked deeper under the stone archway of the bridge and watched. I saw movement so I held my breath and tried not to make a sound. A head appeared and dipped toward the flowing of water. It was a buck—a magnificent animal with a twelve-point rack. He was joined by two does. The buck suddenly lifted his head, looked in my direction, sniffed, and then led the doe up the far bank. My slog across the park continued without incident after that.

A gas-lit road ran along the verge of the park, with blocks of buildings just across the street. The river bisected the district, with walkways running along both sides. The lights from a succession of bridges receded into the distance. Bedford had told me that this part of the citta never slept, except during the HighConjunction. Now that the snows were melting, businesses were reopening and people were moving about on foot and rolling along on carts and wagons.

I passed under the first bridge and came up on the right-hand walkway. The smell of fresh baked goods and coffee lured me up the street to a café. I was supplied with money—not a lot, but more than I had ever had—so I went in and ordered two sticky buns and a cup of coffee. The café was abuzz with talk about the fire at the Grier manor. I became anxious, but no one paid attention to me. I was just another bloke, so I took a seat in a corner and listened to what was being said.

"Sad news about the Grier place."

"One of the original manors, wasn't it?

"I think that's true."

"Things like that happen if you build a bonfire too close to the house, though, don't they? The roof caught fire. Eventually, the gas main exploded."

"Ten dead, including the old Missus and her granddaughter."

My curiosity was piqued. Instead of going to see the barrister straight off, I decided to walk south toward the old citta. I wanted to see the manor from topside.

SolMin was peeking above the tree line and SolMaj was just rising when I reached the Grier estate. A crowd of people were milling around the stone arch, held back by several men wearing green jackets and peaked hats. My memory of my arrival told me that there was nothing to see from the road; the manor was set behind a screen of trees. If it weren't for the arch, you'd think you were looking at the Rim Forest proper.

I melded into the crowd with hopes of gathering more information.

"I heard the Council's going to raze the ruins and fill in the hole," said one man, "bodies and all."

"Let the forest reclaim the land," said his female companion.

"Not true," whispered a wizened old lady. "I have it on good authority that the chancellor is laying claim to the estate."

"How so?" asked the man.

"The young girl was his granddaughter, didn't you know?"

The man's companion shook her head and clucked, "That so?"

"Indeed it is. Come spring, he's going to excavate, recover the bodies, and rebuild from the basement up."

There won't be any bodies to find.

Will excavating the ruins reveal the passage to the Below and the quarters?

Maybe I should abandon the plan and head back right now.

As I wound my way toward the arch, I noticed two Dark Men on the inside, examining the crowd. I pulled up my coat collar as if fending off the morning chill and headed out of the crowd. I started down a street that would lead me toward the heart of the citta and a meeting with the barrister.

I heard footsteps behind me. I resisted the urge to speed up.

Stay calm. Remember the deer in the park. This is probably just someone walking to work, or home, or someplace. The footsteps drew nearer. I willed myself to stay calm. Suddenly, a hand grabbed my shoulder.

"Fallon?" came a hushed male voice.

I turned to confront the man.

"It *is* you!" said the man when he saw my face.

I knew the heavy, high-collared black frock coat, the slick grey hair hanging out from a black wool cap, and the pince-nez perched on a sharp nose.

It was Dean Ambrose.

1.11.3

HE PULLED me down a narrow, walled alleyway. "I came to see Missus Grier the moment the roads were passable. I wanted to sell... to tell her what happened. But she's dead." He glanced down the alleyway in nervous, bird-like head moves. "She's dead!"

When Ambrose first recognized me, I feared that he worked for the Council. But he was just a lowlife skreel trader of information—that's what he was doing in the Great Room the night McCreigh was killed. He had disappeared shortly afterward. I wondered to whom he sold the information.

"Tell Missus Grier what?"

"That... Say, weren't you in the house when it burned?"

Assuming my old manners from the Mount, I looked him in the eyes and lied. "The Missus wanted me to train as her personal baker. She set me up as an apprentice, sir—in a shop in the warehouse district. The baker turned me out when he heard of the fire. 'Who's to pay for your apprenticeship? For your room and board?' he says. 'I'll be glad ta be rid of your smart mouth,' he says."

I pulled my best look of contrition and said, "I wish I had taken your words to heart, sir. I fear I'll not amount to anything in this citta."

"Quite right. Quite right. You praise Below that you found some humility, young man," said Ambrose, regaining his composure and sense of superiority.

I started to walk him farther into the alleyway, away from prying eyes. "Why were you looking for the Missus, sir?"

"I had some information for her. But it's probably too late even if she were alive."

"Too late for what?"

"To save Missy Howard."

"What?"

"It's of no matter to you."

I grabbed him by the lapels of his coat and slammed him against the alley wall. I heard the air expel from his lungs. His hat slid forward, over his face. I flung it down the alleyway and shed my servant boy demeanor.

"It matters a great deal to me. What happened to Jenna?"

"They came and took her."

"Who?" I shook him as if it would loosen him up. "Who took her?"

There was fear in his eyes. "The... the Council, I think."

"When? Why? Where?" It felt as if my heart would pound a hole in my chest. I was sick to my stomach.

"Uh… uh…" he stammered.

"When did this happen?"

"The day after you left."

"Why'd they take her?"

"I wasn't in Hunninger's office, so I don't know."

I pulled him away from the wall, then slammed him back. His skull clunked against the brick.

"I know you, skreel," I said. "You were probably in the servant's passage, eavesdropping." I shook him again. "Why'd they take her?"

"Because they knew she was part of the Movement. That she was working for the old lady," he said sharply. Suddenly, he thrust his right hand in his coat pocket and pulled out a whistle. Before I could react, he blew it—loudly.

I threw Ambrose to the ground and the whistle skittered across the pavement. It was then that I heard the Dark Men coming from both ends of the alleyway.

"They knew," spat Ambrose, "because I told them."

The Dark Men were on me. They forced me to my knees, pulled a bag over my head, and cinched the drawstring around my neck. I remembered McCreigh's bloodied face and braced myself for a beating.

It never came.

1.11.4

AFTER THEY tied my hands behind my back, I was dragged down the alley, hoisted to my feet, spun around until I was so dizzy I could barely stand, thrown roughly onto the floor of a carriage, and carted off. If I had not lost all sense of direction, I would have been able to plot the route we took on the map in my mind. As it was, I was completely lost.

I berated myself for my hubris. I had let the way I was treated by Missus Grier and the others go to my head. I thought I was smart and capable—someone deserving of respect and responsibility. But I was just a kid playing at being an adult. *No one would recognize me.* What a crock of... Tobey or Sean would have fought their way out of the trap in the alley. Then again, Ambrose would never have recognized them. But someone else would have. I'm sure the Council had other plants in the crowd who could identify anyone from the Movement who was dumb enough to come to look at the estate. Dumb. Dumb. Dumb!

The carriage stopped. Two thugs manhandled me, pushing and dragging me along. I could hear water flowing. We ascended stone steps, entered a building, crossed a wide hall, went up more stairs, passed through more doors, and finally stopped. The two men held my arms.

"Unbind him," came a deep voice. The blackness of the bag helped me recognize it. It was the man who had questioned the prisoner McCreigh from the shadows, the one who seemed to be in charge.

The rope fell. I flexed my hands and massaged my wrists.

"Remove the hood," he commanded.

I expected to be in a dark room with a beamed lantern shining in my face, but what I saw was the imposing figure of a man silhouetted in front of an expansive window overlooking the Rim Falls. The Fount of Life soared skyward in the distance.

"You don't believe in the Fount or the Below, do you, boy?"

"Can't say that I do."

The man stepped forward and I could see his face and make out the ginger hair streaked with grey at the temples. Angus Brennan. He was dressed all in black formal wear—pants; shirt; long, open-front jacket. The only flashes of color were red satin gloves and shoes.

"And why is that?"

"The Code tells me that fictions are lies."

He laughed. "Indeed it does."

Angus Brennan walked up to me, bent close to my ear, and whispered, "Missy Howard told us about your talents, boy, and how the old woman was going to use you." He stepped back and gauged my reaction.

"She'd never…"

"She'd never! You are a naïve boy." The chancellor looked to the Dark Man on my right and tilted his head in a silent command. The Dark Man exited through a door somewhere behind me.

Brennan turned his back to me. "I can make anyone tell me anything I want to hear," he said as he moved to the window. "Even if it isn't the truth."

"Did Vernon McCreigh tell you what you wanted to hear?"

He spun on his heels. "What do you know of the blasphemer McCreigh?"

"You came to the Mount in the middle of the night to question him. You! You were the man in the dark. You had him killed."

"Who would believe the word of a one-name skreel like you without proof?"

"I have proof. There was someone else on the Great Room balcony that night. He'll corroborate my story."

"Who? That weasel Ambrose? Don't you think I extracted that information from him while I *convinced* him to watch the crowd at the old woman's estate? I am surprised he didn't tell me you were there, spying on me at the Mount too."

"He didn't see me."

Brennan turned again and looked out over the rushing water. "No matter. Poor Ambrose just had an accident—slipped and fell into the river. His broken body was swept over the falls."

The doors behind me opened. The chancellor turned, came forward a few steps, then waved for the person to come to him. I tried to turn to see who had entered, but the Dark Man punched me in the kidney and I dropped to my knees.

I heard the click of boot heels on the stone floor and, as the person passed, a whimper. I straightened up enough to see a Dark Man leading a woman to Brennan. She was barefoot, had a black bag over her head, and wore a thin, white robe, its back criss-crossed with dried blood. Her head hung low and her shoulders slumped.

"Jenna!" I cried.

She straightened. "Fallon?"

She began to turn toward the sound of my voice, but the Dark Man pulled a stick from his belt and struck her on the back, cracking open old wounds. Fresh blood stained the robe and Jenna cried out in pain.

"Jenna…" My guard kneed me in the back.

She stood facing Brennan, who glared down at me. "Do you doubt that she told me everything, boy?"

He tore the robe from her body, ripping away matted scabs of blood. Jenna screamed. The blood flowed freely.

I shot to my feet. The guard slammed his stick into my stomach. The padding of my overcoat softened the blow, but both Dark Men were on me. They stripped me of my coat, which fell to the floor at my feet, and began to beat me with their clubs. I felt at least one rib crack before they concentrated their blows to my kidneys. Then one of the men cracked me on the side of the head. My vision dimmed as I crumpled to the floor. I managed to cry "Jenna" before spewing vomit and blood.

A Dark Man pinned me down in a crouching position with his knee while the other grabbed my hair and forced me to look up at Brennan.

Jenna was facing me; the chancellor was now holding her to him with his left hand clutching her right breast. He raised his right hand and removed the bag from Jenna's head. The image of

McCreigh's face flashed in my mind. Brennan's hand disappeared inside his coat, then reappeared holding a thin-bladed knife, which he pressed against Jenna's throat.

"Why?" I shouted. "Why all this killing? Because you want to protect some insane story about *kons* and the Fount of Life? Because you don't want the people to know the truth about Neworld? About Earth?"

"Earth?"

"Yes, that's where we came from."

"Where would you get information like that?" He pressed the blade harder against her neck.

"You said Jenna told you everything."

His eyes widened and he withdrew the knife. "You made the descent?"

"Yes."

"Tell me what you saw."

I tapped my head. "You know my talents. I can draw it all for you." I looked him in the eye and said, "That's why I wasn't in the house when you had it burned. I was to contact others in the Movement and draw copies of what I saw. I barely made it out before the snows fell. I can tell you everything. I'll give you the names of my contacts in Primacitta. I can be very useful to you. Just let Jenna go."

"You'll be useful to me if you want to stay alive. This is what will happen to you when you stop being useful." He raised the blade to Jenna's throat and slit it from one side to the other. Blood sprayed everywhere, even hitting me in the face. My screams stuck in my throat. My mind raced with the images of blood and violence I had seen while learning about Earth. But nothing had prepared me for the horrors of such a cruel, senseless act.

I grabbed my chest with one hand, as if in pain, while I groped for my coat with the other hand. I felt like I was moving through mud, but my actions were too quick for the Dark Men to react.

With the taste of Jenna's blood in my mouth, I pulled the pistol from the coat and the magazine from my shirt pocket, shoved it in, cocked the gun, and shot the Dark Man to my left in the thigh—he was so close I couldn't have missed. Then I fell flat to the floor, rolled, and shot wildly at the second henchman, striking him in the shoulder. I continued to roll, got to my knees, and shot blindly at the chancellor twice. Two panes of glass shattered behind him.

Several things happened at once: Brennan started to run away, I staggered to my feet, the rear doors burst open, and a dozen or more household staff rushed in.

"Stop right there," I shouted to Brennan as I shot another round into the window to make my point. "I don't want to kill you. Good... Drop the knife... Now kick it away."

Several of the servants started to advance on me.

"Stay where you are or I'll kill the chancellor." When I was satisfied they weren't going to rush me, I said, "I came to make an offer to the Council. I can only do that through you."

"I... I can't do that," said Brennan.

I walked up to him and pressed the pistol to the side of his head.

"And why is that?"

"Because there hasn't been a Council for many cycles."

I positioned the barrel on the bridge of his nose. "Explain."

"Chancellor is a title handed down through the Brennans for generations..."

"Louder," I said. "I think everyone should hear this." I took a step back from Brennan, lowering my aim to his chest. "What was that about the Council not existing?"

Brennan turned to face the servants. "My family has served Neworld for many generations." Then he raised an arm and pointed at me. "This man is a Solarist who means to destroy our world. He attacked my men and is threatening to kill me."

"Only after you had me beaten and Jenna killed—poor, sweet, defenseless Jenna."

"Seize him!" Brennan commanded.

No one moved.

"Seize him, I say!"

A white-haired man in servant's livery stepped forward. "Those of us chosen to serve here at the Council Hall are never allowed to leave," he said to me. "We cannot leave because, during every HighConjunction, we see the Basin and the Fount for what they really are... We cannot leave because we serve the Council members when they are here and know who they are. Do you understand?"

"Yes," I said.

"Good. Now understand this: we haven't served a councilor in several cycles. We only serve an ever-growing number of the chancellor's Black Coats and Green Jackets. I, for one, want to hear what the chancellor has to say."

I lowered the gun and said weakly, "Whatever game you're playing is over, Brennan. There's an old Earth saying: *The truth shall set you free.* I've struggled with this statement because truth sometimes serves no good purpose. But *this* is a truth that needs to be told."

I raised the pistol again. "Set yourself free, Brennan."

1.11.5

THE CLATTER of running men drifted through the broken window.

"Theodore, see what's happening," said the elder servant to a younger man.

Theodore ran to the window and looked down. "Green Jackets! On the terrace. Coming this way."

The elder came close to me, put his hand on my outstretched arm and gently pushed it down. "You have friends among us," he said. "Your story must not end here, not on this day. Theodore! Take this man. Try to get him safely away from here."

As he crossed the room to retrieve the knife on the floor, he gave orders. "Everyone, get behind the chancellor. Maggie, shove that dust rag into his mouth." The old man placed himself directly behind the chancellor, pressing the knife blade against Brennan's ribs.

"Get going now," he said calmly. "We'll delay the Green Jackets as long as we can, and then I'll stick this miscreant like a pig."

I tucked the pistol in my waistband, reclaimed my coat, and put it on. I picked up Jenna's bloodied robe and limped to where she lay. Dead eyes stared out the window toward the Fount of Life from a nearly severed head. I gagged, then knelt and covered her battered, naked body.

Theodore pulled me to my feet saying, "This way!" We ran through several adjoining rooms, Theodore closing doors behind us—locking those that could be locked. With every step, my body was racked with pain and I struggled to stay conscious. In a dining hall he deftly pressed on a section of woodwork, opening a servant's passage. I ducked in. Theodore followed, again securing the panel. He led me through a maze of passages until we came out in the kitchen. It was empty.

"Stay here," he said before heading down a hall and out of sight. He was gone only a moment before he poked his head back into the kitchen and waved for me to follow him.

"Quickly! The rest of the staff has gone out to the receiving area to see what's going on. This may be your only chance. In there!" He directed me to the back of an empty delivery wagon as its two confused deliverymen looked on.

I climbed up, crawled under the tarp, and snaked my way between the cargo of empty crates and barrels.

I heard Theodore leave, calling from a distance, "All of you, back inside. Don't let the Green Jackets see you." His voice drew nearer as he said, "Bertie, you should leave now. It may be your only chance before the Green Jackets close off the island. Hurry! Hurry!"

The wagon jostled as the deliverymen climbed onto the seat and, with a lurch, whipped their horses into a gallop.

I knew that these were guild teamsters. However, I didn't know if they would head south to the guild section of Primacitta with their wagon full of empty containers, or go north to unload. I had no control over my immediate situation, so I hunkered down and tried to rest. Every bump was utter agony, every corner torture. It was going to be a long, painful ride.

An hour later the wagon stopped. By the way the light hit the tarp, I reckoned it was nearly HighNoon. I could hear the sounds of people, the clopping of horses, and the rattle of wagon wheels. Perhaps the men had stopped for lunch. I slithered to the back of the wagon to sneak a look and try to figure out where I was. Just as I was about to lift the tarp for a peek, it was thrown back.

"Bloody B!" yelped one of the deliverymen, tall, stout and mustachioed. "What are we supposed to do with him?"

"Bloody B, indeed!" said the second man, who was bigger than the first.

"Please don't..." I started to say. Then I blacked out.

• • •

I WAS disoriented when I came to. I was looking at the ceiling of a large room. At first I thought I was back in the quarters.

"He's awake," said a woman somewhere to my left. A ring of people formed around me—a mix of male and female workers including the two deliverymen.

"Where am I?"

"You're in a warehouse on Water Street," said the mustachioed man.

"How long have I been out?"

"More than three days," said a woman, short and matronly, with kind eyes.

"Someone tried to kill the chancellor," said the other delivery-man. "Did you have anything to do with that?"

"Tried?"

"Stabbed, they say." It was the mustachioed man again.

"Brennan's still alive?"

The mustachioed man nodded and asked, "Was it you that stabbed him?"

"No," I said, suddenly remembering the gun. I reached for my waistband. It was gone. I could only imagine what would happen if the pistol fell into the wrong hands.

"I think he's looking for this, Bertie," said the larger delivery-man. He held the pistol out for me to see.

"Careful with that. It's a…" I cut myself off.

"It's a what?" asked Bertie.

"A very dangerous thing. Please. I beg you to put it down."

"Put it down, Jonny," said Bertie to his partner. "Let's hear what the bloke has to say for himself. What's your story, lad?"

The truth shall set you free.

I asked for help sitting up, and then I began to tell them my version of the truth. For, as the captain told Addie, Jo, and me, "The truth is shaped by the historians." What you are reading now is the complete truth as I know it. What I told them then was the truth I needed them to believe. I introduced myself and told them about my talents, the death of McCreigh, my being sold, the raz-ing of the Grier manor, my abduction by the Dark Men, the en-counter with Angus Brennan, Jenna's murder, and Brennan's admission that there was no longer a Council. I left out any men-tion of my trek through the Basin, my descent into the Below, or being trapped the quarters.

"The dirty, rotten skreel," said Bertie.

"All you just told us is real?" asked Julia, the woman who had been taking care of me."

"I assure you that it is. If you can get me paper and pencils, I'll show you what I saw and write down what I've just told you. Then I need to be getting back."

"To where?" asked Bertie.

"Trust me, it's safer if you don't know."

. . .

THE NEXT DAY-AND-A-HALF I drifted in and out of consciousness, still coughing up blood. I couldn't hold down any food—not even broth. I spent all my lucid periods producing three handwritten, hand-drawn copies of what became known as *The Historian's Tale*. It included renderings of the bodies of Vernon McCreigh and Jenna Howard that brought the tough warehouse workers and deliverymen to tears. They took the first copy, delivered the second to Franklin the barrister, and I kept the last. Guildsmen and franchisers worked together to reproduce the papers, first by hand, then in print. Other talented artists faithfully reproduced the images of the slain *heroes*, a word I learned from the captain—and a word that swept through Neworld like wildfire.

I don't know if the decision was mine to make, and maybe it was made in the heat of hurt and anger, but I had sown the seeds of discontent and there was no turning back.

Even though I wasn't healed and was still in agony, it was time for me to return to the quarters.

Two hours before the rise of SolMinor, Jonny and Bertie transported me to the bridge over Little Silver that was closest to the promenade. I rode under the tarp. When they arrived at the bridge, they paused, rapped twice on the wagon bed, gave me a few seconds to climb down, and then trotted off without a backward glance.

I descended the riverbank and worked my way downriver as quickly as possible. The snow was almost gone, so I had no fear of leaving a trail.

The farther I went, the sharper the pains in my side became. I began to feel lightheaded. Twice I stumbled on the river rocks, falling once. My rib cage ached and my left arm tingled, yet I pressed on.

Our plan called for the twins to be at the bridge every day at the rise of SolMajor and wait two hours for my return.

A brilliant red solrise shone through the pines as I neared the Rim. SolMajor would rise within the half-hour. I climbed up the bank so I wouldn't miss the well-concealed entrance to the small cave. Once the leaves of spring sprouted, the opening would be virtually undetectable. I scrambled through brush, slithered through the small tunnel, and descended the tube, careful to mind the broken rung. The tube seemed to spin, forcing me to clutch a rung and hang on tight until my vision cleared.

I was heading home. *Home.* Why did I think of the quarters as home? My heart ached for Aidan. I felt ashamed to admit it, but for a second, as I watched the blood spurted from Jenna's throat, I was thankful it wasn't Addie. My *kon* tore at the thought. No matter what I did, I seemed to betray someone. My deep affection for Jenna betrayed Addie, and my love for Addie betrayed Jenna.

Home. For me, it meant being with Addie and my friends—the only family I'd ever known.

I continued my descent.

Even as I turned the locking wheel, I heard a metallic noise that could only be the extension of the bridge. Within a minute, Sean was grinning at me through the opened hatch. The grin was wiped from his face as soon as I stepped into the light.

"Do I look all that bad, brother?" I said.

"Aye, and even worse," he replied. "You need some help?"

I laughed. "Haven't looked at myself in the mirror lately." Suddenly, everything got blurry. I felt dizzy. I began to fall, then felt myself being caught and laid to the ground. Muffled shouts. I was on my back, being dragged across the bridge. The world faded to black.

When I awoke, I was lying down, gazing at the gallery roof. It was moving fast toward my feet. How could the gallery roof be moving? I lifted my head and saw a welcome sight. Tobey.

"Hang in there, little brother," he said. He tried to smile but I could tell he was concerned. "We're almost back to the aviary."

"Hommme," I slurred. I was beyond pain. I couldn't feel my body.

"Yes, home."

I was laid on the floor. I heard a hatch open. Then I was picked up again and lifted through and saw the high ceiling of the aviary. Sean was shouting: "Call the Missus. Tell her Fallon's back. He's hurt bad."

I drifted off.

My hand felt wet and I saw a blurry mass of red resting on it. Someone was crying. The blur came into focus. It was Addie.

"I lovve youu."

She raised her head, squeezed my hand, and smiled. "Grandmother! Grandmother!"

I drifted off.

"How are you feeling, Fallon?" asked Missus Grier, putting her hand on my forehead.

I felt like a little boy again, Missy Howard comforting me after a beating from Dean Ambrose. I hurt from my head to the very depths of my *kon*. Tears welled up in my eyes.

"Je… Je… Jennna is dead."

I drifted off.

x~11

1.12

Beyond

1.12.1

THEY SAID I died.

They said it was from my injuries.

I say I died from grief… from heartbreak… from shame.

My body lay on the table in the archive. I looked down on the small gathering of people around me—the people I loved and cared for… the people I had failed.

Then I was no longer in the room with my body. I was with Jenna in the courtyard. It was the young Jenna who showed affection to a small, lonesome boy and told him daring tales of spies. I was eager for adventure.

I was in Hunninger's office. He pulled a small bag from his desk drawer, loosened the drawstring, and spilled out a pile of coins. I was filled with rage.

Bedford was leading me through a maze of hanging carcasses. I was afraid. I screamed in voiceless terror when I saw Jenna's body hanging like a slab of meat.

I was holding the pistol to Brennan's head. Voices urged me on. *Pull the trigger. Pull the trigger. Pull it!* I was horrified by the very idea that I wanted to kill the man.

"Or to defend," said Anika.

Theodore was standing by the terrace railing. Behind him, the Riftwater roared toward the falls. Suddenly his throat gaped open and blood flowed down his neck. He tumbled backward over the railing, plunging into the river below. The Riftwater flowed red as a hundred bodies were swept downriver.

I floated in a void. I neither saw nor heard anyone or anything but I felt as if I were being judged.

I knew I deserved to die. I *wanted* to die.

There was heaviness in my chest. Again. Then again.

My body was lying on the table in the archive. The tabletop was alive with graphs and numbers and charts of the human body. Bedford was kneeling on the table next to me. His hands, one over the other, pressed on my chest. A video displayed next to my head, showing a man doing the same thing Bedford was doing to me.

"Don't die on me, lad," he said. "We need you."

Need.

The word tugged on me. It wouldn't let me pass on.

"Come back," cried Addie. "I love you. I can't go on without you."

Love.

I felt it in the deepest recesses of my *kon*. It radiated from every person in the room like the rays of SolMajor.

With a start, I opened my eyes and took a deep gulp of air.

They said I died.

I say I was reborn.

1.12.2

"YOU HAVE the captain to thank, not me," said Bedford. "When the aviary notified us of your condition, the captain said to bring you here. So I took a cart, intercepted the twins, and diverted them."

"Thank *you*, anyway," I said weakly. I felt a squeeze of my hand and knew that Addie was holding it. I couldn't lift my head to see her so I had to settle for the comforting warmth of her touch.

"Anytime, lad. Now rest awhile. Then we'll take you to your pod where you can recuperate."

"But we need to talk."

"You're too weak," said Missus Grier. "It can wait a day or two."

"It can't." But I knew that I was too weak to tell the story. "My coat. Where's my coat?"

"Here," said Lenore, handing it to her father.

"Inside pocket… the papers… read them…"

• • •

WHEN NEXT I WOKE, the archive was dim and I was alone with Addie. My head was on a pillow and my body was covered with a blanket. She was sitting with her head resting on her arms, asleep at the table. I stirred. She awoke.

"How ya feeling?" she asked.

"Not good… but better."

"You need to drink some water. Can you sit up?" She put her hands under my shoulders and helped me up. Set on the table at my feet were two pitchers, some cups, and several bowls filled with fresh fruit and vegetables.

"What would you prefer: water or fresh tomato juice?"

"Tomato juice," I said. "From the hydroponics farm?"

"Yes. It's quite tasty. Cook spices it up."

She poured me a cup and I sipped.

"Strawberries?"

"Yes. And now we have blueberries, carrots, snap peas, and beans as well.

"Blueberries, please. If only I had some fresh milk."

Addie laughed. "Seems like we could have that too. Randall says he can grow us some cows. Imagine that! But it would take a cycle for them to mature."

She ate with me and we talked.

She told me that I had a concussion, several broken ribs, and extensive bruises.

She told me how the twins had laced the bottoms of their coats together to make a sling to carry me in, using the arms as handles.

She told me what she and Jo had learned here in the archive.

She told me that our little group had read the papers and were assembling a team to make handwritten copies and distribute them to the others.

Then she began to cry.

"Do you hate me now?" she asked.

"Why would I…"

"He's my grandfather. The monster who killed Jenna is my grandfather! Brennan blood flows in my veins."

"As does Grier blood."

"What if I'm as mad as he is?"

"You aren't."

"Did he kill my father?"

"No way to know for sure, but I think he did or had someone do it for him."

"And Mother?"

"Probably."

"We need to kill him," said Aidan. "We need to kill Grandfather."

"We do," I said, surprised by my cold determination.

1.12.3

I DREADED the day I returned to the Commons, but I was eager to get back to work. I had been transported to my pod and confined there for almost two weeks, not even leaving our cottage to talk with Lenore, Jo, or the twins. The morning of my release finally came.

"There's work to be done," said Addie, slapping me on the behind as she got out of bed and crossed to the bath. "People to see. Decisions to be made." She threw a towel at me. "So get off your arse, clean yourself up, and come do your part."

I heard the shower turn on.

I swung my legs over the edge of the bed and sat up. My entire midsection ached. I was a little lightheaded when I stood, but I made my way to the bath. The mirror showed that the bruising was changing colors, fading, as was my black eye. I was going to have a small scar on my right cheek. "It'll give you character," said Addie after I had seen myself in the mirror for the first time.

The warm shower was now relaxing instead of causing painful stings.

"Jo and the others got an early start," said Addie as she tenderly bathed my back. "They left us the cart."

I turned to face her.

"That was thoughtful," I said. "But I'd like to walk, if you don't mind."

I pulled her close and we kissed.

"How can I face the twins when they ask why I didn't save their sister?"

• • •

ADDIE AND I walked arm-in-arm to the Commons. The closer we got, the faster my heart beat. Whenever we passed people, they'd stop in their tracks and look at me. I tightened my hold on Addie's arm, feeling more and more ashamed that I'd failed everyone.

When we entered the square, the people sitting closest whispered my name to those next to them, then stood. I heard my name drift through the crowd like a breeze through the trees.

In a growing wave, they all stood. I noticed that some held a copy of the papers in their hands.

The same thing happened as we entered the mess. People parted to let us through as we made our way to the serving line. Some reached out to gently touch me, murmuring kind words and blessings as I passed. I tingled with the realization that I was being offered their kindness, their respect.

Holding back tears, I stopped in the middle of the mess and surveyed the room. Every table had at least one copy of the papers.

"I don't deserve this," I said. "Sit down. Sit down, please."

As they settled in their seats, my gaze landed on Tobey and Sean, who were sitting off to one side with Jo.

"I failed you."

"No, you didn't, little brother," said Tobey.

"You did all that you could," said Sean.

"I could have, I *should* have killed the skreel. I failed you all. The chancellor and his Dark Men know about the passages to the Basin. They're going to excavate the manor ruins. I've doomed us."

"You got the word out!" shouted Frank Bianchi, leader of the right-to-know group. It was more than his cohorts who voiced their agreement.

"You forced our hand, lad," boomed Bedford, who had just entered with the Missus. "But we needed to be pushed off the fence, one way or the other."

"We have all talked and planned while you were recuperating," said Missus Grier. "Lenore and Percy are already topside. They're going to make contact with the guildsmen and franchisers—try to organize them, set up a network of eyes and ears."

"My friends and I will be going topside to fan out over Neworld and spread *The Historian's Tale*," said Frank Bianchi. "It is a version of truth that we can all agree on—that the people can rally behind."

"And Brennan's plan to excavate?" I said.

"We're going to give them the Basin," said Bedford. "It will take them cycles to figure things out."

"But they'll find the quarters..."

He held up a hand to silence me. "The Builders' guides are showing us how to create directed explosives that will bring down the antechamber and the passage to the quarters, including part of the Basin warehouse, sealing the connection between the two."

"We can live in the quarters indefinitely," said Melissa, who was standing behind me. "We've already planted crops of wheat, oats, barley, rice, cotton, and corn."

Jo spoke up next. "The Builders are showing us how to use the biotech bay to create chickens and cows, and how to operate the various manufacturing bays scattered throughout the quarters."

I looked questioningly at Addie.

"It's all true," she said. "We'll be completely self-sufficient within one annum."

"In fact," added Bedford, "We're hoping to give sanctuary to anyone topside who seeks it."

"We aren't prisoners down here now. We're here by choice," said the Missus. "We now have a place of our own and a purpose to pursue."

1.12.4

JO, ADDIE, Missus Grier, Bedford, and I retired to the archive after breakfast. We were sitting around the table talking about stripping the Basin warehouses clean and even destroying the Observation Base and the light runs when the captain manifested himself.

"May I remind you that you still have the option to leave," he said.

"Some of us are leaving," said Jo.

"The quarters, yes," he said. "But not Neworld."

"You mean go back to Earth?" said Addie.

"You would have that option, yes," replied the captain, "but you don't have to leave C-39d to leave Neworld."

"Right! Picture the Earth," I said excitedly. "A big blue ball. Masses of land surrounded by water. Neworld is like one of those masses of land. Don't you see? The Basin used to hold oceans."

"Where are they now?" asked Jo.

I turned to Bedford, "Remember the crusty apple?"

"Yes, lad, I do."

"When this planet cooled, the inside shrank. We are living on the crusty shell. At some point the Basin floor split, perhaps from the sheer weight of the water, and the oceans drained into the Below."

"You are a clever man," said the captain. "Go on."

"It would be safe to assume that Neworld... er... C-39d... has other landmasses like Neworld. Maybe there are other people out there waiting for us—other people who sought to create a better world. Or lands populated only by the native life forms of C-39d."

"Are there?" asked Addie. "Are there other lands?"

"As Fallon says, 'It's safe to assume...'" said the captain. He turned to me. "Please humor me, if you will. Draw a map of Neworld on the table. Just use a finger. Make it big enough for everyone to see."

It only took me minutes to draw the familiar outline. Everyone was satisfied that I had reproduced it faithfully—everyone except me. I looked at the captain, who was patiently waiting for me to have a revelation. "While this *is* Neworld," I said, "It's not the entire landmass."

"By Below!" said Bedford. "We were blind, Mara. We were so busy looking to the stars, we never considered what lies beyond the Rift."

"Captain, please complete the map," I said.

An outline appeared that showed Neworld comprising less than half of the landmass. There was an X marked some distance away from the lip of the Rift, just south of the Rift Falls. It was labeled EAGLE'S NEST.

"What will we find there?" I asked, tapping the X.

"Answers," said the captain.

$$x \sim 1.12$$

PART TWO
THE WARRIORS' TALE

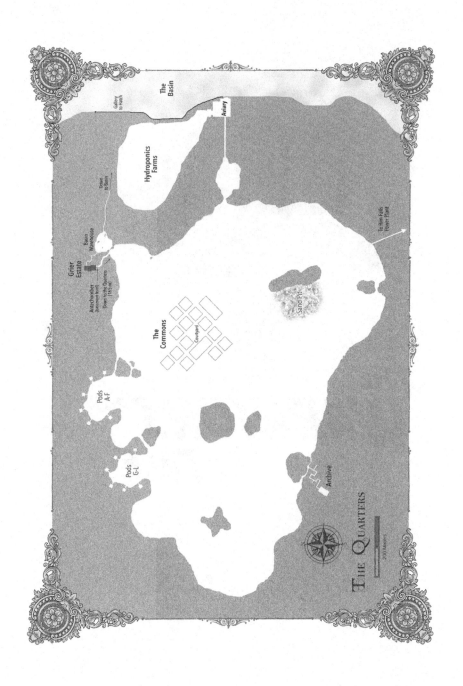

The Basin

Gallery to Hatch

Aviary

Hydroponics Farms

Down to Basin

Basin Warehouse

Grier Estate

Antechamber (basement level)

Down to the Quarters (165 m)

The Commons

Courtyard

Sand Pit

To Rim Falls Power Plant

Pods A-F

Pods G-L

Archive

THE QUARTERS

200 Meters

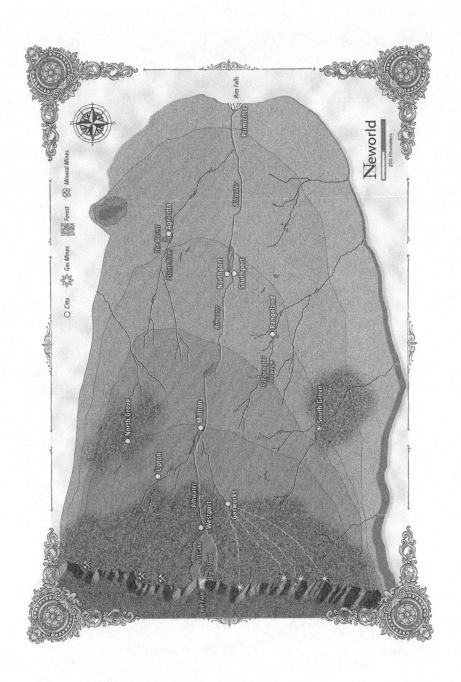

Historian's Note

After much consideration, I must admit that The Historian's Tale is the testimony of an unreliable witness, even if I am that witness. It was written from my perspective without thought of other points of view, but it is accurate as a personal history. And, as you will soon learn, I was in no condition to carry on. For those reasons I have relinquished my duties as historian to far more capable hands.

Mary Jo Wilkinson, who became the keeper of the archive, encouraged everyone in the Movement to keep journals, to log their missions when they returned to the quarters, and to gather and document the stories of the people of Neworld.

In writing The Warriors' Tale, the archive staff used all the resources available to them, including interviews and the journals of people who had experienced the events firsthand. They have written this volume in a style Jo calls narrative history.

— Fallon

2.0
Capt. Gergen

2.0.1

"GERGEN, you old skreel!"

Peter Gergen looked up from his plate of meat loaf and mashed potatoes to see a lithe, strongly-muscled man in stevedore attire approaching his table.

"That's *Captain* Gergen to the likes of you, Barnes!" said Peter, fixing the other man with a hard stare. Then he stood, shoving his chair back with his legs, smiled, and extended his hand.

"Good to see you, Vic. Have a seat," said Peter, motioning to the chair on the opposite side of the table. The head of the dockworkers at Pier 5 nodded and sat, not in the chair offered, but in the one immediately to Peter's right.

"What are doing here, Vic? I'd think you'd want to get away from the docks at the end of the day."

Peter found it curious that his old friend scanned the room nervously before he leaned in and spoke in low tones.

"I came to see you, Pete. I saw you docked this afternoon, so I knew you'd be here for dinner."

There it was again—the furtive turn of the head to the left, then right, eyes darting.

"Is something the matter?" asked Peter in a conversational tone.

Vic motioned for Peter to lower his voice and he stole yet another glance around the public house's dining area.

"What's going on?" asked Peter in a hushed tone.

"Have you read it?"

"Read what?"

"You know… *it*."

Peter answered with a bewildered look and a slight shake of the head.

"The tale… the story."

"I have no idea what you're talking about."

Vic leaned in even closer and barely whispered, "You know, *The Historian's Tale*."

Peter noticed that Vic pressed his hand against the breast of his coat as he whispered the name.

"I'm sorry, Vic. I don't know what you're talking about."

Vic Barnes straightened up in his chair and surveyed the dining room one last time. "I can't say anything more here. May I visit you in your room after dinner?"

"Uh… sure. Room 413. Say, seven o'clock?"

The stevedore nodded, stood, and left Peter to his dinner.

· · ·

IT WAS nearly nine when Peter finally tore his eyes from the drawing of a woman's body lying on the floor in a pool of her own blood. He set the small sheath of papers on the table and addressed his visitor.

"If this story is to be believed," said Peter, the incredulity fairly dripping in his voice, "the Chancellor has dismantled the Council and is gathering a force of thugs—these Dark Men and Green Jackets—by abducting young men from upslope. C'mon!"

"That what the historian says."

"Your precious historian also says that the chancellor kills people who oppose him—that he had his men seal up the Grier estate and burn it to the ground with people trapped inside. Is that what we're supposed to believe?"

"Yes," replied Vic.

Peter snatched the papers from the table and waved them in the air. "Bloody rubbish, Barnes. Bloody rubbish."

"This historian, Fallon, grew up in your neck of the woods."

"Yes," said Peter, "he claims to have been a ward of the Mount. It's a franchiser school outside of the citta. But that doesn't make me believe him."

"It's a compelling story," insisted Vic.

"And that's all it is—a story." Peter tossed the papers back onto the table. "This is why histories and stories are forbidden by the Code."

"Why don't you believe—"

"Because this stinks of Solarist drivel."

Vic looked crestfallen.

Peter slid the papers across the table toward his friend. "I'm sorry, Vic. I just can't believe it."

Vic slid them back. "Do me a favor, Pete. Hire a carriage tomorrow and take a ride through town. Drive by the Grier estate. Then tell me you don't believe it. I'll visit you on your boat tomorrow before you leave the docks."

• • •

AS HE WORKED his way through the citta, Peter didn't see any men in black coats, the so-called Dark Men, skulking in allies or darkened doorways, but he did see plenty of Green Jackets patrolling the citta streets in twos with shiny black clubs strapped to their hips. He stopped several times along the way: for a cup of coffee, to wander through the produce market, and to have lunch. He listened closely to the whispered conversations:

"Burned Missus Grier and her granddaughter alive…"

"Fallon was almost killed by the chancellor's guard…"

"The pictures of that McCreigh fellow and Howard woman brought me to tears…"

"Fallon's disappeared…"

"The historian's dead…"

"People are copying the tale and sending it all over Neworld… In the name of Fallon…"

"In the name of Fallon."

When he turned the corner on the lane that fronted the Grier estate, Peter saw his first Dark Man. He was standing in the shadow of a large stonework arch that marked the head of the drive leading to the estate. Two Green Jackets blocked the drive.

It became real for Peter at that moment. His heart pounded rapidly in his chest. He forced himself to keep looking forward and he feigned a lack of interest. He didn't feel safe until he was in his cabin, preparing to head back upriver.

● ● ●

THERE WAS A KNOCK on the cabin door.

Captain Gergen hastily secreted his copy of *The Historian's Tale* in his desk drawer before saying, "Enter."

Wentworth, the first mate, stepped in. "Sir, Mr. Barnes is here with the bill of lading."

"Show him in."

Vic Barnes entered, clipboard in one hand and a package bound in brown paper in the other. He waited for the first mate to leave and then shut the cabin door behind him. "Well?" he asked.

"Bloody Below! What's happening to Neworld? This is madness."

"Then you toured the citta."

"I did. So what do you want from me? You must have sought me out for a reason."

Vic handed Peter the bound package. "Safe passage for these."

Peter didn't have to ask what was in the package.

"And what do you want me to do with them?"

"We only want you to do your part. Spread the word, in the name of Fallon."

Peter nodded. He took the package and replied, "In the name of Fallon."

● ● ●

IT WAS FULL NIGHT when the rear-wheeler *Queen of the Plains* slipped into her berth at Agricitta. SolMinor had set and SolMajor wouldn't break the horizon for another two hours. The *Queen* was a shallow draft grain hauler that made weekly runs to and from Primacitta. On this leg of the trip she was laden with products manufactured in the capital.

Even at this hour, the dock buzzed with activity as various river packets were loaded or unloaded. Captain Peter Gergen was anxious to get home to Agricitta with the precious packet of papers in travel case. He spent nearly two hours making sure the unloading was safely underway before he picked up his belongings from the cabin and started to head home.

The first mate saluted as the captain approached the gangway.

Captain Gergen returned the salute. "The boat is yours, Mr. Wentworth."

"Aye-aye, Captain, the ship is mine."

Captain Gergen didn't see the mate signal the men lurking behind a stack of crates on the dock. As he stepped off the ramp, three men—two Green Jackets and a Dark Man—confronted him.

Captain Gergen never made it home.

2.1

The Genie

2.1.1

THE FALLON who was quickly becoming a legend on Neworld
was not the Fallon who lay on his back in bed, staring at the ceiling. He was tired to his bones… yet his mind raced with unpleas-
ant images and he fought sleep for fear of the dreams he'd have.

Fallon had become increasingly reclusive over the months
since his encounter with the Chancellor had culminated in the
murder of Jenna Howard. He grew to regret recounting the events
in *The Historian's Tale*, which was, even now, being duplicated and
disseminated across the width and breadth of Neworld. He feared
his disclosures had brought ruin to Neworld.

As his mood darkened, he slipped into self-loathing. Jenna had
been viciously murdered in front of him. He was *there*, just feet
away, and he couldn't prevent it. Nor could he exact revenge on
the man who had slit her throat. That was the dream he feared
most—the dream he was having more and more frequently.

Fallon couldn't bear to be around the people of the Movement—*his* people. It was the way they looked at him, touched
him—almost with reverence, as if they saw him as something more
than he was. Despite the fact that he had "returned from the
dead," he was just a person who had witnessed murder and lived
to tell about it.

The feeling was worst with Addie. Fallon could barely endure
her adoring gaze or gentle touch. He was pushing her away just
when he needed her most. Twisting his head to the side, Fallon
saw her lying close to her edge of the bed, her back to him as if she
needed distance between them. Her long, red hair flowed over her

pillow, reminding Fallon of Jenna lying in a pool of her own blood. Why couldn't he stop having these negative thoughts and feelings? He even questioned their relationship, wondering why he and Addie were together in the first place. It wasn't something he had wanted—something he'd consciously sought. They weren't under contract. They had just sort of happened. He needed time... time alone... time to think things through.

Fallon's eyes fluttered. He tried to keep them open. He didn't want to relive his beating by the Chancellor's Guard or his experience of floating outside his body, watching his friends' desperate attempts to bring him back from death's door. He didn't want to feel the scorching heat of the fire that almost killed Addie. He wished he could dream of the days he had served at the Mount, tending to the snotty sons of powerful franchise families, or relive his whirlwind adventure after being sold to Missus Grier. It was a trek that had taken him from the surface of Neworld down to the Basin and into the depths of the Below. Until his explorations proved otherwise, everyone on Neworld believed the Below was a sacred place where *kons* dwelled. Instead, he found that it was home to fantastic creatures and was the resting place of a ship that could sail to the stars.

Finally, sleep overwhelmed Fallon, his eyes jittering beneath closed lids.

• • •

EERRT! EERRT!

"Aviary door is opening."

EERRT! EERRT!

"Aviary door is opening."

Fallon sprinted down the dark tunnel toward a warehouse-sized cavern that held an array of vehicles and mechanical workstations. The room, normally dark at this time of night, glowed red.

EERRT! EERRT!

"Aviary door is opening."

251

EERRT! EERRT!

"Aviary door is opening."

As the massive door parted, it revealed a clear, starry night sky above the horizon of dense mist that enshrouded the Below.

Through the widening gap, Fallon saw men sliding down ropes. It was the Chancellor's Guard, their green jackets appearing black under the red light. How many men? Too many! They slid down the ropes and flooded into the aviary.

This can't be happening, he thought. How did they find us?

Fallon heard the clatter of footsteps behind him. He turned to see the men and women of the Movement appear like apparitions out of the darkness. They rushed past him as if he weren't there.

The invaders had formed into a defensive line, three-deep. The guards' polished black sticks glinted red as the formation lifted them in unison—as if they were of a single mind.

Weaponless, Addie, Sean, Tobey, Jo—even Bedford and Missus Grier—rushed the invaders.

Fallon's people let out a ferocious roar and threw themselves into the line. But they were no match for the trained, disciplined Chancellor's Guard.

Fallon strained to take action but couldn't move. His heart pounded erratically and he felt like a great weight was settling upon his chest. He just stood there, watching as the guardsmen battered his friends.

The horror of what he was seeing was beyond comprehension. The absurdly loud cracking of bones being broken and skulls being smashed rang in his ears. A mist of blood hung over the skirmish. The cries and moans of the people lessened as they fell, one by one. Only a few were still alive. Sean, Tobey, and Jo were fighting back-to-back. Jo fell first, as ten guards engulfed the trio.

When Tobey finally fell, the guards parted and turned toward the lone survivor. Aidan—Addie, his love—was kneeling next to the body of her grandmother, Missus Grier.

A guardsman waded through the killing field and stood before her. Addie looked up defiantly as the guardsman pulled back his club to strike.

"No," Fallon shrieked, the hoarse sound sticking in his throat like a scream in a nightmare.

The guardsman swung viciously, connecting along the side of Addie's face. Fallon heard her neck snap as her head twisted violently.

Fallon was without voice.

And suddenly he realized there was something in his hand. It was hard, cold metal. He knew what it was without looking down. He flipped off the safety and pulled the trigger.

Tat-tat-tat-tat…

The muzzle flashed and the guardsmen danced a dance of death as they were struck, fountains of black erupting from their bodies. They didn't know what was happening. How could they know? To them, their polished black sticks were the ultimate weapon. The people of Neworld didn't know of guns. Now that his friends were dead, only Fallon knew of guns and their destructive secret.

Tat-tat-tat-tat   Tat-tat-tat-tat

The gun spat an impossible number of bullets.

Tat-tat-tat-tat

The last guardsman crumpled to the floor.

The gun went silent.

Fallon fell to his knees, horrified at the death and destruction and hoping this was just another nightmare…

● ● ●

Fallon was rocking his head from side to side when he woke. His body went rigid and he gasped for air.

Addie stirred, wrapped her arm around him, and said, "That dream again? Jenna's murder?"

"No," he said. "Not that. Something much worse."

Fallon told her of his nightmare and his feeling of helplessness. But he didn't mention the gun—he *couldn't* mention the gun.

Addie leaned her head upon his chest and began to weep.

2.1.2

FALLON and Addie sat at a table in Pod G's common room. The pod's luminescent ceiling depicted an Earthly night sky with a sliver of a waxing moon beginning its descent.

"We need to talk…"

Fallon didn't know where to begin. He looked absently at the floor.

"About your dream?" asked Addie, setting a steadying hand on his.

Fallon jerked his hand away and rested it on his nervously bouncing leg under the table. Then he turned his head toward Addie but couldn't bear making eye contact. "There's something you don't know. Something I don't want you to know. Bloody B, I don't want *anybody* to know."

He glanced up and saw a questioning look on her face. "See this beautiful sky the Builders have left for us?" he said, again breaking visual contact with Addie. "Earth must have been beautiful. You've seen pictures in the archive, right?"

"Yes—the lands, and cities, and oceans. I would love to see an ocean."

"And their art and music," added Fallon, desperately hanging on to hope. "But there's more—a darkness that the founders of Neworld hid from us. A darkness that should be kept locked away."

"I don't understand."

"If you want to understand… come to the archive with Jo and me this morning."

At that moment Sean Halloran came out of his cottage along the back wall of Pod G. He was yawning, with one hand stroking his scraggly black beard and the other in his pants pocket, scratching himself.

"Uh, mornin'," he said. "You're up early."

"Had a bad night," said Fallon.

Sean nodded knowingly before walking a few doors down and knocking. There was no response from inside, so he peeked in the window, then knocked again.

"Up and at 'em!" he called. "The night is wasting."

Sean crossed to Addie and Fallon, a look of concern on his face. "Another nightmare about Jenna? You'd think they'd have stopped by now. What's it been? Three, four months?"

"Five," said Fallon.

"Tobey says Jo's been having bad dreams too. Maybe it's from being cooped up down here for so long."

Fallon shook his head and, with a halfhearted smile, said, "Maybe."

Tobey Andrews, Sean's older twin, came out of the cottage door Sean had knocked on. Tobey was half a head taller than his brother and had long, light-brown hair—in sharp contrast to Sean's short-cropped, dark hair. Both had athletic physiques and sported broken noses from their prizefighting days. "You off?" he asked his brother.

"Yeah, I need to be in Primacitta before dawn," said Sean. "I figure ten days, round trip, then I'll be back the first rainy night."

"Don't forget to pick up what we talked about," said Tobey with a wink.

"Yes, sir. Yes, sir. Two bags full," answered Sean dutifully.

Tobey pulled his brother into a hug and said, "I'll be waiting at the bridge, brother."

"You better be," replied Sean, patting his brother on the back.

"Good luck," said Addie.

"Be careful," said Fallon.

2.1.3

THE TWISTING TUNNEL leading to the hidden archive had no lights, so Mary Jo Wilkinson, the keeper of the archive, led the way with a cranked-up lantern.

"Do you really want to show her?" she asked. She had doubts about letting *anyone* see what the captain had shared with Fallon and her.

"Yes," said Fallon.

"Are you sure you want to see, Addie? I haven't had a good night's sleep since…"

"I'm sure."

Jo sighed. "I haven't even had the heart to tell Tobey the reason for my nightmares."

They continued in silence until they reached what appeared to be a dead end. Jo shone her lantern on a keypad embedded in the wall and then tapped in a passcode. The wall slid away. She stepped into the open space beyond and waited for the others to follow. When everyone was clear, Jo touched a glass plate. The stone wall closed and the ceiling of the small, polished granite anteroom lit up.

They heard a hiss as Fallon opened the secure hatch on the left wall. Lights came to life when the door opened and the three stepped into the spacious archive. Despite its age, the archive was pristine. The lighted, polished metal-and-glass cases that lined three walls from floor to ceiling were filled with artifacts and books that offered insights into life on the planet called Earth—the planet from which the people of Neworld were descended.

Jo positioned three metal stools on one side of a white glass table that dominated the center of the room.

"Grab a stool," she said. As Fallon and Addie took seats to either side of her, Jo expertly worked the controls that appeared in the tabletop display. The archive lights dimmed. The table display came to life and an image that filled the entire tabletop took form.

Jo began to explain the image to Addie. "At one time, Earth used to tell its people what was happening in the world each day through printed materials called newspapers."

"Every day?" said Addie. "It takes months for Neworld's review board to approve a single agricultural pamphlet. What's that mean? *Wahr?*"

"That's W—A—R!" said Jo, her heart sinking. "War. It's a word you won't find in the 1900. I can't adequately explain it, so I'll need to show you. Addie, this is your last chance… As Captain Maczynski told Fallon and me, once you let the genie out of the bottle, you can't put it back in."

"What does that mean? What's a genie?"

"It's a long story, Addie," said Fallon, "but it means that once you've seen or learned something, you can't *un*-see or *un*-learn it."

"If only it weren't true. I wish I could…" Jo gulped down a sob. "It's not too late for you."

"Show me," said Addie without hesitation.

Jo tapped the table and the newspaper was replaced by a cavalcade of images and moving pictures in black-and-white and stark colors:

Dead men in uniforms, lined up like cords of wood on the side of a country road.

"They called that a civil war," said Jo. "Brother fought brother and father fought son as a country, not unlike Neworld was torn apart from within. More than six hundred thousand men were killed."

"Six hundred thousand?" Addie was incredulous. "That's more people than there are on all of Neworld."

"Almost six times more," said Fallon.

Men pointing objects out of the windows of black carriages that didn't require horses. The objects flashed with light and people on the citta street fell to the ground.

"Those dark men were called gangsters. They terrorized cittas in Earth. The things they're holding are called guns," said Jo, as more images flashed on the display.

Guns of every shape and size. Pistols, rifles, machine guns, tanks, cannons.

A huge ditch piled with bodies that were wasted away to skin and bones.

"Millons of people were killed because they believed in something different than the people in charge."

"Millions? said Addie. "It's unfathomable."

"But true," said Jo, tears streaming down her cheeks. "And… the whole… world… fell into… war." Jo couldn't continue her narration, so the images flashed by in an unnerving silence.

Flying machines—airplanes—with guns and… bombs! Bombs falling from the bellies of planes… and cittas ablaze beneath.

Addie clutched her heaving chest with one hand as the other stifled the sounds escaping from her mouth.

A towering cloud that looked like a mushroom.

Two giant towers on fire and crashing to the ground. People fleeing the dust and ash of the collapse.

Repeated headlines detailing "Terrorist Strikes." Bombs exploding in what looked like peaceful marketplaces.

Men and women being beheaded and burned alive.

Rays slanting down from the sky, incinerating everything in their paths.

Destructive flashes of light on the surface of the Earth's moon.

"And if that weren't enough," said Jo, "the people on Earth glorified violence in their entertainment.

Clips of movie and television violence, racing by at an unrelenting pace. Murder, violence, war.

Aidan broke down, sobbing uncontrollably. Jo—who at first look had been enthralled with Earth's beauty and its concepts of art and love—struggled to maintain control. How could people with such beauty in their hearts be so cruel? She reached out and embraced Addie. "That's the genie," she said, tears flowing freely down her cheeks.

"But we've got it contained in this bottle," said Fallon, indicating the archive. "I know that I promised the truth for the people of Neworld... But this...?"

x~2.1

Incursion

2.2.1

A FLASH of lightning illuminated Patrolman 1251 as he stood in the shelter of the warehouse's entrance alcove. His green Chancellor's Guard jacket and black peaked hat were already drenched, but the alcove gave him a short respite from the midnight downpour and the stiff breeze coming off the Rim. The spring rain itself was not cold but the chilling effect of the wind made the night uncomfortable.

The commercial district, which housed franchise warehouses, offices, and distribution centers, was all but deserted at this hour. The calm belied the commotion of commerce that would begin in about four hours as Primacitta woke and demanded the attention required to keep the capital of Neworld thriving.

Patrolman 1251 unclipped the leather-wrapped flask from his belt, thumbed open the lid, and took a couple swallows. Then he surveyed the area in front of him while the liquid warmed him, energized his body, and increased his focus.

The alcove looked out across the Little Silver, a narrow, shallow river that bisected the district. It was a prestigious location because the buildings overlooked the terraced River Walk instead of a street. The view appeared strangely beautiful when illuminated by gas lamps that sputtered in the rain and the wind.

As he slipped the flask back onto his belt, 1251 heard the clopping of horse hooves down at the end of the River Walk, where it terminated at an avenue that skirted the Promenade. The Promenade, a public park, served as a boundary between the city proper and the two to three kilometer strip of wooded wilderness that buffered Primacitta from the Rim. The wilderness beyond the Promenade was off-limits to the people of Neworld.

Assumed I was the only poor bastard that had to work in this slop, he thought.

The clopping stopped.

1251 leaned his head out from under the alcove and squinted against the rain. A teamster wagon, its cargo covered with a waterproof tarp, stood in the center of the avenue bridge, just outside the range of the gaslights at either end. The teamster reined in the horses, which had been spooked by a flash of lightning. He was saying something. *To whom—the horses?* He appeared to be alone. 1251 cocked his head, trying to make out what the driver was saying. But it was to no avail, for the sizzle of the lamps and the patter of the rain drowned out the words.

Then the tarp began to rise and fall as if something was moving underneath, edging toward the rear of the wagon.

Well, that's odd.

As fingers of lightning crawled along the bottom of heavy clouds, a bearded man nimbly slid off the back of the wagon. He was slightly below average height, yet muscular. The young man took a quick look around, then held the tarp up and gestured in a way that suggested he was in a hurry. A second man climbed out. His movement was that of an old man. The pair pulled packs out from under the tarp and slung them on their backs. Then the young man waved to the teamster and, after a shake of the reins, the wagon continued down the avenue.

The two men did not come up the River Walk as the patrolman expected. Instead, they headed east into the Promenade.

What the…?

These weren't warehousemen who had hitched a ride on a rainy night. Anyone going into the Promenade at this time of night and in this weather had to be up to no good.

The patrolman hesitated. When the district was bustling, the patrolmen walked in pairs. In that situation, the course of action was clear: one guard would report the incident to the station while the other would follow the men into the Promenade. So 1251 had to make a snap decision: report or follow?

He decided to track the men and see where they were going. He stepped into the rain and hurried toward the Promenade, keeping just close enough to see the men through the darkness and the rain.

2.2.2

1251 STAYED on the bank as the two men walked in the shallow river. They had traversed the park and had entered the forbidden wilderness. It was obvious they were heading for the Rim.

The trees were just beginning to bud, so they offered no shelter from the rain. Nor did they dim the glare as the jagged lines of lightning snaked along the underside of the clouds. Some displays lasted forty to fifty seconds.

The men's progress was slowed because the older man needed to stop and rest every fifteen to twenty minutes. The younger man relieved the other of his pack and carried it, as well as his own.

1251 had to be particularly cautious when the men rested because the younger one would take the opportunity to look around to see if they were being followed.

For the better part of two hours the patrolman followed, undetected. He had never been this close to the Rim before. He was afraid he'd not see the edge in the dark and accidentally stumble over and plunge to his death in the Below.

What are they up to?

The bank was steeper now as the river ran between two hills.

The sky lit up just as the old man bent over, putting his hand on his knees for support. The young man excitedly pointed to the east. The river disappeared into the lightning's glare some fifteen meters downstream.

1251 knew they could go no farther.

The young man pulled his companion to the opposite side of the river and up the bank. The lightning display stopped abruptly, plunging the men into relative darkness. The old man stumbled, fell, and slid down the sodden bank, crumpling in the shallow water. The young man skittered down, helped him up, and guided him to the top, where they disappeared into a small copse of bushes at the base of a hillock.

The patrolman pulled out his pocket watch and brought it close to his face so he could read the time in the dim light. It was twelve past two. He put the watch away. His energy was waning and he felt a bit listless. He needed a drink. Two swallows from the flask revitalized him.

1251 carefully descended the bank, forded the river, and climbed up the other side. He could easily follow the men's tracks—the old man was dragging one foot, leaving behind a trail in the layers of decaying leaves that lined the forest floor.

The tracks didn't go up or around the hillock. They ended at the bushes. 1251 stood there, silently puzzling out the answer, when he heard an unusual whirring sound. He turned his head slowly, trying to locate the source of the sound. It seemed to come from behind the bushes.

He pushed his way through and found himself in a small cave, as black as midnight on HighConjunction.

A lightning display filtered through the bushes just enough to expose a trickle of water running through the cave.

As the light faded and the cave fell into darkness again, the patrolman noticed a dim, green light close to the floor at the far end of the cave. He crossed the cavern, got down on his knees, and bent lower to peer at the green-lit opening of a tunnel just big enough for a man to crawl through. He lay down on his stomach and began to slither through.

2.2.3

IT WAS standard practice to man the gallery bridge from midnight to dawn on rainy nights. Tobey Andrews was expecting his brother Sean to return with his cargo, so Tobey had bridge duty that night.

The gallery was a narrow walkway, which barely allowed two people to slide past each other, back to back. The Builders had carved it into the sheer face of the Rim more than 160 meters down from the surface of Neworld. Since the destruction of the Grier estate eight months earlier, it was the only way members of the Movement could get topside.

The far end originally ran behind a waterfall but, over the years, the Little Silver had cut a destructive path that resulted in a break in the gallery, cutting off the path to the hatch. To maintain access to the surface, the Movement had engineered a retractable metal bridge that could be extended across the chasm.

Tobey was dozing in an alcove that had been newly carved into the inside wall of the gallery. The nook was located at the end of the retracted bridge and was big enough for two to sit on the alcove-wide stone bench or one to sit with both feet up and back against one side wall. Tobey had his feet up and back against the wall, his chin sunk against his chest. He didn't hear the metal wheel of the hatch spin, or the well-oiled door open. He didn't see the green glow that silhouetted the two men who stood in the chamber beyond.

"Yo," said Sean Halloran as he stepped through the hatch. "Who's on duty?"

No answer.

"YO!"

"Hold your horses, brother," came a sleepy reply. "Can't a fellow catch forty winks without being disturbed?"

"Tobey, is that you?"

"Sure it is. Told you I'd be here, didn't I?" Tobey was behind the bridge now, pushing. "Comin' at you."

A few seconds later the low, covered bridge was extended and Sean handed the old man his pack and motioned for him to crawl through. Then he closed the hatch and spun the wheel before crawling across himself.

Tobey helped the old man to his feet. "Dr. Inoue?"

The man nodded.

"Welcome," said Tobey, talking as he walked the doctor back to the alcove. "As soon as Sean gets across, he'll take you the rest of the way to the quarters."

When Sean arrived at the niche, he slapped his taller brother on the shoulder. "Good to see you, brother."

"New set of clothes," noted Tobey.

Sean held his arms out and slowly spun around, showing off the fresh set of jeans and leather jacket. "Thanks, bro," said Sean. Then he tossed his pack to Tobey, adding, "And this is for the storeroom."

Tobey eagerly opened the overstuffed pack and broke into a broad grin when he saw the contents. "You remembered the wool socks!"

"Like I promised, brother, two bags full. At least fifty pair in there," said Sean. "The doc is carrying another fifty. How're things down here?"

"Moving along. Did you enjoy being topside?"

"Not as much as if I'd been alive."

Dr. Inoue looked confused.

"The chancellor and his thugs think my brother and I are dead... It's a long story. I'll tell you all about it someday. But now, if you'll follow me, I'll lead you to your new home."

Tobey went back to the bridge and began to retract it. When it was about halfway back, he saw the hatch wheel spin. Puzzled, he stopped pulling.

The door swung open and a lean, dark-haired man in a green jacket and black peaked hat stepped onto the landing.

The two men stared at each other, dumbfounded. Then Tobey cried, "Sean! Sean!"

"What?" came a distant reply.

"A Green Jacket! You were followed."

The Green Jacket turned and fled back into the chamber.

Tobey pushed the bridge as hard as he could, and started to crawl through as soon as it was fully extended.

"I'm behind you," called Sean, still some distance down the gallery.

Tobey plunged through the hatch and looked up the tube that led to the surface. He could see the Green Jacket's legs in the dimming green light. He gave the static box a few quick turns and the lights whirred to full brightness. Tobey, who had never been up the tube before, began to climb.

The Green Jacket had reached the top and disappeared. Tobey hastened his pace, pulled himself into the illuminated inner cavern, and dove for the crawl space that he knew led to the outer cave. His bulk hindered his progress through the small passage. The Green Jacket was already outside somewhere.

Tobey plowed through the bushes and into the storm. It was hopeless. He'd never find the intruder...

A dazzling light show lit the forest. Tobey saw movement to the west and gave chase. On open ground Tobey's long legs and athleticism gave him the advantage and he narrowed the gap. He couldn't let the Green Jacket make it to the Promenade.

Green Jacket must have heard Tobey closing in and he desperately called for help. Estimating that they were not even a quarter of a kilometer from the Rim, Tobey wasn't concerned anyone would hear. He was gaining ground fast.

The Green Jacket suddenly turned and stood his ground. He retrieved the patrolman's club from his belt and slapped it threateningly against his own palm.

Tobey's boxing instincts kicked in and he pulled up, just out of range of the man's swing. "Hey brother, nobody needs to get hurt," he said. "Come along peaceably, and I can guarantee that you will come to no harm."

"Who are you?" asked the Green Jacket.

"I'm just a guy out for a walk in the woods." Lightning cracked overhead. "Who are *you*?"

"I'm 1251."

"What's your *name*?"

"1251."

"C'mon, man. You gotta have a name. A *real* name."

"No. I'm Patrolman 1251 of the Chancellor's Guard."

Tobey took a step forward.

Green Jacket swung his club, so Tobey jumped back and began to circle.

The rain quickly went from a shower to a downpour, and it seemed as if the clouds had descended from the sky. Then something happened that terrified even Tobey, who had experienced the "lightning run" down in the Basin. Fingers of lightning forked among the trees, just meters above them, making the hair on their heads stand on end and nearly blinding them. A tree exploded and burst into flames.

Tobey recovered first and lunged at the guard.

Green Jacket had time to make a short swing, catching Tobey in the ribs and sending him sprawling to the ground. The guard went on the offensive and advanced on Tobey, raising the club high. Before he could deliver the skull-crushing blow, he sensed movement to his left and began to spin around.

Sean hurtled himself through the air, ramming his head into Green Jacket's stomach and pulling him down to the forest floor in a vice-like grip.

Green Jacket's head slammed hard against the sodden ground and the club rolled from his hand.

Sean straddled the man's chest and pulled his clenched fist back for a left hook when Tobey grabbed it. "You won, brother," he said. "He's out cold."

Sean looked up at his brother and grinned. "I told you I was right behind you."

2.2.4

EVEN AT DAWN, the quarters bustled with activity. The number of people living underground had swelled from about sixty to nearly four times that number as Lenore Bedford and her growing organization topside recruited new people to fill needs.

The technologies left behind by the Builders were mind-boggling and the Movement needed skilled people to learn their secrets: agrarians to learn hydroponics, engineers to work with electricity, laborers to master the machines that could produce the wide variety of goods required for a self-sustaining community.

The people came in ones and twos. They came knowing they might never again see the open lands and cittas above. They were smuggled in through the hatch on rainy nights like tonight.

The underground complex boasted a medical facility that was beyond the comprehension of anyone in the quarters, so recruiting a doctor was a high priority. When Lenore sent word of a retired doctor from Agricitta, Sean was immediately dispatched to the heartland to contact Dr. Inoue and bring him safely back to the quarters. The rainy night had brought with it high hopes of the doctor's arrival.

Missus Grier, James Bedford, and Fallon waited anxiously in the cavernous aviary. The giant aviary doors were open so they all wore overcoats to fend off the cold, damp breeze coming in off the Below. The yellow disk of SolMajor could be seen through the mist, rising in the east. SolMinor, hidden by the storm clouds, had risen hours before.

"I guess they didn't make it," said Bedford with a sigh.

"I hope they weren't caught by the Guard," said the Missus.

"They could be delayed for any number of reasons, ma'am," said Fallon. "What bothers me is that Tobey isn't back by now. If you don't mind, I think I'll take a stroll out to the bridge."

. . .

It was a long walk from the aviary to the bridge. The rain had stopped, but so much water had drained down the cliff face that it was almost like walking behind a waterfall the whole way.

As Fallon came around a small bend he could see a man in the distance. Fallon waved. The figure didn't wave back. *Perhaps he's facing the other way*, he thought. He waved again and shouted, "Hey, Tobey!"

He saw the man move in response, but he still didn't return the wave. Instead, the man retreated into the alcove and out of sight. Fallon noticed that the bridge was extended and the hatch stood wide open.

Suspecting that something was wrong, he broke into a run. As he approached the nook, he stopped, moved close to the outer stone railing, then edged forward until he could see into the cubby. An old, gray-haired man cowered in a corner, looking cold, frightened, and confused.

"Doctor Inoue?" said Fallon in soothing tones.

The man nodded.

"I'm Fallon," he said as he slipped off his coat and put it over the man's shoulders. "You look familiar... Have we met before?"

The man relaxed a little but still seemed distracted. "Not unless you're from Agricitta."

"I grew up at the Mount."

"Then there is a good chance our paths have crossed... I'm afraid... afraid..." he pointed limply at the bridge.

"What happened? Where are Tobey and Sean?"

"Gone. We were followed... a Green Jacket... they chased after him."

"When?"

"I don't know. An hour? Two? Three?"

"Can you walk another couple of kilometers on your own?"

The man nodded. "If I go slowly."

"Good. Just follow the gallery to the end. It's a straight shot, no turnoffs, so you can't get lost. Okay?"

The doctor gave a nod of acknowledgment before he started down the gallery. He took only a few steps before he turned and said with a weak smile, "Thanks for the coat, young man."

"You're welcome." With that, Fallon headed topside.

2.2.5

THE BROTHERS were carrying the unconscious patrolman through an early morning fog. Sean, who was wearing the Green Jacket's cap, was in front with the patrolman's legs around his waist. Tobey held 1251 under the arms. He had the club tucked into his waistband and the man's utility belt slung over his shoulder. The Green Jacket carried official papers and documents that could prove valuable to the Movement.

"How're we gonna get this sack of bricks through the crawl space?" asked Sean.

"I don't know. We'll figure it out, brother."

"What's that you've got there?" came a voice from the fog. "Some wild game?"

Sean came to a sudden stop, catching Tobey unawares. Tobey's forward momentum drove Sean to his knees, then facedown in the rotting leaves. Tobey lost hold of his load and the Green Jacket's limp body fell on top of Sean. Tobey stumbled over the pile and went sprawling himself.

Fallon appeared out of the fog. "Was he the only one?"

"Can't be 100 percent sure," said Tobey.

Tobey and Fallon dragged the Green Jacket off Sean.

"Is he alive?" asked Fallon.

"I think so," said Sean. "Would've been a waste of time and effort to be lugging a dead man around."

Fallon knelt down and checked the man's neck for a pulse, then examined his head for injuries. "Doesn't seem to have anything more than a lump on the head. Here, give me a hand. Let's take him down to the river."

The three men skidded and slid down the steep bank, trying not to lose control of their unconscious captive.

"Lay him down on his back... his head upstream," said Fallon.

The edge of the river was so shallow, the water didn't even reach the man's ears. Within seconds Green Jacket began to stir.

"Did you get his name?"

"Yeah..." Tobey began.

"Get this," Sean interjected.

"His name is 1251," finished Tobey.

"1251? That's not a name. He must've had identity papers on him. Did you search for them?"

Tobey patted the utility belt. "Yeah, it's in here. His only identity is Patrolman 1251."

The man began to shiver and moan, so Tobey dragged him out of the river and laid him on the steeply sloped bank.

"Yo, Green Jacket. Can you hear me?" Tobey grabbed the front of the patrolman's coat with both hands and shook him.

"Gently, Tobey!" said Fallon. "Gently."

Tobey changed tactics. He patted the man lightly on the cheeks and repeated his question.

The man mumbled a reply.

"What was that?" asked Tobey. "I couldn't make it out."

"Yes... I can... hear... you..."

"That's good. You remember me? From last night?"

"Yes..."

"I told you you'd come to no harm if you just came with me."

"Have… to report… hooligans in the night…"

"We're not hooligans and you wouldn't have that nasty bump on your noggin if you hadn't tried to beat me with your club."

"What's your name?" asked Fallon. "1251 is *not* your name. You must have a name…"

Green Jacket shook his head groggily. "1251… my name… is… 1251. I'm Patrolman 1251 of the Chancellor's Guard."

"Where'd you come from?" asked Tobey.

"I'm stationed in Primacitta."

"Yes, we know that," said Tobey. "But where're you *from*?"

"Where were you born?" asked Sean.

Green Jacket shrugged and slowly shook his head.

Fallon said, "Where were you before you came to Primacitta?"

"Upland…" 1251 shook his head violently. "No… no more talk." Then he fell silent.

With a signal from Fallon, the brothers hoisted Green Jacket to his feet.

"Can you walk?" asked Fallon.

No answer.

"Okay, let me put it another way. You need to walk… to come with us quietly…" The man shook his head stubbornly. "…or we'll… You do know where we are, don't you?"

No answer.

"I think you do. You saw it for yourself last night. We're at the Rim—the edge of the world. If you don't come with us, I'll have my friends here take you down the river, to the very brink, and throw you over."

Fallon saw the fear in 1251's eyes.

"We'll throw you over without a second thought," said Sean.

"And you'll plunge into the Below," said Tobey. "Ever consider what would happen to a living *kon* if it entered the Below? I wonder if you'd die or if you'd just keep falling forever."

"Now c'mon," said Fallon as the three men half-pushed, half-dragged Green Jacket up the embankment.

. . .

THE HATCH was secured, so Fallon knew that the bridge would be retracted and someone was probably on duty. He spun the wheel and stepped through. "Yo," he called. "It's Fallon, Tobey, Sean, and a guest."

Jerry Franz from the mechanical team stepped from the alcove and started to push the bridge forward.

Green Jacket had not resisted, said anything, or shown interest of any kind until he stepped through the hatch for the second time. He couldn't help but be awed by the view. The rain clouds had given way to blue skies. SolMin had completely risen and the glow of SolMaj made the horizon look as if it were ablaze. And there, so close it seemed you could reach out and touch it, was the Fount of Life, rising like a flame.

Fallon noted Green Jacket's expression. "Yeah, it's pretty spectacular, isn't it?"

"So close to the *kons*." There was concern in Green Jacket's voice. "We can't be safe."

"*Kons*? Sorry, bub, it's just mist," said Sean. "Fog, low-lying clouds."

"I don't believe it."

"It's a fact," said Fallon. "We can say with all certainty."

"How..."

"'Cause we've been down there, man," said Tobey.

"Down there? No... you couldn't."

The bridge slid into place.

"We could and we did," said Fallon. "And I went into the heart of the Fount and saw things that will change this world."

Green Jacket's eyes went wide with recognition. "You're him... the historian... the blasphemer."

Without comment, Fallon motioned for Green Jacket to crawl across.

2.2.6

WHEN DR. INOUE walked through the gallery door alone, wearing Fallon's coat, Missus Grier was both elated and concerned.

The Missus and Bedford made their way across the aviary to greet the man.

"Dr. Inoue, I'm Mara Grier. Welcome…"

The doctor wavered, then put his hand against the wall to steady himself.

Bedford grasped the man around the waist to keep him from falling. "Doctor, are you okay?"

Inoue took a deep breath and exhaled slowly. "Yes… I'm just worn out." He took another breath. "It's been a long night."

"We were going to take you back to the cottage we prepared for you." Missus Grier's comforting tone did not betray her concern for Fallon and the twins. "But first, I think we'd better take you to the small mess here in the aviary. We can get you something to drink and eat. Can you walk a bit farther?"

The doctor laughed weakly. "Seems like I've been asked that constantly for the last few days." He straightened himself as best he could and said, "Lead the way."

Bedford stayed on the ready in case the man faltered. "Where is the young lad who brought you here and the one at the bridge?"

"And the young fellow who gave you his coat?" added Missus Grier.

"Uh… yes," the man stammered. "We were followed…"

"Followed!" boomed Bedford's baritone voice. "By whom?"

"A patrolman from the Chancellor's Guard. You know, one of those young thugs Brennan's unleashed on us."

"How far did he follow you?" asked the Missus calmly, while giving Bedford a troubled look.

"As far as the bridge," said the doctor.

Missus Grier felt the great weight of responsibility fall upon her. *I'm the reason all these people are down here.* "What happened?"

"When the patrolman turned tail and ran, your men lit out after him. I don't know how long it was before the other fellow showed up and gave me the jacket. He pointed me this way and then he took off too."

"Bloody B!" cursed Bedford. He looked around the aviary for someone, anyone, to whom he could give orders. "Grab some-one," he called to the first person he saw, a woman from Randall's engineering team, "and the two of you hustle out and secure the bridge."

Missus Grier deferred to James Bedford's ability to command in times like these. She had known him since she was a teenager and he was just a little boy. She trusted him implicitly. Together, they had discovered and explored the secret passages that were hidden beneath the Grier family estate—an estate that was de-stroyed by the chancellor's agents, trapping her and sixty of her followers beneath the surface of Neworld.

"We'll need to have someone out there at all hours from now on," said Bedford. "We should ask Randall if his team can hook up some way to communicate between the quarters and the bridge."

"I agree, James," said the Missus. "I can take Dr. Inoue to the mess. You have things to do."

She and Inoue were just about to enter the office complex in the aviary's north wall when she heard a commotion behind them. People were rushing toward the gallery door. She assumed it was the team going to secure the bridge, but then she heard Bedford call out from one of the transportation bays: "Fallon!"

She turned to see a knot of people watching a short parade that included a black-haired young man wearing one of the infamous green jackets she had been hearing about.

Melissa Chawla, head of the hydroponics farm, came out of the office to see what the commotion was about, but she stopped short when she saw the Missus.

"Missus Grier," she said cordially. "Is something the matter?" The Missus was distracted, so she asked again.

"Oh, Melissa," said Missus Grier, turning her focus on the engineer. "Yes, I'm afraid there is."

"Can I be of help?"

"Melissa, this is Dr. Inoue. He just came down from topside."

"The new doc!" Melissa offered her hand. "Boy, we're glad you came."

Missus Grier noted the doctor's growing smile as he shook Melissa's hand. "Can you please show him to the mess and get him some warm food and drink?"

"Yes, ma'am. Right this way, doc. Can you walk just a bit farther?"

Missus Grier and Dr. Inoue shared an amused look before she crossed to Bedford, who was standing with the boys and their captive.

"The hatch and bridge are secure, sir," said Tobey.

Bedford nodded acknowledgment before turning to the engineer he had talked to minutes earlier. "You and your mate still need to hurry to the bridge to keep guard. We'll always have two people out there from now on, so one can run back if there's trouble."

"And who do we have here?" asked Missus Grier. Close up, she noticed mud and grime on his clothes, bruises on his face, and a mixture of fear and wonderment in his eyes. She realized that his presence threatened the lives of everyone in the quarters, but she felt compassion for the fellow.

"Are you all right, young man?" She pressed a hand gently against his shoulder and smiled warmly. "What's your name?"

Green Jacket looked at Missus Grier, his expression becoming one of confusion. His eyes became vacant and he crumpled to the ground.

"He needs medical attention," said Fallon, kneeling by the unconscious man.

"Just so happens," said Missus Grier, "we have a doctor in the house. Unfortunately, he will have to treat this patient in the brig."

As a child, and even as a young woman, Mara Grier had no conception of a cell, or jail. If anyone broke the Code, the rules everyone abided by on Neworld, they were dealt with swiftly by local authorities. The word "murder" did not appear in the 1900—at least not in the common issue of the dictionary. Only after years of trying to gain access to a hidden vault did she and Bedford unlock the door that held an archive of documents and artifacts left behind by the Builders. In this archive they learned the origins of Neworld and the horrors and wonders of the planet from which their ancestors had come. They learned of war and weapons, plenty and poverty, murder and hate. All these things did not exist on Neworld—or at least *seemed* not to exist.

While she was not aware of any jails topside, she knew there were two, called brigs, in the quarters: a small one in the aviary and a slightly larger one in the Commons.

"Someone give Bedford a hand carrying…" She looked down at Fallon. "What is his name?"

"1251," said Fallon.

Missus Grier raised a questioning eyebrow, to which Fallon just shrugged.

"Someone please help Bedford carry 1251 to the aviary brig. I'll fetch the doc…"

Tobey, Sean, and Fallon moved to help pick up the Green Jacket.

"No… Not you boys," said Missus Grier. "You three go back to your cottages. Clean up, eat, and get some sleep. We'll bring our guest to the Commons brig as soon as he's able to be moved."

x~2.2

2.3
Hiding

2.3.1

PART OF the reason Dr. Inoue decided to join the Movement was that he was tired of Agricitta. He was born there and lived his entire life there—except for the years he studied medicine in Primacitta. His desire for adventure, even at his age, was not dampened by the arduous travel and days in hiding. Now, his mind raced as he rode through an enormous cavern on a horseless cart, preparing to tend to an injured Green Jacket.

Like most people, the doctor was at first skeptical when he read *The Historian's Tale*. He couldn't believe the Solarists' claim that the people of Neworld had come from another world. But the doctor's heart sank when he read how the chancellor had broken the people's trust by usurping the power of the ruling Council. He was outraged by the deaths of Vernon McCreigh and Missy Howard and the burning of the Grier estate with its occupants trapped inside—all at the hands of the Dark Men, the chancellor's secret guards. What the doctor was not prepared for was the scene before him now: an underground village bustling with activity.

The dark-skinned fellow, Bedford, was operating the cart.

"Mr. Bedford…"

"Please doctor, call me Jim."

"Tell me, Jim, what is this place … where did it come from?"

"We call this the quarters, doctor. The number of people living down here has grown to nearly a hundred in the past few months. The technologies left behind by the Builders are mind-boggling and we need capable people to learn their secrets: agrarians, engineers, skilled workers and, of course, a doctor. My daughter, Lenore, is topside recruiting people to fill our needs."

"The quarters? The Builders? There was no mention of these in *The Historian's Tale.*"

"Fallon had to protect us and the secrets we discovered. Look at all the lighted areas spread throughout the cavern. They're all work bays, each with a special function. We have mastered a few of these technologies, are just starting to learn others, and some are still beyond us. In a couple of minutes, we'll arrive at the Commons and I'll show you the reason you're here."

The doctor didn't notice the Green Jacket's eyes flutter, then open, look furtively around, and close again.

In the distance, Inoue saw an arrangement of two- and three-story buildings bathed in what appeared to be sol-light.

"Is that the Commons up there?" he asked.

"It is."

"Does the cavern open to the sky there?"

"No, that is one of the many marvels of this place. It's artificial light displayed to look like the sky—but not our sky, the sky of Earth, the planet our founders came from."

"The sky of… planet…" The doctor shook his head in wondrous disbelief. "How does it work?"

"A force called electricity. No need for gas down here, though we do light the gas lamps at night for effect."

"Night?"

"Yes, the overhead display cycles through day and night, but with a difference. Earth had only one sol, which was called the sun. They also had a small, barren world that was best visible at night. It was called the moon. You'll see. No RedNights down here."

The immense size of the Commons and the artificial sky above became apparent as they approached. Dr. Inoue craned his neck to take it all in as Bedford brought the cart to a halt next to several similar vehicles parked on the outer edge of the Commons.

2.3.2

EARLIER...

1251 had heard everything since he first woke in the aviary brig. Although he was groggy, he was aware enough to know his situation. He both cursed and praised his predicament, for he was a prisoner of the Movement and the only man in the Chancellor's Guard to know where they were hiding. He decided to feign unconsciousness until he could devise a plan of action.

The old man, who was most certainly a doctor, came in to examine him. It took a supreme effort to keep his reactions to the man's poking and prodding to a minimum.

How long had it been since his last drink? He took a chance and fluttered his eyes, smacked his lips weakly, and mumbled somewhat incoherently, "Thir... sty... Drink..."

"He needs some water," said Dr. Inoue.

The man with dark skin and deep voice spoke. "Manion!"

"Yes sir," came a younger voice in reply.

"Run to the mess hall and fetch some water," said Deep Voice.

"My... my belt... Water..."

"Hang on there, Manion. Check that belt on the table over there. Do you see a canteen?"

Manion held up the leather-wrapped flask. 1251 smacked his lips in response.

"Yes, that's it," said Deep Voice. "Hand it to me through the bars."

1251 didn't hear a reply but heard the shuffling of feet, a clank, the slight pop of the flask's lid being opened, and the sound of someone inhaling through the nose.

"No smell," said Deep Voice. "What do you think, Doctor?"

A second later the old man said, "Seems okay to me."

1251 felt the doctor's hand slide beneath his head and gently prop it up. Then he felt the cool lip of the flask against his lips, the slow tip, and finally the flow of fluid—two sips, just two sips. He refused any more. Even as his body was refreshed and his focus renewed, he once again feigned unconsciousness.

"What's wrong with him?" asked Deep Voice.

"Nothing I can see," said the doctor. "Maybe a slight concussion, but nothing life-threatening."

"I'd like to get him to the Commons as soon as possible. Do you think he can be moved?"

"As long as he's lying level, I see no problem."

The cart upon which he was placed scarcely made a sound as it moved—just a low hum, which threatened to lull 1251 to sleep for real. But he listened closely to every word that came from Deep Voice's mouth during the journey, occasionally stealing glances as his head lolled from side to side. What he saw astounded him—a dark, mammoth underground cavern dotted with lighted areas that contained machines and devices he could not comprehend. But the dark spaces... A man could hide in those spaces... Get lost in those spaces. He would stay hidden, maybe do a little spying, until he could devise a plan of escape.

He sensed a growing brightness beyond his eyelids. Deep Voice, the man called Bedford, was talking about things called a sun and moon when, all of a sudden, the cart came to a standstill.

"Wait here with the patient, doctor," said Bedford. "I'll get some people to help us take the Green Jacket to the brig in the Commons. I'll be back in a minute."

1251 listened for the footsteps to fade away before opening his eyes and sitting bolt upright.

The doctor let out a startled bark.

1251 could see the shock in the old man's face. He only had time to hop off the cart and search for his belt and flask—gone— before the doctor began to yell, "Help! James, help!"

No time to waste! 1251 sprinted into the largest expanse of darkness he could find. The cavern floor was smooth and clean.

They wouldn't be able to track him. No one would find him in the black void.

2.3.3

ADDIE was concerned about Fallon, who had walked by her without a word and lain down on the bed. She stood in the doorway between the bedroom and the living area, listening to his slow, steady breathing. He wasn't the same as before—curious, brash, and outgoing. He hadn't touched her in the same way either—eagerly, passionately, and frequently. Since his deadly encounter in Primacitta, he rarely went to the Commons with her to socialize with their friends.

Her concerns were interrupted by the low buzz of the com by the front door. Aidan closed the bedroom door, crossed to the com, and touched it. "This is Addie."

"This is Mike Goldman in the aviary. Bedford and the doctor are on the way to the Commons. He requests that you and Miss Wilkinson meet him there."

"Thanks, we're on our way."

Jo Wilkinson lived with Tobey Andrews in the same pod as she and Fallon. Until recently, the only other residents were Sean and, for a short time, Lenore Bedford. Now, seven more of the thirty cottages in the pod were occupied, and the pod's communal space was seldom empty.

Addie knocked on Jo's door, waited, then knocked again a bit louder. The door inched open and Jo looked through the crack. Seeing it was Addie, Jo swung the door open and let her in. Addie noted the slightly disheveled hair and the disarray of Jo's clothes. Jo and Tobey were a contracted couple and, obviously, Addie had interrupted something.

"I'm sorry," she said, "but Bedford wants us to meet him in the Commons as soon as possible."

"I'll be ready in just a minute," said Jo.

"I'll wait outside," said Addie.

Jo, as always, was true to her word. As they walked down the pod's access tunnel, a thought came to Addie: Jo was the glue holding their little group—their team—together. She was three cycles older than the twins, which made her about six annums, or Earth years, older than she and Fallon. Jo had a maturity and solidity about her that raised the level of all their work.

They entered the main cavern and started walking through the darkness toward the lights of the Commons.

"What do you and Fallon think about the Green Jacket?" asked Jo.

Aidan just gave her a puzzled look.

"You mean Fallon didn't tell you that a Green Jacket followed Sean and the doctor down the hatch?"

"No, he just walked into the bedroom and went to sleep." She tried to hide her anger. "He must have been tired."

"He's been different since…"

"You've noticed?" said Addie.

"Tobey and Sean, too. We're all worried about him."

"What can I do? He seems fine when we're working, but he shuts down when we're alone. And he goes off by himself, who knows where, for hours at a time. Anyway, enough of our personal troubles… Tell me, what's this about a Green Jacket?"

"Tobey said he was just going to retract the bridge after Sean and the doctor arrived when this Green Jacket pops through the hatch, sees Tobey, then hightails it back topside."

"Bloody B! The chancellor will be sending his goons to root us out!"

"Not to worry, Tobey and Sean chased him down and, with Fallon's help, brought him to the aviary. He was unconscious. Bedford must be bringing him to the Commons with the doctor."

After a considerable silence, Addie said, "I had a crush on him, you know—on Fallon—even before I ever laid eyes on him."

"How... When?"

I was a young girl when Jenna Howard..."

"Missy Howard? From the Mount?"

"Yes. The Howards and the Griers have ties going back a long time. When I was quite young, Jenna came to visit and told Grandmother and me about this beautiful boy who was a servant—a ward—of the Mount. She spoke of the boy's drawing talent and showed us some of his sketches of plants and animals. I've been infatuated with him ever since."

"When did you first meet?"

"I first *saw* him last spring while on an extended visit to the Howard farm outside Agricitta. I spent many hours sitting high in a chestnut tree just outside the walls of the Mount, hoping to catch a glimpse of the amazing boy."

Jo smiled. "None of this is in *The Historian's Tale*. Tell me more!"

"Well, spring grew into summer. I came of age during Ninth Month. It was about the time Jenna began her relationship with Fallon."

"Missy Howard and Fallon..."

"Yes."

"She must have been eight or nine annums older than him."

"Six, actually, but that made no difference. It was a brief but beautiful time for the both of them."

"He told you this?"

"Yes, but Jenna told me first. We were always close. We chatted like sisters, or maybe like mother and daughter. And since I had come of age, she talked openly to me about coupling and reproductive contracts, and what a fantastic partner Fallon would make."

"What did she tell you?

"Everything!" Addie giggled at the remembrance. "'You could do far worse than Fallon for your first relationship,' she told me.

'And since he's stemmed, you don't have to be concerned about contracts. The two of you can practice all you want.'"

"So you got together that summer?"

"No, not until we were down here."

"Really?"

"Yes. Later that summer, things changed. Jenna became serious. She broke off her relationship with Fallon and hardly visited with me. She never told me the reason. I only learned of the Dark Men and the murder of Vernon McCreigh when Grandmother came to the Mount that fall and bought Fallon from the headmaster."

"Missus Grier *bought* Fallon?"

"Grandmother always said that Headmaster Hunninger was a greedy, untrustworthy little swine. He sold Fallon into servitude just weeks before he came of age—or at least he thought he did.

"I met the carriage just outside the Mount's gate. My pulse raced, and I flushed when I climbed into Grandmother's carriage and met Fallon for the first time, face-to-face."

"What happened?"

"I acted like an impetuous child is what happened. I shudder to think about it now. He must have found me brash and off-putting during our brief encounters. I did things…"

"Like what?" Jo coaxed.

"No… I can't."

"Come on, it's just the two of us."

"You won't tell a *kon*?"

"I promise."

"I ambushed him while he was taking a bath at one of the inns we stopped at."

"What'd you do?"

"I rubbed him, kissed him on the cheek, and said things to… um… rile him up. And I succeeded. I know because I reached into the tub and checked. And he was everything Jenna said he was."

"But you never coupled until we got down here."

"I wanted to, but he seemed so timid and, besides, we never had a chance. As you know, the moment we arrived home, he was gone, along with Grandmother and Bedford, down to the Basin to descend into the Below. My heart ached. I hardly knew him, but my heart ached just the same. I felt connected to him as if he was part of me."

Jo smiled. "Back on Earth, they called that love. It's a messy thing, love is, but I think it's a beautiful idea."

"It *was* love. I know it now. But did he feel the same toward me? He didn't show it. You know the rest. You were trapped down here with the rest of us."

"I remember when Tobey, Sean, and Fallon broke through that wall between here and the passage to the Basin. You ran to Fallon first, and hugged and kissed him."

"When I saw his face, he seemed embarrassed and was looking at Lenore. He was interested more in Lenore than in me. I felt humiliated. I let go and rushed to Grandmother, crying."

"You and Lenore were very close before then."

"We practically grew up together. If it hadn't been for Lenore, I might well have died in that fire."

"As I recall, your relationship with Lenore became frosty, almost hostile at times."

"You're right. I couldn't deny my feelings. I comforted Fallon and helped him settle in that first night, and it just sort of happened—a full- blown and passionate relationship. To this day I don't know what changed in him, but I'm happy it did."

Suddenly, something came hurtling at them through the darkness and knocked Addie off her feet. Whatever it was fell on top of her like a dead weight. She closed her eyes, wincing in pain and gasping for air. She felt the pressure of a hand on her left breast and heard a man grunting as he pushed down on her in an effort to rise to his feet. Addie opened her eyes and saw a frightened look on the face of a dark-haired man about the same age as the twins.

Jo grabbed the man by the collar and yanked him to his feet. He thanked her with an elbow to the gut that doubled Jo over.

Before Addie could get to her feet, the man disappeared into the darkness.

* * *

BEDFORD didn't send a search party after the Green Jacket. After all, where could the fellow go? Instead, he warned all the work stations to be on alert and he posted extra sentries at the aviary entrance.

He then took Dr. Inoue to the former bedding storehouse, a space that Randall's engineers discovered was actually a small hospital—what the Builders called an infirmary. It was the reason the doctor was recruited.

They had barely stepped through the door when he heard Jo calling, "Bedford..."

He turned to see Jo and Aidan supporting each other as they limped into the light of the Commons.

"Bloody B, lass, what happened?"

"It sounds crazy," said Jo, "But we just ran into a Green Jacket."

"You saw him?" asked Bedford.

"Then he *was* a Green Jacket!" said Addie. "How's that possible? He's out there somewhere, in the dark."

"Yes, I know," said Bedford. "I've sent out an alert. Everyone will be on the lookout by this evening. Now get yourself in here, Jo. You look hurt."

"Oh, it's nothing..."

Bedford cut Jo off. "Our new doctor just arrived, so let him check you out. This is Dr. Inoue. Doctor, this is Mary Jo Wilkinson, and this is Aidan Brennan."

Dr. Inoue raised an eyebrow. "Brennan?"

"Yes, the chancellor is my grandfather, but I was raised by my grandmother, Mara Grier. I just had the wind knocked out of me, but you'd better have a look at Jo. The Green Jacket gave her a blow to the ribs."

This news angered Bedford. "He struck you?"

"It was more like he ran into me," said Jo. "It was an accident, really."

Inoue didn't need the technology in the room to examine Jo. "No broken ribs," said the doctor. "But you're going to be sore for a few days. If I knew where the medicines were, I'd get you some aspirin."

"I've got some back at the pod, Dr. Inoue," said Jo. "Thanks."

Bedford turned his attention to Inoue. "Are you okay, doctor? You seem worn out."

"I'm fine, James. This has all been a lot to take in and comprehend, don't you know?"

Bedford nodded agreeably. "Jo and Aidan were supposed to give you a tour of the quarters and settle you in your new rooms but, tell you what, it's probably best all around if we postpone it until tomorrow."

"Why don't we take him to the mess hall, then we'll show him his rooms," said Aidan.

"Is that okay with you, Doctor?" asked Bedford.

"That'll be fine," said Inoue.

"Then I'll leave it to you," said Bedford. "I have matters that need my attention."

Bedford was angry that 1251 had injured Jo, but time was his side. They would eventually catch the intruder.

2.3.4

From the Journal of Lenore Bedford

> I must be honest: I did not volunteer to leave my father
> and the relative safety of our underground community
> because of the importance of the work that I do. It was

because I could no longer bear seeing my love living with someone else. My heart does not ache so much when I keep myself busy. However, it wants to burst when I am alone and free of immediate duties.

Yet, my brief study of Earth's history gives me hope. Not that my love will ever be mine but that, perhaps, there are others like me on Neworld.

• • •

LENORE BEDFORD had just returned to Primacitta from a trip upslope. She fought an urge to visit the grounds of the Grier estate so she could see, with her own eyes, the devastation the chancellor's thugs had wreaked. Even with her close-cropped hair and teamster attire, she couldn't take the chance of anyone recognizing her, for she was well known in the district—and she was supposed to have died when the Dark Men burned down the Grier estate. Instead, she decided to exercise caution and return directly to the warehouse that served as her base of operations topside.

She stood on the warehouse roof. The red glow of SolMinor was about to give way to the dawn of SolMaj. By her side stood Julia, the matronly warehouse worker who had nursed Fallon back to health after his escape from the chancellor.

Lenore's stomach churned as she scanned the activity on the street below. It seemed like every large, open expanse of wall exhibited the giant image of Chancellor Brennan, made even more menacing by the amber light of solrise. The bastard had never denied the historian's revelation that he usurped the powers of the ruling council. Below Brennan's stern face were the words:

One World. One Vision.

Lenore had not seen these images on her trip upland, but she suspected the chancellor's authoritative gaze would be ubiquitous by the time she went back.

"When did those monstrosities go up?" she asked Julia.

"The day Bertie dropped your man and the doctor off at the bridge... that makes it three days ago," said Julia. "'Twas a terrible storm that night, Miss Gabby—the same night that Green Jacket went missing."

"A Green Jacket went missing? The same night Sean took the doctor through?"

Julia nodded. "That's what people're sayin'."

"Went missing... where?"

"He was on night patrol here in the district."

This was troubling news.

Lenore's heart seemed to stop beating in her chest. She pointed at a gap between some buildings a block to the north. Julia gasped. Twenty or more men in black clothing were assembled in ranks on the darkened street. But these weren't Dark Men in their long coats. Who were they? Their identity was revealed as SolMajor crested the Rim forest and illuminated the east-west–oriented street. The men's jackets transformed from black to the distinctive green of the Chancellor's Guard.

The everyday morning clatter of the warehouse district was pierced by the shrill blast of whistles. Lenore comprehended the full import of what was happening when she realized the sounds were coming not only from the direction of the throng to the north but from locations all around them. The men she was watching drew out their clubs and dispersed at the sound of the whistles. People screamed and the sound of broken glass punctuated the cacophony of distress and destruction.

Lenore grabbed the older woman by the shoulder and pulled her toward the roof stairs. "Come! They're going from building to building. Probably searching for their missing comrade. We have to act fast!"

"We don't have him... He's not here..."

"But all our historian materials are," said Lenore as she swung open the door and rushed down the stairs.

A large room above the warehouse proper served as the production space for the hand-scribed copies of *The Historian's Tale*. Thankfully, production was done in the dead of night and all but two of the volunteer scribes were already gone and safely home—if they hadn't run into and been detained by the gathering bands of Green Jackets.

"Go down to the first floor, get help, and head to the basement," said Lenore. "We'll gather the documents together up here and drop them down the trash chute. You toss them into the incinerator. Hurry now!"

As Julia ran off, Lenore shouted to two men who were looking out the windows, trying to figure out the cause of all the commotion outside. "Quickly, we need to dispose of everything. Down the trash chute—*everything*. Not just the finished copies, but all the blank paper, pens, ink. Everything."

They set into action without question or pause.

The noise on the street grew louder as one of the Green Jacket squads came closer. By the time the havoc reached their street, there was no trace of Solarist activity in the upstairs room of the warehouse. They had even cleared the tables and chairs and redistributed the normal packing materials that had been shoved against the walls to make room for their clandestine work.

"You two go downstairs and grab yourself some work clothes. Look like you belong here."

"What about you, Miss Gabby?" asked one of the men.

"The chancellor knows me…"

"The chancellor…?"

"Yes… Gabby's not my real name. It's…"

The man held up a hand to stop her. "I don't want to know."

"Let's just say that if I were captured, the chancellor would recognize me and know our secret—a secret not revealed by the historian. Off with you."

Lenore heard the smashing of street-level windows. The guards were approaching the street from the west. Soon they'd be at her building. Were they going inside the warehouses to search, or were they just terrorizing the district? She dared not look out the window for fear of being seen. Where to go? Lenore sprinted to the stairway that led to the roof and took the steps two at a time. She cracked open the roof access door and surveyed the rooftops of adjacent buildings, looking for any sign of Green Jacket activity. She was surprised to find the district rooftops empty.

Even though there was no movement on the rooftops she could see from the access door, she couldn't walk right out into the open. There might be men on roofs she couldn't see or she might be spotted by thugs searching the upper floors of buildings across the street.

So, before moving onto the roof, she took the canvas teamster's cap from her waistband and pulled it low on her head, then removed the work gloves from her canvas coat pocket and put them on. She was thankful for the padded knees in the teamster's thick, leather pants. The gloves and padded pants would lessen the pain of crawling across the tar-and-pebble roof on hands and knees.

Lenore patiently crawled around the perimeter of the warehouse roof, listening and occasionally stealing a glance over the low, crenulated parapet. She considered her options. She couldn't safely descend the fire escape ladder because of the constant patrols on the ground. However, she could easily jump the distance between her roof and that of the building to the rear—but to what end? Until the streets were clear, Lenore couldn't go anywhere. And even if she could get to street level, where would she go? She wouldn't take the chance of stealing her way to the Promenade, through the forest, and to the cave.

Another quick peek revealed silhouettes of men searching the roofs several buildings to the west. She was trapped and odds were that it was only a matter of time until a Green Jacket came through the access door.

2.3.5

AT FIRST, 1251 found it curious that no alarm was sounded after he escaped. Three days had passed but nobody in the Solarists' underground hideout had chased him. No one probed the darkness with lanterns. Then his situation slowly became apparent to him. He was not bound and chained but he was a prisoner just the same.

It took him a full day to even find a passage that led to the room that afforded an exit to the outside world. Then he discovered that it was effectively guarded.

He became hungry and, even worse, thirsty. They had his belt and flask. He needed his flask to stay energized and focused.

By the third day he had to keep repeating "I'm patrolman 1251" in his mind just to remember who he was. In the middle of the night he was able to scavenge an odd cup of water from various work stations that had been shut down. He even found part of a sandwich and some half-rotten strawberries. Still, he knew he was starving. He needed food and water. His vision was blurry and he walked erratically.

The work stations were closed and the only light came from an area called the Commons. It was a soft, cool light, the likes of which he had never seen. As he staggered slowly toward the light, he heard the distant sound of people talking, laughing. He was drawn onward, drifting to the right a few steps, then to the left.

As he drew closer, he could see stars in what looked like the night sky. Hanging in the sky was a silvery half-circle that bathed the cluster of buildings in a soft, bluish-white light.

The noise was coming from the center of the complex. He reeled down a narrow walkway between two buildings, toward the inviting sounds. Then it washed over him—the overwhelming aroma of hot food. It fortified him. Motivated him. He tried to straighten himself up. He attempted to walk in a straight line.

He came upon an open, gas-lit square in the center of the complex. People were relaxing, conversing, and eating at tables scattered around the square.

His mind seemed to be in a fog. He couldn't understand why the people stopped and stared at him. The smell of food came from a lighted building at the side of the square. He forgot to tell himself who he was.

"I'm... 12..." he rasped through a parched throat and cracked lips, his chin resting on his chest. "12... I'm... I'm 51..."

He stumbled on the curb in front of the building with bright lights, and then he lurched toward the door.

• • •

Francis Bianchi was eating dinner with some of his old friends. He told them of his recent mission topside and grumbled about the Green Jacket that was on the loose in the quarters.

Everyone who had read *The Historian's Tale* knew Bianchi's story. He was a simple farmer from a small town in the middle of the upland plains and had joined the movement after the Green Jackets beat his son and then carried him and the other young men of the village away in barred wagons.

"I begged Bedford to let me lead a search party, but he refused. He knows my story, but he refused," said Bianchi.

Just then, the mess hall door banged open and an unkempt man in a green Chancellor's Guard jacket stumbled through, mumbling something. The slouching posture, the downcast, slightly bobbing head, and the dust in his hair made the man appear to be old.

While the mess hall fell into stunned silence, Bianchi's blood boiled. He rose to his feet, his hands balled into fists at his sides.

The woman sitting to his left tugged at Bianchi's shirt. "Frank, don't," she said.

Bianchi brushed away her hand, then purposefully wove through the tables toward the Green Jacket. As he got nearer, Bianchi could hear what the man was saying, "I... I'm... I..."

The man must have sensed Bianchi's approach, for he looked up with dark, pleading eyes, stammering, "I'm... I'm... I..."

Bianchi stopped dead in his tracks, dumbfounded. Tears welled up in his eyes and began to flow freely down his cheeks. "You're Danny," he sobbed as he embraced the ragged man. "You're my Danny. Danny Bianchi!"

2.3.6

LENORE removed the grate from a ventilation duct, took off her belt, looped it through the grate, and secured the buckle. She then lifted the grate in front of her and slipped one arm, then the other, through the looped belt and lowered the grate until the belt was positioned under her arms.

Next came the difficult part. She slid into the duct feet-first and backward, her gloved fingers gripping the duct in front of her. She tried to control her descent by pressing her legs tight against the sides of the duct but, partway in, she lost her grip and slid. The grate lodged into place, arresting her fall. The sling stung as it bit into her breasts and armpits.

Now that she was in place, she had second thoughts about her hiding place. First, her own weight was keeping the grid in place. Would she be able to climb back out if she couldn't gain purchase with her legs or feet and undo the sling? Second, the sling held her suspended in a manner that kept her head at the level of the grate. Anyone who looked in could see her canvas cap. She pulled the cap from her head and let it drop down the vent, hoping that her black hair and dark features would help hide her.

She heard sounds coming up through the duct. Shouting. They *were* searching for the missing patrolman. A slap. Someone crying. A few minutes later Lenore heard the roof access door swing open and the crunch of boots on the tar and pebble roof.

"You take that side," someone said. "I'll take this."

The footsteps came in her direction. Lenore closed her eyes and bent her head forward so her cropped black hair faced the grate. She held her breath.

Bloody B! she cursed to herself. *What if he sees the belt loop?*

The man circled the duct slowly but at a distance. Lenore could imagine the guard being wary of someone hiding *behind* it, ready to attack, not hiding *in* it. It felt like hours but Lenore knew the men were on the roof for no more than five minutes.

By middle of the night, Lenore's body was drenched in sweat under the heavy teamster's livery despite the cool night air. It seemed as if all the latent heat from the warehouse was escaping through the vent. Her shoulders ached and her arms were numb. The district was quiet, without even the rattle of normal business. The Green Jackets were gone. Lenore felt it was safe to climb out.

She tried to apply pressure with her feet but the heat and sweat had sapped her strength. She couldn't even muster the strength to call for help. She wanted to go to sleep. *No, she couldn't. She had to stay awake. She had to call for help.*

Muted voices wafted up the duct. *Bertie? Jonny?* Someone was on the floor below her. She couldn't push hard enough with her feet to climb out, but she could certainly swing her leg and kick the shite out of the duct.

CLANG… CLANG CLANG…

Hey guys, I'm up here, she thought. *You have to hear this.*

CLANG… CLANG… CLANG…

The voices beneath her became excited.

CLANG CLANG…

She heard the access door slam open. People were running toward the duct. It was Jonny and another man.

"Hang on," said Jonny. "We've got you."

She saw Jonny reach for the grate, then she went limp—almost passing out. Her shoulders caved, her arms slid up, and she slipped through the sling. She couldn't even manage to scream as she fell.

It was a short fall—only a couple of meters before the duct made a 90-degree arc and flattened out. The duct wasn't designed to bear a load. It groaned under her weight, separated at a seam, and spilled Lenore's limp body feet-first onto the floor three-and-a-half meters below.

$$x \sim 2.3$$

Recovery

2.4.1

DR. INOUE paid no attention to the two burly men seated to either side of the infirmary door. He was busy hanging an intravenous bag that would help rehydrate his sedated patient. There were three glass-topped tables in the infirmary. Danny Bianchi, clad only in undershorts, lay on the middle table.

Brian Randall, the Movement's head engineer, was standing with Dr. Inoue at the side of the examination table. "All these tables are basically the same throughout the quarters, Doctor. They can collect and dispense information. Look here."

Using two fingers, Randall double-tapped the tabletop by the patient's left shoulder. A graphic that Dr. Inoue didn't understand instantly displayed. "This is the control panel. If the table is asleep..."

"Asleep?"

"When the table is not in use, the Builders say it's asleep."

Dr. Inoue nodded but his expression betrayed his confusion.

"Don't worry, Doc. The only thing you need to know right now is how to wake the table. Watch... You tap with two fingers, anywhere you wish..." Randall tapped by the patient's hip. "...and that's where the control panel will appear." The panel snapped off and reappeared under Randall's fingers. "Or you can slide it like this..." He dragged the panel back up to the patient's shoulder.

"See? Simple, huh? To put it to sleep, tap this button." The table went dark. "Okay, you give it a try."

Dr. Inoue tentatively gave the table a two-fingered double-tap and reflexively yanked his hand back when the display appeared.

"That's it, Doc. You're now the only doctor in Neworld who knows how to use this diagnostic table."

"I don't know a thing… except how to turn the blasted machine on."

"That's all you need to know… how to turn the blasted machine on. Now here's the exciting part. Dr. Hadjh?"

Before Inoue could correct Randall on his name, an image of a man only about a third of a meter tall appeared on the table.

"Ah, Brian, how can I be of service today?"

"Dr. Hadjh," said Randall, "Let me introduce you to Dr. Mathew Inoue. Dr. Inoue has just joined us down here in the quarters."

The little man turned and looked up at Dr. Inoue. "Welcome, Doctor. It will be nice to have a colleague to work with again."

"I… I… Uh…"

Dr. Hadjh laughed. "You'll soon get used to me. What would you have me do, Doctor?"

"Uh…"

"Just talk to me as if I were a real person."

"Uh, do we have a stethoscope?" asked Inoue.

In a flash, a graphical display next to the patient's head lit up. It showed blood pressure, heart rate, and jagged lines that Inoue reasoned corresponded to the man's heartbeats.

"The table is your stethoscope and any other diagnostic tool you're familiar with," said Randall.

"And I can show you many more tools you may never have thought of," added Dr. Hadjh.

Inoue ducked and stepped back from the table as he sensed movement overhead. He looked up and saw a framed glass plate the same size as the table lowering from the ceiling. The tabletop and glass plate began to glow green.

"By Below!" Dr. Inoue was astounded as he watched a small picture of the man's skeleton take shape next to the control panel. "X-rays?"

"Nothing so primitive," said Dr. Hadjh.

"Go wake the table behind you, Doctor," said Randall.

Dr. Inoue brought up the display panel on the empty table—more confidently this time.

"Display scan, please," said Randall.

The table was filled with a detailed, life-sized, three-dimensional image of the scan as it took form.

Dr. Inoue was wide-eyed. "This is amazing."

"This level of technology was commonplace for the Builders, Doc."

"It appears as solid as the real thing," said Inoue as he leaned in for a closer look. Dr. Inoue could clearly see evidence of trauma to the young man's skull and what looked like healed fractures on the left humerus and right fibula.

"Are those old fractures?"

"Yes, Doctor," said Hadjh. "By the remodeling, they seem to be about a year-and-a-half old."

"Year?"

"Sorry, Doc," said Randall. A year is what we call an annum. A year-and-a-half is equivalent to our full cycle."

"Yes, yes. So much to learn. If only I could look at the man's back…"

Randall extended his hand toward the image and appeared to gently roll it over on its side. "You can roll, flip, twist, spin, or even zoom in." Using both hands, Randall manipulated the now-complete scan of the skeleton, enlarging it to magnify the fibular fracture. He ended by bringing his hands toward each other until the scan returned to life-size.

"Dr. Hadjh has a library of scans you can study and practice with." Randall then turned to the hologram and said, "Show the doc the other views available, if you please."

Dr. Hadjh appeared on the table displaying the skeleton. "This scan is live," he said, "as you will see when we render the circulatory system."

Inoue was stunned to see the man's heart, arteries, and veins fade into view. They pulsed with the ebb and flow of blood. But he was transfixed by the rhythmic contractions of the living heart.

"The patient is in excellent health, doctor," said Hadjh. "Except for the evidence of earlier trauma, and..." Daniel Bianchi's skull faded, revealing an image of his brain that, in turn, faded to reveal an amazingly intricate network of flashing points of light and tenuous luminescent strings. "...a minor anomaly in the neural network."

Again, Inoue was at a loss. "Neural..."

"Neural network," said Dr. Hadjh. The electrical pathways in the brain."

"I'm overwhelmed."

The hologram smiled. "That's why I'm here to help. Might I suggest a course of action, Dr. Inoue?"

"A course...? Why, uh... Certainly... yes."

Dr. Hadjh disappeared and the scan faded from view.

"If you please," came Dr. Hadjh's voice.

Inoue turned to see the hologram standing on the darkened center table. He was next to the patient's hand, and as the glass plate rose to the ceiling, a small shelf extended from the side of the table. On it was an outline of a hand.

"If you can position the patient's hand on the pad," said Dr. Hadjh, "we can do some blood work."

2.4.2

A SHARP PAIN in her legs woke Lenore. For a moment she was confused. Walls of boxes and crates surrounded her and a woman holding a cup of water sat next to her. *Julia?*

Lenore was parched and her lips were dry and cracked, so she propped herself up on one arm and seized the proffered cup of water. She drained the draught, held out the tin cup for more, then drained it again. Temporarily sated, she set the cup down on a crate next to her makeshift cot of folded cartons and shredded packing material.

"Does it look like rain?" Her voice was dry and raspy, but urgent.

"It does, Miss Gabby," said Julia. "But if you're hoping to go back to wherever you all come and go from, you won't be able to manage it, I'm afraid. You sprained both ankles when you fell out of the ductwork."

With her thirst quenched, the throbbing in her feet became overwhelming, eliciting a groan. Regardless, Lenore sat up and swung her legs over the edge of the cardboard cot.

Julia made no effort to restrain or assist.

"I have to report what's happened to Missus… to my superiors," said Lenore as she tried to stand. "They have to know about…" She winced in pain and began to collapse.

Julia caught her under the arms and guided her back onto the cot. "There was no use trying to stop someone of your mind, Miss. You learn from experience, not words." She refilled the cup and held it out to Lenore. "But take my advice, and learn to take advice. It can save you pain in the long run."

Judging from the walls of crates that formed her little room, Lenore surmised she was still in the upper floor of the warehouse.

"Was anyone hurt? Did they find anything?"

"Drink," said Julia. She didn't respond until Lenore had emptied the cup once more. "That's a good lass. No, no one was hurt and we were able to destroy all the materials well before we had to let the bastards in. We *let* them in, and they still smashed the front windows."

"What now?"

"We knew you'd want to send a message to your group, so Bertie put the signal in the usual place. Next time any of your people…"

"Our people," said Lenore.

Julia nodded graciously. "Next person to see it will know to stop by. In the meantime, you stay hidden here until you can walk again. We're ceasing operations for a few days, then we'll get back at it."

"But everything is gone," said Lenore. "There's nothing for the scribes to copy."

"If we needed them, we could fetch a copy or two to work from, but our scribes have made so many copies they can reproduce *The Historian's Tale* by heart. So we've spread production around. Some people are working from their homes and others are headed upland to distribute and train other scribes. There's no stopping the Movement now."

Lenore's chest so swelled with emotion that she could hardly catch her breath. Her eyes stung with tears. For the first time, Lenore's return topside was more than a form of self-exile. She no longer dwelt on her emotional distress over Addie. She had found purpose. She finally understood and believed in what Fallon had started.

"There's no stopping us now," she said.

2.4.3

DESPITE her sore ribs, Jo was in a good mood—a great mood, in fact. She was adjusting the shower water when Tobey arrived.

"Jo, you here?"

"Back here, hon." Jo was enthralled with the Earth concept of romance and love. She had tried to explain terms of endearment such as *hon* and *honey* and *dear* to Tobey, but she wasn't quite sure that he understood. "I'm just getting in the shower. Why don't you come join me?"

She was lathering her hair when Tobey came into the bathroom. It hurt to raise her arms, but she'd put off washing her hair too long. She'd just have to endure the pain.

"That bastard!" said Tobey when he looked at the purple and greenish-black bruising on Jo's side. He disrobed and stepped into the shower. "How's it feeling?"

"My side? Sore." Jo turned to face him, raised herself on her toes and said, "But my lips are perfectly fine."

"Perfectly fine," said Tobey as he leaned into the kiss and started to hug Jo.

Jo stepped back. "No hugging," she cautioned.

"I'm sorry…"

"Not for a while at least. But these are perfectly fine." She guided Tobey's hands to her breasts.

"Perfectly fine," he repeated, and he bent in to kiss her.

"You're no longer under contract," she said. "I didn't conceive within the allotted time. Why are you still here?"

"What are you talking about?"

"I'm older than you. *I* contracted *you*. And we didn't make a baby, so you're free to go. There're a dozen or more women in the quarters who would enter into contract with you. Why are you still here?"

Tobey pulled away. "To Below with contracts, Jo. We've had this conversation before. Contracts mean nothing anymore. We're both dead as far as the world topside is concerned. I… I…"

"Go on, say it. I've told you all about Earth mating customs. Go on… say it."

"You *know* it. I don't have to *tell* you."

She pressed her hands against his chest, then slid one hand down until she found what she wanted. "Say it."

Tobey smiled, kissed her and said, "I love you. Is that what you wanted to hear?"

She let go her grip, grasped his right wrist and placed his large hand on her belly. "And will you love our child as well?"

"Wha…?" He was beaming. "You're pregnant?"

"Dr. Inoue confirmed it when I went back for a follow-up this morning."

"You're going to have the baby you wanted."

"Not *my* baby. No contract, remember? *Our* baby… I mean… if you want."

"Of course I want," he said as he embraced her and lifted her with joy. "I love you."

Jo's side ached, but she didn't complain.

2.4.4

"WILL I see you at lunch?"

Fallon looked up to see Addie coming out of their cottage. He didn't know how long he'd been sitting at the table, drawing, in the Pod G meeting room. He flipped the sketch he was working on upside down and laid it atop a pile of completed drawings.

"Nah," he said.

"Doing important work there, are you?"

Fallon understood Aidan was trying to goad him out of his melancholy, but her comment only irked him. "Yah, actually, I am."

Aidan walked up to him, started to put her hand on his shoulder, hesitated, then withdrew it. "I appreciate what's on your mind—the weight of it all. But you have to eat. Come to the mess hall and relax with Jo and the twins."

"Too many people…" He sighed and said, "You know…"

"Yeah, I know."

Fallon saw a hardness in her expression that he'd never seen before.

"You need to pull yourself out of this," she said. "We need you…"

They need *me!* The thought made him bristle. *They'd be better off if I didn't exist… None of this would have happened if I…*

Addie rested a hand on his shoulder. "*I* need you."

Fallon looked into her tearing eyes. He desperately wanted to say something reassuring but all he could manage was, "Bring something back for me, will you?"

"Sure," she answered coldly. "Will you be here when I get back?"

Fallon cocked his head and shrugged.

He sat in the common room for another hour, shuffling through drawings that depicted the nightmare battle in the aviary. He hadn't drawn much since he became trapped in the quarters— only the set of sketches he included in *The Historian's Tale*: most notably the murders of Vernon McCreigh and Jenna Howard.

They used to watch images like this for entertainment, *for Below's sake. I should never have included the images of Jenna and McCreigh.*

He felt ashamed and fought back tears.

One by one, he tore the new drawings into strips.

I won't draw again unless it is something worthy of remembrance.

He collected the shredded sketches, took them into the cottage, burned them, and flushed the ashes down the commode.

Then he left Pod G and headed into the darkness. But instead of taking one of his meandering walks, there was purpose in his stride. He knew where he had to be.

• • •

FALLON checked the hallway to make sure nobody was around before he pressed his hand against the security plate. The door in front of him slid open, revealing a brightly lit, windowless cube of about four meters to a side. The walls were lined with racks of guns and drawers of ammunition. This was the genie's bottle—the armory.

These machines of death could be the salvation of his people… or they could be Neworld's doom. In the hands of someone just, they could help keep the peace. In the hands of someone like the chancellor, they could be used to dominate and bend the will of the people.

One of the Builders' glass-topped tables stood in the center of the room. On the table sat a pistol. It was a semiautomatic and Fallon knew how to use it. He sat on a stool, lifted the gun, and turned it over in his hands as if examining it. But his eyes were closed.

His mind was back in the Council Hall, several of its tall windows shattered. Jenna's naked body lay on the stone floor in a growing pool of her own blood. Fallon raised the pistol and held it to the chancellor's head. *Pull the trigger... pull the trigger, you coward... pull the trigger!*

Fallon slowly opened his eyes. His face was covered in perspiration. He was holding the pistol to his head.

Pull the trigger... I'm the genie... Keep the genie in the bottle. No one else can open the bottle... They'll never find me in here... Pull the trigger.

Fallon slammed the pistol down on the table and began to cry. *Coward.*

2.4.5

JO HAD hoped to share her good news with the group at lunch, but the time wasn't right. Even the faux sky over the Commons was filled with dark clouds—a sign that a cleansing "rain" would wash away the quarter's dust overnight.

"I'm concerned about Fallon, but it's getting to be too much," said Addie. "I know he'll be gone when I get back with his food, and he'll probably be gone all night again. Then he'll sleep the day away."

"He's been through a lot," said Sean.

"Haven't we all?" snapped Addie.

"None of us has *seen* a close friend murdered," said Tobey.

Jo saw Sean clench his right hand into a fist as he said, "Jenna was our sister. Tobey and I are torn up inside just *knowing* she was murdered."

Jo laid a comforting hand on Sean's.

Sean choked on his words: "But Fallon *saw* the chancellor slit her throat."

"She was Fallon's first lover…" said Jo, glaring at Aidan. "Fallon was there and couldn't stop it. I can't imagine how I'd feel. He needs time to heal."

"I agree, but sitting alone, brooding, is not doing him any good," said Addie. "In fact, I think it's making him worse."

"He needs your support now, more than ever." Jo was upset with Addie's attitude, especially since she and Fallon had shared the war video with Addie. "Nobody knows that better than you and I do."

Addie crossed her arms as Jo continued to vent:

"Think of what he's been through since that pig Hunninger sold him to the Missus. What? Just a few months ago? He wasn't even of age then—he was just a boy. He's gone from being a ward of the state to being "the historian"—the public leader of a movement. He's gone from caring for only himself to being responsible for the fate of Neworld. If you can't give him your unconditional support, at least give him time. Give him space."

2.4.6

MISSUS GRIER made her way to the infirmary as soon as Bedford called her on the com link. As she entered, she saw Frank Bianchi seated next to his son, who had been moved to one of the beds in the rear room of the facility.

"In here, Missus," called Bedford from an office near the examination tables.

He and Dr. Inoue rose from their seats when Missus Grier entered, and Bedford offered her a seat.

"How is your patient doing, Doctor?" she asked as they settled into their chairs.

"First," said Dr. Inoue. "I have to thank you for bringing me here. Half a day with Dr. Hadjh and already I've learned so much."

Missus Grier turned to Bedford. "Who's Dr. Hadjh? I wasn't aware that we already had a doctor…"

"He's another avatar, like Captain Maczynski and Anika," said Bedford. "Dr. Hadjh is the guide for the infirmary."

"Ahh." She nodded.

"And to answer your question," said Dr. Inoue, "the younger Mr. Bianchi is doing well. He's still sedated but we've finished the intravenous hydration. We also learned something interesting. A skeletal scan showed that he may have been beaten about a cycle ago."

Missus Grier didn't know what a "skeletal scan" was, but she did grasp the "what" and "where" of Danny Bianchi being beaten. "That'd be about when he was taken from his village, wouldn't it?"

"Indeed," said Bedford. "But wait until you hear the interesting part."

Missus Grier heard the excitement in Dr. Inoue's voice as he spoke. "We, Dr. Hadjh and I, scanned Mr. Bianchi's brain…"

"You did what? Scanned his brain?" Missus Grier and Bedford had been exploring the quarters since they were children. Recent discoveries such as the aviary and the generation station under Rim Falls were surprises she could understand. But this?

"The diagnostic table lets us examine every system within the body—*every system*—and make a diagnosis. We found abnormal activity in the brain, so we took a blood sample and did some tests. Danny Bianchi was drugged."

"Medicated?" she asked.

"In a way… in a bad way," said Inoue. You know how some medicines can make you drowsy?"

"Yes. Go on."

"Well this medicine, this *drug*, can make a person susceptible to suggestion. It allows someone to control the drugged person's mind."

"*Below!*" Mrs. Grier seldom cursed, but she instantly grasped the implications. "The chancellor made Danny Bianchi into 1251."

"Yes," said Bedford. "And used the drug to build the ranks of Green Jackets."

"Do you have any idea how they did it, Doctor?"

Dr. Inoue opened a desk drawer, withdrew 1251's flask, and set it on the desktop. "It was in the water."

2.4.7

BOHDAN MACZYNSKI had been the captain of the *IE Neworld*, the interstellar ship that Fallon discovered on his descent into the Below. He was also the leader of the Builders, workers who had been hired to terraform Neworld. Now he "lived" on as the main holographic guide within the Builders' computer network. To Fallon, the small man standing on the table in front of him wasn't a hologram. He was the closest thing to a father Fallon had ever had.

The disassembled parts of the pistol lay scattered on the table at the captain's feet.

Fallon was exhausted from his bout of sobbing. Still, he resisted falling asleep for fear of the dark images that haunted his dreams.

"Why don't you try to sleep?" said the captain. "You need rest."

"I can't go back to the pod. I can't face Addie."

"Then crawl up on the table and stretch out. Let yourself go. I can run a scan while you're resting."

"Uh... I don't know. I couldn't rest even if I did fall asleep."

"Still dreaming about the chancellor and Jenna?"

"It's more than that now. Jo's having nightmares too."

"Really? Why?"

"Look at the video file she's culled from the restricted archives you gave us access to."

"Which file?"

"The one labeled *WAR*."

The captain was able to assimilate the video in a few seconds. "Those images *are* disturbing. I understand your distress."

Fallon nodded. "At first, the artifacts you stored in the archive showed us a beautiful world. Art, music, poetry…"

"And Earth was that, and more," said the captain. "But we could never completely free ourselves of our animal instincts. *Countries* didn't go to war, Fallon. Countries' *leaders* took their people to war.

"That's why the Neworld Foundation was started—three generations of searching for and developing people who were genetically free of ailments such as cancer, Alzheimer's, heart disease, or diabetes. These are afflictions you won't find in the 1900 because they had been genetically eradicated from the population. Your genetic code is what makes you what you are: it determines the color of your skin and hair, your body type, whether you're a man or a woman, and other physical characteristics.

"Mental conditioning was another matter. The Neworld founders cut themselves off from the rest of society and they began the slow process of creating a new social structure. Two more generations of conditioning were accomplished on the ship as we made our way here, before we entered the long sleep. We engineers woke first and terraformed the continent. Then we roused our passengers to populate Neworld. After three generations on Neworld, no living soul had a firsthand memory of Earth."

"Then what went wrong?"

"Nothing went *wrong*, Fallon. There's an old Earth saying, 'shit happens.' It's amazing to me that you made it this far, because the human body, the human mind, isn't perfect. Even though your ancestors were selected for their 'perfection,' genetic code will develop flaws over time. It doesn't appear that any genetic diseases have reappeared on Neworld. That could take thousands of years.

"But there's also human nature—and that's a different beast. For instance, did you know that everyone was equal when Neworld was founded? There were no wealthy and worker classes like you have now. Absolute equality was part of the mental conditioning that took generations to achieve. Yet, less than two hundred years on, you have separated into classes.

"And murder! The very concept of killing another human being was wiped from collective social memory. But now you know that murder has existed on Neworld for some time, even though the word is not in your dictionary. It's just that the Council covered it up."

"Greed, passion, anger, and jealousy are all part of human nature. It was only a matter of time before the Neworld Foundation's conditioning would give in to human nature."

Fallon spread his arms to encompass the room and said, "I don't know what to do with this. Should I arm the Movement so we can defend ourselves and maybe go topside and take the fight to the chancellor? Or should I keep the armory hidden and see the people of Neworld live under the chancellor's rule?" Fallon felt his pulse race and his chest tighten with anxiety. "It's all too much for me. I should tell the others about this place. Let them decide."

"If you do that, son, the genie's out of the bottle, you understand? Look, it took us thousands of years to invent the weapons we did. It started because we weren't civilized and had to defend ourselves from all sort of predators. Neworld was created with a full-blown, unified civilization, and no predators. It took more than two hundred years for one crazy guy to arm some henchmen with clubs. Do you really want to jumpstart an arms race? Go from shiny black sticks to automatic weapons and machine guns?"

Fallon pondered the question before replying, "You mean, fight clubs with clubs."

"Not necessarily," answered the captain. "Let me give you something to view and read. Then you can go back to your pod and sleep on it. Promise?"

$$x \sim 2.5$$

New Directions

2.5.1

ADDIE was angry after her lunch with Jo and the twins.

Who is she to speak to me the way she did?

There was no way Addie could tolerate being cooped up in the small confines of the archive with that woman, so she sat alone in the courtyard of the Commons and sulked.

She had been sitting for several hours when she saw her grandmother and Bedford leaving the infirmary. She followed the pair toward the administration offices.

"Grandmother?"

Missus Grier stopped and turned. "Addie. Are you looking for us?"

"For you, actually," she said, giving Bedford a sheepish look.

Bedford picked up on the cue. "Well, I've got things to attend to, Mara," he said.

"Come to my room, Aidan. We'll have some privacy there."

• • •

MISSUS GRIER sipped tea and listened patiently as Addie vented her growing frustration with Fallon and her annoyance at Jo's rebuff.

"I can't stand it down here anymore," she said. "I've got to get away. Is there anything I can do topside, Grandmother?"

Missus Grier pulled Addie to her, holding her granddaughter's head to her chest. "It's your grandmother you're asking, is it?" She stroked Aidan's hair a few moments before going on.

"As your grandmother, I only want to ease your pain. But as the leader of this group, I can't show you any special favors. Plus, you're just too well known topside." She lifted a strand of coppery red hair. "Too noticeable."

Aidan pulled away from her grandmother's embrace. "I can cut it. Dye it brown."

Missus Grier's tone became matter-of-fact. "We have nothing for you to do topside."

"But..."

Missus Grier raised a finger to silence her granddaughter. "However, we do have something you can do down here. Something vitally important. Bedford and I hesitated to ask because of your relationship with Fallon, but now that you and he are cooling off..."

"What? What is it you want me to do?"

"It's about Daniel Bianchi. We need to know what he knows. He's still in bad shape. Withdrawal from that drug causes bouts of delirium, and whatever mental conditioning he was put through has left him distrusting to the point of paranoia. He's been unresponsive to all our questions and even his father has had no success. We don't have any experience in interrogating people."

"Interrogating?"

"Rough questioning, like what Fallon described when the Council brought Vernon McCreigh to the Mount. And you know how that turned out."

Addie covered her mouth and closed her eyes as she recalled Fallon's drawing of McCreigh's limp, dead body lying in a heap on the stone floor.

"So Bedford and I consulted with Captain Maczynski, who left us with another of his quaint Earth sayings: You can catch more flies with honey than vinegar."

"What is that supposed to mean?"

"Master Bianchi won't respond to our old, sour faces, but maybe, if we offered him something sweet—some*one* sweet..."

"Me?"

. . .

"AIDAN, is it?" asked Dr. Inoue.

"Most people call me Addie."

"Okay, Addie, I hear you've moved in upstairs and are going to help me with our patient," said Dr. Inoue.

"Grandmother... the Missus suggested that I help. Maybe gain his trust."

"I understand."

Addie surmised the doctor was aware of her true mission.

"But I really could use some help here," the doctor continued as he escorted her toward the patient ward at the rear of the infirmary. "There aren't any nurses or orderlies down here. Perhaps you'll become interested in medicine."

"To tell you the truth, doctor, I need to take my mind off things, you know. I just want to do something different than what I've been... Oh, my!"

Daniel Bianchi's arms and legs were strapped to the bed and a wide band of cloth was pulled tight around his midriff and tied on each end to the frame of the bed. His black hair was matted and his sweat-soaked hospital gown was in disarray, exposing one shoulder and his genitals. A tube ran from his arm to an IV bag hanging next to the bed.

"We haven't been able to get him to eat or drink, so we're keeping him hydrated through the drip. He had an attack of delirium about a half hour ago, so I sedated him. He'll be out for hours. Here, help me free him."

Aidan went to the far side of the bed and mirrored Dr. Inoue as he unfastened the straps.

When she started to pull Bianchi's gown to a more modest position, Dr. Inoue asked, "You've seen a man naked before, young lady?"

Addie nodded as the doctor detached the drip bag from Bianchi's arm. "I'm older than I look."

"Have you touched a man's..."

"Yes," she said, cutting him short.

"Good, because I need you to strip him and give him a sponge bath. I don't want you to be surprised if he reacts to your ministrations."

Addie nodded. "I understand."

"We need to clean him up, and by we I mean you," said the doctor. "He reeks of perspiration and vomit. Take a pan from over there, fill it with warm water, then grab a sponge and soap. If you need help rolling him over, call me."

After she bathed the patient and got him into a clean gown, Addie and Dr. Inoue moved him to a clean bed and strapped him down once more.

"Well, there's little else to do," said the doctor. "No IV until he wakes in the morning and we see how he reacts. So why don't you grab yourself something to eat and get settled in upstairs?"

* * *

ADDIE didn't want to run into Jo, the twins, or Fallon so she loaded a tray of food from the mess and took it to her new room above the infirmary. She picked halfheartedly at the meal as she sat alone in the sparsely furnished one-room apartment.

She felt sick. Not *sick* sick. But the kind of sick she'd felt that night the Dark Men boarded up the Grier house and poured rivers of kerosene down the chimneys. If it weren't for the Builders' hidden caverns beneath the estate, she and the rest of the Movement would have been burned alive. In fact, those topside believed they were all dead.

She slid the tray away and sat staring at the tabletop.

What have I done?

She missed Fallon. But then she had been missing him even while they were together, hadn't she? He just seemed to have withdrawn from their life together.

He shouldn't have gone topside. He was changed when he came back. He was broken. He was dead.

The memory of his lifeless body lying on the archive's table sent her into a fit of uncontrollable sobbing.

He was a hero. How can I abandon him?

Fallon's "Historian's Tale" gave enough truth about the Council and the chancellor's corruption of their social order to foment a revolution, but it was not the whole truth. He had left out details—details so fantastic that his story of the chancellor's crimes would not be believed. He didn't tell of the secret passage that took him on a journey that ended with the world-shattering discovery he had made in the depths of the Below. He didn't tell them that the inhabitants of the Grier estate were alive and well, hidden safely underground. Instead, he told them how Chancellor Brennan had usurped the powers of the Council and was behind the brutal deaths of Vernon McCreigh and Jenna Howard. Fallon drew gut-wrenching images of the slain bodies. He told how the Chancellor's Dark Men had savaged the Grier estate.

My grandfather, the chancellor.

Choking back more sobs, Aidan rose unsteadily, staggered the short distance to the small bed, and collapsed.

• • •

AIDAN didn't know she had fallen asleep until she woke with a start.

"Ahhhh!" she screamed in the choked way one does when awakening from a nightmare.

What was that? Where am I?

Had something disturbed her? She raised herself on an elbow and listened as she tried to perceive her dark surroundings.

The Commons… above the infirmary, she told herself.

The room was silent.

She slid her feet off the bed, stood up, and crossed to the sole window in the front wall. She peered up at the simulated night sky and realized that it was the middle of the night.

Then she heard a muffled CLUNK, CLUNK, CLUNK.

She cocked her head and tried to determine where it was coming from.

CLUNK, CLUNK, CLUNK.

The sound was emanating from below her feet.

Downstairs... The infirmary.

Addie started to look for clothes to put on before she realized she was still fully dressed.

She hurried out of the room, down the stairs, and into the fully lit infirmary, where she found Dr. Inoue fumbling with a drip line while trying to hold down a bucking and writhing Daniel Bianchi.

"Doctor!"

"Good. Give me a hand here, will you?"

As Addie took up position beside him, the doctor said, "Try to hold his shoulder and arm still while I hook up an IV."

Because of her size, Addie had to crawl onto the bed and lean her full weight onto the patient's chest and shoulder to have any effect.

"That's the best I can manage, Doctor. Please hurry."

"Okay... One more second... That's it. Give it a moment..."

Aidan could feel Bianchi's muscles un-tense beneath her as the sedative did its job.

"What happened?" she asked as she slid off the bed.

"The sedative wore off sooner than I thought. Obviously, the Green Jacket's drugs are still racking his body."

Dr. Inoue held the patient's wrist and took his pulse. "He'll be okay now. You can get back to sleep."

"I don't think I can. Mind if I sit down here with him for a while? Just in case?"

"Suit yourself, but you'll want to be fresh in the morning if our patient is coherent enough to talk."

Addie nodded and Dr. Inoue returned to his upstairs apartment. She wandered idly about the infirmary, turning off the lights in the front room before returning to the back.

Addie examined Daniel Bianchi from the foot of the bed for a few minutes before turning down the lights in the patient ward. She moved to the head of the bed and eased herself into a chair there.

In time, her eyelids grew heavy and her chin sagged to her chest. She was on the edge of sleep when Bianchi began to mumble. Her head snapped up and she became alert, trying to make out what the Green Jacket was saying. She leaned in and held her breath. She was disturbed by what she heard.

Below! This is important. I wish Fallon was… I don't have his memory. I need to write this down.

She sprang up, went to the front room, and rummaged through the doctor's desk, retrieving a pencil and some paper on a clipboard. She hurried back to the chair, positioned herself, and began to write.

2.5.2

FALLON returned to Pod G early in the evening, his mind racing with the images and ideas the captain had used to challenge him. The fog that had enveloped his brain was now blown away by the powerful winds of hope. He was eager to share his newfound hope with Addie.

As he entered the pod's entrance tunnel, he saw that a few newcomers were sitting at tables in the common room. By the changing colors within the room ahead, Fallon surmised someone was fiddling with the ceiling illumination controls. As he entered the room, the ceiling changed from a creamy orange to a depiction of the Earth's night sky, to images of bright points of light enveloped in awe-inspiring clouds of deep, vibrant colors.

"Captain Maczynski says that those are stars being born."

The three men and two women fell silent when Fallon spoke. He didn't know their names, or even if they all now lived in Pod

G. He saw that expression of awe, almost reverence, on their faces as they turned to look at him. It was the look he had grown to hate because he knew he didn't deserve their trust, much less their admiration. Fallon felt the heaviness in his chest return and beads of sweat formed on his forehead. He wanted to escape, to slink back into his cottage and crawl into bed. Instead, he forced a smile.

"Hello, I'm Fallon. Glad to finally meet you."

He dutifully introduced himself to each newcomer in turn, asking their names, where they were from, and how they were recruited. They all worked in the hydroponics farm and, to his delight, came from small villages around Agricitta.

"I'm from the area myself. I grew up…"

"In the Mount," said a young woman with short-cropped brown hair. "We've all read your papers."

"Of course you have." He wanted to gracefully retreat somehow. "Here, let me show you something." He moved to the illumination control by the tunnel entrance. "This is my favorite."

The ceiling returned to the night sky—with a half moon on the rise.

"We've seen this before," said a stout, balding man. "It's the Earth's…"

Fallon held up one hand to silence the man and pointed skyward with the other. "Wait for it…"

There was a soft pop to one side of the room, then a shrieking sound as a trail of sparkling light shot toward the domed ceiling's zenith, where it exploded into a multicolored blossom of dazzling light.

One woman shrieked in fright and the others barely contained themselves.

A second trail arced across the ceiling, bursting into a massive ball of white sparks punctuated with noisy, spiraling pinwheels of fire that whistled and popped.

Other bursts filled the night sky, and Fallon smiled gratefully as the newcomers began pointing upward, instinctively "oohing" and "aahing."

"Enjoy," he said as he slipped, unnoticed, into his cottage.

The kitchen was dark, as was the bedroom beyond. He whispered, in case Addie had already gone to bed. "Addie?"

Fallon set the kitchen ceiling illumination to a low, soft-blue and then sat at the table to remove his shoes before padding quietly into the bedroom.

"Addie?"

When he approached the bed, Fallon discovered it empty and still made. His enthusiasm again began to drain from him and the fog in his brain returned. He felt sleepy and his body seemed heavy. He sat wearily on the foot of the bed, his chin drooped to his chest, and his mind became a jumble of contradictory thoughts. He fought back tears.

Where's Addie? Why do I feel this way? I felt so good a few minutes ago. Depression... that's what the captain called it. Try to stay focused. Where's Addie? There's a way to keep the genie in the bottle. Take a deep breath... exhale... again... Lie down. Sleep it off. There's hope. Breathe... exhale... again.

He crawled into the center of the bed, curled into the fetal position, and drifted off.

* * *

FALLON was still alone when he woke. His senses remained dulled and he had no idea what time it was. The dim blue light still filtered in from the kitchen. He reflexively reached for the spot on the bed where Addie should have been. She wasn't there.

His body went limp and he let out a deep, trembling sigh. He was unsure how long he lay there before drifting back into a restless sleep.

* * *

THIS TIME Fallon woke to the sound of knocking on the door.

"Little brother, you there?" It was Tobey.

More knocking. Fallon sat up groggily and swung his legs over the side of the bed.

"Fallon, if you're there…"

"Yeah, I'm here, I'm here." Fallon instantly regretted the edge in his voice.

What's wrong with me? He stood and moved toward the dimly lit kitchen. *I have no reason to be sharp with anyone. What did the captain call it? Projection. I'm projecting my anger with myself onto others.*

Unable to make it to the door, he collapsed into a chair by the kitchen table. "Come in."

The front door opened. Tobey and Jo entered, with Sean close on their heels.

Sean reached for the illumination control and set it to mimic daylight. Fallon flinched and squinted at the sudden brightness.

"Bloody B," Sean began, "you look horri…"

Jo elbowed Sean in the ribs and shot him a glare.

"Horrible," said Fallon. "I'm sure I do." He gestured for his friends to have a seat.

The twins sat as Jo moved toward the cupboards. "Let me make some coffee. You can use a little lift this morning."

"Where've you been keeping yourself?" asked Tobey.

"I've been around. Here and there. You know?"

"Not so much here as there," said Tobey.

"Not so much," Fallon conceded.

"And where's the *there*?" asked Sean.

"Walking around. I like being alone in the dark."

"Like the Green Jacket," said Tobey.

"No, but I'll keep an eye out."

"Below, you really are out of it!" said Sean. "He stumbled into the Commons days ago. Doc Inoue and Addie are…"

"Addie? She's working for the new doctor?"

Jo approached the table and set a cup of coffee before Fallon. "Yes. We sort of had a… falling out."

"When?"

"The night before last," said Jo. "We haven't seen her since, but Missus Grier told us she was going to stay in the room above the infirmary for a while and help the doctor."

Fallon sipped the coffee as he tried to unmuddy his mind. "Night before last?"

Jo sat next to him and nodded. Fallon could see the sadness in her eyes.

Night before last, he thought. *Below, I must have slept yesterday away.*

"Sorry. I've just been so... so... out of it, I guess." He drank more coffee and began to feel some of the fog lift from his mind. *Depression*, he reminded himself. *I have to fight it.*

"Well, we need you back," said Tobey.

Fallon didn't reply. *Need me.* Fallon took a deep breath and exhaled slowly, fighting back the weight of phrase. *Need me. They* need *me.* He finished the coffee and turned his thoughts to his last conversation with the captain. He remembered his newfound hope— and his promise to get some rest, read the book the captain had suggested, and make a decision. *Well, I'm certainly rested. Now I need to keep the rest of my promise.*

He looked into the eyes of each of his friends and nodded. "I've got something to do," he said. "Something I promised the captain. Give me a few days, okay?"

Jo rested a reassuring hand on his, and squeezed.

"Whatever you need, little brother," said Sean.

"Just a few days," said Tobey.

"Yeah," said Fallon, feeling a surge of energy. "Just a few days. But first, tell me about the Green Jacket. You say he's in the infirmary?"

2.5.3

LENORE stood at a rear window of the warehouse, staring into the rain that threatened to flood the narrow alleyway. She hoped the downpour meant someone would be coming from or returning to the quarters. She was able to hobble about, but there was no way she could make the trek to the quarters.

Bertie, an old teamster, approached and stood next to her. "I checked the signal, Miss. It was still there. If anyone's out 'n' about, they'll drop by sometime tonight. It's still early. Good news is we're back up 'n' running. Not here, of course, with the Green Jackets buzzing about the way they are, but we got scribes all over Primacitta. Less traffic coming 'n' going from any one place, don't you see?"

Lenore gave Bertie a warm smile. "That's good..." Her reply was cut short by the sound of steps on the stairs. She and Bertie turned to see a man silhouetted in the doorway, his long oilcloth teamster's coat dripping from the rain.

"Father?" said Lenore as she started to hobble to the man.

"Lenore," said the man in a voice that was not her father's. The man stepped into the light. Lenore hesitated but quickly set aside her disappointment and greeted the man with a hug.

"Percy, it's so good to see you."

Percy Williams had been on the staff at the Grier estate and had posed as James Bedford when the Dark Men searched the house, concealing the fact that Bedford had taken Fallon on the momentous mission to the Below. Percy was younger and darker skinned than her father, but the subterfuge had worked.

Percy looked at Lenore with concern. "You're hurt. What happened?"

"Long story. Come, sit." Lenore led Percy to a table and eased herself into a chair. "Bertie, can you give us a few minutes?"

Bertie nodded and went downstairs.

"Bertie and the crew here are the people who nursed Fallon after he was beaten. But it's best they don't hear our business. They don't know about the quarters. They only know we come and go from someplace. It's safer like that. Which way are you headed?"

"I'm heading down with a cook in tow. With so many new arrivals, Effie and Anne need some help in the kitchen. I saw the signal, so I came. What do you need?"

"Heading down, that's good. I need to get a message to Father and Missus Grier. Look, a Green Jacket went missing from this area some time ago and it's unsafe to make the transit."

"We noticed the patrols. We had to have papers authorizing our movement after dark. We were stopped twice. Thank Below for Franklin! It's good to have a barrister who can get his hands on legal forms."

"That settles it. We need to suspend movement up or down for a while. In fact, we need to figure a way to get you and your companion safely away. No papers are going to get you into the Promenade at this time of night."

Lenore bent over to massage her ankles, groaning at the effort.

Percy winced in sympathy. "So, how'd that happen?"

Lenore sat up straight, stretched her legs out in front of her, picked up a slim notebook from the table, selected and removed some pages, and then handed them to Percy. "From my journal, just as Jo suggested. It's all in here. Be sure to destroy it if you get caught, right?" Percy took the pages with a quick nod and slid them into an inside coat pocket.

"Now, would you please go downstairs and send Julia up? We need to plan your safe departure."

. . .

IT TOOK longer than Lenore had hoped to set everything up. Percy and his companion would have to enter the Promenade a few blocks south of the Little Silver River and then cut north until they were deep in the safety of the wilderness beyond. Making the journey even more dangerous, the rain was easing.

They would have to put the plan into action during this circuit of the Green Jacket patrol or the travelers would be stranded topside until the next rain. Lenore surveyed the area from a darkened window overlooking 52nd Street. The street dead-ended at the block wall of a foundry two streets to the west. Hanging on the wall was one of the garish banners bearing the image of the chancellor.

She saw the patrol turn east onto 52nd and slowly make their way toward her, one guard down each side of the street. She knew that more patrols were on nearby streets.

She watched two dark figures scurry into view at the end of the street, staying close to the foundry wall. One carried a bucket and the other a shielded lantern. The figures stopped beneath the banner. The one with the bucket splashed its contents against the banner, while the other unshielded the lantern and flung it against the wall.

I hope it's not too wet, thought Lenore as the figures darted off in opposite directions.

The wall exploded with flame as the lantern shattered against it. A moment later, Lenore heard a WHOOOSH and the windows rattled in their frames.

The patrolmen turned and screened themselves from the blast of hot air. The Green Jacket on the far side of the road reacted first, pulling out his whistle, signaling for help, and running toward the conflagration. His partner was close on his heels. Two more patrolmen raced up the street from the direction of the Promenade to assist.

Lenore smiled. Every Green Jacket in the warehouse district would be heading toward the fire as Percy guided his companion down the alleyway behind the warehouse to the Promenade.

2.5.4

FALLON cloistered himself away in the armory, where he had set up a cot and stockpiled food he scrounged from the hydroponics farm's mess hall. He began his sequestration by reviewing the materials Captain Maczynski had shown him. He thought about the message the captain was trying to convey and how it impacted his decision.

If he turned these weapons over to the Movement, they could mow through scores of Green Jackets, armed with only their feeble clubs, and exact revenge on the chancellor in a single day. His emotions urged him to avenge the abhorrent murder of Jenna Howard.

Yet his logical mind told him that doing so would endanger Neworld. There was a reason the words "weapon" or "war" or "murder" couldn't be found in the 1900. The people of Neworld had existed for more than 190 cycles—280 annums—in peace.

Chancellor Brennan was the bringer of war and murder, but Fallon would be committed to the Below before he'd unleash wholesale death and destruction on the people of Neworld. He couldn't allow the concept of the weapons to become known. He was determined not to let that particular genie out of the bottle.

Fallon hadn't called up his holographic mentor during his deliberations, and that was intentional. He knew the decision was his to make, and his alone.

He sat on a stool at the glass-topped table, eating a bowl of fresh vegetable soup. He had made his decision and his hermitage was almost over.

For days now, Fallon had been meticulously disassembling the weapons. In the dead of night, he had commandeered a small wagon to cart the pieces to a smelting station in a corner of the aviary, where fumes could be vented to the outside. The smelter reduced the pieces to their base metals while vaporizing the plastic. Fallon then carted the stockpiles of ammunition out onto the aviary gallery and dumped them over the railing and into the damp depths of the Below, where he hoped they would corrode before anyone stumbled upon them.

The armory walls were now barren. The last weapon lay on the table next to his bowl of soup. Fallon set down the spoon, tapped the tabletop, and the holographic figure of Captain Maczynski appeared.

"Do you know what this is?" asked Fallon.

"It's the pistol you used when you tried to kill Brennan."

"And I failed."

"You survived. I count that as a victory."

Fallon sighed and grunted, "Maybe."

"Life is always better than death, my boy."

"To be or not to be? Right?"

"You finished your reading, then?"

"I did."

"And...? What's your opinion?"

"About what?"

"About Hamlet."

"He was crazy."

"Was he? Or was it an act?"

"He was driven crazy."

"What drove him?"

"Vengeance."

"If it had been vengeance, he could have just killed the king. It's a simple cause and effect—you killed my father, now I'll kill you."

"Simple in *your* world, maybe. We don't think like that."

"Come on, son, you know better than that. We've been over this before. People killed each other on Neworld long before Brennan took power. It was just hidden under the surface, swept under the carpet by the Council. The Dark Men have been around a long time."

Fallon knew it was true and truth was often painful.

"So what drove Hamlet crazy?" the captain prodded.

Fallon considered the question from a new perspective. "You're right. He could have justly killed the king and maybe gone mad with guilt."

"But that's not the story Shakespeare chose to write, is it?"

"No… no, it's not. He wrote about a man who knew what he should do but couldn't bring himself to act on it." Fallon's eyes widened as he comprehended the answer. "That's what drove him crazy—his *inability* to act. And he left a trail of victims in his wake, including himself."

"It was, literally, a tragedy." The captain let that sink in for a minute before asking, "And why do you think I suggested you read the play?"

Fallon didn't reply.

"Come on, son. If it doesn't come from inside you, it will be meaningless."

Fallon wouldn't reply.

"I know you are not a vain person, Fallon. I know you to be selfless and compassionate. A man of action. Aidan needs you. Missus Grier and Bedford need you, and the twins, and Jo and… Maybe all of Neworld needs you. You can't hide away from them in here, talking to an avatar of a long-dead Earthman."

"I'm driving myself crazy. I don't know what to do."

"But you do know. You've made your decision, haven't you? You've already taken action." The captain motioned to the empty wall. You've destroyed those weapons, haven't you? You can destroy that pistol and wipe them all from your mind now. Banish them from your dreams."

The captain paused so his last words would be absorbed. Fallon nodded in reply.

"Good. So, what's next?" prompted the captain.

"We take back Neworld."

"Exactly."

"But how?"

"Don't be coy with me, son. You know how. You don't need me to validate your decision. And you know where you need to go, don't you?"

"Eagle's Nest."

"Right. Then it's time you came out of hiding."

$$x\sim 2.5$$

2.6

Ascension

2.6.1

MISSUS GRIER called her inner circle into the library conference room. "Much has happened overnight," she said as she entered the room and took her seat at the middle of the table. She surveyed the group, evenly split on the two sides of the table: Bedford, Aidan, Dr. Inoue, and Brian Randall, on her side; Sean, Jo, Tobey, and the newly arrived Percy Williams on the other. As she surveyed the group, she was struck by the contrast between the fresh clothing of those who had recently been topside and the threadbare clothes of those who hadn't. She noted the fraying on the sleeves of her own sweater and Bedford's shirt collar.

"Where's Fallon?" She instinctively directed the question toward Addie. "Oh, sorry dear. Forgive an old lady's memory." Then she turned toward Jo and the twins.

Sean shrugged and Tobey shifted uncomfortably in his chair.

"We haven't seen him in days, Missus," said Jo.

Missus Grier grew concerned. She turned to Bedford. "Has he gone topside?"

"Percy and his recruit have been the only ones to come or go in the last week."

"Well, a person can't just disappear down here," she countered.

"The Green Jacket did," said Sean.

"He has a name," shot Aidan. "Daniel Bianchi!"

"He's still a…"

Bedford held up his hands to put a quick end to the skirmish. "But no one was looking for Master Bianchi."

"And nobody is *looking* for Fallon, sir," Sean retorted.

An uneasy silence settled upon the room.

Where is the boy? thought Missus Grier. *Doesn't he realize he is our anchor?* "Well," she said, deliberately breaking the tension, "we shall proceed without him. We have several things to discuss. First, Randall, are there any operational problems we need to address?"

"Nothing to report, Missus. Percy's recruit filled our only need."

"And Percy has brought news from topside as well," said Missus Grier. "It seems that the Bianchi boy's disappearance has stirred up trouble in Primacitta. Percy…"

Percy slid the papers that lay in front of him across the table to Jo. "This is from Lenore's journal. As I told the Missus and Bedford, she's injured and couldn't make the trip herself."

"Is she hurt badly?" asked Jo.

Ah, Jo, thought Missus Grier. *What would we do without you?* She had become fond of the shy young woman over the past few months as Jo grew into her role within this little group. Jo was always a voice of reason, with a curious mind and an openness to new ideas. She was the heart of the team, caring as much about feelings as actions.

"Sprained both ankles," answered Percy. "It's a long story and those pages tell everything, but she's on the mend. The short of it is that the Green Jackets and the Dark Men have torn apart the warehouse district searching for the Green Jack… uh… Master Bianchi. Lenore says we need to…"

Missus Grier's attention was pulled away from Percy as a shadow moved along the shades on the conference room windows. Someone was in the hall. She held up a hand to silence Percy.

Then the door opened.

Fallon! Inwardly, Missus Grier was happy to see him but she addressed him with a hard look. "We're glad you could find the time to join us."

"I apologize. I was busy, Missus. I was not well, actually."

Missus Grier noticed the look that Fallon directed toward Aidan. Was it sorrow? Regret?

"Not well *and* busy. I had to deal with something."

The Missus saw Fallon shoot a knowing glance in Randall's direction with that statement. *They share a secret*, she thought as she studied the chief engineer's face.

"And I eliminated the problem," Fallon concluded.

Now the Missus detected the trace of a smile on Randall's face.

They're both relieved, she thought, and she decided to trust in their judgment.

"Pardon the interruption, Percy," said the Missus. "Please continue.

"Uh… yes. Lenore says we need to suspend all movement to and from topside until further notice. She'll come down when she thinks it's safe to resume operations."

"What about the estate?" asked Fallon, closing the door behind him.

Percy looked confused by the question.

"Has the chancellor begun excavating the manor ruins yet?"

The Missus had been wondering about that herself. If the chancellor decided to excavate the ruins, he would learn that she and the others had not died in the fire and, most likely, would discover the tunnels leading to the Basin. For that reason, the Movement had all but ceded the Basin tunnels to the chancellor and his henchmen—after taking care to hide the access route to the quarters. They had gone so far as to dismantle the strings of static lights that illuminated the long descent and the path to the first waystation. They did all this in the hope that their pursuers would believe Missus Grier and her followers had taken refuge in the Basin.

Percy addressed the group: "I asked around and even took a stroll by the estate entrance. Nobody has seen or heard any activity in the area and my surveillance backs that up. Just a couple of guards at the entrance arch."

"Why's that, now?" Tobey asked of no one in particular.

"Perhaps they believe we are indeed dead," suggested Bedford. "There's nothing in Fallon's *Historian's Tale* to make them think otherwise."

"Maybe he's too busy flushing out the organization Lenore is putting together," said Percy.

"Think about it," said Fallon. "If Brennan excavated the ruins, he'd just confirm what I wrote in *The Historian's Tale*. No, I think he wants to keep us buried along with the Movement."

Missus Grier nodded. "I agree. So that takes some of the pressure off us. Any technical reason we can't stay down here indefinitely?"

"None, Missus," answered Randall. "We have an endless supply of power and the hydroponics farm can sustain two, maybe three, times the number of people we currently have."

"Meat would be nice," said Tobey jokingly.

"You, brother, will have to be the one to smuggle a cow down through the hatch," replied Sean.

Even Missus Grier smiled at that. She saw the twins as the arms and legs of the team—the muscle. Still, she valued their ability to lighten the mood even in the direst of situations.

The Missus shifted her focus to her granddaughter, and her heart sank. Addie, her hair pulled up severely in a bun, sat straight-backed with her hands clasped in front of her, a look of indifference on her face. Where had Addie's spark gone? It wasn't like her to give up.

Fallon took a seat at the end of the table.

The significance of the position he assumed did not escape the Missus. She could only imagine the emotional strain of Fallon's ordeal. She and Bedford had used him like a pawn in a game he didn't even know he was playing. Now he sat at the end of the table, no longer a pawn but the king of the board.

And, with a glance toward Addie, the Missus thought, *Who will be the queen?*

2.6.2

FOR THE first time since the Missus had purchased him from the headmaster of the Mount, Fallon felt in control—of himself, at least, if not the situation. He would not be paralyzed by the inability to act. He would speak his mind, make his case, and follow the consensus.

"That's dangerous, Missus," he began. "Thinking we can bide our time down here is risky. We need to plan our move and be ready to execute it by the time Lenore returns. Right now we have the element of surprise on our side—they think we're dead. And Lenore's efforts topside have given us the start of a force we can bring to bear."

"Welcome back, brother," said Sean with a grin.

Fallon could feel the tension in the room ebb as the others expressed agreement with Sean's sentiment. All, that is, except Addie. But Fallon couldn't worry about her feelings at the moment.

He continued, "Forgive me if I'm asking you to rehash old news, Doctor, but what have you found out about your patient? I heard he was drugged somehow?

"Yes, that's correct," said Dr. Inoue. "Apparently the Green Jackets are conditioned to self-dose at regular intervals."

This surprised Fallon. "They drug themselves?"

"It's in the water flask they each carry," said Addie.

"And how do you know this?" asked Fallon.

"He talked while under sedation."

"About what?"

"Lots of things," she replied curtly. "That was days ago. I gave my notes to Bedford."

Fallon was relieved he could get more information about Danny Bianchi from someone else. Not trusting his emotions, he preferred to keep his contact with Addie to a minimum.

Jo spoke up, "So, Doctor, Master Bianchi wasn't necessarily responsible for his actions?"

"That's correct. He seemed to be acting under the influence of the drug and some sort of mental conditioning."

"Can we reason from that, the Green Jackets might not be true converts to Chancellor Brennan's cause?" asked the Missus.

"I think that would be a safe assumption."

"Then if we can cut off their supply of whatever they carry in those flasks of theirs," Bedford theorized, "we can break the chancellor's hold on them?"

"No," answered Aidan emphatically.

Fallon redirected Addie's statement to the doctor. "Is that true, Dr. Inoue?"

"It is. After all these days, Danny is just now fighting off the effects of the drug. I'm convinced that if he hadn't been under our care and sedated repeatedly, the strain of the drug withdrawal would have killed him."

"Is he better now?" asked Jo.

"Yes and no," said the doctor. "The withdrawal crisis has passed but it will take time to work through his mental conditioning. He's confused at best and paranoid at worst. We're relying on Addie to gain his trust."

"I'm sure Aidan will win him over." Fallon caught the brief, fiery glance Addie threw his way. Then he sighed and concluded, "So we can't effect change on that front."

Dr. Inoue held up his hand in disagreement. "That's not what I said, is it? I said cutting off their supply would probably kill these young men."

"Pray tell, Doctor," said Missus Grier, "What exactly are you saying?"

"Dr. Hadjh…" Dr. Inoue began.

"Doctor who?" Fallon hadn't heard that they'd brought down a second doctor.

"Dr. Hadjh is the holographic assistant in the infirmary," Dr. Inoue explained. "He suggested we make an antidote."

"Then why haven't you, man?" boomed Bedford.

"We need a sample of the drugged water to work from, and Danny Bianchi's flask was dry when he staggered into the Commons."

"Percy," said Fallon, "I'm afraid you'll have to make one more trip up and back before we take Lenore's advice. We need a Green Jacket's flask. And we need it as soon as possible. Next storm, you're going up."

Percy nodded his assent.

Fallon again avoided Aidan by addressing Bedford. "Has Danny Bianchi been able to tell us how many Green Jackets the chancellor has created?"

Bedford replied, "Aidan?"

"No," said Aidan. "But his comments support what Lenore's investigation suggested: he and the other abducted men were taken to an island on Rift Lake."

"That's good to know. Thanks." Fallon offered Aidan a smile, which she returned with an almost imperceptible nod.

"Percy, add this to your list: Have Lenore's people determine the number of Green Jackets—how many in Primacitta and how many spread around the rest of Neworld. We need that information when she comes down. Okay?"

"Got it," Percy acknowledged.

"Good." Fallon stood. He couldn't sit still and be able to say what he was about to say. "Now, on to my news. While I was in seclusion I talked at great length with Captain Maczynski. I've been troubled by the danger I put you all in by going topside."

He moved slowly around the table as he spoke, keenly aware of the attention focused on him.

"I've had nightmares most of you couldn't imagine. Addie knows what I mean. So does Jo. Those of us who have been studying the history of our ancestral home, Earth, have learned disturbing things. The humans who grew up there were a violent lot. They rained death and destruction on their fellow men for the most insane of reasons. There was a time on Earth when people like Bedford and Percy could have been killed simply because they were darker skinned than those in power.

"Mankind had to fight to survive on a primitive world and fighting became an ingrained part of human nature. Violence was hard to unlearn as a society. Before coming to Neworld, our founders spent generations in isolation on Earth, unlearning violence and cultivating the type of society we have here. Over the more than two hundred annums that we've been on Neworld, our society has proved to be mostly successful. But there are problems under the surface. The existence of murder and even madness on Neworld was hidden, swept under the carpet by a group of men created just for that job—the Dark Men.

"The chancellor himself has shown evidence of some regressive human nature. He craves power. He does what he does simply because he desires complete control.

"Those of you who have read Earth's history know the word *revolution*. For you who don't know, revolution means "to tear down one system and replace it with a, hopefully, better system." That's *not* what I'm proposing.

"The captain has expressed, to many of us, his amazement that we've survived this long. He thinks, as do I, that we should try to stay the course. Maybe human imperfections will insinuate themselves upon us over the generations, but we can strive to overcome them as they do.

"The Builders left us tools with which to defend ourselves—tools so powerful they would allow us not only to easily defeat the chancellor's forces, but to impose our will upon the people of Neworld."

He gave Randall a knowing look before proceeding. "But I have taken it upon myself, without your advice or consent, to destroy these tools."

A general outcry of concern ensued, save from Jo, Addie, and Randall.

"How could you?!"

"What were these tools?"

"You had no right!"

Finally, Jo shot to her feet and yelled, "Just stop it. All of you!" When the dissent died down, she continued in a calm voice. "I don't know what exactly Fallon is referring to, but I can make a guess after watching the video logs in the archive. I wouldn't wish those sort of tools upon Neworld."

Aidan rose in support of Jo. "I believe I *do* know the tools Fallon is referring to. And Jo is right."

Immediately, Randall got to his feet. "I've *seen* these tools, and I fully support Fallon's actions."

Sean pounded a fist on the table. "But the chancellor's men have their bloody black clubs, don't they? You've left us defenseless."

"We'll make our own clubs, then," said Tobey.

"No clubs," said Fallon. "We will not be beating upon our fellow men. Remember, they too are victims in this affair."

He moved to stand between Sean and Tobey, resting a hand on each twin's shoulder. "I have a plan and the two of you—Sensei Halloran and Sensei Andrews—you're crucial to its success."

"Sensei?" the twins said in unison.

"I'll explain later," answered Fallon with a grin on his face. "I believe you'll enjoy it. You'll have to work fast, because we need to be ready by the time Lenore returns. Okay?"

"Whatever it is, you can count on us," said Tobey.

"And Dr. Inoue, you'll need to find that antidote in a hurry when Percy brings back your Green Jacket flask. Addie, I know your charms, so I trust you can win Danny Bianchi to our side and secure whatever information he has."

He stopped at the head of the table, resting his knuckles on the tabletop, and took a deep breath. He had never felt so alive.

"So when Lenore returns we need to be ready to go topside and take back Primacitta, then march on to Capital Island, confront the chancellor, and reestablish the council. Are you with me?"

Fallon's question prompted a rousing response.

"One more thing." He paused and resumed his seat. "I need to leave as soon as I can."

Another general outcry erupted. "Why? Where? How can you?!"

"I'll try to go out with Percy in the next storm. I have another task. I need to go to the Eagle's Nest."

"What?" said Bedford. "What the B do you need to go there for?"

"The captain says that's where I'll find answers… and I have so many questions."

"But that's on top of the Rift." Fallon heard the concern in Addie's voice. "Nobody's ever scaled the Rift."

"And nobody had ever descended into the Below," said Fallon.

"You have all our support, little brother," said Sean.

"Sean's right. It'll be dangerous," said Tobey. "I'll go along."

"No, you won't, Tobey Andrews," Jo protested. "Not with a baby on the way."

Fallon's spirits leapt at the news. He knew how long the couple had been trying—even after the lapse of their contract.

Once more the room was chaotic, but this time with proffered congratulations and questions about when the baby was due, and why Jo hadn't shared her good news with anyone.

"I tried," offer Jo, "but events got in the way and…"

Fallon looked to Missus Grier to take control of the meeting, but she only smiled and gestured that he was in charge. So he got to his feet and proclaimed, "This is cause for a celebration, don't you think? I propose we adjourn to the mess and share the news with the others. I'll talk with each of you later about the details of our plans."

As the jubilant crowd filed out of the conference room, Missus Grier drew close, put her hand on Fallon's arm, and whispered, "Fine job, young man. They're *your* people now."

Fallon's heart skipped a beat. A week ago, Missus Grier's statement would have been an unbearable burden. But now, it filled his heart with appreciation for what the Missus had done for him. His emotions welled up and his eyes teared.

As the matriarch of the Movement approached the door, she stopped, faced Fallon and said, "I knew you'd be a leader when I first examined your teeth back in Hunninger's office."

"You can't be serious…"

Then, with a sly smile and wink, she turned and left.

Fallon fell back into his chair, laughing.

2.6.3

AIDAN felt uncomfortable as she worked her way through the crowd in the mess hall and tentatively approached the happy couple. "What was that Earth saying you like so much, Jo? Love always wins?"

Jo replied warmly, "Love will conquer all."

That may be true for some people, thought Aidan.

"I'm so happy for you," she said, giving Jo a hug and a kiss on the cheek. "Really, I am."

Aidan was sincerely happy for Jo, even joyous, but it only served to magnify her own feeling of loss. She wondered if she could ever regain the friendship she had shared with Jo and the others.

"I appreciate it," said Jo.

Aidan turned to Tobey, put on her best attempt at a smile, and opened her arms wide. "Daddy!"

Tobey grinned with pride as he took Aidan into his embrace and said, "That'll be Da, if you please." Then he held her out to arms length. "We miss you, Addie." And with a tilt of the head, he said, "And I'm sure Fallon does too."

Aidan's heart sank. "Maybe. Maybe not. I don't have a contractual hold on him, but thanks for the thought."

She retreated into the crowd and threaded her way toward the door, where she stopped to look over the gathering. Off in one corner, Fallon was having an animated conversation with Percy Williams. *Love will conquer all. Hah!* Love was an alien concept on Neworld and she doubted that Fallon believed in it. She wondered if she believed in love herself. Certainly she and Fallon shared a passionate physical relationship, but was there anything more? That intangible something that could keep them together without the binding of a contract? That something that Jo and Tobey had? Was love some regressive bit of human nature, as Fallon had called it? Or was it something special, as Jo seemed to believe?

She shook her head and tried to curtail this line of thought. Well, Fallon said he knew Aidan's charms… said he wanted her to use them to secure the information they need. So that's what she was determined to do.

• • •

PERCY couldn't explain it but he felt privileged in some way, honored maybe, to be having a private conversation with Fallon. He didn't understand the feeling of giddiness—yes, that was it. Percy was twice Fallon's age, yet he felt like a young boy meeting an important elder.

"I'm sorry to ask so much of you, Percy, but I believe you're the best person for the job."

"I'll do anything you ask. I just want to make a difference."

"Well, finding an antidote to the Green Jacket's drug is as important as anything we need to do and without a full flask to work from, we don't have a hope of breaking the drug's control. But how do you get it? You can't just up and ask a Green Jacket to give you his flask, and you can't steal it without it being noticed."

Percy wasn't sure if Fallon had gently led him down a trail of thought or if the idea had come to him on its own, but he had a spark of a plan.

"I may have a thought or two about that," he said. "But I'll need Danny Bianchi's flask and uniform."

Percy was encouraged by the gleam in Fallon's eyes as the young man slapped him on the back and said, "I knew I could count on you."

• • •

BEDFORD and the Missus retired to an office near the conference room to discuss the events of the day.

He had his suspicions, but he wanted to hear it from the Missus. "What happened this morning, Mara?"

"What do you think happened?"

"Don't play coy with me, old woman," he chuckled. "But I asked first."

"As they used to say on Earth, age before beauty, James."

"Since you have both," said Bedford, taking Missus Grier's hand into his, "I suppose I must defer to your wishes."

"A gracious concession."

"I believe we no longer lead the Movement. I believe the young lad has accepted the weight of his position."

Missus Grier nodded and smiled.

"Did you plan this all along?"

"I wish I could claim I did, but I'm as surprised as you. When we took that ride to the Mount, all I saw was a boy with talents that would fit our immediate needs for the descent—a tool to be used. With that ironclad mind of his and the ability to draw... an unimaginably useful tool. I never suspected that the chancellor would react as he did and that we'd be trapped down here like skreel living under the floorboards."

"Mara, what are we to do, after all these years? You and I discovered this place when you were what? Twelve?"

"Thirteen. And you were a skinny little runt of nine annums. You found the way in when you hid in a box in the basement, remember?"

"Yes, in the granary. Quite an exciting game of hide-and-seek. I somehow released the panel and fell through into the ante-room..."

He sat silently with his old friend, replaying the discovery and exploration of the quarters in his mind. Then, with a wistful sigh, he said, "We really need to tell Fallon that story."

"I agree," said Mara. "The historian needs to hear it and to write it down. But, if you truly understood what happened this morning, you'd know we need to have this conversation with Jo, not Fallon. Jo's the historian now—she's the heart of our leadership. Fallon is now the head."

"And where does that leave us, then?"

"It leaves us in a good position to watch, consider, and advise."

x~2.6

Jobs to Do

2.7.1

AIDAN lingered in the Commons courtyard a moment, watching Jo and Tobey through the mess hall windows. She swore she could see it in their eyes, in the way they looked at each other, in the subtle, gentle way they held hands or leaned against each other. *Love*. The thought caused a physical sensation in her chest that welled up and rose, catching in her throat.

Was this another "regressive Brennan trait"—envy?

Then she saw Fallon and Sean making their way toward the door, so she quickly left the courtyard and headed for the infirmary. She had a job to do.

• • •

SEAN was bursting with pride as he and Fallon left the mess. "I'm going to be an uncle, how bleeding great is that?"

"It's fantastic," said Fallon, slapping Sean on the shoulder. "Let's make sure your little niece or nephew is born in the Neworld we thought we knew."

"Aye to that, brother. And I mean that too, Fallon. You're our brother true. You're going to be 'Uncle Fallon.'"

Fallon stopped and squeezed Sean's shoulder. Under the gaslight, Sean noticed a glistening in Fallon's eyes.

"I've never had a family, Sean."

"Yeah, it must've been tough, being a foundling."

"Until the Missus took me away, my whole world was contained inside the walls of the Mount.

"Must've been tough."

"It was the world I knew, and I thrived in it, thanks to your sister, Jenna…" Sean thought he heard a fondness of sorts in Fallon's voice.

Fallon turned his head away, but Sean heard him sniff and saw him wipe his eyes with the back of his hand. He put a comforting hand on Fallon's shoulder.

"Because of the complicated family structure our contract system tends to create, you knew her better than Tobey and I did. You loved her, didn't you, brother?"

Fallon nodded.

"We'll get that bastard Brennan for what he did to her!"

"We'll get him for what he did to Neworld," said Fallon.

Sean knew he wasn't the deepest thinker around, but even he could appreciate the subtle distinction Fallon made. "I hear you, brother," he said.

Sean also wasn't one to wallow in dark thoughts. He liked to be active, whether it was physical activity or prodding and teasing others in conversation. Right now he craved physical action.

"So, tell me, brother. What's this sensei stuff you were talking about this morning?"

"I want to tell, or rather, show you and Tobey together. You both were pugilists, right? Your obviously broken noses tell me this job is going to be right up your alley."

Sean's interest was piqued. "It's fisticuffs then, is it?"

"Welllll… I need to show you. Come to the archive tomorrow morning and we'll get started. For now, go back in and enjoy the party with Tobey and Jo." Fallon gave him a little shove toward the mess.

"Good night, brother."

"Good night, brother," repeated Fallon, managing a half-smile.

As he watched Fallon walk away, Sean felt sympathy. He knew what it was like to return home to an empty bed. Through the mess hall windows, he saw the steady stream of people congratulating his brother and Jo. He was going to be an uncle! But his heart longed for a woman as fine as Jo. To the B with contracts, Sean wanted someone to love. He took a deep breath, put on a smile, and returned to the mess.

• • •

FALLON felt suddenly exhausted as he walked from the courtyard, but he needed strength to fight off that niggling doubt that could drag him back into the pit of depression.

His path led him past the infirmary, which appeared dark. No, wait, a rectangle of pale light shone through the door to the patient ward. Fallon paused when he saw Addie's silhouette move into the backlit frame. She reached up, removed something from her hair, shook her head, and the bun released, allowing her hair to cascade to her shoulders. She then stepped into the light and her coppery hair glinted, even in the pale illumination. Fallon's heart leapt.

Then she closed the door and she was gone.

• • •

ADDIE stood in the darkened infirmary, gazing into the dimly lit patient ward. She was hesitant to undertake this task, but determined to do her job. She was intent on "using her charms" to win over Danny Bianchi and there was no time like now to start. She moved toward the door, removed the pins holding the bun in place, and shook her red hair free. Then she stepped into the room and closed the door.

Danny Bianchi's hands were still strapped to the bed rails but, since he no longer suffered fits of pain, the other bindings had been removed. The drip bag was also gone. Instead, some berries, bread, and a half-full pitcher of water sat on the rolling tray at the foot of the bed.

She moved to the side of the bed and whispered, "Are you awake?" No reply. Seeing beads of sweat on Bianchi's brow, Aidan gently touched the back of her hand to his forehead. He felt a little warm.

She crossed to the sink, filled a small bowl with cool water, and soaked a clean cloth. She then carried the bowl and cloth back and set it on the stand at the head of the bed, where she removed the cloth, wrung out the excess water, and then tenderly mopped his brow. She dipped the rag a second time and laid it across Bianchi's forehead. She wanted to be the first person he saw when he awoke; so she positioned a chair next to the bed facing Bianchi's head. After settling into the chair Aidan slipped her hand through the side rails and took Bianchi's hand in hers.

When she felt his fingers respond to her touch, she sat erect and moved forward on the chair. *Use my charms*, she thought, almost bitterly, while she smiled demurely.

"Danny, are you awake?" she asked in a soft, soothing tone.

Danny Bianchi groaned, groggily moving his head from side to side.

"Is there something I can get for you? Water?"

"Uh-h-h..." He opened his eyes and looked vaguely in Aidan's direction.

Perhaps Addie's anger at Fallon clouded her judgment. *Use her charms, indeed!* She slowly moved her hand to his leg and seductively slid it toward his inner thigh. "Anything I can do for you?"

Addie's seduction of Fallon while he sat in a hotel tub flashed into her mind. It was a special memory and made her current actions seem crass, disgusting. She felt queasy and started to pull her hand away.

Bianchi grabbed her wrist in a viselike grip and squeezed hard. Pain shot up Aidan's arm, causing her to yelp, then whimper.

"Danny, stop! You're hurting me."

"Who are you?" asked Bianchi as he thrashed about with his legs. "Where am I?"

She saw the crazed look in his eyes and instantly knew he was suffering a bout of paranoia caused by his mental conditioning.

Aidan was afraid Bianchi's struggle would break her wrist. She tried to pry his fingers open with her free hand. No success.

"Patrolman," she shouted, "unhand me!"

His legs became still.

"Officer 1251, unhand me this instant! That's an order."

Bianchi's grip loosened and the look in his eyes faded, then his lids drooped closed, his head lolled to one side, and his body went limp.

"Bloody B," sobbed Aidan, rubbing her aching wrist. She wondered how they—how *he*—could ask her to do this.

She would have hated Fallon if she didn't... what? Love him so much?

Aidan swallowed her sobs, told herself she had a job to do, and steeled herself to the task.

2.7.2

THE MAN moved quickly. He lunged at the woman, grabbing the front of her garment, and tried to pull her toward him. But the woman didn't panic. She didn't kick or scream. Instead, with a flurry of arm and legs, she shed the aggressor's hold and went on the attack herself. In a matter of seconds, the man was on his back and the woman was kneeling on his chest, threatening a fingered jab to his eyes.

"It's called martial arts," said Fallon as the twins watched two holographic figures take turns fending off blows and throwing each other to the cushioned matting beneath their feet. A different number displayed on the tabletop for each move, along with words Tobey did not understand.

"All you have to learn," Fallon continued, "is a few basic defensive and disarming moves. Remember, the chancellor's men you'll be fighting are not at fault. We don't want to do them serious harm. We just want to deprive them of their clubs and subdue them."

Tobey nodded his agreement. "Can I see the one where the girl takes down the guy again?"

"Watch as I do it, okay? Sean, you too. These are your *sensei*—your teachers. Yamada-san..." The male avatar stood up, faced the twins, and bowed from the waist. "...and Bennett-san." The female avatar rose and repeated the bow.

"Sensei, please enlarge 50 percent." The figures increased in size.

"Bennett-san, please perform 114."

The two avatars took opposing positions. Tobey felt his brother's shoulder against his as they both leaned in close to watch. He figured that, in real life, Yamada must have had a least a quarter of a meter and forty kilograms on Bennett. Yamada stepped in to attack. Bennett did something with her hands, shifted position, and Yamada was suddenly flat on his back.

Tobey was flabbergasted. He turned to his brother and asked, "Did you follow that?" Sean shook his head.

Bennett got to her feet and offered Yamada a hand up. Then the two bowed to each other and turned to face their audience.

"It happened so fast," said Tobey, turning to Fallon. Do you know how she did that?"

"The captain explained it a little, but I haven't studied the simulation. That's your job."

"Can you make them bigger and slow them down?"

"Sensei, please enlarge by 30 percent." The figures affirmed the request with a slight bow from the waist, then increased in size.

"Bennett-san, please perform 114 at 25 percent speed and explain each move."

The avatars resumed their defensive positions before the action began in slow motion. Bennett's disembodied voice could be heard over the action. "The attacker comes at me. When he grabs my left shoulder, I come across with my right hand and pull his hand down my arm until I can hold his right wrist in my left hand. He comes at my right shoulder. As I wrap my right hand around his left wrist, I twist my upper body so my elbow makes contact with his left wrist and I pop his arm free.

"He pulls his left arm into a defensive position tight against his body. I am still holding his right wrist, so I pull it toward me and across my body. At the same time, I swing my right hand between us, grabbing his right triceps, then I take a step back with my left leg and pull his arm across my centerline. This motion forces the attacker to step into me with his right foot.

"Notice, I don't keep my hold on his wrists. Instead, I shift my position downward, grasp his right thigh with my left hand and his left thigh with my right hand. Now, going down on my left knee, I hook my right leg around his left ankle and drive my body forward, collapsing his knees."

Tobey looked to Sean, who smiled and nodded in appreciation. Then Tobey said to Fallon, "The captain gave you these?"

"Yes." Fallon retrieved a folded piece of paper from his pants pocket and handed it to Tobey. "I've written down the moves he suggested we learn. There are only five or six, but each one has multiple variations."

Tobey unfolded the paper and held it so Sean could read it as well.

"We can learn this in no time, brother," said Sean.

Fallon said, "I know you can. But you need to teach the others by the time Lenore returns and gives you the okay to move topside."

Tobey thought the job would be easy. "How many do we need to train?"

"Everyone."

"Everyone?!" He gasped.

"Yeah. When it's time to bust out, we'll need every able body topside. We have fewer than 250 people down here and we don't know how many Green Jackets we'll confront in Primacitta."

"Whew," Sean whistled.

"As we speak, Jo is getting the work schedules from the department heads and she'll figure out a training schedule."

Tobey was eager to get started. "We can clear out the tables and benches in Pod G's common room..."

"Hold on there, brother," said Sean. "See our friends back there?" He hitched a thumb over his shoulder. "They're holograms, but they had padded mats beneath them, if you didn't notice. The pod floor is hard stone. And we ain't got any mats that I know of." He gave Fallon a questioning look. "Do we?"

Fallon shook his head. "Afraid not... but we do have the playground."

Tobey was at a loss. "The what?"

"You know," said Fallon, "that big sandy area south of the Commons?"

"Yeah?" Tobey, like the others in the quarters, thought the expanse was just an unusable sand pit the Builders had uncovered as they developed the natural cavern for their own purposes.

"The captain called it the playground. Said it was used for exercise and games. Brian Randall is working with Anika to restore power to the ceiling lights over the area. In the meantime, I've asked Randall to have a hologram table installed in Sean's front room. Bedford assigned a few people to gut the room and cover the floor with as many mattresses as we can spare. You have three days to teach yourselves, then you need to start training the others."

Fallon bowed to Sean... "Halloran-san."

Then to Tobey... "Andrews-san."

Tobey was impressed with Fallon's planning. Fallon wasn't the young kid he and his brother had taken under their wings during that historic journey through the Basin and descent into the Below. He had liked Fallon from the start, but now he admired him as well.

2.7.3

"IT'S A BIG JOB," Fallon conceded. "But it needs to be done."

"You're kidding, aren't you?" boomed Bedford.

Fallon was in the conference room with Bedford and the Missus, and he wished that he was kidding. "No, sir. I think we need to reopen the ramp up to the antechamber and the crossover to the passages to the Basin warehouse."

"Whatever for?" asked the Missus.

"But we gutted the warehouse of everything that could be moved," said Bedford. "The static lights, the excursion suits, tools, spare parts... everything."

"That's because we thought the chancellor might excavate the ruins and find the tunnels. But now, we think he chooses not to go looking for them."

"So?" asked the Missus.

"To effect change, we need to be topside, right?"

"We discussed that already, lad."

"Well, consider the problems of sending everyone up through the hatch, one by one: how much time it would take; the risk of failure if even two Green Jackets were waiting inside the exit cave."

He paused to let the two of them think about what he had just said. "We need a better way to break free."

Bedford and the Missus nodded.

"That means clearing the ramp to the antechamber and the Basin passage, then excavating up through the burned-out ruins from the granary and the butcher's room."

"That'd give us three exits," said Bedford, signaling his tacit approval.

FALLON ate alone at the mess; the rest of the team was busy preparing for their jobs. He returned to his cottage early, showered, and fell into bed. He missed Addie but he knew that he had let her down. He shook his head and told himself he couldn't think about relationships. Relationships would be impossible until this was over—not only for him, but for every person in the quarters. They would all be busy preparing for the move topside and the confrontation with the chancellor's men... a confrontation he would not be part of.

Fallon was satisfied. He had done everything he needed to do down here. Now it was time for him to think about *his* job, to think about how he would make the journey to Eagle's Nest, how he would scale the two-kilometer high Rift. The captain hadn't told him of any passages the Builders might have made. But that didn't mean there weren't any.

As the thoughts roiled in his head, Fallon drifted into an uneasy sleep. He was in the Basin. A translucent organism floated through the mist. The animal looked too heavy to float, with a body that looked like a fancy gelatin mold of unique design with a swarm of delicate tentacles dangling and writhing beneath.

$$x \sim 2.7$$

On the Move

2.8.1

BEDFORD had not seen this level of activity in the quarters since the ragtag group had sealed themselves in—after the Grier estate burned—but they'd only had sixty-odd *kons* at the time. Now they had four times that many and all of them were busy.

As he descended the granary entrance ramp, Bedford was careful not to get in the way of the people hauling carts of stone down the narrow passage. It was more than 160 meters from the basement of the Greer estate's burnt-out ruins to the quarters. They had been working for less than a day, yet Bedford could tell that progress was slow. He smiled ironically as he realized they had sealed themselves in maybe *too* well.

The diggers would clear the crossover to the Basin tunnels before they reached the antechamber. At least that path would be relatively easy to unblock and, since they had left the Basin tunnels undamaged as a diversion for the chancellor's search, they could breach the hidden door to the butchery without much trouble. That would give them one more route to the surface, even if they couldn't clear the antechamber in time.

Bedford was thankful for the open space of the quarters when he exited the passage. He turned toward the Commons and saw a flicker of light in a portion of the cavern ceiling beyond. For some reason, the power to that section of "sky lighting" had malfunctioned during the 280 annums of disuse. The engineering avatar, Anika, was helping Randall and his crew track down the problem so the twins could use the so-called playground for training.

The twins... he wanted to check on their progress, so he turned right and started the long trek over to Pod G.

• • •

ENTERING Pod G's entrance tunnel, Bedford felt a bit ashamed that he had never before come to visit Fallon or the twins. He didn't even know which cottage was Sean's. He'd just have to knock on the first door he came to and ask.

When he entered the pod's meeting room, he knew he wouldn't have to ask directions because several people were maneuvering for position to see in one cottage's window and open door.

He approached the small knot of men and women blocking the door and placed a hand on the shoulder of a tall man at the rear of the group. "Excuse me," said Bedford in a pleasant tone.

The man simply shrugged off Bedford's hand and, without turning to look at the interloper, muttered, "Bug off. I was here first."

Bedford clasped the man's shoulder, twisted the fellow in his direction and boomed, "Excuse me!"

"Uh... M-Mister B-Bedford," he stammered as he stepped back, pulling the woman in front with him.

She turned to see Bedford and immediately dragged a shorter woman with her. "Mister Bedford!"

By now the entire gathering at the door and at the window were looking at Bedford.

He didn't want to come off as superior or officious, so he gave them a nod and a smile and asked, "How are the lads doin'?"

The short lady shook her head and clucked, "Tsk. They're throwing each other around like rag dolls."

"Is it true," asked a slightly built man at the window, "that we're going to learn to fight like that?"

"Aye, 'tis true. We'll tell you all about it at tonight's meeting in the courtyard. Be sure to be there. Now, if you can give me some private time with the lads, I'd appreciate it."

As the group broke up and drifted away, Bedford stepped up to the door, leaned a shoulder against the jamb, and watched Sean slam his bigger brother onto the mattress-covered floor.

The twins were drenched in sweat and a rank odor emanated from the room's interior. Sean offered Tobey a hand up.

"How long've you lads been at it?"

Bedford's question and appearance at the cottage door must have startled Sean, for he lost his grip and Tobey fell flat on his back.

"What the B, brother?" griped Tobey.

Sean simply stood up and nodded in Bedford's direction.

Tobey had to roll over and get to his knees before he could see the old man. "Heya, Bedford. What brings you to our humble dojo?"

"Your what?"

"Dojo," answered Sean. "It's what you call the place where you learn this type of fighting."

"So, how long?"

"Since late yesterday afternoon, when Randall's people hooked up the holo-projector." Tobey pointed to the kitchen table, where two avatars stood in silence.

The twins turned to face the avatars, bowed slightly from the waist, and Sean asked, "How was that one, Yamada-san?"

"I think," answered the male avatar, returning the bow, "that you have mastered the move."

"Bennett-san?" asked Tobey.

The female bowed and said, "I concur. I believe you are ready to teach the moves you have studied to others. We hope you will continue your lessons for your personal pleasure after the immediate crisis is over."

Sean and Tobey looked at each other and grinned, and then Tobey said, "We thank you, sensei. We hope we can continue learning from you when this is over."

At that, the avatars faded.

Bedford was more than impressed. "You've mastered the material already? Good work, lads!"

Sean beamed.

"It's only ten moves," replied Tobey.

Bedford raised an eyebrow. "You know the moves... but can you teach them to others?"

"Sure we can," said Sean with his usual swagger.

"Even an old man like me?"

"You?" Tobey shot Sean a questioning glance.

Bedford stepped into the center of the room and removed his jacket. "Fallon said 'every able body,' didn't he?"

2.8.2

Addie worked to gain Danny Bianchi's trust with friendly attention and small talk, but she also encouraged the perception that she held an official position of some sort. Again, her hair was fixed in a tight bun. She wore a simple green dress to which she had added black trim, reminiscent of a Green Jacket's uniform.

She closed the door behind her as she entered the ward with a salver holding a mug of vegetable soup, a half loaf of bread, and bowl of assorted berries.

"Here's some lunch." She smiled kindly and set the salver on the rolling tray at the foot of the bed.

"If you promise to behave, I'll let you feed yourself."

Bianchi's now-bearded face contorted with frustration. He clenched his bound hands into fists and rattled the bed rails.

"That's not an answer, 1251, now is it?" She gave Danny the same look she had received from the Missus all those times she had misbehaved. She must have gotten the look down pat because Danny Bianchi withered under it.

"That's better." Aidan moved to the left side of the bed. "Now do you promise?"

Bianchi nodded.

"I need to hear you say it, 1251."

"Yes... I promise."

After a friendly hand on his shoulder, Aidan moved to his wrist and loosened the strap. When his hand was free, she said, "You can undo the other one and sit yourself up while I move the tray into position. This is a very special loaf of bread, Danny." She positioned the rolling tray so it extended across Bianchi's lap. "Would you like to know why?"

"Uh... Yeah, sure."

"It's from the first batch of flour made from wheat we grew down here."

"Down here?"

"Don't you remember where you are?"

"Base camp."

"Base camp?" As she talked, Aidan casually removed the pins that held her bun in place. "You think you're up at Rift Lake?"

Bianchi's nod was tentative, yet Aidan knew she had his attention by the way he watched her loosen her bun.

Aidan shook her head and her red tresses fell to her shoulders. *Use my charms.*

"Mind if I sit?" she asked demurely. "We can visit as you eat?"

"Uh, sure... why not."

Aidan could see the change that came over Bianchi as he tucked into the meal.

"You're not at base camp, but I'd love to hear about that in a moment or two. You were stationed in Primacitta. Do you remember?"

He paused long enough to close his eyes, as if trying to recall the events of the past few days. "I... I think so."

"Good. That's a good sign, Patrolman. Go on, eat up. As I was saying, that bread was baked with flour made from wheat we grew

165 meters under the surface of Neworld. You're in the infirmary of what we call the quarters. Do you remember that?"

Bianchi's mouth was full, so he shook his head in reply.

"Maybe this will help. Do you remember your last patrol?"

Again, he closed his eyes, giving the question consideration as he chewed. Suddenly he gulped and his eyes snapped wide open.

"You do remember, don't you?"

"It was raining…"

"Yes, 1251, it was raining. You were in the warehouse district…"

"Uh… yeah. It was late. There was a wagon down toward the Promenade… Two men crawled out from beneath the tarp. A grey-haired man and a younger fellow. Something was wrong about them. Something suspicious in the way they moved into the Promenade."

"What did you do?"

"I was alone. I didn't know if I should return to headquarters to report them or follow them myself."

"You followed them, didn't you, 1251?"

"Yes. I'm sorry. I should have reported back."

"No, you did the right thing. Do you remember where they went?"

"Into the wilderness, toward the Rim."

"That's forbidden, isn't it?"

"Yes."

"But you followed."

"Yes…"

"Where did they lead you?"

"Almost to the edge of the Rim. There was a cave… and a ladder down into the ground."

"You followed them down?"

When Aidan saw Bianchi gulp a breath of air and stiffen, she knew he remembered everything.

He pushed the tray away and cowered against his pillows.

"Who are you?" he asked.

"My name is Aidan. My friends call me Addie. But the real question you have to ask is who are you?"

"I'm Patrolman 1251."

"Yes, you *were* Patrolman 1251 but that's not who you really are, is it?"

"I'm... I'm..."

"Think hard. You're not just a number. You have a name?"

"I'm..."

"Do you remember the man you met in the mess when you stumbled in?"

Bianchi shook his head. He looked dazed and tears were forming in his eyes but Aidan pressed on.

"Do you remember the man who sat with you the first night and day you were in the infirmary?"

"No."

Aidan rose and looked down at the frightened and confused man. She held his hand between hers and softly pleaded, "Please try."

"I... I can't remember... Sorry, I can't."

Aidan held his hand a moment longer, then set it down gently. She rolled the tray away from the bed and crossed to the door. As she grasped the knob, she turned to Bianchi and said, "Perhaps this will help."

She opened the door and nodded to the man sitting in a waiting room chair. The man rose and came to the ward door.

"Do you know this man?"

It almost broke Aidan's heart to see the range of deep and conflicting emotions that registered on Bianchi's face before he began sobbing.

Frank Bianchi crossed to the bed, caressed the young man's forehead, and laid a comforting hand upon his cheek. Then, with a trembling voice, he said simply, "Danny."

"Dad," said Danny Bianchi.

2.8.3

ONCE AGAIN, Fallon secluded himself in his cottage. However, this time he wasn't trying to avoid people. He had assigned tasks and trusted that his friends would carry them out. Now he set about *his* business.

He was well rested after a long, peaceful sleep and eagerly started the project he wanted to complete before returning topside. He needed to draw again. It was a way to work through his experiences—to make sense of things.

Jo had his original drawings catalogued in the archive. They included the sketches Missy Howard had taken from him at the Mount as well as those he'd made during his excursion in the Basin and his descent into the Below. All those images still lived vividly in his mind and he could redraw them whenever he wanted to. However, since they had returned from the Basin to find themselves trapped underground, he'd had neither the time nor inclination to draw—except for the dream drawings, that is. He had used them to help exorcise his demons, then destroyed them.

Now he wanted to capture the people, places, and events that shaped their lives underground. So, armed with a sheath of blank paper and a pouch of pencils and charcoals, he set out to create a visual document of life in the quarters.

He drew portraits of every one of the original captives. He documented the structures they'd discovered: the Commons, the aviary, the generator beneath the Rim Falls, the hydroponics farm, the gallery, and the hatch with its cave entrance topside. He purposefully neglected to draw the armory.

He sketched people performing their tasks: cooking, sewing, raising vegetables, or learning about the Builder's technology with the help of the avatars. Each avatar got his or her own portrait because Fallon thought them as real as any living being in the quarters.

He lingered on his drawings of Addie. He thought he'd caught her fiery spirit, but he might be attaching his own feelings to the work. His body responded to the images of her lying nude in bed, washing in the shower, or sitting at the kitchen table with her robe half open.

Was this just biology, this stiffening in his loins? That's what the books at the Mount taught. It was a natural biological urge— the need to procreate. You needed a man and a woman to bring children into the world, and the children needed to be raised. That was the purpose of the contract system.

The Code stated that when a person wanted a child, that person, whether a man or a woman, would contract with a partner and accept full responsibility for the child if the contract was successful.

Biology explained the physical response, but what explained the sense of loss and emptiness he felt without Addie by his side? What explained the ache in his heart?

As he had done with the dream drawings, Fallon ultimately weeded the overly intimate sketches of Aidan from the portfolio and burned them in the kitchen sink. These were personal memories not to be shared.

He bound the other drawings between two pasteboard cover sheets, wrote a note to Jo on the top one, and set the portfolio on the kitchen table in the corner closest to the door.

Still, his project wasn't done. Next, he drew things he could only imagine, things that did not yet exist on Neworld, things he might need to reach Eagle's Nest. Then one last drawing to remind him of his final goal—a sketch of the IE Neworld, the starship waiting for him on an island in the depths of the Below.

He folded these few drawings and secured them in waxed paper. He had to protect them from the rains that would mask his return to Primacitta.

He took the package into the bedroom and tucked it into an inside pocket of the hooded jacket he had laid out on the bed. He made a cursory examination of the other clothes and items he had arranged on the bed and was satisfied that he could throw them into a small backpack and leave at a moment's notice.

Suddenly he was hungry. He craved a good meal and the company of his friends one last time.

He left his cottage and went to call on the twins at Sean's. He was surprised to find the cottage dark and locked.

"Yo, brother," came Sean's voice from behind.

Fallon turned to see Sean stepping out of Tobey and Jo's cottage. "You looking for me?" asked Sean.

"The three of you, actually. Can you all spare the time to come have dinner with me?"

"Perfect timing, brother. We're just about to head over to the Commons." Then Sean called into the house, "Yo, Tobey! Fallon's here."

Tobey stuck his head out the door and said, "Be right with you, Fallon." Then he ducked back in and Fallon could hear Tobey shout, "Hey, Jo! Get a move on. Fallon's here!"

● ● ●

THE FOUR of them sat at a table out in the square. Because of the community meeting scheduled that evening, only skeleton crews were working at the hydroponics farm and the power plant, and everyone else seemed to be eating at once.

Sean was gesturing wildly with his hands and half laughing as he said, "And the old man went flying ass over teakettle!"

"I thought I'd killed him," said Tobey, who obviously took the incident more seriously than his brother. "I honestly did."

"Bedford's a tough old bird," said Fallon. "You know that as well as anyone, Tobey. Now shut up and let Sean finish the story."

"Well, within a half hour, the old man puts Tobey on his back."

"Were you going easy on him, Tobey?" asked Fallon while looking past him at the man approaching.

"Fallon, I swear I wasn't," replied Tobey with a sheepish expression. "Like you said, he's a tough old bird."

"Tough old bird, indeed," came the baritone voice of James Bedford.

Tobey turned, his face red with embarrassment. Sean chuckled and Jo grinned and rubbed Tobey's shoulder soothingly.

Fallon chuckled and asked, "So, Bedford... How many moves have you mastered?"

Bedford rubbed his side and arched his back as if trying to stretch out a pain. "Just the one, he groaned." He put a hand on Tobey's back and said, "I'm looking forward to learning the rest, lad. The both of you are fine teachers."

It was Sean's turn to blush. "Thanks, Bedford. That means a lot to me."

"And to me," added Tobey.

"Now, I'm sorry to break up your little party, but we received word from the gallery. Seems a storm is moving in already. I know it's a bit of a rush, but probably a good thing 'cause the rainy season will soon come to an end and RedNights will be upon us. Can you and Percy be ready to go at midnight?"

"I know I am," answered Fallon. "I'll find Percy and let him know."

"Missus Grier and I will be there to see you off." With a nod of the head, Bedford took his leave.

Fallon saw the sad look in Jo's eyes as she asked, "Want me to go tell Addie?"

"Thanks, but no. I want to stop at the infirmary to find out if Danny Bianchi has any information to give. I'm sure she's there."

As he got up to leave, his friends rose as one. Sean and Tobey shook Fallon's hand and wished him luck. Jo hugged him, kissed him on the cheek, and said, "See you when it's over," but it came out more as a question than a statement.

Fallon squeezed her tightly and said with certainty, "See you when it's over." Then he held her at arm's length and added, "You keep these two scoundrels out of trouble."

He released Jo and addressed the twins: "No matter what the old man says, Bedford stays down here with the Missus and Jo, you hear? And Jo, you find out if there're any other pregnant women down here, will you? And keep them safe when you make the break."

No more words were exchanged but the bonds of promise passed between them just the same.

* * *

FALLON found Percy and gave him the news, then went to check on Danny Bianchi.

The front of the infirmary was dark but Fallon could see lights in the ward so he let himself in. He heard several voices coming from the back room: Dr. Inoue, an older man, a younger man—that must be Danny—and Addie's unmistakable laugh.

Laughter?

As Fallon entered the ward, the conversation stopped and everyone turned to look at him, making him feel like an intruder. Dr. Inoue and Frank Bianchi stood on the left side of the bed, while Addie sat in a chair on the right side.

Fallon's eyes locked on hers for just a second. He saw a small change in her expression that told him she knew it was time for him to go topside. Fallon's throat went dry and he shifted his attention to the younger Bianchi.

"You must be Danny," he said, offering a warm smile.

"Fallon, my boy is back," said Frank Bianchi, waving him forward. "Come. Come meet my boy."

Fallon was grateful that Dr. Inoue backed away to make room for him next to the bed. He wasn't sure he could handle standing close to Addie.

He offered his hand. "Fallon."

"Danny Bianchi." The young man didn't hesitate to shake Fallon's hand.

"I heard laughing when I came in. So, what did I miss?"

Addie didn't seem as anxious as he was to avoid direct contact. "Danny's quite the storyteller. He and Frank were telling us about a misunderstanding two fellows had up at their village inn. But I think Danny has more to talk to you about than family memories." She stood and signaled for the doctor and Frank Bianchi to leave. "Danny, you need to tell Fallon everything you told me. I'm going to give him my notes before he leaves, but I want him to hear it from you. I want him to hear your voice and know that it's all true. Do you understand?"

Danny nodded.

"Good," replied Addie before looking Fallon squarely in the eyes. "I hope he has the information you're looking for." With that, she turned and left, closing the door behind her.

Fallon spent the next hour-and-a-half—all the time he could spare—talking with Danny Bianchi.

The patrolman provided more than Fallon could hope for: the number of Green Jackets in Primacitta, how many were at the base camp and its location on Big Island, the largest island in Rift Lake. Danny told them about the Green Jackets' flasks and how the water gave them energy and made them alert. He detailed the command structure of the Green Jackets and the control the Dark Men had over them. It was evident that he felt guilty for his actions as a patrolman.

Fallon ended his visit by saying, "Once the people know how you were drugged, they won't hold a grudge against any of you. They will only demand justice for the chancellor."

When he left the ward, the doctor and Frank Bianchi returned to Danny's bedside. Fallon surveyed the room but saw no trace of

Addie. He thought to call for her, but then he decided to leave without saying good-bye. It would be easier that way.

"Time to go?" asked Addie as he stepped out of the infirmary.

She was standing near a gas lamp that made her hair seem to dance with fire. The sight of her took Fallon's breath away.

He wished he could have said what was in his heart, but all he could get out was, "Yeah."

Addie stepped forward and handed him a notebook. "I know you have a steel trap of a memory, but this might be helpful to Lenore. You will see her, won't you?"

"Yes. At least, I plan to." Fallon took the notebook and said, "Thanks."

He stood there awkwardly, all the while wanting to apologize... wanting to take her into his arms and kiss her.

"Well, I gotta go."

"Yeah," she said before heading in the direction of the Commons.

$$x\sim 2.8$$

2.9
Moving Forward

2.9.1

THE COURTYARD was jammed with people standing shoulder to shoulder. The tables, chairs, and benches had been moved up against the walls of the surrounding buildings. This allowed access for as many of the 240 *kons* as possible and provided places for those in the back to stand and see over the crowd. The overflow spilled into the lanes separating the structures that bordered the Commons.

Bedford stood on a large rock that dominated one corner of the plaza. Its top had been ground smooth by the Builders and steps had been carved into one side. Missus Grier sat in a chair slightly behind him and to his right. Stacks of papers were lined up along the front edge of the platform.

"No doubt you've all heard the news about our impending move topside." Bedford surveyed the faces before him—most of whom, he was sad to admit, he didn't know. "I can't call them rumors because, as you all know, it's impossible to sneeze down here without everyone knowing."

Laughter rippled through the crowd.

"Just the same, I'm here to confirm the news. We need to be prepared to move topside shortly after Lenore gives us the 'all clear.' You've heard, if not seen, the activity in the passageway that leads up to the estate. We're clearing that route to the surface because the chancellor has shown no interest in excavating the ruins as we first feared, and it's just not feasible to quickly move everyone topside through the hatch.

"Those of you who have joined us down here over the past few months know how the Dark Men and Green Jackets have instilled fear in the people of Neworld. Some of you have been beaten with their clubs, or had sons abducted and carted upslope."

Bedford saw a smattering of heads nodding.

"You all are aware that a Green Jacket found his way through the hatch and that he was our own Frank Bianchi's son, Danny."

As Bedford gestured to the doctor who stood at the foot of the platform with Jo and the twins, he scanned the front of the crowd. *Where in the Below is Addie?* he thought. "Dr. Inoue and Aidan Brennan have tended to the Bianchi boy in the infirmary."

There was grumbling among the throng.

Bedford held up his hands to silence them. "Now, now. The lad's had a rough time of it. He nearly died trying to fight off the effects of the drugs he had been given."

The grumbling instantly turned to utterances of disbelief and anger.

"Danny Bianchi, and all the Green Jackets, are being forced, against their will, to obey the commands of the Dark Men. In other words, they are being used—nay, abused—by Chancellor Brennan. But, armed with their clubs, they're still a threat to us when we move topside."

"I can make clubs in the metal shop," shouted a man from the middle of the gathering, eliciting a frenzy of agreement.

"We'll have none of that," boomed Bedford, silencing the crowd.

"What then?" asked a woman near the front.

"What then? That's a fine question. That's the right question. Sean. Tobey. Please come up here."

"For those who don't know," said Bedford as the twins mounted the platform, "this is Tobey Andrews and Sean Halloran. Sean's the bearded fellow. They're brothers, twins in fact. They were responsible for the historian's safe descent to the Below."

372

This elicited a respectful "Ooo" from the new arrivals.

"These lads will be teaching most of us how to defend ourselves against the Green Jackets. Defend… not attack. Those of you who live in Pod G now know what the brothers have been doing."

"I seen it with my own eyes." It was the slightly built man who had watched the martial arts practice through the window. "Sean, the little one, was throwing his lug of a brother around like a sack of flour!"

"And by the time you're done with training," said Sean, "you'll be tossing my brother to the ground yourself. And I gotta tell you, it's rather satisfying." The assemblage roared with laughter.

Once more, Bedford raised his hands to quiet the gathering.

"But that's only the half of it. As long as the drug is still in their systems, the Green Jackets will continue to fight. We can take away their water flasks, which contain the drugs, but the effects are long-lasting and the withdrawal could kill the innocent lads. But Dr. Inoue has given us hope. We can make an antidote if we get a sample of the tainted water. To that end, Percy Williams is going topside tonight. His incredibly risky mission is to secure the sample the doctor needs."

"Now, on the front of the platform…"

"Where's the historian?" It was a woman's voice, her question then repeated by other men and women throughout the court-yard.

This was the question Bedford had hoped would not come up, especially considering Fallon's position in the minds of the people gathered before him.

"Yeah, where's Fallon?"

"He's leading us topside, isn't he?"

"So why isn't he here?"

"We haven't seen him for some time. Is he okay?"

Bedford wasn't sure he had an answer that would satisfy the people. "The lad's fine," he shouted over the growing din. "He's been working on this plan—among other things."

"Where is he?"

Bedford hesitated before answering. "He's going topside with Percy tonight."

The crowd grew agitated.

"He won't be with us, then?"

Bedford shook his head and the crowd erupted.

"He's the reason I came down."

"Me, too."

"And me."

"He has other things to do," barked Tobey. "He's given us everything. Now he has to go."

Bedford wished Tobey hadn't taken that tone. The crowd was growing hostile. Bedford, for the first time in his life, didn't feel up to the task he faced. The Movement had always been small. He knew everyone and everyone knew him. Again, he looked at the crowd and took in all the unfamiliar faces. *Who are these people?*

"Where is Fallon going?" asked some anonymous person.

"How can he leave?" asked another.

"His place is here!" yelled a third.

All Bedford could think to do was to shout at the crowd, demanding silence. He was about to open his mouth when Sean stepped forward, pointing a finger at the man who just spoken. "*Your* place is here. *My* place is here." He then spread his arms, taking in the courtyard and, ultimately, the entire quarters. "This is where we're needed. Fallon is needed elsewhere. He's put his trust in us to get our jobs done. And I put my trust in him. If he needs to go somewhere, he *needs* to go. Give him your trust even as you work to earn his."

In the silence that followed, Bedford moved beside Sean and put an arm around his shoulder. He finally accepted the fact that the Movement's leadership was now truly in the hands of a younger generation.

"Well said, lad. Well said, indeed." Bedford addressed the now-quiet crowd. "Sean spoke true. We have to work to earn Fallon's trust. We need to work hard. Before you leave, come grab a work and training schedule. You'll find them on the front of the platform. It's an arduous schedule and it starts tomorrow morning, so return to your pods and get some rest."

Bedford sensed movement behind him and turned to see Missus Grier rising from her chair. He knew the Missus was going to speak, so he pulled Sean to one side with him and made room for her to step forward.

The courtyard seemed to freeze, and Bedford could hear the sizzle of the gas lamps surrounding the area. All eyes were on the Missus. Were the people hoping for a better explanation from the Missus—a deeper insight into Fallon's situation? Bedford knew he was. He was soon disappointed.

"One last thing," the Missus began, "the aviary is off-limits tonight. And you in Pod G, no loitering in the meeting room, you hear? I want to give Fallon some peace before he leaves."

2.9.2

MISSUS GRIER, Bedford, and Percy were waiting for Fallon when he entered the otherwise vacant aviary. The Missus and Bedford were dressed in rain gear and Percy was wearing Danny Bianchi's patrolman uniform. "I'm not late, am I?" he asked.

"You're early, actually," replied Bedford.

"It's just that I couldn't sit around in my cottage any longer," said Percy. "I came while the meeting was still going on. I didn't want to give anyone a fright, being in this uniform and all."

"Good thinking," said the Missus, pulling up the hood of her rain jacket and offering Fallon her arm. "Mind if we walk with you to the hatch? I've never been there, you know. About time I see it, don't you think?"

When they opened the small door that led from the aviary to the gallery, they faced the double assault of wind and rain. Fallon was grateful for the lack of lightning, at least.

Bedford and Percy led the way, single file. Fallon followed with the Missus, shifting her to his left arm to keep her to the inside of the narrow gallery and shield her from the bad weather.

Since the wailing of the wind made it impossible to converse, they walked in silence. Fallon knew that he and Percy could have double-timed it to the hatch in less than a half hour, but progress was much slower with the Missus in tow. More than an hour later, they reached the hatch. The guard on duty stepped to the mouth of the bridge, allowing the four arrivals to slip into a small alcove Randall's crew had carved out to provide shelter to the men and women who guarded the sliding bridge.

The Missus turned to face Fallon, slid her hood back, then pulled Fallon down to kiss him on the cheek. "You'll be okay, won't you?"

Fallon couldn't be sure, but he suspected that not all the moisture on her cheeks was from the rain. "I will. Thanks for asking, Missus."

"Mara, please."

Fallon took her right hand in his, raised it to his lips and kissed the back of her hand. "I'll be okay, Mara. Now you promise me that you and Bedford will stay below ground during the fracas."

He saw that defiant look in her eyes, the look that Addie had either inherited or learned from her.

"Mara?!"

The look faded as the old woman nodded and squeezed his hand.

Fallon hugged her and said, "Thanks for giving me a life." He felt her chest heave as she started to sob. He patted her on the back, kissed her on the forehead, then gently loosened his grip and turned to Bedford, who was shaking Percy's hand. It was a tight squeeze, but Fallon and Percy managed to exchange places.

Bedford and Fallon just looked at each other, saying what needed to be said without words.

"The bridge is across and secure," said the guard.

Bedford offered his hand. Fallon clasped it, but instead of shaking, he pulled Bedford into a hug, then stepped back and said, "Gotta be going."

. . .

MISSUS GRIER found the walk back down the gallery a struggle. It was surely a physical struggle as she and Bedford braced themselves against the wind, but it was also an emotional struggle. It had been less than an annum since she took Fallon from the Mount. Yet, to the Missus, tonight felt like she had lost a child. But Fallon wasn't a child, was he? And not *her* child, for sure.

After Missy Howard's first report about the foundling boy with extraordinary talents, she and Bedford had looked into his past. Who were his parents? How had he come to be left on the steps of the Mount?

Missy Howard suspected that young Fallon was the out-of-contract child of someone who worked at the Mount—staff or faculty—or perhaps the child of someone's daughter. But over the years, she couldn't detect anyone secretly looking after the boy so she took him under her wing, telling the Missus with a laugh, "I'm sure they gossip that I'm his mother."

Mara Grier leaned into the wind and sighed deeply. Fallon had thanked her for giving him life. Her maudlin reflection was broken when Bedford stopped walking, pulling her short. Someone had appeared out of the rain ahead of them. The Missus raised her hand to her face as a shield and squinted into the rain.

"What are you doing here?" she asked.

2.9.3

ABOUT HALFWAY along the Little Silver's course through the wilderness that screened the Rim from Primacitta, Percy led Fallon to the south to avoid exiting the Promenade at the bridge. Now they paused just inside the tree line that marked the border between the wilderness and the Promenade.

"So, what's your plan?" asked Fallon as he surveyed the relatively open area that lay before them. "How're you going to get a sample of the drugged water?"

"I had a chance to talk with Danny Bianchi and he called it his juice—the drugged water, I mean. I'm not quite sure how I'm going to get a sample," said Percy. He looked around. "Okay, I think it's safe now. Let's move."

Fallon pulled up his hood and the two ventured closer to the Promenade and, without the protection of the dense forest, into the full fury of the storm.

"You're going to try to steal a flask?"

"I hope it doesn't come to that." Percy took the flask from his belt, held it up to Fallon's ear, and swished the contents. "I put about one swallow of water in." He returned the flask to his belt. "I really don't want to get more than a block into the citta if I can help it."

"I wouldn't either," said Fallon.

"Danny and I went over patrol schedules and the way the patrolmen interact with each other."

"That was good thinking."

"They have a particular sign they use to identify themselves. It goes like this…" Percy casually touched his right earlobe with his right index finger and then, making a V with the index and middle fingers, touched his left shoulder.

To Fallon, Percy could have been shooshing a bug away or brushing a loose hair or piece of lint.

Fallon suddenly stopped in his tracks, raising one arm across Percy's chest and signaling him to be quiet with the other.

"What?" whispered Percy.

"Did you hear that?"

Percy shook his head.

"A noise behind us, back in the tree line. Like something fell."

The two men cocked their heads to listen.

Nothing.

Percy used his hands to communicate a message. Fallon immediately understood. He continued on their original course and began talking conversationally, as Percy stealthily backed off perpendicular to their line of travel and concealed himself behind a tree. Eleven or twelve paces on, Fallon heard a scuffle and swiveled to see Percy struggling with the hooded figure that had been following them. He heard the person mumble, "filthy Green Jacket."

Percy slipped on the wet leaves and lost his grip. The figure broke free and started to kick him in the ribs, but Percy caught the assailant's foot with his hands, twisted, and brought him to ground.

Fallon straddled the fallen figure and pinned his arms to the ground, allowing Percy to regain his feet.

"Fallon, behind you!" shouted the struggling figure. "It's a Green Jacket!"

Fallon shot to his feet. "Addie?!"

Aidan's hood fell away as she scrabbled backward, pointing at Percy. "Fallon!"

Percy stepped around Fallon, leaned over, and offered Addie a hand up. "It's me, Addie. Percy."

"Percy? What the…? Why…?" she stammered as Percy pulled her to her feet.

"He's wearing Danny Bianchi's uniform." There was anger in Fallon's voice. "It's a ploy to get close to a Green Jacket and secure a sample of the drugged water. Now what the Below are you doing here?"

Rather than being contrite, Addie went on the offensive. She walked up to Fallon and hammered her fists against his chest. "I used my charms, you asshole. I used my charms and did my job."

Fallon wrapped his arms around her, pulling her close and pinning her arms between them.

"And... and you... you were going to leave..." Addie laid her head on his shoulder and began to cry. Fallon could feel the fight drain from her body. "And maybe I'd never see you again... And... and your last word to me was 'yeah'?"

Fallon's arms loosened to a hug. He kissed her on top of the head and said, "Yeah..."

Addie's ire was rekindled and she tried to push away but Fallon held her tight and continued, "Yeah, I know. I'm sorry. There was so much I wanted to say, and the words just wouldn't come out. I'm sorry for what I put you through. I really am." He loosened his grip, looked Addie in the eyes and said, "I love you."

The emotion in Addie's eyes was like none Fallon had seen before. It was more than lust, or friendship, or whatever it was they'd had up till now. It made his heart race and his cheeks warm. He pulled her into a passionate embrace.

"Ahem!" interrupted Percy. "We've got to keep moving."

• • •

THE TRIO walked toward the amber haze of gas lamps diffused through the rain. When they were close enough to the edge of the warehouse district to hear the gas lamps sputter in the rain, two silhouettes of roughly the same height materialized before them.

"Halt! Who goes there?" It was the thinner of the two. The shape of the silhouette's peaked hat identified the speaker as a Green Jacket.

Fallon sensed Percy moving behind him and Addie, followed by a rough shove in the back. He and Addie went stumbling forward, Addie landing on her knees at the feet of the two patrolmen. Fallon bent over to help her up.

"What's going on here?" asked the heavier man.

"My partner and I found these two skulking through the Promenade," said Percy after giving the secret sign of recognition.

Fallon saw the two patrolmen repeat the sign. He pulled Addie close.

"Solarists," said the thin man.

Because of the rain and being silhouetted against the amber glow of the warehouse district, the men's faces were indistinct and Fallon couldn't read them. Addie trembled in his arms.

Percy snorted. "Solarists? Bah! We checked their papers and questioned them. Apparently, the two were running away. The girl was skipping out on a contract, it seems."

The heavy man moved close to Addie and tugged off her hood, then held her by the chin and positioned her face so it was faintly illuminated. "She's too young to be under contract," he said.

Addie snapped her head back, freeing herself from the patrolman's grip, and said, "I'm older than I look."

"Feisty miss," said the thin one. "And who's this? The man you'd prefer to couple with?"

Fallon was about to take a challenging step forward, but Addie stopped him.

"Hardly," she sneered. "He's my brother. He came to help me escape."

"They have papers to travel to a small village upslope," said Percy. I was escorting them back to the edge of the citta and sending them on their way. Say, could you do me a favor, and take the time to make sure they go into the city and not back into the Promenade? I should really catch up with my partner."

"Well…" said the heavy one.

"C'mon. Three, maybe five minutes. You don't have to leave your patrol route. Just watch them."

The thin one jabbed his partner with an elbow. "Sure. Now you two get moving, 'cause we have to be on our way. And be quick about it."

"Thank you, sir," said Fallon.

Behind them Fallon could hear Percy say, "One more favor. My partner and I are both low on juice. Can I swap my flask for one of yours?"

Fallon smiled as he and Addie walked toward the lights of Primacitta.

$$x\sim2.9$$

2.10
Revelations

2.10.1

ADDIE'S naked body was inviting. The smell of her hair was exquisite. Her kiss was tender and passionate. They fell into bed locked in a lover's embrace, which was at once both surprising and comforting.

A rude shaking of the shoulder shattered the forbidden fantasy. "Gabby! Gabby!"

The loss of the dream almost brought Lenore to tears when she opened her eyes to see Julia standing above her cot, holding an oil lamp. Lenore sighed as she became aware of her makeshift cubby, formed by crates and boxes. It was still dark. She shook her head and complained, "What in the B, Julia?" Then, becoming fully alert, she asked "Is something the matter?"

"We have visitors." The older woman sounded excited, but before Lenore could ask who they were, she had gone.

Lenore swung her legs over the edge of the cot, sat up, and rubbed her eyes. She knew it was raining but thought that Percy would have delivered her message by now. She grew concerned. Had Percy been captured? Had he never made it to the quarters?

Lenore stood and left the cubby, hobbling to the table and four chairs in the center of the warehouse floor.

Julia was almost to the stairwell door when Lenore called after her, "Is anyone else here with you?"

"Both Bertie and Jonny, Miss. They're downstairs with the callers."

"Okay, that's good. Have them escort the visitors up to me, will you please?"

She sat down, removed the glass chimney from the lamp on the table, then struck a match and lit the wick, adjusted the flame, and replaced the chimney.

Lenore thought Julia was acting strange. Who could be calling at this time of the night? There was no one from the quarters topside who might use the cover of the storm to return below ground, and she had asked for a suspension of traffic coming up. Could the chancellor's men have found her hiding place?

A minute later Bertie stepped into the room, holding a lantern, followed by the hooded visitors—who were drenched to the bone. Jonny, holding another lamp, brought up the rear.

The visitors approached Lenore as the two teamsters assumed positions to either side of the door some ten meters away.

Lenore was shocked when the callers came within the range of her oil lamp and folded back their hoods. Her mouth opened as if to say something, but she was without words.

Addie crossed to Lenore, her arms held wide. "Don't just sit there. Give me a hug."

Lenore rose and put her arms around Addie. Being taller than Addie, Lenore felt Addie's sodden hair against her cheek. She closed her eyes and her dream came quickly to mind. "Addie."

Then Lenore looked beyond Addie and said, "Fallon."

Lenore chided herself for her cool reception of Fallon. She knew it wasn't his fault that Addie was attracted to him—and not her. In fact, until she started learning about the customs of Earth people, she had thought there was something inherently wrong about her desire for another woman.

Lenore broke off the embrace and gestured to the chairs. "Take off those wet coats and have a seat. Jonny, Bertie, these are two friends: Aidan and…"

"We know Master Fallon, right enough," said Bertie. "We're glad to see him back in good health. That was quite a beating he took. But Julia took good care of him."

"Well, would you please take their wet coats and have Julia set them out to dry? And maybe bring them a pot of hot tea and some cream?"

"Cream!" said Addie. "That's something we don't have…"

Lenore shot Addie a sharp look. The cavern and all its hidden technology was still a well-kept secret topside.

Addie caught her mistake and said, "Um… uh… cream would be very nice."

Fallon pulled out a chair for Addie, then another for Lenore. Before she sat, Lenore moved close to Fallon, gave him a hug, and kissed him on the cheek. She was amused to see the confused look on his face. After all, she had once threatened him bodily harm if he caused Addie any pain.

"Didn't Percy make it…?"

"No need to worry. He's fine, and he delivered your message," said Fallon. "In fact, he came back with us."

"Where is he? Is he coming here?"

"No," said Fallon. "He should be back to the hatch by now."

Addie took up the story. "He only came up to get a sample of the water the chancellor uses to drug the Green Jackets."

"Wait a moment there! The chancellor? Drugs?"

It took till dawn and two pots of tea for Fallon and Addie to bring Lenore up to date on everything that had happened in the quarters since she left—including the details of Addie and Fallon's falling out.

Lenore's first reaction was to follow through on her earlier threat but, as she listened, she felt compassion for Fallon and even sided with Jo on Addie's failure to stick it out—an opinion she would never share with Addie.

But most of all, Lenore was moved by the fact that she was one of the very few Fallon trusted with his struggle over the destruction of the weapons the Builders had left behind.

Lenore saw the lightening skies outside the warehouse windows. Addie's eyes were drooping and Fallon slouched in his chair.

"I'm sorry. You're exhausted," she said, suddenly yawning herself. "Perhaps we should all get a few hours' rest before you tell me why you've come topside."

2.10.2

LIKE LENORE, Dr. Inoue had been up since the early hours of the morning when he was awakened by a pounding on his apartment door.

"Coming… coming," he muttered while fumbling to slip on his pants. Aging was no fun. He was in good health overall, but his body was a collection of minor aches and pains. He adjusted the ceiling illumination, then stretched his back and ran his hand through his tousled grey hair before opening the door.

"Percy!? I thought you went topside."

In reply, Percy simply grinned and held the flask in front of the doctor's face.

Inoue snatched the flask greedily and shook it. "It's nearly full," he gushed. "How did you get it so quickly?"

"I asked."

"You what?"

Percy held his hands out, palm up, and shrugged. "What can I say? I met a couple of patrolmen and asked them for it."

The doctor's aches and pains seemed to dissolve away as a wave of adrenaline coursed through his veins. He felt young again. "Well, why are we standing here? I need to get this down to the infirmary."

"And I'll go let Bedford and the Missus know you've started your work." Percy turned to leave.

"Thanks," the doctor called after him.

Inoue finished dressing and went downstairs to the infirmary, not turning up the ceiling lights until he had quietly closed the patient ward door. He set the flask on the center examination table, and activated Dr. Hadjh.

"Great news, Doctor," said Inoue, sliding the flask in front of the medical avatar. Inoue had so completely accepted Dr. Hadjh as an associate, he did not dwell on the fact that the flask was half as tall as the hologram.

"Is that the sample, Mathew?" asked Hadjh.

"Yes, Vahin. It is. Tell me, how do we proceed?"

"How much liquid do we have to work with?"

"I'd say slightly less than a liter."

Dr. Hadjh beamed. "Oh, that is most sufficient!"

Inoue heard a whirring sound and looked toward the foot of the table where a panel had slid open.

Dr. Hadjh walked to the end of the bed and Inoue followed. He had seen this panel before. It consisted of a transparent surface that covered a revolving tray with small, round-bottom dimples evenly spaced around its circumference. The tray rotated, aligning one of the dimples with an opening in the transparent cover.

"This procedure is much the same as the blood test we ran earlier, Mathew. Let's start with five samples of ten milliliters each."

After retrieving a small glass bowl and an eyedropper from the supply cabinets, Inoue carefully poured a little of the tainted water into the bowl, then skillfully extracted ten milliliters of fluid with the dropper and deposited it in the exposed dimple. The tray rotated, and Inoue repeated the process until all five samples were distributed. The tray rotated once more, moving the samples away from the opening, and the panel closed.

"How long will it take to find an antidote?"

"That depends upon the composition of the drug," said Dr. Hadjh. "However, I would argue that any drug your people may have concocted will be rather primitive... no offense intended, Mathew."

"None taken, Vahin."

"As I was saying, to formulate an antidote for a simple drug, it will take less than an hour, I estimate."

"That quickly?"

"If it's simple."

Inoue was filled with optimism. "Then we'll be ready in plenty of time."

"Don't be so hasty, Mathew. We may have a formula but it will still have to be tested."

Inoue was crestfallen. "How are we going to do that, Vahin? Who would we test it on? Do we need to capture another Green Jacket? All hell would break loose topside if we did."

"We have a substantial supply of the drugged fluid left, Mathew. We can ask for a volunteer to take the drug and..."

"He's right here."

The doctors turned to see Danny Bianchi standing in the patient ward door. "What are you doing up?" as Inoue

"Couldn't sleep and I heard you talking to someone out here, Doc, so I came to see who it was."

"How much did you hear?"

"Enough to know you need someone to test the antidote on." said Bianchi. "I'm the logical choice to experiment on. It took several doses to have an effect, I think, so maybe I'd be affected by it more quickly than someone else."

"But you've been through the withdrawal, Danny," said Inoue. "If the antidote doesn't work, you might not survive a second time."

"That's just it, Doc. I'm the only one down here who understands the risks. I'm the only one who doesn't have a job to do. Let me do this. Let me contribute to the effort."

THE PLAYGROUND was more than just the sandy pit Tobey originally thought it was. The large rock lining the east side of the pit had been carved to form three tiers of seating that could easily accommodate the thirty people in each defensive training session. The ceiling light above the area was a simple white light with no ability to change color or show images such as clouds or the sun.

When the ceiling light was finally repaired by Randall and his crew, they made a discovery. Hanging from the ceiling on the east side of the playground was what could be best described as an extremely thin, white wall. After making the find, Randall called Tobey and his brother to the pit and told them what he had learned from Anika, the engineering avatar: the wall was a video screen that could be operated from a control panel at one end of the seating platform.

Sean was sitting next to this control panel while Tobey stood in the sand in front of the stands. This was the first of eight training sessions scheduled for the day.

"Welcome," said Tobey, sizing up the group sitting in the stands. "We're not all in the best of shape. You won't be tossing anyone about today." This elicited chuckles from the students. "We need to work up to that. Mostly, we'll exercise and loosen up for the first couple of sessions. For future reference, please wear loose clothing so you can move easily. And make sure you can shed a layer or two, because you're going to sweat."

Tobey nodded to Sean and the screen lowered from the ceiling behind, stopping less than a meter above the sand. It was roughly sixteen meters wide by nine meters tall.

"Before we begin, we want to give you a little taste of what's in store. Please meet Yamada-san and Bennett-san." The avatars appeared as twelve-meter-tall projections on the screen—not live, interactive avatars, but recorded images. "They will guide us through the moves we need to learn in order to defend ourselves when we move topside. Sean, start the video."

The students ooh-ed, aah-ed, and winced as the people on the screen progressed through the sequence of moves and their many variations.

When the picture went dark and the screen began to rise, someone called out to much laughter, "I'm sore just from watching."

"Okay," said Tobey, backing up from the stand. "Come out here and form three rows. Let's learn how to loosen up so you don't hurt yourself when we start getting serious the day after tomorrow."

. . .

THE COMMONS COURTYARD was empty except for two men sitting at a table. The older man picked at his scrambled eggs while the other ate eagerly.

"You can't do it, Danny," said Frank Bianchi. "I've almost lost you once…"

Danny Bianchi set down his fork and reached across the table to touch his father's arm. He hated to put his dad through this, but he felt a sense of duty. "You heard the doctors. The antidote has to be tested. And I'm the logical person to test it on."

"But what if the drugs make you violent again… make you forget me? What if the antidote doesn't work?"

"It won't make me violent, Dad. I discussed it with the doctors. We think it was the mental conditioning that did that. All the drug does is make a person open to the mental conditioning."

"But maybe you're still under the drug's influence and the doctors are manipulating you to do this."

That possibility hadn't occurred to Danny and gave him pause. He hoped his father didn't notice the flash of doubt in his eyes. "I'm volunteering of my own free will, Dad. Honest."

"And if the antidote doesn't work?"

"They can keep me drugged until they have another formula to test."

"They can't do that forever. They only have the one flask of the drug."

"That's true, but they now know the drug's composition and can make more if they need it."

"That's little consolation, son."

Danny wanted to stop thinking about the drug and what he had done while under its influence so he leaned back in his chair, clasped his hands behind his neck, and gazed at the morning sky. "It looks so real. You say Earth has only the one sol?"

"They call it a sun. And there's a moon that shines with a silvery light at night."

Danny had never heard of such a thing as a moon. "Then it's a second sol... er... sun, surely."

"No, no. It doesn't make its own light like a sun. It reflects the light from the sun."

Danny shook his head in amazement. "You've learned a lot about the Earth, haven't you?"

"It's very fascinating. I've been working for one of Randall's engineers in the hydroponics farm and she explained it all to me."

It gave Danny joy to see his father so excited. "Dad, what are these hider pond farms you work in?"

He laughed. "Hydroponics farm. Let's see... How can I explain them? They're..."

"Can you show me?"

"It's quite a walk. Are you up to it?"

"After all that time in bed, I could use some exercise. I just have to be back in the infirmary after dinner."

"Well then, let's return these trays and get going."

Danny Bianchi wanted to enjoy one last day with his father... just in case something went wrong.

● ● ●

SEAN led the first session after lunch so Tobey sat in the stands with Jo, watching.

"You and Sean were born to this," said Jo, laying her head on Tobey's shoulder.

He put his arm around her and considered what she'd said. "I suppose we were," he replied. "I was thinking that martial arts is worth teaching even after this is over. There's a code of honor that goes with it, y'know."

Jo smiled and patted his leg. "Yes, I know. You've told me several times."

"Oh... uh... sorry."

"I think you're right, though. It would be worth teaching when this is over. Maybe, if people had had the ability to defend themselves, the chancellor wouldn't have been able to frighten them into submission."

Tobey had been watching a woman with an athletic build and shoulder-length, dark brown hair pulled into a ponytail. "Who's that woman?"

"Which woman?" asked Jo.

"The one on this end, in the second row. The one with the ponytail."

"Melissa Chawla. Why?"

"She's been giving Sean the eye."

"Oh, the eye!" teased Jo.

"No, I'm serious."

"Well then, I hope you're right."

"One of Randall's engineers, isn't she?"

"She was," said Jo. "Now she runs the hydroponics farm."

"Really?"

"Yes, really."

Tobey was duly impressed and hoped that she *was* interested in Sean—he deserved to be with someone exceptional. "Yes, I think she'll do."

2.10.2

IT WAS mid-afternoon when Lenore finally roused Addie and Fallon. "Hey, you two," she called. "It's after HighNoon. Bertie brought us some food. Beef stew... with baking soda dumplings..." After receiving no response, she rapped her knuckles against the wall of boxes that gave the couple some privacy and said, "Come join me at the table."

Lenore was starving so she went to the table, sat down, and dug heartily into her bowl of stew.

Addie wandered out of the stacks of boxes. "Beef? Really? I can't remember the last time..."

Lenore gave her another warning look. "Really, Addie. You need to be careful what you say when anyone is around. I trust these people to keep our secrets, but I don't want them to have to lie if the Dark Men show up. In fact, they don't want to know any more than they need to at the moment. So watch yourself, and please remember to call me Gabby."

Lenore was afraid that she had come down too hard on her friend and she was relieved when Addie said, "You're right" and sat across from her at the table.

"Where's Fallon?"

"I don't know," said Addie. "I was going to ask you. He wasn't there when I woke up."

"When did he get up?"

Addie shrugged.

Lenore felt a growing anxiety in her chest. "He wouldn't have gone into the citta, would he?"

Then Lenore finally processed the scene before her. There were only two table settings. Fallon was gone, and Julia knew it. Lenore rattled the plates on the table as she shot up from her chair and headed for the door. "Julia... Jonny... Bertie...?!" she called.

Addie was close behind.

Lenore stopped when she heard the rapid fall of footsteps; several people were rushing up the stairs. She stepped back from the door when Bertie appeared, followed by Julia and Jonny, who stopped just inside the warehouse.

"What is it?" asked Bertie.

Julia held her hand to her chest and asked, "Is something the matter?"

Lenore was furious. "When did Fallon leave?"

"I haven't gone anywhere," said Fallon, stepping between Julia and Jonny, carrying his and Addie's now-dry coats.

Lenore was surprised, relieved, and embarrassed, all at once.

Fallon continued, "I couldn't sleep, so I went down to visit with my old friends. If it weren't for them, I'd be dead."

"Do they know you *did* die?" asked Lenore.

Fallon didn't respond. Instead, he said, "Why don't you and Addie finish lunch, then we need to talk—all of us."

● ● ●

SOON, the whole crew was standing around the cleared table; the chairs had been removed so they could all gather in close. Fallon set the waxed paper package on the table, untied its bindings, and carefully unfolded the wrapping, which he set aside.

He looked solemnly at the teamsters and Julia. "It's time to tell you things I didn't reveal in *The Historian's Tale*. All of Primacitta knows the Dark Men burned the Grier estate to the ground after trapping everyone inside. What you don't know is that Lenore and Addie, here, were in the house."

Julia was confused. "Lenore?"

"My real name is Lenore… Lenore Bedford."

Julia looked at Lenore and gasped. She knew the name from *The Historian's Tale*. "But you're dead."

"I never wrote that they died," said Fallon contritely. "I only said that they were trapped in the manor."

"It's true," said Lenore. "Everyone was safe in the quarters, but Addie and I almost did get trapped when the Dark Men set the house ablaze."

"The quarters?" asked Jonny.

Fallon resumed the story, telling them of the tunnels and caverns beneath the estate grounds—how they were trapped below ground—and describing the amazing inventions the Builders had left behind."

Bertie was puzzled. "Who are these Builders?"

Fallon then unfolded the drawings, revealing his sketch of the IE *Neworld*. He told of the mad dash through the Basin and his descent into the Below. "I know it's a lot to take in, and hard to believe even, but this is the craft—this starship—that brought our ancestors across the vastness of space to settle this world—or rather, a small piece of this world."

"And this 'craft' is just sitting down in the Below?" said Bertie with a touch of doubt in his voice.

"Waiting to be reclaimed," beamed Fallon.

"Then what?" asked Julia. "Say you can get to this... What did you call it? Starship? What then?"

Fallon's eyes brightened as he pointed skyward and said, "We go to the stars."

Jonny gave Fallon a stern look. "After you set things straight here, you mean."

With an inclusive gesture, Fallon said, "*You* will set things right. The Movement is planning to bust out by RedNights. They're preparing for the move as we speak. But they'll need your help topside." It was time to tell them about the Green Jackets, about Danny Bianchi, and the drugged water.

As the story unfolded, Julia was nearly in tears and the men were outraged.

"I promise," said Fallon, "that I'll explain my plan to you all before I leave..."

"Leave?" snapped Jonny. "Where are you going?"

Fallon slid the drawing of the IE *Neworld* off the stack. "This is a map of Neworld." He saw the confusion in the teamsters' eyes.

It looks a bit like the bottom of a boot, doesn't it?" He used a finger to trace around the right side of the map. "This part—the sole, if you will—is our world as we know it, and the heel is the Rift, rising upward. And much like a heel, it is about half as large as Neworld."

Then he pointed to an X centered on the edge of the Rift. "And this is Eagle's Nest." He tapped the mark with his finger. "That's my destination."

"Our destination," said Addie.

Fallon saw the look Lenore gave Addie, but he knew better than to object. "Our destination," he said.

Jonny threw his hands up in the air. "That's crazy."

"Impossible!" said Bertie flatly. "How are you going to scale the Rift? It's two kilometers tall, don't ya know? The weather's bad, the cliff is sheer, and then there's the problem of the gas vents."

"That brings me to this," said Fallon, revealing the next drawing.

Even Addie and Lenore were amazed at what they saw.

"I need to get one of these made before I head to the Rift. Or rather, we'll need two." Then, turning to Addie, he said, "If you're still set on going with me."

Addie responded without missing a beat. "We'll need two."

x~2.10

2.11

Logistics

2.11.1

PLANS are one thing, but execution is another.

• • •

"Maybe I can come work at the farm with you, Dad," said Danny Bianchi from his position on the center examining table. He wanted to part with his father on a note of hope. "Maybe get to know that cute redhead a bit better, you know?"

His father smiled, but he seemed just as tense. "Are you sure I can't stay with you during this?"

"No, Dad. Dr. Inoue thinks it'd be best if it was just me and him." Danny could tell his father was exhausted after the tour to the hydroponics farm and his first training session in the playground. Danny had sat in the stands and watched his old man perform the regimen of stretching exercises led by a tall man with sandy blond hair. Danny had been enthralled with the moving images of people on the screen and the physical feats they performed.

"You're exhausted," he told his dad. "Really, you should head home and get some rest. I'll be okay."

Dr. Inoue entered the ward carrying a glass of what appeared to be water. "Listen to your son, Frank. All we're going to do tonight is have Danny take an initial dose of the juice."

Danny took the glass from the doctor and held it up in front of him. "It looks so innocent, doesn't it? Just a cup of fresh water. We all were parched—all the young men who were marched upslope. Then, when we reached the island, the Dark Men offered us each a single glass of water."

"The skreel," spat his father.

"The Dark Men *are* skreel, Dad. They choose to do the things they do."

Danny looked gravely at the glass and then said, "Just a cup of fresh water" before gulping down the fluid.

"Now go home, Dad. Everything will be fine." He smiled at his father and lay down, adjusting a pillow under his head. "Today was a good day. I almost felt at home in those farms. Come see me after your training session tomorrow evening. I want to hear all about it."

. . .

MARA GRIER couldn't catch her breath.

"We just don't know what happened, Missus," said Dr. Inoue.

She and Bedford had been summoned to the infirmary just before breakfast. When she saw the lifeless body of Danny Bianchi lying on the table, the Missus felt faint and Bedford had to guide her into a chair. She barely registered the conversation that followed.

"Did the antidote kill the lad?" asked Bedford.

"That's just it," said Dr. Inoue. "We never had a chance to administer it. I stayed with the boy all night. He fell asleep easily enough on the hard table, and I dozed in that very chair, Missus. Then about forty minutes ago, he seized violently. It took all my power to hold him down so the convulsions wouldn't send him flying off the table. When I was able to control him with just one hand, I summoned Dr. Hadjh. We tried everything."

Mara struggled to maintain focus. *Was all of this my fault? Was this the result of a young girl's stubborn curiosity? How did that old saying go? "Curiosity killed the skreel."*

"What have I done?" she moaned.

Bedford crouched before the chair and took her hands into his. "You've done nothing, Mara."

She looked at her old friend with rheumy eyes and saw he was crying too. "We're responsible, James. Our childish explorations have led us to this point."

Bedford sank to the floor and laid his head in her lap, as he had done so often as a child. She softly stroked his greying hair, then lifted her head to address Dr. Inoue. "You'd better have someone fetch his father."

"Yes, Missus."

"No, wait," she said, tapping Bedford on the shoulder and starting to rise. We should be the ones to tell him. Come, James. We have to go tell a man his son has died."

• • •

FRANK BIANCHI was devastated. Jo Wilkinson escorted him from the infirmary to his cottage in pod C. He sat with the young woman at his kitchen table, but what he wanted to do was die. He wanted to curl up on his bed and die. The only thing that kept him going was his determination to see his son's body returned home.

"He can't stay here," he pleaded. "I need to get him home. Back among friends."

"We can't do that right now, Mister Bianchi," said Jo. "We can't get him home until we move topside. But I promise, we *will* get you and Danny home. On Earth they called people who sacrificed their lives trying to save others *heroes*. Your son was a hero. Neworld will always remember Danny Bianchi as a hero."

Frank wiped his nose on the sleeve of his sweater. "You promise?"

"I promise."

• • •

DR. INOUE was worried about Bedford and the Missus. They looked drained—defeated, maybe. "The two of you had better get some rest," he said.

Bedford waved the suggestion off and asked, "Any idea yet on what killed the lad?"

"We've analyzed the blood samples and it appears that his body had developed some sort of resistance to the drug, probably as a result of the withdrawal process. Remember, he hadn't been dosed on the days before he stumbled into the Commons. So he was fighting off trace amounts of the drug. When we gave him a full dose, it triggered the body's resistance, but it was just too big a dose for his system to handle."

"What do we do now?" asked the Missus somberly.

Dr. Inoue's mind was clear on this. "We need to find another volunteer. The antidote has been formulated and is ready to be tested."

Missus Grier's response was less than enthusiastic. "How can we ask anyone to volunteer now?"

"Nobody else has the resistance in their blood, Missus. They shouldn't react to the drug the way Danny did."

"I'll do it," said Bedford.

"No offense, Jim," said Inoue, "but you're too old. It's the same reason I gave his dad. We need someone about the age of the Green Jackets. I'll spread the word. Hopefully, someone will step forward."

● ● ●

BY THE TIME Dr. Inoue returned to the infirmary after lunch, more than fifty young men were standing in line, led by Tobey and Sean. He was overwhelmed with the response.

"Thank you for your willingness to help," he said, "but you can all return to your scheduled duties." He rested his hand on the back of the man with whom he had eaten lunch. "Percy Williams has already volunteered."

2.11.2

THE SECOND DAY after his return to Primacitta, Fallon sat at a table on the third floor of the warehouse. He had shoved it close to the window because he needed better light for the job he was doing.

Franklin, the barrister friendly to the Movement, had secured blank official travel papers and several certified real documents. Fallon was using his artistic talents to fill out the required information and forge the necessary signatures.

The teamster documents didn't have to be forged. The members of the guild that moved food, products, and people across the length and breadth of Neworld were fully behind the historian. They had created a number of fictitious member documents that allowed people like Lenore, Sean, and Percy to go upslope and return with new recruits. And they served as the distribution network for *The Historian's Tale*. There wasn't a citta or village in the land that hadn't heard of the historian and learned the truth about Neworld.

Fallon was grateful for the work Julia, Bertie, and Jonny had done. Even now, Julia and Bert were coordinating the manufacture of the objects he had designed and Jonny was securing the use of a wagon and booking passage up the Riftwater.

He was anxious to move upslope but the fabrication of his designs would keep him and Addie in Primacitta for a number of days.

Once everything was in motion, Fallon would lay out the exact plan and timing of events surrounding the breakout. He wished there was some way to know how the search for the antidote was going. It had to succeed. It just had to.

2.11.3

PERCY lay on the examining table, looking at the ceiling. Aside from its slightly acidic taste, the "juice" wasn't hard to swallow.

He twisted his head to the right and saw the blurred faces of Dr. Inoue, Bedford, and the Missus. He couldn't make out if they happy, sad, or angry. Their faces looked as if they were melting.

He turned his head to the left. If he hadn't already known who was there, he would not have recognized Jo and the twins.

"Why donnn't yooo all go-o-o to bed," he said with a slight slur and a crooked smile. "Ah'll be ohh-kay."

Percy felt a hand on his forehead and then heard a man say, "Percy, look at me." It seemed to be an order, so he turned toward the direction of the voice. By the splotch of grey on the blurry figure's head, it must have been the doctor.

"Sorry, Doc. Buut it doesnnn'tseem to be a… afec… affecting mmme. Mmmaybee I need annnother d-d-ossssse."

"Percy," said the doctor, "Raise your right hand."

"Sssurre, doc." His arm felt as if it fairly floated off the table. When his hand came into view he wondered whose hand it was.

"Okay, Percy. You can put it down."

His arm grew heavy and fell with a thud against the hard surface of the examination table.

"Good. Good," said the doctor. "Now Percy, sit up."

Without being aware of how, Percy found himself sitting on the table with his legs stretched in front of him and a man's hand in front of his face holding a glass with no more than a swallow of green liquid in it.

"Percy, drink this," came the doctor's order.

He wasn't thirsty. He didn't really want a drink but he took the glass and downed the liquid.

"Timer started." It was a woman's voice. Jo? "Five seconds…"

His eyes were droopy and he felt tired.

"Ten seconds…"

He felt hands on his back lowering him to the table as his body went limp.

"Fif…"

Then all was silence. All was darkness.

A second later Percy opened his eyes and looked around the examination room. Everyone was still there.

"I told you, you can go home and sleep. This drug just doesn't have an effect on me."

He was confused by the laughter and attention he was getting.

"We did go home," said Sean, patting him on the arm. "It's lunch break, so we came back to check up on you."

Jo picked up a tray from the exam table to Percy's right and showed it to him. "We brought you some soup and fresh fruit and uncooked green beans, the way you like them."

He still didn't fully understand until he tried to sit up. He felt drained and had to ask Tobey for help.

Doctor Inoue placed his fingers on Percy's wrist and took his pulse.

"How do you feel?" asked the doctor.

"A little weak," he replied, "but otherwise I feel fine."

He gave the doctor a questioning look. "Do you mean to say, the drug worked?"

The doctor nodded as Sean said, "You'd do anything the doctor asked. Raise this hand, then that. Cluck like a chicken and kiss my hairy ass."

Jo punched Sean hard in the shoulder.

"You were very open to suggestion," said the doctor. But the antidote put you to sleep in about fifteen seconds and you slept for almost fourteen hours."

Percy was ecstatic. "Then it was a success."

"Yes, Percy," said the Missus. "It was a resounding success."

"However, there is a problem," cautioned the doctor.

"What's that?" asked Percy.

"How do we take the antidote to the surface and administer it in the middle of a skirmish?"

2.11.3

DRESSED in a baggy, white cotton shirt and canvas cargo pants held up with suspenders, Fallon was ready to go. He was practically climbing the walls of the warehouse. He pulled out his pocket watch and checked it for the hundredth time.

He and the team had exhaustively discussed, planned, and replanned every move of the breakout and every contingency that might arise. It would be up to Lenore to put the plans in motion topside, then take them to the Missus and Bedford at the time Fallon had chosen. The teamsters would have to organize and act independently topside, having no way to communicate with those coming up from the quarters.

"It's here," said Bertie, hollering up the stairwell.

Fallon went to the table and picked up the waxed paper package and tucked it inside his white shirt.

"Addie, time to go!" he called.

Addie and Lenore appeared from behind the wall of boxes carrying two teamsters' long-haul travel bags. Addie was wearing the same type of shirt and suspendered pants as Fallon.

Fallon liked Addie's new haircut. She'd had Lenore cut it into a short shag in the tradition of female teamsters.

Fallon grabbed a set of goggles from the table and handed them to Addie, who slid them over her head and let them dangle from her neck. He then placed a billed driver's cap on her head and gave her a kiss. "I like the look," he said.

Donning his own goggles and hat, he took his travel bag from Lenore and gave her a kiss on the cheek. "You take care."

"I will," she said.

Addie set down her bag and hugged Lenore. "See you upslope," she said.

"See you upslope," said Lenore.

Addie lifted her bag and followed Fallon downstairs, where Bertie took Addie's bag from her. "It's in the back. This way," he said.

Jonny, Julia, and several other teamsters were waiting on the loading dock.

"We thought it would be good to keep you among friendly faces while you go through the city," said Jonny. "You sure you can find your way to the docks, now?"

Fallon replied with a good-humored smile, "The map's in my head as clear as day. I can draw it for you if you want."

The other teamsters were driving open-bed, short-haul wagons so it was easy to identify the one he'd be driving. Fallon's transportation was a box-lorry with a semi-enclosed driver's cab. He lowered the tailgate and lifted the back tarp to inspect the interior of the box. His two crates were secured against the front wall of the box and the rest of the bed was stuffed with crates that smelled of soap and cleaning supplies.

Jonny gave Addie a hand up into the covered cab as Bertie introduced Fallon to the oxen. Fallon had tended the Mount's stables so he was familiar with the grooming and feeding needs of horses, but Bertie taught him everything he needed to know about oxen.

"This is Paddy, and this is Troy. Remember, Paddy is always hitched on the right, looking from the cab. Got it?"

"Got it," said Fallon.

"They're as fine a team of long-haulers as you'll find."

"Thanks, Bertie." With that, Fallon climbed into the cab, took the reins, and followed the other wagons into the citta.

x~2.11

On the Move Again

2.12.1

THE SHORT-HAUL WAGONS, with their empty flatbeds and teams of horses, soon outdistanced or peeled away from Fallon's ox-drawn lorry. He lost himself in the jostling of the wagon and the rhythmic CLOP, CLOP, CLOP of the ox hooves on the cobblestone road.

"On the move again," said Addie, breaking a long silence. "Feels good."

Fallon was thinking the same thing. All those years, growing up at the Mount, he had dreamed of leaving and making his way to Primacitta. Dreamed. Ha! It had turned into a nightmare. Now all he wanted was to put as much distance between him and the citta as possible—quite literally. Primacitta and the Rift were on opposite ends of Neworld.

"You're right." Fallon felt the excitement of being on the road. "It feels good." His adventure had begun with a road trip and a mad dash through the Basin to his destiny. He had descended to the lowest depths of the Below and now he would scale Neworld's highest height.

Maybe it was just a projection of his own feelings, but Fallon thought he sensed a tension in the air. People didn't look at each other or offer a friendly greeting or touch of the cap. When a man walked blindly into the street, causing a carriage driver to suddenly rein in his team, the coachman didn't so much as give the pedestrian an angry look. It didn't help matters that there seemed to be a Green Jacket on every corner.

When they reached Port Street, Fallon turned the team south and headed down the brick-paved thoroughfare toward the docks on the Riftwater. He had never seen this part of Primacitta. To him, it was all just a grid of streets on a map. It took all the discipline he could muster not to gawk at his surroundings like the upslope bumpkin he was.

"Another kilometer to the docks," offered Aidan. "You're doing fine. When does the boat start loading?"

"HighNoon."

"We'll be there in plenty of time," she assured him.

Their talk didn't flow as easily as it once had. Fallon felt like he needed to be careful about every word he chose to say. To make it worse, Aidan's remarks were as short and clipped as his. He wondered if she'd ever forgive him for his withdrawal into himself and his dark mood. The relatively smooth passage over the paved street added to the strained silence.

The closer they got to the docks, the more long-haul wagons joined them on the street, both coming and going. Eventually they came to a halt in a long queue outside the entrance to the east-end docks. The street was lined with produce warehouses and vendors, storing and selling every kind of fresh fruit or vegetable that came downriver from the west, and the occasional café that catered to the teamsters and locals. The morning smell of fresh baked bread, coffee, and sausage wafted on the breeze.

The midland docks about two kilometers upriver received raw materials for manufacturing and building supplies like lumber and bricks.

The west-end docks were outside the boundaries of Primacitta and were home to the livestock yards, slaughterhouses, tanneries, and rendering plants. Neworld's predominantly westerly winds carried the smells of these operations inland, dispersing them well before the next town, more than 150 kilometers to the west.

Fallon wanted to ask someone what the holdup was, but he cautioned himself that such a question would show that he wasn't a regular. He was leaning to his right, trying to look down the line of wagons, when he sensed Addie moving. Before he could say anything, she was out of the carriage and moving down the sidewalk, along the row of vendors, toward the docks. Fallon tried not to look upset as she disappeared from view.

The queue moved a few meters, stopped, then moved a few more. Where was Addie?

Then she appeared, a smile on her face as if returning from a pleasant stroll, carrying a cloth sack in her hand.

She climbed into the cab, set the bag on the seat between her and Fallon, and said, "Have an apple."

Fallon half expected her to say, "We don't have those in the quarters." But she just leaned back and propped her feet on the dash of the cab before taking an apple, polishing it on a shirtsleeve and biting in.

"Mmm, crisp and juicy."

That was one of the things he loved about her. She was smart and brash.

"Thanks," he said, taking an apple for himself. "Went shopping, huh?"

"There's a bag of summer cherries in there for later."

Fallon bit into the apple and held it between his teeth as the queue moved a few more meters. He laid the reins on his lap when they came to a halt and started to eat the apple and savor its flavor before asking softly, "What did you see?"

Addie continued to look ahead as she said, "Green Jackets. They're checking the wagons."

"For what?"

"I don't know. I didn't get close enough and couldn't linger to hear what was going on."

Fallon tried not to sound concerned. "They're probably just checking travel papers." He was confident his forged documents would get them through.

"No," answered Addie. "It's more than that. They're checking the beds."

That was troubling. Fallon didn't have a credible explanation for what was in his crates.

The queue moved meter by meter. Soon enough, they reached the front of the line, where two wagons could stand side by side. Fallon's stomach churned as he caught sight of a Green Jacket sipping from his flask. He hoped Danny Bianchi and Dr. Inoue were making progress with the antidote.

"Step down and present your papers."

Fallon slid his goggles off and climbed down. Out of the corner of his eye he saw that Addie had gotten off on her side as well.

Fallon withdrew the leather folio from the pocket on the bib of his apron and handed it to the patrolman. Fallon didn't know how to react to this inspection. Should he smile? Should he look perturbed at the delay? He chose to remain impassive.

After inspecting Fallon's teamster registration, travel papers, and bills of lading, the patrolman closed the folio and handed it back to Fallon without comment.

"Show me your freight," said the patrolman as he stepped to the rear of the wagon.

Addie and another Green Jacket were waiting for them when they got to the back of the box.

"Open," said Fallon's guard.

He and Addie unpinned the tailgate, and then Addie hopped up and drew up the canvas cover.

Fallon noted the patrolmen's initial reaction to the smells that wafted out of the wagon's box.

As Addie's guard inspected the undercarriage, the other patrolman had them remove several crates. Addie slid each one to the end of the tailgate and Fallon manhandled it to the ground.

"What's your cargo?" asked the patrolman while Fallon opened a crate.

"It's on the bills... Bath soaps, mostly," said Fallon.

"I guessed as much when the woman opened the box."

"But also a variety of cleaning supplies," Fallon was quick to add. "And some shop displays in the two larger crates up front."

The patrolman seemed to lose interest quickly and indicated they could put the crates back into the wagon.

"No false bottom," reported the patrolman who searched the undercarriage.

"A man would likely die from the fumes if he stowed away in the box," said the other.

So they were looking for people, thought Fallon. Had the Green Jackets or the Dark Men found out the teamsters were helping smuggle members of the Movement across Neworld?

Just then, there was a commotion in the wagon next to them as someone inside the wagon's cargo box shouted, "We got one!"

The patrolman drew a shiny black club from his belt, motioned for Fallon to be on his way, then rushed to the other wagon, where a Green Jacket was holding a small woman on the tailgate. Fallon didn't recognize her.

"Found her crammed in a side compartment," said the Green Jacket, one hand clutching the woman's neck. He raised the other hand, brandishing a sheath of paper. "She had several copies of *The Historian's Tale* and drawing pencils with her."

The woman took a swing at the Green Jacket's arm in a vain effort to knock his hand from her neck. The man squeezed her neck in retaliation, causing the woman to shriek and resist all the more.

The Green Jacket shoved her violently off the tailgate toward a knot of patrolmen who had gathered at the rear of the wagon with their clubs drawn. They parted, letting the woman crash, screaming, to the ground. Then they encircled her and thrashed her with their clubs mercilessly until the screaming stopped.

Fallon pulled Addie forward and pushed her up into the cab. He followed, grabbed the reins, and urged the ox team through the entrance and onto the dock.

ADDIE fought to hold in the rage. Had they killed that woman? How many members of the Movement had they caught? At the same time, Addie felt ashamed. She should have done something. She should have fought her way through the Green Jackets and shielded the poor woman—the woman who was stealing away upslope to spread the word of the historian.

She felt Fallon's hand settle on her leg. "You'd be dead too," he said softly.

It was as if he had read her mind. Of course he knew what she was thinking! He must have felt the same way after seeing first McCreigh, then Jenna, murdered right in front of him and being unable to do anything about it.

"We need to kill my grandfather."

"We need to bring him to justice, Addie," said Fallon. "We can't just execute him summarily. Earth had a system of courts… trials by jury."

Addie folded her arms and looked straight ahead. She wanted him to hold her, to comfort her, but she closed herself off, not re-alizing that she was doing to Fallon exactly what he had done to her. She felt Fallon remove his hand as he guided the team toward Pier 4. Addie felt alone. She felt like curling up into a ball and going to sleep. She felt like she wanted to die.

"We'll get through this," said Fallon. "I can guess what's going on inside your mind, Addie. Believe me, I can."

"Don't leave me the way I left you," she whimpered, one hand pressed to her heaving chest, the other covering her trembling lips.

"You didn't leave me," said Fallon. "I withdrew from you, from everyone. Stay with me, Addie. I'll always be here."

2.12.2

PIER 4 came into view. Their boat, a side-wheel freighter named the *Misty Waters*, was backed into its berth, allowing its rear railing to lower and form a ramp from the dock to the boat.

Fallon had seen illustrations and plans of various riverboats in the books at the Mount. Every franchise student had to study commerce along the *Riftwater*. With a width of more than thirty meters—including the wheel housings, freighters like the *Misty Waters* could only navigate upriver as far as the twin cittas of Northport and Southport. Fallon and Addie would disembark at Southport.

Beyond that, travel upriver was done in shallow-bottomed stern-wheelers that carried mostly passengers and personal cruisers, so Fallon would take the lorry overland to Gasworks.

He saw a queue of wagons waiting to be loaded onto the *Misty Waters*. In this queue, the wagons stood side by side. He took up station at the end of the queue, tied the reins off on the dash, and turned to Addie. He was concerned for her. "You okay?"

She nodded slightly.

"No Green Jackets here. See?"

Another nod.

"Good. Now, the other teamsters are taking the time to feed and water their teams. We should follow their lead, don't you think? You get the grain and I'll get the water, okay?"

Addie stepped down from the cab and went through the motions of the job. Fallon hoped the work would distract her enough to get them through the loading process without attracting attention.

As they tended to the oxen, Fallon watched SolMajor slowly climb to its zenith. They had barely stowed the feed and water bags when the freight master came down the ramp and approached the line of twelve long-haul wagons. She was a petite woman with a big voice. Her attire was a cross between that of a teamster and a boat captain: canvas pants and white cotton shirt topped with a brass-buttoned, deep-blue wool coat and soft, black officer's cap with a silver braid over the bill. The master unbuttoned her coat, lifted her cap, ran a hand through her short, greying hair, replaced the cap and called, "Get ready to load!"

All the teamsters stowed their gear and climbed into the cabs of their box-lorries.

"They load the wagons going the farthest upriver first, so we should be called soon." Wanting Addie to relax, Fallon tried to start a genial conversation. "Ever been on a boat before?"

"Yes, but not a freighter. Grandma and I took a solrise cruise around Capitol Island once. It was a small stern-wheeler."

Fallon had almost been killed in his encounter with the chancellor on Capitol Island, but he tried to keep the conversation going. "Must have been beautiful."

"It was."

"Roux and Newman," called the master.

Fallon saw Addie's eyes soften with the memory. "This is the first time I've seen the Riftwater, much less a boat. I'm glad you're here with me."

That elicited a trace of a smile. He was making progress.

"Roux and Newman!"

Addie managed a laugh. "That's us. Isn't it?"

Fallon snapped the reins and urged his team toward the boat. As they came alongside the glaring master, Fallon slowed the team and said, "Sorry, Ma'am. This is our first time upriver. Our first long-haul, actually."

"Well, it's not mine," replied the master. "Get a move on. You're on the port side."

Fallon moved the wagon toward the mate signaling him from the left side of the stern ramp. "Hey, I read about Earth boats in the archive." He tried to sound cheery. "Want to hear where the terms *port* and *starboard* came from?"

"No," said Addie with a tone of finality. Then she softened and said, "Sorry. I know what you're trying to do. I appreciate it. Maybe later. Okay?"

"Later," he said with a smile.

It took some urging and the deck mate pulling Troy's collar to get the team up the ramp.

"Keep it close to the rail," said the mate.

The open-air cargo deck began directly behind foredecks, slightly ahead of the wheel housing's axis. It was sloped slightly from front to rear and was covered with wide hardwood planks spaced in a manner that allowed water to be quickly channeled aft. To the fore of the cargo deck was the four-story passenger and crew deck structure.

At less than half the length of the boat, the cargo deck was long enough to easily allow six rigs to line up nose to tailgate, leaving an open area between the cargo and the foredecks. The *Misty Waters* was not an ordinary cargo boat with lines of crates stacked two-high covering the deck. It was a freighter designed specifically to accommodate long-haul rigs. To that purpose, the cargo deck was divided into three parts. Lanes for the wagons ran down each side, and the center consisted of twelve paddocks for the livestock—six to a side. At the front-side of each paddock was a small, white-washed-plank bunkroom where the teamsters would sleep.

"Okay, hold 'em steady there," said the mate as two more of the crew came to help lash the wagon into place. They had stopped just short of the port side paddle-wheel housing.

"Secure," called the crewman on the left side of the wagon.

"Secure," called the crewman on the right.

By this time, a second wagon was pulling in behind them and the crew moved aft.

The mate came alongside the cab and handed Fallon a piece of paper. "Settle your team in Paddock 1. Have you ever sailed with us before?"

"No, sir," said Fallon.

The mate replied, "Meals are served in the crew mess, just forward of here, through those doors, one deck down. You aren't to go on the fore- or upper-decks, okay? Those are for passengers only."

"Okay," said Fallon.

"Obey the rules and you'll have a pleasant enough cruise."

2.12.3

WHEN SHE entered the bunkroom, Addie discovered that it was just that—a narrow room with a set of bunk beds against the left wall. Cabinets with open shelves above lined the far wall. There were no tables or chairs and barely room for two people to squeeze by each other in the alley between the beds and wall.

"Cozy," she said as she hoisted her travel bag onto the cabinet counter. She opened one of the cupboards and found blankets, sheets, and pillows.

She tossed a set of sheets and a pillow onto the bottom bunk and said, "I'm too short to reach up there. You get the top bunk."

"But I thought you liked being on top," said Fallon.

At any other time Addie would have smiled, but not now. She set about making her bunk, taking out her feelings on the sheets and mattress as she snapped, spread, and tucked. She fairly punched the pillow into its case.

She didn't once look at Fallon, who stood out of her way by the door. She could feel him looking at her—could see in her mind the look of concern on his face.

"Are you going to be okay?" he asked in a soft voice.

She threw the pillow at the bed and stood with her back to Fallon, her head bowed and face pressed into the palms of her hands, her nails digging into her skin. She wanted to scream but knew she couldn't let the others hear. She wanted to be alone but she knew she'd have to share this tiny coffin of a room with Fallon for the next five days.

She swore she could feel a claustrophobic compression of air on her back as Fallon drew near. She wanted to retreat, to put more distance between them. When his hands caressed her shoulders and his thumbs gently massaged the back of her neck, the tension and anger began to drain.

After a few moments, she turned to face him and tilted her head back, inviting him to kiss her. He pulled her close and leaned into the kiss—a long, tender kiss.

Addie sagged to the bed, dragging Fallon with her. She rolled away and drew his arm tight around her. She fully understood the heaviness in Fallon's heart.

They lay still in that cramped space, locked in embrace, sharing their overwhelming sorrow.

* * *

THAT EVENING, Fallon stood with Addie at a short stretch of open rail between the last of the lorries and the rear of the boat. They looked across the water that shone blood-red under the light of SolMinor, which had already risen in the east. RedNights had arrived.

The other teamsters were gathered in an area between the paddocks and the forward deck that was set up with tables and benches.

Fallon looked over his shoulder to see if anyone was close enough to overhear before he answered Addie's question. "No, I didn't know who she was, but it's obvious she was one of Lenore's network of scribes." Fallon's hands tightened on the railing as he was overcome with a sudden pang of guilt. He took a deep breath and exhaled slowly, trying to calm himself.

He felt Addie sidle a bit closer, barely touching his arm with her shoulder—a gesture of closeness that wouldn't arouse the curiosity of their fellow travelers.

"You know," she said after a long silence, "I hated those men. I wanted to snatch away one of their clubs and beat them the way they beat her."

Fallon knew the feeling all too well.

"She's dead, isn't she…" Addie said it more as a statement than a question.

Fallon took another deep breath and held it before exhaling.

"Yes," he said simply.

"And you feel responsible, don't you?"

"No, Addie. I don't feel responsible. I *am* responsible. If I hadn't written that blasted tale and drawn those pictures for Julia, Bertie, and Jonny to copy…" He had to pause to collect himself before continuing. "I should have come back to the quarters and talked it over with the Missus and Bedford… I shouldn't have taken such an action on my own."

Addie didn't say anything. She only leaned a little bit closer. He appreciated that she didn't offer any platitudes.

"Excuse me, but I heard you tell the freight master this was your first long-haul."

Fallon turned to see a tall, large-framed woman approaching. She wore a blue kerchief around her neck and short-cut grey hair framed a round, affable face. "Bernice Jepson," she said, holding out a hand in introduction.

Addie stepped forward first and shook the woman's hand. Looking up past the lady's ample bosom, Addie said, "Amanda Roux."

Turning to Fallon, the woman said, "That'd make you Newman."

Fallon nodded at the woman who stood half-a-head taller than him and took her proffered hand. It was a firm grip, but not overpowering. He looked into her bright hazel eyes, accented with deep laugh lines, and instantly took a liking to her.

"That'd be me," he said, not offering a first name.

Bernice Jepson kept a grip on his hand and cocked her head as if to say she was waiting for his given name.

"I just go by 'A.'"

"That's curious," said the woman as she let go her grip.

Fallon laughed and said, "Long story short: My mother named me after her best friend."

"What's wrong with that?" asked Bernice.

"Her best friend was a woman."

"Ah!" said Bernice through a widening grin. "How bad is it?"

"Alman. My given name is Alman."

"Ouch! Friend's name was Alma, eh?"

Fallon nodded sheepishly.

"Then Newman it is." Bernice positioned herself on the side of him opposite Addie and said, "Care to escort a couple of lovely women forward?"

Fallon offered an arm to each woman and started to move along the aisle between the secured lorries and the paddocks.

"I'll introduce you to the others. I think you'll find us long-haulers a friendlier lot than our more competitive short-haul brethren."

The housing that covered the upper halves of the giant paddles dampened the noise of the constantly rotating wheels. In fact, Fallon grew to find the blend of sounds—the churning of the water and the *thrum* of the steam engines below deck—somewhat comforting. The others sat at tables casually arranged among four gas lampposts that ran in a line bisecting the open area between the wheel housings.

Bernice first introduced them to her partner, Mary, a woman about Bernice's age but about Fallon's height and build, and then to the other teams. They moved from table to table, becoming acquainted with their fellow travelers and listening to their lively tales about the long-haul life. There were stories of harrowing moments like being trapped on a burning boat, and a humorous anecdote about the teamster who contracted with three women along his route at the same time.

"Now a woman couldn't do that," said Bernice with a burst of laughter.

Fallon looked across the table at Addie, who was sitting next to Bernice. He was pleased to see Addie's eyes sparkle with excitement as she lost herself in the moment.

"Why not?" asked Addie.

"Think about it, Amanda," said Bernice. "If I wanted to cash in my reproductive chit, it'd be a waste to spend hard-earned credits on multiple contracts when one stiff Rodney will do the job, if you know what I mean."

Fallon's spirits soared when Addie reflexively turned toward him to share her smile.

"And if I contracted to three men seeking heirs and got a bun in the oven, how could I prove whose kid it was?"

Fallon laughed with all the others and the conversation shifted easily from topic to topic until a short, muscular man with biceps the size of Fallon's thighs came from the next table and stood next to Fallon. He tried to recall the man's name... Nelson. The man's name was Nelson and his partner was Fred.

"You was next ta the wagon where they found the woman, wasn't ya?"

The entire table grew silent.

"Yes... Yes, we were," said Fallon.

Nelson looked around and nodded to the men and women at the other tables, who seemed to take it as a signal, for they all rose and gathered in a circle around the table.

Bernice's face had transformed. *A look of suspicion,* thought Fallon.

"We don't know ya," said Nelson.

Addie started to say, "This is our first..."

Nelson cut her off. "So you say… so you say. As I said, we don't know ya, so maybe you're who you say you are, and maybe you aren't."

Fallon heard the threatening tone of Nelson's voice, but he couldn't be sure of the reason for the threat. He looked Nelson in the eye and asked, "Who else would we be?"

"You could be a spy," said another man.

"A spy for whom?"

"For 'whom,'" said a woman. "Did ya hear that?"

"Fancy language for a guildsman," said Nelson. "Sounds like a franchiser education to me."

In fact, during his years at the Mount, Fallon had stolen the best franchiser education any young man could have. He also knew that spying between the franchises and the guilds was a common practice. As a boy, he had even dreamed of becoming a spy for some franchise family or trade guild.

Fallon laughed. "I'm definitely not a franchiser. I was a ward of the state and I grew up as a servant in a franchise school."

"Yeah," challenged Nelson. "Which one?"

"The Mount," answered Fallon without hesitation.

"Neither a franchiser nor a guildsman," said Bernice. "How did you come to get teamster papers?"

Addie turned to face Bernice. "We earned them."

Bernice seized one of Addie's hands, turned it palm-up and shoved it toward the center of the table where everyone could see.

Fallon tried to jump to his feet but Nelson and someone else forced him back down onto the bench.

Bernice turned her free hand palm-up next to Addie's. "Then where are your calluses, young lady?"

The crowd grumbled angrily.

Addie snatched her hand away and hid it on her lap.

A man said, "They're the chancellor's spies!"

"He's a bloody Green Jacket," said a woman.

The crowd tightened in around Fallon. Someone slapped him alongside the head. Another man had Addie by the hair.

All my fault, came Fallon's tormented thought.

Bernice leaned forward and addressed Fallon directly. "Let us make this clear, Master *Newman*, the men who were driving that wagon were friends of ours. They were beaten and hauled away to who knows where."

This raised the ire of the teamsters to another level. Fallon feared where this was headed.

"We knew what they were hauling," said Bernice. "I can tell you this because unless you can convince us otherwise, you're never going to make it off this boat. You heard our stories… bad things can happen to inexperienced drivers."

Fallon winced as Nelson dug powerful fingers into his shoulder. "Those skreel you report ta will never know what happened to you."

"To a person, we're supporters of the historian," said Bernice. "If that's what you're trying to find out, you don't have to go snooping about. That woman? She was a trained scribe who could copy the tale and the historian's drawing, to boot. Our guild has dedicated itself to spread the word across Neworld. Is that clear enough for you?"

"Clear enough," said Fallon.

Nelson grabbed Fallon's hair and yanked his head backward. "So what do you have to say for yourself, Master *Newman*?"

$$x \sim 2.12$$

Stories Told

2.13.1

FALLON lifted his hands in surrender, hoping Nelson would release his head, and was stunned when the muscular man slammed his face into the table.

Nelson withdrew his hand and took a step back, which allowed Fallon to lift his head and try to staunch the flow of blood from his nose.

Bernice undid the kerchief around her neck and tossed it toward Fallon, who picked it up without comment. "Well? What have you got to say?" she said.

Fallon closed his eyes as he tilted his head back and pinched the bridge of his nose. "Nudd-ing," was his nasal reply. Even without seeing them, he could feel the knot of teamsters tighten around him and Addie. These were the historian's followers. They were *his* people. He started to laugh at the irony of the situation, but coughed instead. He convulsed forward and hacked a clot of blood onto the table.

He saw a blur of motion as Addie wrenched herself from the hands gripping her shoulders and headed across the table to stroke Fallon's head.

Addie faced the crowd. "How could you? Do you know who…?"

"No!" barked Fallon. Then he took Addie's hand from his head and held it in his. "No," he repeated, more gently this time.

He sat up straight, dabbed at the blood drying on his upper lip and chin, and then threw the sodden kerchief in Nelson's face.

He stared at the teamster and said, "Get me some paper and a pencil." It was a command, not a request.

Nelson clenched his hands into fists and started toward Fallon.

"Get Master Newman his paper and pencil," said Bernice. When her partner began to get up, Bernice motioned for her to sit. "Nelson, I think he was asking you."

Nelson gave Bernice a defiant look before leaving the table.

With that, Fallon knew who the leader of this little group was. He nodded his appreciation to Bernice and then said, "Back off" to the men and women immediately behind Addie.

Bernice gave them a look, adding the weight of her power to Fallon's order.

Again, Fallon closed his eyes, took a deep breath, and exhaled slowly. Finding some calm within himself, he opened his eyes and greeted his captors with a genial smile. He locked eyes with Addie, telling her that everything was going to be fine, and they sat silently until Nelson returned and tossed a few sheets of paper and a couple of pencil stubs on the table.

Fallon picked up a pencil and positioned a piece of paper in front of him, hunched over, and began to draw. "This is where I grew up," he said, spinning the finished drawing to face Bernice and shoving it across the table.

He didn't wait for a response. Fallon pulled another paper to him and began another sketch.

Nelson pushed his way through the others to take a position behind Bernice. "That's the Mount, all right," he conceded. "But that proves nothing."

"It proves that he knows the Mount," said Bernice.

"Any franchiser snot who went there would," countered Nelson.

Fallon turned the second drawing and slid it slowly with both hands, a dour expression on his face.

"But no franchiser snot witnessed this."

All the teamsters had seen one or more copies of *The Historian's Tale* and immediately recognized the image of Vernon McCreigh's lifeless body crumpled on the floor.

Bernice looked up from the drawing, her expression shifting from suspicion to sorrow.

Nelson began, "So he can copy…"

"Just close your piehole, Nelson," snapped Bernice. She lifted the sketch and handed it to Nelson. "Just look at the drawing, will you? Look at the detail. There's more there than in the *Tale*'s sketches."

Fallon leaned over the last piece of paper. This drawing took longer as he labored over it, wiping away teardrops so they wouldn't smudge the drawing.

"This wasn't in the *Tale*. It's too horrible to look at and I'll destroy it as soon as you all get this image in your head. That's Missy Howard. Jenna was her name. She was my only friend at the Mount, and I cared for her deeply. That's Chancellor Brennan slitting her throat, spilling her blood over her naked body."

Fallon was careful to make eye contact with each teamster as they handed the sketch from one to another.

The last teamster solemnly set the paper in front of Fallon. He picked it up and displayed it for all to see one last time, the teamsters averting their eyes when it came within their view.

"This image haunts my dreams," said Fallon with a grim look. "As it will now haunt yours."

He then shredded the drawing and stood up. The teamsters parted, giving him room to leave the table. Fallon made his way between the wagons to the side rail. He gazed out over the water, which looked black now that SolMinor had set. Ceremoniously, he dropped the torn pieces over the side, like the spreading of ashes. He knew he would never again draw that image and wished that he could wipe it from his mind.

Addie came to stand beside him, putting her arm around his waist. He, in turn, wrapped his arm around her shoulders and held her close. They stood there in silent thought for what seemed like hours.

2.13.2

ADDIE acceded to Fallon's wish that they seclude themselves in the tight bunkroom as much as possible. She had sneaked off early and fetched some scrambled eggs and toast from the crew mess, hoping to avoid the others. Now he sat next to her on the bunk, their plates in their laps.

"What if one of *them* is a spy?" asked Addie as she idly pushed her eggs around the plate.

Fallon had been pondering that question all night, replaying the events in his restless dreams. "I still can't believe you put hot sauce on your eggs."

"No, seriously," said Addie. "That Nelson was awfully eager to accuse us."

He looked at Addie and shrugged. "I don't know—not for sure anyway—but I think not. I think they were just angry about what happened on the docks yesterday. You know how you felt…" Addie bit her lower lip and looked down at the still-full plate on her lap. "…and we didn't even know them, personally. Those drivers were their friends."

Fallon pulled her close and kissed her on the side of the head, then leaned his head against hers.

Their somber mood was broken by a soft knock on the door.

"It's me, Bernice. Can we talk?"

Fallon looked to Addie, who nodded her assent. He handed Addie his plate, stood, and in two paces was at the door.

Bernice stood in the cool morning fog, her hat in her hand and a contrite look on her face.

"We were hoping that you and Amanda would come have breakfast with us."

Before Fallon could turn to ask, Addie was already at his side. "We'd love to," she said, bowing her head graciously to Bernice.

Fallon let the ladies lead.

Through the morning river fog, Fallon could barely make out the teamsters scattered among the tables. They all appeared to be involved in deep conversations. As Fallon approached, the conversations died as the teamsters turned to look at him. Then, one by one, they removed their caps and got to their feet.

Images of his first visit to the quarters' mess hall after his beating flashed in Fallon's mind. It was a scene that weighed heavily on him—the look of reverence on the people's faces, their hands reaching out to touch him. These people had the same look. He felt flushed and uneasy.

Nelson, with a look of shame on his face, stepped forward and extended his hand.

Fallon instantly wanted to recoil, to retreat back to the bunkroom and shut the door. He fought the urge and accepted Nelson's hand.

Nelson began to speak in a choked voice, "I'm sor…"

"I understand your sorrow. Believe me I do. And I accept your apology."

He saw Nelson's face transform from shame to tearful joy. At that moment, Fallon understood the power of forgiveness.

"And to you too, Miss Amanda," said Nelson, offering Addie his hand.

Addie reached up, pulled Nelson's face to hers and kissed him on the cheek, then whispered something into his ear. Fallon was surprised to see the man nod and openly weep. He wondered what she had said to the teamster.

Fallon was no longer uncomfortable. He moved freely among the tables, Addie at his side, accepting offered hands and apologies.

Bernice eventually guided them to a table stacked with platters of eggs, sausages, toast, and fruit. Fallon watched as Addie loaded a plate with food. He laughed and said, "Is that for both of us?"

"Absolutely not," Addie replied. "I just suddenly feel really hungry."

Fallon felt it too. The release, even temporarily, from the pressure and the sorrow had allowed him to hear his body's demands—it needed food and it needed rest.

They were allowed to eat in peace. After a hearty meal—the most he had eaten in weeks—Fallon made their need for sleep known and he and Addie retired. They snuggled in the lower bunk and almost immediately fell into a deep, restful slumber.

2.13.3

FALLON was shocked to see the red glow of SolMinor outside when they awoke. He figured they must have slept almost twelve hours.

"Wonder if we missed dinner," said Addie.

"Are you hungry again?"

"Not really. But I sure could stand to clean up," she said, fanning her hand in front of her wrinkled nose. "We've been in these clothes for two days now."

"There're towels and soap on the shelves," said Fallon, "so they must have facilities. Grab some clean clothes and let's see where they are."

A female teamster guided them to the crew shower below decks. "Good idea to go this time of day," she said. "You should have the showers practically to yourselves."

They were alone, but they didn't linger—the water was cold. They quickly showered and were soon in fresh shirts and pants.

Fallon reached out with both hands and tousled Addie's damp hair. "I really like this wet-skreel look on you." Addie punched him playfully in the stomach.

Before stowing their gear in the bunkroom, they had dinner in the crew mess.

When he and Addie came out onto the rear deck, Fallon was intrigued to see that the teamsters had pulled a table to the side and arranged the benches almost like a classroom at the Mount. Two rows of benches were set in a semicircle around one central bench. Fallon gave Bernice a questioning look as she approached.

"Some of us have helped move your people to and from Primacitta," she began. "I don't mean some scribe. I mean someone on a mission. Mary and I have never had the privilege, but one team onboard has—Harry and Jan. Do you know who I mean?"

Fallon wondered what this was all about. "Yes, I remember."

"Well, anyway, they said that the gal they took, Gabby was her name…"

Fallon and Addie exchanged knowing looks.

"She said part of her mission was to gather stories for you… the historian. That you were putting together a history of Neworld."

Resisting the urge to clarify that he was no longer the historian, Fallon simply said, "Yes, we are."

Bernice's eyes lit up. "That's what this is," she said, sweeping her hand toward the arrangement of benches. "It's a long trip upriver, and we want to tell our stories to the historian."

2.13.4

JAN WALSH'S TALE

Jan was a short, stout woman in her fifties. Everyone who knew her said she was the best horse and ox wrangler on Neworld.

"Like many men, I suppose, my father, Walter Beecham, contracted with hopes of siring a colt, not a filly. He was a franchiser who contracted with a guildswoman from Rangeland he came to know while managing his family's property up that way.

"Hazel Walsh ran the day-to-day operation of the Beecham family ranch—although she was only twenty-four annums, she managed the place with great skill. Hazel wasn't beautiful but she was a sturdy woman with wide hips and stamina—features my father calculated were perfect for breeding the son he desired.

"Hazel conceived early on in the contract and disappointed my father by giving birth to me. He felt like he was deceived—cheated somehow—and demanded his contract money and reproductive chit back.

"Hazel never told him, but from the first moment she held me in her arms, she didn't want to give me up. She was a shrewd woman and protested father's reneging on the contract, threatening to take the issue before the local board. In the end, she gave him back his chit and used hers instead..."

And with a grin and a wink, Jan continued, "...and kept the contract money for herself, plus a bonus that she held in trust for me. Like I said, she was shrewd woman.

"So I grew up on my father's ranch in a small house over the rise from his. As I grew, my mother had me work at every job on the range. I was taught by the toughest, meanest, most caring people on the range. That's where I learned everything I know about livestock."

"How did you come to leave the ranch and become a teamster?" asked Fallon.

"Well..." said Jan turning to look fondly at her partner. "There was a man."

"But that's a story for another time," said Harry, patting Jan's knee.

• • •

EDDIE FLICK'S TALE

Eddie was a man of average build with sun-bleached hair and a weathered face that made him look ten annums older than his thirty-seven.

"I was destined to be a teamster. Like you, Master Newman, I was a foundling, but my story is quite different from yours.

"My pa, William Flick, was what people call "ruggedly handsome." He was a teamster and was much sought after by women all along his route looking to scratch their itch, if you know what I mean.

"Pa had a certain reputation that made him desirable to women seeking to cash in their reproductive chits. The gossips along his route called him "One-shot Willy" because he sired six offspring in only eight conjugal visits. That appealed to many women, don't you know, franchisers and guilders alike.

"Old Willy was in his forties when he decided to cash in his chit, so he negotiated with my mother, Sally Winters, a woman from Millton who had previously contracted with him. She was the woman who took Pa three couplings to fulfill his contract. She was also the only one to bear a son—and Pa wanted a son.

"Well, it took Dad many trips up and down this here river to get the job done. Wanting to finish the contract, he accepted Sally's invitation to spend HighConjunction with her in Millton. After the first week of being snowed in, Sally had practically wore Pa out—two, three times a day, don't you know?

"Then he discovered that Sally had been taking precautions, keeping Pa coming back for one more try. Seems Sally just liked coupling with Pa. She enjoyed his company, that's what she told him later.

"Anyway, Pa refused to couple with Sally the rest of Conjunction, promising her just one more attempt before he left. For two months he kept her company and told their son—*her* son—stories of his travels. They shared the comfort of her bed but did no more than affectionately cuddle and spoon.

"Then the thaw came and Pa could begin his trip back to Primacitta. The night before he left, Pa made good on his word.

"On his next trip upslope, he went to see Sally and was ready to try one more time. However, when he reached Millton, she gave him the news he had hoped for.

"He completed his route and returned to Millton, giving up his long-haul route to stay close to Sally until I was born and weaned.

"As soon as I was fit to travel, Pa signed on to a new long-haul route in the plains, moving grain and supplies to and from Primacitta.

"As you probably know, the guild provides child care when members are on the road. Well, when I was a little over a cycle old, Pa drove a load of wheat to Primacitta and pulled into the Casey Granary..."

Fallon sucked in a breath and Addie clutched her chest. "The Granaries Fire!" she gasped.

"Yeah. Pa was among the unidentifiable bodies after Casey's exploded and set fire to the district. It was a chain reaction—embers from Casey's ignited the grain dust in every granary that was downwind, don't you see?

"Simply put, Sally already had her son, so the guild took me in, raised me, trained me, and granted me my father's papers when I reached age.

"So you see, I was destined to be a teamster."

● ● ●

JOE AND JOEY'S TALE

Joe and Joey Jones were a father/son team who came from a small town on the south fork of the Plains River. This was the return leg of Joey's first haul. Both were tall and muscular with windblown ginger hair.

"My boy Joey was going to be a farmer," said Joe. "I didn't want the hard, lonely life for him. I gave up my route and made a home in Golden, where his mother lived, so he'd have family around. I worked in the general supplies store and made short hauls between Golden and Agricitta. For twelve cycles it was a good life."

Joey sat next to his father, looking at his feet. "I miss my Ma and sister and all the cousins," he mumbled. Then he looked up and spoke in a clear, proud voice. "I miss the days working in the fields. We ran the Grier's corn farms in the region. But I'll get used to the road, I guess."

Joe set a reassuring hand on Joey's knee. "This is just temporary, son. We'll get back to our life just as soon as we rid ourselves of them Green Jackets. I promise."

"What do you mean?" asked Fallon, wanting to collect as much information on the Green Jackets as he could. "What do they have to do with Joey being on the road with you?"

"You don't know?" The expression on Joe's face seemed to ask *Where have you been?*

"We've been away," said Fallon. "Secluded."

"Hiding?" Fallon saw the challenge in Joe's eyes.

"No…" Fallon hesitated, choosing his words carefully. "More like caged. But that's *our* story to tell… later. Now, about the Green Jackets?"

Joe rubbed his stubbly chin and his eyes displayed a deep sadness. "It was almost a cycle ago, during RedNights last. I was heading home from a haul to Agricitta and I stopped into a public house in a little village west of the citta. I got myself a room and went downstairs to the common room for a bite and a drink. It was fifthnight, a special night in the village when the publican served something called ale. Most of the men who were of age in

432

the village must have been there that night. Enjoying themselves, just letting off some steam."

Fallon and Addie exchanged looks as he continued his story.

"I was sitting in the corner with a father/son long-haul team who were heading back to Primacitta with a load from North Grove. We were having a good ol' time when the locals started pressing a young man to tell a story. He must've had a reputation and they started to chant his name… Dave…? Davey…?"

"Danny," said Fallon.

"Danny!" said Joe. "Why, that's right. Danny. How in the B did you know?"

Fallon felt Addie's hand searching for his. He clasped it and gave it a gentle squeeze. "We've heard a version of the story before. His name is Danny Bianchi. We know that the Dark Men—the Blackcoats is what Danny's father called them—we know that they came and abducted the young men of the village that night and took them upslope."

"Y-yeah," stammered Joe. "B-by Below, that's exactly what happened."

Fallon felt as if he had stolen the thunder from Joe's story. "I apologize, Joe. Please tell us how this affected your son. He was still working on the farm, wasn't he?"

"Yeah, up at Golden. Well, here's the thing: They never laid a hand on the teamster's son. Never even approached our table. In the middle of the fray, the old man grabs me by the collar and says, 'We best be getting out of here.' So we left a few chits on the table and made our way to the stables.

"'What was that all about?' I asked. And he tells me about the stories of Blackcoats coming in the night and stealing young men from small villages, farms, and ranches and taking them west. 'But they don't touch long-haulers for some reason,' he says. Claims he heard that from several teamsters. It doesn't take much thought to put two and two together, now does it?"

"No, it doesn't," said Fallon. "Golden is upslope from the village Danny came from."

"You got it, sure. We helped each other harness our teams and I headed west and they headed east before the ruckus in the public house died down. When the Blackcoats arrived in Golden two nights later, there were no young men to be found, only a thousand acres of cornfields standing two-meters tall."

"You warned them," said Fallon, with a look of admiration.

"He did," said young Joey. "And we lost ourselves deep in the cornfields until HighNoon the next day, just like he told us."

"I couldn't take a chance of them ever coming back, so I told the guild my story and they issued my son apprentice papers and he joined me on my short-hauls until he was able to qualify for long-haul duty. I reckon… I hope… he's safe for now."

• • •

AFTER HEARING Joe Jones's story, Fallon asked for a table, paper, and pencils. The rest of that night's story session became more focused as Fallon and Addie directed the conversation with questions designed to gauge the strength, numbers, and distribution of the chancellor's men.

2.13.5

THE NEXT DAY, three of the teams disembarked at a remote landing along the way—two landings, actually, one on each side of the river. One team got off on the north bank for its route into the lower plains, and two on the south, both heading to Rangeland.

Fallon reveled in the new mental images he could match with descriptions he'd read in the Mount's textbooks. He knew the Riftwater bisected Neworld from the Rift in the west to Rim Falls in the east and was the line of demarcation between the north slope and the south, between the agricultural plains and the sprawling rangelands. From the middle of the river, which was nearly a kilometer wide as they approached the landings, Fallon could not see any noticeable difference in the terrain. However, differences became clear after the *Misty Waters* visited the opposing landings.

The north bank wharves were lined with warehouses that protected and stored unprocessed grains and nuts until they were shipped downriver. One wharf was dedicated to fresh produce, which was loaded onto a steady stream of smaller packet boats.

The south bank could be smelled before it was clearly seen. It was covered with stockyards as far as one could see. On the upriver leg of its cruise, the *Misty Waters* dropped off rigs headed onto the range. On its trip downriver, it would stop and fill any empty livestock paddocks with cattle, horses, sheep, and goats bound for the rendering plants west of Primacitta.

But there was something just inland from the south bank that Fallon could not see, but knew was there—a number of gas lines. Engineered by the Builders, these lines were the arteries that carried the refined gas to power and light all of Neworld. When he had discussed his plans with the captain, Fallon learned everything there was to learn about Gasworks and the gas-vent mines at the foot of the Rift. In fact, he now knew more about them than anyone on Neworld. He knew their secret.

x~2.13

2.14
The Quarters

2.14.1

PERCY was breathless when he finally tracked Bedford down in the stands at the playground. "We're through! We've cleared the antechamber and breached the granary room in the manor!"

Bedford was elated. That meant they would have three routes ready for the breakout. Crews had already broken through to the Basin warehouse, giving them access to the northern end of the manor's basement. The antechamber now gave them access to the south end. And, of course there was the hatch.

"That's excellent news—excellent news, indeed." Bedford wiped perspiration from his forehead and neck with a towel, then patted the empty spot next to him on the carved stone bench.

"Have a seat. I think we both need to rest a minute or two." He took a deep draft from a bottle of water. "You should grab a drink yourself. That's a long run, from the anteroom." He asked the woman in front of him to pass a fresh bottle back to Percy.

"What are you doing here, anyway?" asked Percy. "You don't need to train. You're not on the list to go topside during the breakout."

Bedford chose to answer Percy with a hard stare that said: "No way in Below am I going to stay down here. And don't even think of challenging me on this."

He took another pull of water, stood, and said, "If you've caught your breath, I'll walk with you back to the anteroom and inspect the progress." He held his mostly-empty bottle in front of him and swished its contents. "But first we have to make a side trip to the infirmary. There's a meeting I need to attend."

2.14.2

THE NEWS of the breakthrough spread through the people in the stands like ripples on a pond.

Sean was complimenting the trainees from his just-completed session while Tobey was organizing the next group out on the sand. Sean could feel the charge of energy the news had instilled in them.

He felt a hand on his back and turned to see Melissa Chawla.

"It is true?" she asked. "They've broken through to the granary?"

"I didn't hear it myself, but Percy just gave the Old Man the news and the two of them headed off in that direction."

Melissa's almond-shaped brown eyes lit up as she took Sean's hands in hers. "That's great news!"

Sean's heart skipped a beat.

"How 'bout we talk about it at dinner?" she said.

Sean was stunned. Beads of sweat broke out on his forehead. "Uh, that'd be great," he said.

"It's a date, then," said Melissa.

"It's a date," repeated Sean, his mouth widening into a smile.

She leaned in and gave him a peck on the cheek. "I'm late for a meeting." She picked up a small cardboard carton from one of the bench seats. "Gotta run. See you tonight." With that, she headed toward the Commons.

Sean felt lightheaded—dazed, even. He caught sight of Tobey in his peripheral vision and turned to find his brother looking at him with a stupid grin on his face. When Sean made full eye contact, Tobey irked him further by lifting his eyebrows twice and pursing his lips into a mock kiss.

Sean felt his face grow hot. He scowled at his brother and made a rude gesture.

2.14.3

BEDFORD greeted the Missus, Doctors Inoue and Hadjh, and Brian Randall, who were all gathered around the center examination table in the infirmary.

He set the empty water bottle on the table and turned to Percy. "See this bottle, Percy? Can you imagine us all carrying enough bottles of antidote to a fight topside where we're likely to be outnumbered three-to-one?"

Percy shook his head slightly.

"Neither can we," said Bedford. "The good doctors and Randall were charged to come up with a way to easily get the number of doses we need to the surface." He gave Randall an inquiring look.

"We have a solution that I hoped to show you but…"

The infirmary door opened and Melissa Chawla entered.

"Ah!" said Randall. "Have you got them?"

"Right here." Melissa laid a small carton on the examining table and opened the lid, revealing a handful of shiny, translucent spheres.

"What are those?" asked the Missus.

"They're what we call gelcaps," replied Dr. Hadjh. "Soft capsules that dissolve quickly in the stomach. Engineering and hydroponics have worked to prototype these from vegetable-based gelling agents."

Bedford instinctively grabbed Melissa's wrist when she suddenly slammed her fist on top of the carton. "What in the B…?!" he yelled. But when he saw the capsules were undamaged, he was struck dumb and let go of her arm. "What in the B…?" he repeated, this time phrasing it as a question prompted by curiosity.

Randall laughed. "See that, Jim? The capsules are tough but flexible. When packed together, they distribute the weight of a blow."

Melissa removed a capsule from the carton and held it between two fingers. The gelcap flexed as she squeezed

The importance of this fact was not lost on Bedford. "They could survive a blow, like from a club, maybe?"

"Like a club, exactly," said Randall.

"How then do we get the antidote out?" inquired the Missus.

Melissa put the capsule between her teeth, back on her molars, and bit down.

Again, the young woman from hydroponics managed to catch Bedford off-guard. Melissa swallowed and said, "Don't worry. These are only filled with flavored water."

Dr. Inoue picked up the carton. "If we can't get the Green Jackets to bite down, we only need to get them to swallow." He popped a capsule in his mouth and then passed the carton around, inviting the others to try.

"Mmm, strawberry," said the Missus after she decided to bite first.

Melissa looked pleased with her reaction. "Our research indicates that the strawberry flavor will make the antidote-sedative compound palatable."

"Great work, everyone!" said Bedford. "How long before you can produce enough capsules for the breakout?"

"We've already started production," said Randall. "Will tomorrow be soon enough for you?"

For Bedford, this was quickly becoming the best day he'd had since Fallon made his descent into the Below. He felt five cycles younger. Well, everything here seems to be well in hand," he said. "So, Percy, what do you say we take a stroll up to the manor?"

2.14.4

"I'M GOING to go soak in the hot spring before dinner," said Sean as he and Tobey neared the two-story public bathhouse on the south end of the Commons. They had secured lockers in the seldom-used facility when they started to teach their defensive arts classes so they could wash off the sweat and sand before lunch and dinner. In fact, the building had become a widely used facility since the classes began.

Tobey responded with a sly grin. "Something so special to-night that a shower isn't enough?"

Sean ignored the comment and was relieved that Tobey didn't press the matter. When they reached the upstairs locker room, the brothers were greeted by many of the men and women from their last class.

Sean shed his clothes and dropped them on the floor of his locker. Then he pulled clean pants and a shirt from his duffel and hung them on a hook. He grabbed a white cotton towel from a table, secured it around his waist, and headed downstairs to the hot mineral spring the facility was built over.

Steam wafted out of the bath's door as the woman in front of him opened it. He hadn't visited the bath before, preferring a quick shower, but today he wanted to be both clean and relaxed at dinner.

His body was enveloped in moist, warm air as soon as he stepped into the room. The steam was so thick, he couldn't see halfway across the pool. He wasn't sure of the etiquette of such a facility but watched as the woman who entered before him hung her towel on a wall hook and stepped under one of several contin-ually flowing showerheads.

Sean was accustomed to public facilities. He always felt some-what anonymous in the communal showers of the public houses back home. If anyone drew attention, it was Tobey, who had won some notoriety as a pugilist. But now he felt awkward as he hung up his towel and crossed to an open shower. The woman, who was about Jo's age, looked him up and down and flashed a smile when her eyes came back up to his. *Awkward! Why was that?*

He returned the smile and watched her fade into the mist as she waded into the pool. Instead of following in the woman's wake, he walked along the perimeter of the pool, past other bathers gathered in groups of twos and threes. He found a spot where he could sit alone and barely see the nearest bathers on either side. He found that it was two tall steps to the floor of the pool, the first step forming a bench. As he entered the pleasantly warm mineral waters, he could make out small, benched "islands" deeper into the pool. The pool bottom sloped downward, eventually forcing him to paddle to keep his head above water. This was not something he was used to, so he quickly turned back until his feet reached the bottom and returned to the step.

He sat down and found that he could lean back with his arms stretched out on the pool's deck, relax, and enjoy the muscle-relaxing effects of the mineral water. He leaned his head back, closed his eyes, and drifted off.

He was startled awake when he heard and felt the splash of water to his left. He twisted his head to see a pair of shapely calves descending the steps. His eyes drifted up the athletic body of a young woman until they locked onto a pair of almond-shaped brown eyes framed by shoulder-length brown hair.

The woman sat down beside him and said, "You'll be late for our dinner if you nod off in here."

"Did I...? Was I...?" Sean stammered.

Melissa giggled and said, "Yes, you were."

"I'm sorry," said Sean, who silently chastised himself for nearly standing up his first date in forever.

Sean's body tensed when Melissa slid close to him, set a hand on his thigh, and rested her head on his outstretched arm. "Lucky I tried to find a spot that wasn't so close to other people," said

Melissa. "If I hadn't, we could have been sitting across from each other, alone, hidden in the mist."

Sean closed his eyes and willed himself to relax. Melissa must have been able to feel his tension fading for she said, "That's better, isn't it?"

Aside from the intimate body contact, Melissa made no overt sexual moves. Sean shifted his hand to rest on her shoulder.

"We can't be late if we *both* rest for a minute or two, can we?" she asked. She lifted her hand from his thigh and moved it across her body, taking hold of Sean's hand. Leaning forward, she slipped his hand behind her, then pulled his hand forward so he could pull her closer.

She leaned her head toward his, and he leaned his toward hers. Sean found an inner peace he had never known before when he heard her contented sigh and felt the slow rhythm of her breathing as she drifted to sleep. Then he too succumbed to weariness.

2.14.5

BEDFORD and Percy were alone in the antechamber, bathed in the greenish glow of the static lamps. Bedford observed the water flowing from the granary breach, across the floor of the antechamber, and down the ramp. The two men stood near the antechamber wall, where the floor was beginning to dry. "Just like the meat locker," he said.

"Yeah," said Percy. "The late snow that covered the ruins melted and drained to the basement floor—then all the spring storms came. The water had to go somewhere. We're going to let it drain overnight before we start clearing the rubble."

Bedford nodded his approval. "Then we need to hurry because we don't know how soon Lenore will return and give us the go-ahead."

"We have a path topside nearly cleared through the old meat locker," said Percy. "We'll go the last distance right before the breakout. That means we can concentrate all our effort here, so it should go quickly."

"Good work, Percy. You and your team have done a fine job."

"I'll give them your thanks."

"If I can make it back down without slipping and breaking something, we should go report to the Missus."

2.14.6

JO SAT in the Commons courtyard with Tobey. "It's not like your brother to miss a meal. I'm worried."

"I'm not. He's old enough to take care of himself."

She thought Tobey had been acting strange all night. He wouldn't give her a straight answer about where Sean was and he seemed distracted at dinner, turning to look at the mess hall door every time someone entered. Then he insisted on sitting in the courtyard when they had finished eating.

Suddenly, Tobey elbowed her in the side and pointed toward the southern corner of the courtyard. There was Sean... with a woman on his arm. Melissa Chawla, the head of hydroponics.

"Told ya," said Tobey. "Told ya she was giving him the eye. And him giving her extra one-on-one instruction during class." Tobey stood and waved, a broad grin on his face.

Jo could see that Tobey was the last person Sean wanted to see right then. He glanced their way but continued to lead Melissa toward the mess.

"Heyya, Sean!" called Tobey, catching Melissa Chawla's ear.

To Sean's apparent dismay, Melissa turned, smiled, and pulled Sean in their direction.

Jo elbowed Tobey back and said sternly, "Wipe that grin off your face, Tobey Andrews. Why are you embarrassing your brother this way?"

"Believe it or not, I'm not trying to embarrass him. I'm feeling really happy for him. He deserves it."

Jo welcomed Melissa while Sean glared at his brother.

Tobey ignored the glare and said, "I'm Tobey Andrews, Sean's…"

"Bloody B" said Sean. "She knows who you are by now, after how many days of classes, and I'm sure Jo's told you who Melissa is. We've been in meetings together, for cryin' out loud."

"But never formally introduced," said Tobey. Then Tobey bowed to Melissa. "Tobey Andrews."

Melissa proffered her hand, "Melissa Chawla."

Tobey raised her hand to his lips.

With a roll of the eyes, Jo scolded Tobey. "Okay, let's let them go have a quiet dinner."

"Where have you been all this time, brother?"

Sean ground his teeth.

Tobey leaned close and smelled Sean's hair. "You smell so… clean. You *both* smell so clean."

Jo saw the amusement in Melissa's eyes but knew Sean was about to take a swing at his brother. Then she found a way to defuse the situation.

"Oh, look, here comes the Missus," said Jo. "She's with Percy and Bedford."

"They look happy for a change," said Tobey.

"It's good news about breaching the granary," said Jo.

"And about the antidote," added Melissa.

"Go on," prompted Jo. "Spill the beans."

"Spill what beans?" asked Bedford as he and the Missus drew near.

"News about the antidote," said Jo.

"Why don't all of you come sit with us in the mess," said Missus Grier. "Miss Chawla can tell you about her team's marvelous work, Percy can tell you of the progress in the ruins, and you two boys can tell me about the training."

The stately woman put her arm in Jo's as they walked. "And you, Jo," she said. "You record their words. Be sure to mark this day in your history. Mark it as a turning point—as the beginning of the end of our captivity. Tell the story of how a small band of people clawed their way home and sought to restore justice and bring hope to all of Neworld."

x~2.14

Topside

2.15.1

SIX WAGONS continued with Addie and Fallon up to the twin cittas. It was the night before they'd disembark and Fallon had rethought part of his plan. "Things are going to happen in Primacitta before any of you get back."

"What sort of things?" asked Nelson.

"The teamster's guild is going to help my people take back Primacitta and bring the chancellor to justice."

"I tell you, I'd love to get my hands on some of those bloody Green Jackets," said Nelson.

Fallon gave Nelson a harsh look and told the group the truth about the Green Jackets and the chancellor's drugs.

"Once again," said Bernice, "your thoughtless words have made an ox's ass out of you, Nelson."

Fallon and Addie then went on to tell of their life trapped underground, carefully omitting any mention of the trip to the Below or the remarkable technologies the Builders had left behind. Finally, Fallon divulged the plan he had laid out for Lenore, who they knew as Gabby.

"You won't be able to make it back to Primacitta in time to help, but I have an idea how you can be useful out here. He gathered his companions close around the table and began drawing a map of Riftwater Lake. "This is what you can do, and spread the word to anyone else who might have an available wagon, cart, or carriage…"

2.15.2

LENORE was thrilled to be out of the warehouse on this beautiful day. She was traveling as Bertie's short-haul apprentice, Gabby Davis. She breathed in the scent of the pine trees that lined the Rim-side of the road leading north from Primacitta. It was more of a trail than a road and it led into a rarely visited part of Neworld.

Lenore had grown up in the Grier household but had never traveled outside of Primacitta until she took charge of organizing the people topside. In slightly less than six months, she'd traveled the length and breadth of Neworld and one thing stood out in her mind: Neworld was mostly empty. She had seen the images of Earth in the archive. She knew how that planet was overcrowded, and forests and farmland and water had been ravished. On the long overland hauls, Lenore had plenty of time to think. She wondered if the same thing would happen on Neworld. She supposed so… but it wouldn't be anytime soon.

An hour and a half out of the citta, Lenore and Bertie arrived at an abandoned outpost, its original purpose unknown to anyone now alive on Neworld. It was a sprawling, one-story affair with no windows and few doors. Not a *kon* was in sight. Bertie slowed the team and turned them off the road when they reached the far edge of the stone-block building. She directed the team through an arched opening in the middle of the north-facing wall and found two carriages and several horses tied to hitching posts at the far end of the square atrium.

From the looks of it, Lenore thought everyone had accepted her invitation. She pulled off her hat and goggles, set them on the seat, and jumped from the wagon. She then headed to the nearest opening, its wooden door long ago rotted away. She waited there for Bertie to tie off their team and join her before venturing farther into the structure.

"This way," she said, following the dusty footprints that marked the recent passing of people.

The building looked like it might have been a large stable originally. Rotted remnants of wooden stalls lay strewn across the floor, providing concealment for an assortment of skreel that scurried for cover as the intruders passed by. The ceiling had collapsed in several places and shafts of light slashed through the mote-filled air. The people Lenore had come to meet stood in one of the pools of light.

She shook the people's hands as Bertie introduced them. "This is Averill Harper, head of the Guildsman Association. Sarah Fleming, supervisor of the Teamsters Guild. Henry Conrad of the River Pilots and Dock Workers Guild. Helen Hobbs, chairperson of the Merchant's Guild. And these are Jean Connelly and Jasper Ingram, executive officers of the Franchise League. Everyone, this is Gabby Davis."

Jasper Ingram cocked his head and gave Lenore a curious look over his wire-rimmed glasses as he shook her hand.

"Let me be blunt," said Lenore. "None of you would be here if you hadn't read and lent some credence to *The Historian's Tale.*"

Jean Connelly stepped to the front of the group and took stock of Gabby Davis. "Perhaps, Miss Davis, we've come to see exactly what sort of person would spread these accusations against the chancellor and incite unrest in Primacitta."

"Primacitta?" laughed Lenore. "You think the unrest is confined to Primacitta? When's the last time any of you've been upslope? Visited any of the dozens of farm villages on the plains or ranches on the range? The people upslope have lost their sons to the chancellor, who's systematically abducting young men."

"Abducting? For what purpose?" demanded Henry Conrad.

Lenore gave Conrad a hard look. "Where do you think the Green Jackets came from? They've been taken from their homes and forced to serve the chancellor."

"Nonsense!" said Conrad, turning to face the others. "You've seen these men. Do they look like they're being forced to do anything?"

The group began to argue the question among themselves.

"Listen to me!" shouted Lenore, quieting the group and pulling the focus back onto herself. "Remember the brouhaha over the missing Green Jacket a while back? We took him and discovered the chancellor is drugging them."

"*We?*" said Averill Harper. "Who is *we*, Miss Davis?"

"Miss Davis is a ghost, Averill," said Jasper Ingram, separated from the group to stand face to face with Lenore.

Again, Lenore saw that curious look on Ingram's face.

"It's been years," he said with a trace of a smile. "You were probably too young to remember me." He turned to Jean Connelly and said, "Don't you see it, Jean? It's Jim's daughter. It's Lenore Bedford, all grown up."

Doubt shown on the franchise woman's face. "But… she's dead." Jean Connelly came forward and gave Lenore a penetrating look. "They're all dead… Jim, Mara, the two girls, and the entire staff… all dead."

"Yet here I am, telling you that my father, the Missus, Aidan, and the rest are alive… and we need your help."

Jean Connelly, eyes welling with tears, pulled Lenore into her embrace.

2.15.3

FALLON looked at his watch, then slipped it back into his pocket. It was two hours after HighNoon. He stood with Addie at the rear of the boat, watching SolMinor rise on the horizon, right where Primacitta would be. It was easy for him to imagine the citta being consumed in fire. He closed his eyes and tried to picture something more pleasing: like the golden waves of wheat at harvest time or the wondrous flora and fauna he'd seen on his excursion through the Basin.

Addie must have sensed Fallon's withdrawal into his mind, for she bumped her shoulder against his. "You all right?"

Fallon smiled and bumped her back.

"It'll be good to have Bernice and Mary with us all the way to Gasworks," said Addie.

"You know what's really good?"

"No. What?"

"Having you here with me." Fallon pulled her close and kissed her tenderly on the lips.

"Take it to the bunkroom, you two," came Bernice's voice, teasing. "We still have a couple of hours before we have to prep the teams and hitch up the wagons." The older woman came to the railing and stood beside Addie. "Looks like Primacitta's ablaze, doesn't it? Even it was, we couldn't see it this far upriver."

"Reckon not," said Fallon, his arm still around Addie's waist.

"If everything you told us about the Builders is true…"

Fallon and Addie had pulled Bernice and Mary aside after the others retired the night before, and in low tones they entrusted them with the whole truth.

"It is," he said.

"…and they're so smart and all…"

"They are."

"Then why'd they come up with such simple names for places? *First Lake, Second Lake, Third Lake*… C'mon! Take this lake, for instance. I know it's the first lake west of Primacitta, but look at the gorgeous stands of birch trees on the island to our left and on the shore on our right. Why not call it *Birch Lake*? Or since it's the end of the line for boats like this one, maybe *Terminal Lake*? I don't know, but anything would be better than *First Lake*. And this island on the port side—it's called *Long Island*. What kind of name is that?"

Fallon thought a few seconds before responding. "I think that when the map was originally drawn, they scribbled down descriptive or functional names, and nobody took the time to change them. I remember the captain telling me that he wanted to call this river the *Crimea River*, which he thought was very funny." Fallon shrugged. "But I never got the joke."

Bernice shook her head in bewilderment. "I don't get it either."

"What about Gasworks?" asked Addie. That seems like a horrible name for a place to live."

"Wait until you see it. The name is perfect, if you get my meaning," said Bernice with a wink. "Anyway, I just came to tell we'll be unloading before you two but we'll wait for you just outside the Southport Docks gate. It'll be evening when we get underway, but the teams are well rested and we're heading into RedNights so we'll have light after SolMajor sets. If you don't mind, I'd like to push on to the first public house out of town."

"Let me guess," said Addie. "Is it called *First House*?"

Bernice laughed. "No. It's the *Come On Inn*, actually. If the weather holds, we should make it to Gasworks in ten days, just about the time things will get exciting back home."

Fallon stared into the boat's wake, which shone like a trail of liquid fire in the red glare of SolMinor. Fallon had a pang of guilt. Was he leaving a path of destruction behind him?

2.15.4

THE TWO officials from the Franchise League were close personal friends of James Bedford and Mara Grier. Lenore's visceral, horrifying tale of the harrowing night the Dark Men sealed them in and burned the manor to the ground both outraged the assemblage and excited them into action.

Her improbable revelations about the underground facilities and the unbelievable discovery deep in the bowels of the Below utterly confounded them.

"Then our whole existence on Neworld has been a lie," said Averill Harper, shaking his head in disbelief.

"No, you can't think that way." Lenore strove to set an encouraging tone and not sound like a scolding schoolmarm. "That's the very type of thinking that worried the historian when he wrote his tale. That's why he didn't tell the whole story—why *we* shouldn't tell the whole story—not just yet."

"But our life here *has* been a lie," said Sarah Fleming.

"Our life here is *our* truth," countered Lenore. "It gave us a framework that has worked and kept us prosperous for 280 annums. Where's the lie in that? Learning about our origins poses less of a threat to our truth—to the life we enjoy—than does the chancellor. He is corrupting the system that has kept us safe."

Lenore paused to let her comments sink in. "Understand this: The actions I'm about to propose are meant to restore our truth, not to destroy it. The six of you and Missus Grier will constitute the new Council and will be entrusted to keep the secrets that should be kept and judge which, if any, of the discoveries we've made can serve the better good of Neworld."

"And who'll be the new chancellor?" asked Helen Hobbs. "Brennan's son is dead, isn't he?"

"Yes, he is," answered Lenore. "But Brennan has an heir. However, first things first." She pulled some folded papers from the front pouch of her leather teamster's apron. "These are the detailed plans we've drawn up. I'll be returning to the quarters tonight, so this is our only chance to coordinate our efforts. For safety's sake, I'm going to talk to you individually—you'll only know your own part of the plan."

After reviewing the plans in detail with each of the new Councilors, Lenore reassembled the group. "Now I suggest that that you separate and don't contact each other again until we meet in the Council chamber. Hide yourselves and organize secretly. Since we'll have no way to communicate between now and then, I cannot emphasize enough how important keeping to the timetable is. Is that clear?" Everyone nodded. "Good." She pulled out her watch and said, "Let's make sure our watches are synchronized. Everything begins in ten days when we break out of the quarters..."

2.15.5

THE GREEN JACKETS only inspected teams that were queued for the return trip downriver, so Fallon had no trouble unloading and meeting up with Bernice and Mary.

Mary was waiting on the curb with two box dinners when they pulled up behind. "To hold you over. It's three hours to the Come On Inn. Just follow us."

They were the only traffic on the paved road after SolMajor set. Fallon considered the type of person it took to be a long-hauler—someone who liked solitude, for sure.

Almost three hours later he spotted the flickering pinpoints of light that could only be gas lamps. The Come On Inn sat on the north side of the road. It was tall and narrow, sandwiched between a general store on the near side and a tackle outfitter on the far. Five small houses lined the south side. Farther to the south, almost to the horizon, Fallon could see two lights that must have been kilometers apart. This was ranch land.

Mary led them past the general store, the inn, and the tackle outfitter, which had a small livery stable tucked in the rear. Bernice jumped to the ground as soon as Mary brought their rig to a halt. She had a puzzled look on her face.

Fallon reined in the oxen and Addie deftly dismounted. "Something wrong?"

"Don't know for sure," said Bernice, looking toward a blue-painted house across the road. "Usually, Sam is right out to meet us."

Just then, Fallon saw the door on the blue house crack open and an elderly man came out on the porch, waving. "Be right there," he called.

"Hmm, that's Ol' Pete, Sam's grandpa."

"Is that you, Mary? Bernice?" called Pete as he crossed the road.

"Sure is," answered Mary. "Where's Sam?"

"Gone west," said Pete. His tone told Fallon the all-too-familiar story.

Bernice shook the old man's hand and said, "Sorry to hear that, Pete."

"Not a young man left on the Beecham and Randall spreads." Fallon thought the man sounded defeated.

"Well, we've got some friends here that'd like to hear your story," said Mary. "Let's get the teams taken care of and then we'll sit and talk a spell. I think you'll feel better afterward."

2.15.6

LENORE wouldn't have the cover of rain, so she wanted to cross into the wilderness boundary where she'd likely not encounter a Green Jacket patrol. She had Bertie drop her off a good kilometer outside of Primacitta. She changed into the clothes she had originally worn the night she came topside, and then she took the backpack and canteen she had stuffed under the wagon seat.

"Take care," said Bertie.

"You too. See you in ten days. Okay?"

"Ten days!" He urged the team on and headed into Primacitta.

Lenore walked straight east until she was no more than one hundred meters from the Rim, then cut south. It was slow-going over the unfamiliar terrain but she reached the Little Silver River before SolMinor had set and was soon crawling through a low tunnel to the ladder that led down to the hatch.

Down the ladder, through the hatch, answer the challenge, across the bridge, and she was home.

Home? she thought. *How strange that this feels like home.*

She was tired from the long walk but anxious to get things moving, so she double-timed it along the gallery. The aviary was empty when she arrived. She commandeered an electric cart and drove to the northeast side of the Commons, then parked in front of the building in which her father had a ground floor room.

Lenore entered the building and knocked softly on the first door to her right. No answer. She knocked a bit harder, and put her ear to the door.

"I'm coming. I'm coming."

She rejoiced at the deep baritone grumblings. Lenore pulled her head back and stuck a finger in the door's peephole. She chuckled when her father complained, "I'm in no mood for..."

The look on his face was priceless.

"It's on in ten days! Are you ready, old man?"

"We're more than ready!"

$$x\sim2.15$$

2.16

The Tenth Day

2.16.1

THE FARTHER west they traveled, the hillier the terrain became. It was like going over a succession of ever-taller waves. In the morning of the tenth day of their journey, Fallon and Addie entered the eastern boundary of the rain forest. There had been trees along much of their route, but the forest grew dense about twelve kilometers before the town of Gasworks. And the trees were taller and thicker than those downslope. The plant life changed from pines, grasses, and bushes to broad-leafed plants and ferns.

Fallon explained the differences to Addie. "The books say the trees and other plants are so different here because of Neworld's weather pattern. You know which way storms mostly come from, right?"

"From behind us," answered Addie. "From the east."

"Right. As the air gets pushed upslope, even on a day like today with only puffy clouds scattered about, the rise of the land squeezes the moisture out. So during our dry periods downslope, they still have frequent precipitation up here. And then there's the Rift, where the humidity is so high, the land is shrouded in constant fog and a permanent bank of clouds obscures the cliffs."

A little before HighNoon noon the trees thinned out as the wagons struggled up a long incline. *This is why long-haulers use oxen,* thought Fallon. He saw Bernice pull to the side of the road and rein in her team. Mary waved for them to come alongside.

As their wagon crested the hill a wide, treeless valley came into view. A lake of brownish haze filled the bottom of the valley and metal spires jutted skyward, periodically spewing columns of flames. From the hilltop, it appeared to be one large tangle of pipes and tanks. A scattering of houses and buildings dotted the far slope above the line of brown haze.

"Welcome to Gasworks," called Bernice. They'll sure be happy to get your soaps." Then she pointed high above the far side of the valley. "That's where you're headed. This is the only spot I know of in all of Neworld where you can hope to see the top of the Rift on a clear day. There, above the cloud bank. It looks like a distant shoreline."

Fallon's heart pounded as he strained to see. *Yes! There it was.* Up there, somewhere, was Eagle's Nest and the answers the captain had promised. He clasped Addie's hand and gave it a squeeze.

"Come on," said Mary. "Let's make our deliveries, and then we'll meet at the Gasworks Lodge. It's up there on the far side, above all the gunk. It's easy to find. Just ask anyone for directions."

* * *

THE FOUR of them ate dinner on the lodge's veranda. The female teamsters made short work of their food, but Fallon and Addie just picked halfheartedly. Fallon kept glancing over his shoulder to the east.

"Tonight's the night, isn't it?" asked Mary.

Fallon had knots in his stomach. "It is."

"Are you worried?"

"I am."

Bernice put down her fork and folded her hands in front of her. "Tell me, do you trust your friends?"

"I do."

"Then trust that they'll do what they have to do, and you concentrate on what's ahead for us."

"Us?" said Addie.

Bernice nodded. "Look, Mary and I've talked it over. It sounds like you might be making a one-way trip so we thought we'd tag along and bring the team home once you've done whatever it is you're going to do. Besides, we've never been further west than Gasworks. So, tell us. Where *exactly* are we going? And what is it you have in those crates?"

Fallon took a pencil and a piece of paper from his pants pocket and began to draw a detailed map of the area. "We're going to take this service trail over to this gas mine here."

"Why there?" asked Mary.

"It's closest to Riftwater Falls."

"No… Why a gas mine?"

"Uh, sorry. It has something I need for these…" Fallon began to sketch.

The teamsters' eyes widened as the drawing took shape, revealing a sphere draped in netting, a thick belt that supported poles evenly spaced around its circumference, and a person suspended below, sitting on a circular platform.

"That's what's in the crates?" asked Mary.

"Two of them, to be exact," said Addie.

Bernice was incredulous. "And they'll get you to the top of the Rift?"

"We hope so," said Fallon only-half jokingly. "The idea came to me when I was dreaming about a creature I had seen in the Basin. It floated through the mist. Remarkably, when I told the captain about my idea and sketched it for him, he didn't scoff. He just said, 'I can help with that.' That's when he told me about the gas mines and their secret."

Fallon let the last comment hang in the air, piquing the teamsters' curiosity.

"Okay, out with it," said Mary. "What secret?"

"You see all that?" Fallon gestured to the hazy valley floor. "All the piping and spires and brown air? It's all for show and it's meant to be unappealing. It's a version of technology that fits within the design of Neworld and it keeps a few hundred people busy. The workers here keep the gas flowing and little else. They think they're processing natural gas that's piped down from the mines, but they aren't. That's all done much more efficiently with the Builders' technology at the mines themselves. Even the Gasworks Council doesn't know how the mines work. They only know the maintenance routines that are performed twice in a cycle."

Bernice looked troubled. "This place... the Fount of Life... the Below... Is our entire life a sham designed to keep us busy?"

Fallon had feared this reaction to the truth. "It's not a sham, Bernice. It's our life. Our work gives us purpose. It's in the Code: We pledge our lives to the service of today and the building of tomorrow. What each and every one of us does, day in and day out, is important to the survival of Neworld."

2.16.1

THE COMMONS was empty. The ceiling sky was off and only the amber light from the gas lamps illuminated the courtyard.

The men and women of the Movement were divided into two groups. Half, with Tobey in the lead, huddled quietly in the Basin warehouse, waiting for the word to make the push to the surface.

The other half was queued down the ramp below the anteroom. Sean stood with Percy at the top of the tunnel that wormed its way up through the charred ruins.

Sean's nose and eyes burned from the acrid smell of scorched timbers and mold. Quietly, he and Percy dislodged the last of the debris, passing bricks and chunks of charred wood along the line of people. The passage was strung with a run of static lamps cranked to give a soft green glow.

"That's just enough room to slip through," whispered Sean. He hoisted himself through the hole and discovered that he was still three meters below ground level. He looked down the hole at Percy and said, "Send up my team, then sit tight until we get back."

Percy's face disappeared and a man's hand reached up through the hole. Sean grabbed it and pulled Frank Bianchi through. No one could deny Frank's request to be part of this team.

Together, Sean and Frank helped the rest of the team to the surface. Roddy Markham, Sandra White, Jerry Franz, and Melissa Chawla were four of their most athletic trainees.

Sean moved toward the remnant of the basement wall and motioned for Frank to give him a boost up. Frank crouched and locked his fingers together. Sean put his foot in Frank's cupped hands and stretched for the surface after Frank stood. He started to pull himself over the edge when the wood he had used as a handhold snapped in two with a loud crack. Sean tottered backward and was about to fall when the fingers of his other hand found purchase. He steadied himself, took a calming breath, and carefully felt the lip of the pit for a solid anchor.

Safely on the surface, Sean cleared the area of loose debris, lay on his belly, and looked down into the pit. "Hey, Rod. Tell Percy they'll need a ladder or three up here." He then offered his hand to the next person in line. As soon as the whole black-clad team was topside, Sean took a moment to get his bearings. Without the reference of the manor house, it was a challenge. Finally, he located the gravel drive and led his team toward the estate's gate.

The drive was a long *S*. Twenty meters from the gate, around the last curve, Sean halted and observed the gateway—an open stone arch with decorative walls that extended no more than three meters to either side.

No guards.

He split the team in two, going the rest of the way in the trees that bordered the drive. Sean, Roddy, and Sandra took the left side while Frank, Jerry, and Melissa took the right. Sean didn't see any guards until they were just meters from the arched entrance. He signaled Frank, who was across the drive, back pressed against the stone arch, to take that group around the wall to the front of the gate.

Frank nodded and made his move. As the group disappeared around the wall, Sean saw the guards suddenly turn in Frank's direction. With a wave, Sean sprang forward, Roddy and Sandra to either side, catching the two guards by surprise. In the blink of an eye the Green Jackets were on their backs, with Roddy kneeling on one's chest and Sandra on the other. Frank and Jerry had already retrieved the antidote cartons from their jacket pockets and each inserted a capsule into the Green Jackets' mouths, which were held open by their captors.

Sean caught some motion in the corner of his eye, swiveled toward it, and saw Melissa sprinting just inside the tree line paralleling the lane that fronted the estate. Then Sean saw the reason for her move—two more Green Jackets standing in the middle of the paved lane, looking toward the gate. They were immobilized by the initial confusion over what was happening, so Sean bolted into action.

The taller of the two patrolmen told the other to go for help. Then he lifted his club, pulled out a whistle, put it to his lips, and started to blow. The whistle flew from his mouth as Sean's head rammed the man's abdomen at full speed. The patrolman dropped his club when his back and skull struck the hard pavement. Sean had trouble controlling the guard as he thrashed his arms and kicked his legs. "Sorry, brother," said Sean before striking the man's chin with a left hook and rendering him unconscious.

The shorter patrolman made the mistake of starting back to help his partner. Melissa darted from the tree line and called, "Hey, you!" in a low but forceful voice. The Green Jacket was quick and well trained. He pulled his club, spun to face his attacker, and took a vicious swing at the side of her head. But Melissa was quicker. Her left arm flashed into a defensive pose, blocking the man's swing. She reached across her body—just like she had practiced—grabbed the man's wrist, pulled his arm toward her, stepped into her off-balance opponent, and swung him to the ground.

Frank appeared at her side and handed her a capsule. Melissa held it in front of the patrolman's eyes and said, "See this? I suggest you bite down on it and swallow. If you don't, say goodbye to your left testicle. Got it?" She cautiously placed the antidote into his mouth. "Now bite."

The man did as he was told and ninety seconds later he was out cold.

Frank and Melissa each took a leg, dragged the Green Jacket to the gate, and leaned him against a wall, next to the other three unconscious men.

Sean watched as Frank unclipped each of the patrolmen's flasks and ceremoniously poured their contents to the ground, then spit in the small puddle he'd made. Frank looked up and saw Sean staring at him. Sean gave him a nod and Frank nodded back. No more needed to be said.

"Sandra," said Sean, "We've got it here. Time to run back and let Percy know it's safe to bust out."

As Sandra ran down the drive, the remaining team members fished strips of white cloth from their pockets and helped each other tie them around their left arms.

"Our day is done," said Sean, feeling satisfied. "Now all we can do is wait until dawn."

x~2.16

Day 11

2.17.1

PERCY checked his watch, then stared impatiently up the hole. He could sense the pent-up excitement of the people who waited in line below him. "Ladders ready?" he whispered, and not for the first time.

"Three of 'em right here," came the reply.

There was a loud *thud* topside and an instant later, Sandra White's smiling face looked down at him.

"It's a go!" she said, gasping for air.

Percy hesitated, as it took a moment to sink in. *This is really happening!* "A go?"

"A go!"

Percy turned his head to look down the tunnel and shouted. "Crank the lights to full power and pass the word, 'It's a go!'"

The sound of the words being passed down the line filled the tunnel and quickly receded into the distance like a fading echo.

Sandra offered Percy her hand. He grasped it, pulled himself through the narrow hole, and then assisted two others to the surface. The four feverishly began to widen the opening.

• • •

AT THE Basin warehouse, the excavators had more time to prepare the passage through what had been the manor's meat locker. The route was wide and well-braced, with a wooden ramp providing an easy climb to the spot where Tobey, Lenore, and two other men crouched below the last layer of timbers separating them from open air.

Tobey could see the night sky through gaps in the debris. He strained to get a whiff of the pine trees that surrounded the manor, but the smell of charred ruins was too much. He could sense it before he heard it, like a pressure growing; then the mass of people waiting in the warehouse erupted in cheers. Tobey didn't wait for the words to make their way to the end of the line. He crouched below a blackened timber, pressed his back against it, and heaved, using his powerful legs like pistons. The charred wood wasn't much more than a husk, so it snapped in two instead of lifting— and there he was, standing waist-high in a pile of rubble. Lenore and the two men shoved the fragments of broken timber upward and Tobey tossed them clear of the opening.

Two minutes later, the men and women of the Movement, white bands tied around their left arms, were streaming to the surface.

• • •

AT THE CRACK of dawn Sean and Melissa stood in front of the gate, looking at the two Green Jackets—a hundred meters away on either side—and listening to the shrill alarm of their whistles. Every Green Jacket within earshot would soon be on them. Then there were three on the left, five on the right... eight and seven... more than a dozen coming from each direction.

The two patrolmen who had sounded the alert marched toward the gate, their reinforcements in tow.

With a jerk of the head, Sean indicated that it was time to beat a hasty retreat. Shoulder to shoulder, he and Melissa went through the gate and ran down the drive.

Sean looked back over his shoulder. The two patrolmen who had summoned the others turned into the drive, where they stopped and waved the others on in hot pursuit. Sean lost sight of the Green Jackets when he and Melissa rounded the first curve. Twenty strides past the curve, they stopped and listened to the rapid pounding of boots on the gravel.

The patrolmen barreled blindly around the bend in the drive. The first line of Green Jackets stopped in their tracks when they saw the wall of people standing behind Sean and Melissa. The patrolmen who followed plowed into the others and many were sent crashing to the ground.

"You know the drill," shouted Tobey, and the mass of warriors engulfed the floundering patrolmen.

They worked in pairs, one person pinning a Green Jacket to the ground while another administered the antidote. It was all over in two minutes.

Sean separated himself from the cheering throng and saw the two leaders of the pursuit walking around the bend, white bands tied around the left sleeves of their green jackets. "Great work, you two," he said, slapping Jerry Franz and Roddy Markham on the back. He looked around, trying to locate Melissa, and saw her working her way through the crowd with Sandra and Lenore.

• • •

LENORE was exuberant and only hoped the rest of the day would go this smoothly. "That went well," she said when she reached Sean.

"Piece of cake," said Sean, grinning.

Lenore pulled out her watch and checked the time. "The wagons should be here any minute. We'd better get back to the gate."

She led the warriors in a trot around the curve. As they neared the front gate, she noticed Frank Bianchi tending to the four Green Jackets who were still propped up against the inside of the gate's wall. Lenore had been devastated by the news about Danny and could only imagine the grief that Frank must be feeling.

The first wagon appeared in front of the gate as they drew close. The driver wore a white armband and ten or more men and women sat in the bed of the wagon.

"Bertie!" called Lenore.

Bertie jumped down from the wagon and took a defensive stance. "All's well?" he asked, eyeing the two Green Jackets at Lenore's back.

"White bands," answered Lenore, stepping into the lane to shake Bertie's hand. "They're our people. Did everyone get the word out?"

Bertie pointed in the direction from which he had come. "Jonny's right behind... as well as a few others." A long line of short-haul wagons was approaching. Lenore was pleased to see that they all were filled with people.

"Great! Unload your people here, Bertie. We need to put a few of our unconscious friends on the back of your wagon."

"So it worked? The antidote, I mean."

"Perfectly." Lenore pointed to the four young men propped against the wall, dressed only in their skivvies. "There're more down the drive that need to be picked up too. Frank, here, will help you load these boys into your rig and return with you to the warehouse to tend to them. Jonny and two other wagons will be right behind you as soon as they drop off their people. And Frank..."

"Yes, Lenore?"

"Tell Dr. Inoue to ride to the warehouse with Jonny."

The Movement's warriors walked down the drive, led by two-dozen white-banded patrolmen, all of them parting to make room for the wagons as they passed.

Lenore picked two men at random and pointed them to the patrolmen's uniforms Frank had folded and stacked neatly by the wall. Then she wrangled several others to help her manage the flow of the wagons.

As each warrior was paired with a citizen, Lenore noted how pallid her comrades looked compared to the people from topside. The citizens each received a carton of antidote capsules and brief instructions on what to do. Then the loading process began. Lenore figured each of the first eight wagons could carry ten citizen/warrior teams, making an initial strike force of 160 people.

Sixteen people sat in the bed of each of the eight wagons, with two faux patrolmen standing in the rear corners and one in the seat next to the teamster driver. As each wagon was reloaded, it moved down the lane.

When the eight rigs were queued, Lenore walked down the column, making sure everyone knew what was to happen next and wishing them luck.

Sean and Tobey stood in the rear of the first wagon. "You're good to go," she said. "We'll be a half hour behind."

2.17.2

TOBEY held tight to the side rail and tailgate as the small caravan clattered down the lane. The wagons turned west at the first crossroad, heading into the heart of the citta, where the Dark Men had commandeered a trade school building and turned it into a headquarters and holding pen for prisoners.

The lead wagon slowed as it neared two Green Jackets on patrol. Tobey gave them the signal of recognition and motioned for them to come near.

"Big ruckus out at the Grier estate," said Tobey, giving the patrolmen the spiel they had cooked up. "A small mob came over from the warehouse district. Said it was some sort of protest." Tobey withdrew his club and slapped it into his palm. "But we got 'em under control in short order. Grab hold of the tailgate and climb up on the running board—we'll need all the hands we can get taking 'em into the pen."

By the time they reached their destination, four or five more patrolmen were hanging onto the back of each wagon. Tobey was satisfied there would be no one left behind to raise an alarm.

The wagons came to a halt in front of the former school. The solid, four-story brick structure consumed an entire block, with wide, stepped entrances in the center of each side. It had once been a boarding school for the sons and daughters of guildsmen. The Movement's reconnaissance indicated that the building housed the Green Jackets and served as their headquarters.

The hangers-on dropped to the street and Tobey helped Sean lower the tailgate, then they started shoving their captives into the waiting arms of the Green Jackets. "Move it. Move it, you scum," Tobey shouted. The same was happening all along the line of wagons.

Tobey followed Sean to the street, where Sean singled out a burly Green Jacket. "Lead 'em in. My partner and I will make sure there're no stragglers."

Tobey gave his brother a quick nod and a wink to say "good thinking!" He and the other warriors knew the general layout of the school but had no idea of procedure once they were inside. Burly Guy would take them right where they needed to be.

With the help of the Green Jackets, Tobey herded his people up the stairs into a large, oval foyer. Curving staircases ran up the side walls, ascending to an iron-railed balcony.

Burly Man led the procession through the foyer, past an intersecting hallway, and toward a rear exit that opened onto the old school's central courtyard. But the way was blocked by a recently added iron gate.

He stopped at a large wooden desk in front of the barred wall. Two hatless Green Jackets, a blond and a ginger, sat behind the desk and gave Burly Man a challenging look. Burly Man gave the signal, identified himself as Patrolman 917, and proceeded to repeat the story Tobey had fed him.

The two men at the desk seemed at a loss for what to do. "How many do you have?" asked the ginger.

Burly Man looked behind at the growing lineup. "Somewhere around a hundred, I reckon."

The blond man whistled. "It'll take forever to process them all."

The ginger scratched his head. "Well, we can't have them all loose like this in the building. We'll pass them through and sort them out later." He stood up, removed a ring of keys from his belt, and crossed to the iron-barred wall.

Tobey leaned close to his brother and whispered, "Hang back and make sure the last of our people are still out here when we make our move." Sean drifted toward the entrance and Tobey followed the first group through the bars, along a short stretch of hall, and through a set of double doors that opened onto a four-sided courtyard. The four sets of steps leading down to ground level were identical to those at the front entrance. The patrolmen stayed on the steps, forming a gauntlet through which the prisoners had to pass.

Tobey positioned himself next to Burly Man on the top landing, just to the left of the double doors. He was repulsed by the smell and outraged at what he saw. Maybe 150 men and women in filthy, tattered clothes wandered listlessly about the courtyard or lay in the shadow of the east wall. The ground was strewn with straw that was clotted with human waste.

Burly Man must have seen the disgust on Tobey's face. "Yeah," he said, "the stench is enough to gag a skreel." Then he unbelted his flask and started to raise it to his mouth.

"Hey, haven't you gotten the word?" said Tobey. "No more juice." He fished a capsule out of his pocket and held it up for Burly Man to see. "They call it *the berry*." Here, have one of mine." He handed the capsule to Burly Man. "Just put it between your teeth and bite. It'll fix you up for hours."

Burly Man took the capsule and was about to put it in his mouth when he looked hard at the prisoners going down the stairs. "Did you notice that?" he asked.

"Notice what?"

"The armbands. They're all wearing white armbands." He inserted the capsule and held it between his molars, pausing as if considering the significance of the bands. Then he noticed the band on Tobey's arm and his eyes widened in realization.

Tobey's pugilistic training kicked into gear. He seized the moment, the fraction of a second it took Burly Man to make the connection, and unloaded an uppercut that slammed Burly Man's teeth together and smashed the capsule.

Burly Man's face registered a rapid succession of expressions: realization, the shock of the blow, and a fleeting look in the eyes that seemed to say, "Mmm, strawberry."

Burly Man tensed, reached for his club, then crumpled into a heap. "Now!" shouted Tobey, and chaos ensued.

● ● ●

THE WARRIORS still in the space between the iron gate and the door surged forward, forcing the assembled Green Jackets into the courtyard proper.

Confusion was rampant as the citizens mistook more than one faux patrolman for a genuine Green Jacket. But this had been foreseen and they dispatched the errant citizens as gently as they could.

One disheveled prisoner crawled from the shadows and snatched up a loose club that came skittering her way. Her face was contorted in hatred. She struggled to her feet, propping her back against the wall for support. A Green Jacket tumbled backward and landed at her feet.

"You skreel!" She kicked him in the side and struck at his head with all her might until a warrior's hand grabbed her wrist on the downswing and pushed her gently against the wall.

"It's all right," consoled the warrior. "It's all right. My partner's taking care of it."

A petite woman in shop-owner's attire straddled the Green Jacket and forced a capsule into his mouth, holding his lips and nose closed until he swallowed. Just before he fell unconscious, the woman tenderly pushed the hair out of the patrolman's eyes and said, "We forgive you."

Inside, Sean and the warriors he had held back stormed the desk and easily disabled the blond and the ginger. The other three sets of door guards must have seen the fight in the courtyard; they set off an alarm and ear-piercing whistles reverberated down the corridors.

Green Jackets came running down the foyer stairs. Sean swiftly divided his forces, each half defending a staircase. No need to advance; just keep the Green Jackets bottled up and the gate open.

• • •

THE OTHER THREE courtyard doors flung open and a stream of green flowed into the battle. "Form up on me!" shouted Tobey as he backed toward the door through which they'd entered. "And lose the hats and jackets!"

They retreated to form a semicircular cordon around the base of the stairs. The Green Jackets formed up into a line four men deep—two hundred men, at least, to the sixty-or-so warriors huddled by the stairs.

The line of Green Jackets advanced, stepping over their unconscious comrades as they came.

• • •

ALL THE GREEN JACKETS' attention was on the incursion in the courtyard. If any of them had looked outside, even drugged, they might have been terrified.

A long caravan of wagons transporting the remaining warriors and their citizen partners clogged the streets surrounding the school and warriors were forming assault groups at each door for their final attack. Behind them came the people of Neworld—franchisers, guildsmen, traders, and laborers—shoulder to shoulder, from every direction, making the street impossible to pass.

The leader of each of the four assault groups cautioned the assembled townspeople to stay out of the building until it was secured. All four groups surged at roughly the same time. Percy's group entered through the south entrance and reinforced Sean's group, fighting their way up the curving staircases.

The other three groups surprised the Green Jackets from behind, giving Tobey's warriors an opening. Confusion was the warriors' worst enemy. Some of the Green Jackets fought their way through the tumultuous mob and made a dash for the front doors, only to be repulsed by the mass of citizens jamming the streets.

• • •

LENORE BEDFORD appeared at the top of the east entrance stairs and shouted, "We've taken back the school and the Green Jackets are subdued." The same announcement was being made at the other three entrances.

The crowd erupted in cheers, and Lenore had to shout above the clamor. "If there are doctors or nurses in the crowd, please come forward. People in the courtyard could use your help. The rest of you, please clear a passage for the wagons. We have other business to take care of. We're going to pay a visit to that man on Capitol Island."

The windows of the school shook from the thunderous cheers.

• • •

THE SOUND of cheers from the streets blasted down the corridors and echoed off the courtyard walls. But the warriors and citizens gathered around the south courtyard stairway didn't feel like cheering. Many were hurt and all were dazed by the horror of the battle. It was an experience few would ever feel like sharing with someone who wasn't there.

Tobey and Sean, sans patrolman hats and jackets, stood in front of a knot of people in the south courtyard entrance. Tobey addressed the crowd from the top of the stairs while Sean scanned the group for Melissa.

"Thank you all for what you did here today. You're all my brothers and sisters." He pressed his right palm to his heart. "I heard one of you tell a Green Jacket, 'We forgive you.' Remember her words, because we must forgive them. We know now that they couldn't control what they were doing. These men will need time to recover and reclaim their lives. And thanks to Danny Bianchi, they will all get their lives back."

The warriors nodded in unison and repeated Danny's name.

"If you don't know Danny's story, ask one of us about him, ask us how he made today possible, and give him life after death by keeping him alive in your stories of this day."

"Now it's not yet HighNoon, and there's more work to be done. We need to move on to Capitol Island. We're going to run into the Dark Men and the Chancellor's Guard out there and I don't have to remind you, those folks are not victims like the young men here who were taken from their homes. They're a nasty, ruthless bunch. It's a job for only our trained warriors. So the rest of you, please stay here and help tend to the young men. Warriors, assemble at the doors you entered."

Tobey turned to his brother and saw the worried look on his face, then looked back at the crowd as it sorted itself out. "I'm sure she's okay. Did you see her during the fight?"

Sean nodded. Tobey took his brother by the shoulder and they began walking toward the front of the building. "You'll find her."

"Find who?" said Melissa as she appeared out of a cluster of people who had been standing behind them.

Sean took her into his arms and they kissed.

"Hey there, save that for later," said Tobey. "We need to get a move on!"

"Mind if I ride with your group this time?" asked Melissa.

Tobey stepped between the two and laid an arm over each of their shoulders. "That's not a problem," he said, guiding them to the front of the building.

When they exited, Tobey was awed by the size of the crowd. Even the side streets were filled with people as far as he could see.

The throng pulled back to the middle of the street, giving the teamsters room to pick up the warriors at each gate. As the warriors settled into the wagon beds for the move to Capitol Island, people broke through the line to lay food and drinks on the lowered tailgates. Some even brought damp washcloths and clean shirts.

2.17.2

THE TEAMSTERS had been active since dawn. The short-haulers helped mobilize the warriors while the long-haulers had another task—to block access to the north and south causeway bridges that led across the Riftwater Delta to Capitol Island.

When the procession of short-haul wagons from the north came into view, the long-haul rigs began clearing a path.

The teamsters watched silently as Tobey's lead wagon rumbled by. Driver after driver tipped his or her cap to warriors as they rode by. The plan was to reseal the bridge, but the road was filled with people following on foot.

The warriors' wagons formed into two columns once they reached the bridge. They had expected to meet a blockade—probably when they were bottled up on the bridge and had little room to maneuver. Tobey was both relieved and concerned that they hadn't met any resistance as they traversed the causeway.

He directed his driver to pull alongside the steps that led from the flagstone plaza up to the grand stone and glass Council Hall. He sat in the wagon seat, staring toward the building as the other wagons pulled forward and came to a stop. He felt the men and women in the wagon bed crowding forward to look for themselves. Looking left, then right, he saw all the wagons following suit. The last four wagons stopped on the bridge, forming a barricade to keep out the townspeople who followed.

"Whaddya think?" called Sean from the wagon to Tobey's right.

Tobey shook his head and shrugged. He considered the situation, then stood, dismounted, and started up the first flight of terraced steps. Stopping on the first terrace, he waved for the warriors to follow and form a skirmish line along the width of the steps, with him at the center.

When all were in place, he turned to Melissa and Sean, standing to his right, and said, "Keep your eyes open and be prepared. Pass it down the line." Then he turned to his left and gave the same message to Lenore and Percy.

The center of the line thrust forward, forming a shallow V as each person to the outside of the line started just a fraction of a second later than the person to the inside. Tobey's height and long stride meant that his head was the first to clear the top of the upper terrace. The pavement stones were awash with a tide of browns, blacks, and greys. He couldn't believe what he was seeing: the terrace was covered with an undulating, swarming mass of skreel.

As the warriors warily mounted the terrace, the skreel began to scatter like so many leaves on the wind, revealing the true horror—twelve or thirteen bodies rotting in dried pools of their own blood. The sounds up and down the line ranged from sobs to cries of anger to retching.

"What the B?" gasped Lenore.

Tobey fought back the bile as he crouched next to the nearest body to examine it. It was a servant woman—her eyes and much of her flesh eaten by the skreel. They were all servants. Tobey turned away, fell to his hands and knees, and vomited. Sean was instantly by his side, a friendly hand on his back. Slowly, Tobey collected himself and Sean gave him a helping hand up. He beckoned Melissa to join him and Sean. "Look, you two. This is really bad stuff. These people've been dead for days. Maybe weeks. Go back to the bridge and see if you can organize some way to handle these bodies."

As Sean and Melissa sprinted down the steps, Tobey shouted for the others: "Nothing we can do here. Go around!"

The line split as it skirted the gruesome scene.

Tobey didn't see any movement within the glass-walled atrium of the Council Hall. His stomach churned and the roar of Rim Falls was all but drowned out by the beating of his own heart. He didn't turn to the left to see the magnificence of the Fount of Life spewing its towering, cloudlike column of moisture. He saw only the desiccated bodies lying on the terrace. *Were they supposed to be some sort of warning? Were there more bodies on the southern terrace to deter intruders coming from that direction?*

The warriors gathered along the length of the glass wall, waiting for the signal to move in.

Tobey tented his hands over his eyes to block the glare and leaned his head against the glass. The entrance hall was empty.

"Might as well go in," he said to Lenore then turned to Percy. "Take a small group all the way through the hall and out onto the south plaza… Check for bodies."

"I had the same thought," said Percy.

As soon as Percy had gathered his team, Tobey opened the door and went in. Every door in the north wall opened and the warriors flooded the entrance hall, Percy's team dashing to the far side and out onto the south terrace.

Tobey angled left to the wide stairs leading up to the Great Hall. When he was halfway up, one of the south doors swung open. He turned and saw the grim expression on Percy's face. Tobey's blood boiled. All he wanted at that moment was to get his hands on the chancellor and his men, to beat them within an inch of death. His rage erupted as a primal scream and he charged up the stairs, oblivious to the consequences. The sound in the cavernous entrance hall was deafening as the screaming warriors raced up the steps and through the doors into the Great Hall.

The sounds died as they swarmed into the hall and found it empty. Framed in the expansive, east-facing glass wall was the roiling tower of mist—the Fount of Life—thrusting into the clear blue sky.

This is a place of life and death, thought Tobey.

Percy approached from behind and whispered in his ear, "There's something you should see."

. . .

THEY STOOD over a body on the south terrace. A partially eaten index finger still pointed to the word it had scrawled in blood—WEST.

"The poor fellow's telling us where the chancellor and his men have gone," said Tobey.

"But the whole country's west of Primacitta," said Percy.

"True, but all the stories Lenore's people collected suggest the Dark Men took the boys they abducted west. No matter how far upslope their captives were seized, the Dark Men took them west… to the stronghold on Big Island!"

"The very place we were going to visit next," said Percy.

2.17.4

THE FOUNT OF LIFE looked like a pillar of fire in the glow of SolMinor. Citizens made the pilgrimage to Capitol Island from the north and the south, laying flowers and lit candles around each dried pool of blood. The north and south terraces began to look like lakes of flickering flames surrounding a series of dark islands. The incessant roar of Rim Falls embodied the grief and anger of the people.

Six of the new Council members sat at a table in what had been the chancellor's private residence. It was high in a tower that offered a 360-degree view of Primacitta, the Riftwater Delta, and Rim Falls.

The leadership team from the quarters also attended: Bedford, Lenore, Jo and the twins, Randall, Percy, and Melissa.

Henry Conrad was giving his report. "My people say that three private launches left Capitol Island eight days ago. Being private, there are no logs of their destination."

"Eight days ago!" said Sean. "How did the bastard know to leave?"

Jasper Ingram looked at Sean over the rim of his wire-rimmed glasses. "Helen Hobbs was part of our little meeting with Lenore. She's not here and nobody has seen her in more than a week. We can all work that one out now, can't we?"

Sean was puzzled, "If the chancellor knew our plans, why didn't he strike first?"

"Lenore told us only our own part of the plan," said Jasper Ingram.

"And none of us knew where the others were until today," added Jean Connelly. "Brennan must have known he didn't have enough men in Primacitta to be victorious."

"My question is, how far west can those boats travel?" asked Tobey.

"All the way," replied Conrad. "Brennan's probably regrouping at, what did the Bianchi boy call it?"

"Base camp," said Jo.

Tobey looked at Bedford. "It all fits."

Bedford rubbed his stubbly chin. "I agree," he said decisively. "Tobey, Sean, assemble our warriors—and as many citizen volunteers as you can get—on the north plaza. You're heading upriver sooner than we planned."

Tobey slammed his fist on the table. "Yes!"

"Sarah," continued Bedford, "We need your wagons to get our people to the docks... Henry, get with Sarah and work out which docks to go to, and how many people to send to each one. The rest

of you, we need to supply the boats with enough food and water.
We want our people heading upriver as soon as possible.

$$x\sim2.17$$

2.18
Up

2.18.1

DAY 12

The chancellor had fled upriver and he, Henry Conrad, controlled the boats and the docks. It would be up to him to coordinate assets and mobilize a veritable flotilla of packets, freighters, and launches to transport nearly five hundred people—warriors and volunteers alike—to Big Island.

It was after midnight when the Council adjourned. It had been a long, trying day but there was no time to sleep. Conrad hurried through the milling people and makeshift shrines on the north plaza, then down the steps to his carriage. He climbed in and barked at his driver, "To the docks, with all due haste!"

Progress was interminably slow as the carriage made its way through the throngs of people coming and going from Capitol Island. Conrad rapped on the carriage ceiling and shouted, "Stop here."

Even before the carriage came to a full halt, he jumped to the pavement, scouted his surroundings, and saw what he was looking for—a middle-aged man on a sleek-looking horse.

Conrad ran up to the man and asked, "Your name, sir?"

"Thomas... Thomas Hoch," replied the man.

"I need your horse, Thomas."

The man tried to rein the steed away from him but Conrad grabbed hold of the man's coat and yanked him to the ground. The horse reared and whinnied, causing the people nearby to dash away. Conrad grabbed the reins, brought the horse under control, and swung himself into the saddle.

"No time to explain, Thomas, but you will get your fine animal back. I promise." Then Conrad cried, "Make way! Make way!" As the crowd began to part, he spurred the horse into a gallop.

As soon as he arrived at Dock 1, Conrad organized a system of runners to augment the semaphore communication among the docks, gathering information about the number and types of boats in port. Then he set his people in motion, and it was a wonder to behold.

By the time the first teamster wagons arrived at Dock 1, the dockmaster was able to efficiently reroute people and supplies to their points of embarkation.

The warriors and citizen volunteers worked side by side with dockworkers and deckhands to load supplies and erect temporary shelters on the rear decks of freighters. Finally, the motley assemblage of boats headed upstream two hours after HighNoon—under threatening skies.

DAY 15

The fastest of the boats, a private cruiser, reached Northport three days later, landing in a driving downpour. Henry Conrad accompanied Bedford, Lenore, and the twins to add weight to the orders that were to be given. They would use Northport to unload boats too large to continue upriver, with the men, women, and supplies onboard transported across a bridge that connected the twin cittas.

The boats that could navigate the western run of the Riftwater would anchor just above Southport and wait while every other available upriver packet of any size could be docked, loaded, and sent to join them.

• • •

IT WAS sunny near the Rift, but Fallon couldn't tell for all the fog-like mist that reminded him of the Basin. The ever-steepening incline and muddy conditions made for slow-going, but the trees began to thin out as they got closer to the two-kilometer-tall cliff. They never feared losing their way, for the service trail paralleled the gas pipeline between Gasworks and the mine.

"Humid enough for you?" asked Addie, whose rain gear dripped with rivulets of water. Like Fallon, she wore her goggles around her neck since they were rendered useless in these conditions.

"At least it's not windy," said Fallon. "Wind is our enemy."

Without warning, a jet of fire erupted with a loud whoosh and shot into the air some distance ahead. The oxen became startled but Fallon easily reined them in.

"Must be close," said Bernice from the relative comfort of the lorry's box.

After they unloaded their soaps and other cleaning supplies in Gasworks, Fallon acquired a well-padded sofa, a table, and a mattress for the back of the wagon. He fastened the sofa to the front wall so it faced the back of the box. Then he bolted the table in front of it. He placed the mattress on the floor of the box between the table, the two crates, and spools of lashing cord snugged tight against the tailgate. This living space allowed two or three people to rest while someone else drove the team on their long, arduous trip.

"How did you ever come up with this idea, Fallon?" asked Mary.

"It was my idea, actually," said Addie. "They called it an RV back on Earth."

"RV?" said Bernice.

"A recreational vehicle," said Addie. "People used to travel just for fun."

"Travel for fun?! Unbelievable," said Mary, shaking her head.

But now, the two women knelt on the sofa and looked forward over the shoulders of Fallon and Addie.

"There it is again," said Mary, pointing into the mist.

The pipeline took a sudden nosedive, disappearing into the ground and, twelve meters beyond, the framework of the mine loomed through the mist. Directly behind the mine was the sheer, black cliff face of the Rift. Fallon craned his head upward, imagining he could see the top almost two kilometers above.

Bernice was awestruck by the sight of the mine. "Why, I've never... I thought I'd seen everything. Two hundred years old, you say?"

"Yep," said Fallon.

"No rust..." said Mary. "Not a dent. Bet it would gleam in the sunlight."

"It would," assured Aidan. "It's the same metal the Builders used in the quarters and the electrical generators we told you about."

Bernice shook her head. "Then why does everything we have rust and have to be replaced?" Before Fallon could say a word, Bernice held up a hand and said, "Don't tell me... To give us something to do. *In the service of today*, blah, blah, blah..."

The mine was not large, consisting of two cubes stacked atop one another, each ten meters to a side. The bottom cube appeared to be a solid block of the Builders' stainless metal. Only a hatch with a spinning wheel lock—similar to the ones down in the quarters—broke its seamless surface. The upper cube's open framework of beams and pipes housed a large metal sphere. The fire-spouting spire rose from one corner of the framework. The gas pipeline rose out of the ground some twelve meters east of the structure.

To the left of the mine, a small, covered stable leaned against a moss-covered log cabin like someone too tired to stand.

"See that," said Bernice, pointing first at the mine, then the cabin. "Them... and us."

"We'll be here overnight," said Fallon, "so we should unhitch the team." He halted the wagon in front of the cabin and the four of them tended to the oxen before taking shelter.

It was dark, damp, and chilly inside the cabin but Aidan had the gas heater and lamps working in no time. The single room's layout could accommodate four people, having two sets of bunk beds and four chairs around a square table. The top of the gas heater also served as a stove, and the cabin soon smelled of bacon, eggs, and toast.

They talked about many things as they ate. Mary set her hand in Bernice's and said, "Tell us again about love." Fallon studied the two teamsters as Addie told them about the Earth concept that had found favor among those living in the quarters. Fallon saw Mary and Bernice look into each other's eyes and squeeze hands. He thought about Lenore, the most beautiful woman he had ever seen. He hadn't understood Lenore's initial hostility toward him, but on seeing the interactions of Bernice and Mary, it was all too obvious. Lenore loved Aidan. Did Addie know?

His study of Earth culture told Fallon that love wasn't bound by contracts and reproductive needs. It was messy, complicated, often fleeting, and sometimes painful.

The conversation drifted to the viability of the contract system versus the Earth institution of marriage. These were complex questions for which they had no sure answers.

Fallon cleared the table and cleaned the plates while the women continued to talk. Then he put on his rain gear and slipped quietly out the door.

The mist glowed yellow as a gas flare *whooshed* from the spire.

Fallon headed toward the mine, dragging his fingers along the slick, wet surface of the cube as he walked along. He didn't even pause as he came to the hatch. Rather, he continued around the corner of the cube, to the edge of the north wall. And there, at about chest height, right where the captain said they would be, he saw the only other blemishes that could be found on the structure—two rectangles etched into the wall, their outlines a hair's breadth wide. You wouldn't see them if you weren't looking for them. Fallon ran a forefinger across one of the outlines and could barely feel it.

Whoosh!

The bigger of the two rectangles started a hundred centimeters from the ground and was a meter tall by a half-meter wide. The other, to the top-right of the first, was small enough to be covered by the palm of a hand. Fallon pressed firmly. With a hiss, the rectangle popped open and slid upward, revealing a lighted keypad identical to the one outside the quarter's archive.

Whoosh!

He entered the code the captain had prescribed and the larger rectangle hissed open and slid to the left, revealing an illuminated recess about thirty centimeters deep. It contained a coiled hose on a mount that swung outward. The hose was thick, like those used by fire brigades, and had a similar nozzle.

Fallon swiveled the hose mount, grabbed the nozzle, and pulled out a length of hose. He extended the nozzle forward and clamped his arm down on the hose to control it when he opened the nozzle. He eased back the nozzle control bar and braced himself against the expected flow, but there was very little pressure as the colorless gas cut a path through the mist. Fallon smiled with satisfaction and pushed the control lever forward, shutting down the stream.

Whoosh! The amber glow revealed Addie and the two women standing by the front corner of the cube.

"What is that?" asked Addie.

"Helium," said Fallon. "It's a by-product of refining the gas. We've had no use for it yet on Neworld, but the Builders apparently did."

"And how's it useful to us now?"

"It's lighter than air, Addie." Fallon was exuberant. It's going to get us up there," he said, pointing skyward.

· · ·

THAT EVENING Fallon redrew his plans. "I've had some time to think. Addie is a lot lighter than me. I'm pretty sure that means she'll ascend faster than I will. You follow so far?"

The women told him they did.

"Also, the poles will keep us from smashing into the rocks but there's nothing to keep us from spinning round and round. So I propose we lash the two balloons together, like this."

His drawing showed the two spheres butted together, their poles crisscrossing on each side.

"We can lash the poles together where they cross and bind the netting by weaving rope through and through, like this. We'll begin first thing in the morning and we should be on top of the Rift by the rise of SolMinor."

· · ·

THE UNPRECEDENTED procession of boats sailing upriver faced the dual hazards of driving rain and the proximity of the boats.

Sean huddled with Melissa and ten others under a waterproof tarp. The deckhands had built low, square walls from supply crates, with a taller stack of crates in the center of the open area. They covered these improvised rooms with tarps secured with cargo netting fastened to recessed cleats that dotted the deck. The rain drummed against the oiled canvas that protected the occupants from direct assault; however, it didn't keep the water from flowing under. But, at the moment, none of this mattered to Sean and Melissa.

"I've wanted to get to know you for more than a cycle," said Melissa. "But you never even gave me a look."

Sean didn't know what to say. Of course he'd noticed her. He knew she was working with Randall down in the quarters while he and Tobey were busy preparing for the descent. He'd run into her a couple of times up in the manor.

She continued, "I'd planned to say something to you before you all left for the Basin, but things got crazy and we were all busy moving anything that had to do with the Movement down to the quarters."

"Yeah, I remember. Tobey and I wondered at all the commotion, but we needed to get down to the warehouse and prepare for the descender—for Fallon. We had no idea the Dark Men were going to do what they did."

Melissa smiled. "Then Brian kept us busy learning all the new technology we were finding and I ended up spending 99 percent of my time in the hydroponics farm. I saw you and Tobey in the aviary a couple of times as you were coming and going. I was even there when you brought poor Danny Bianchi in."

"I didn't know," said Sean.

"Why didn't you ever look at me?"

"You're… I'm… I mean, you're smart and beautiful, and I'm just…"

"Just what?"

"Look at me. I'm nothing. If I get noticed it's because I'm Tobey's brother."

"You're your own man, Sean. You're the man I wanted to contract with."

Sean clasped her hand. "I didn't know. Maybe when this is over, we can…"

"But I don't want that now," she interrupted.

Sean was crestfallen.

"I've seen what Jo and your brother have. There's something more there than two people under contract. There's a deeper bond."

"*Love* is what Jo calls it," said Sean.

"I think that explains what I feel for you. But I'm not sure you feel the same toward me."

Sean was hesitant to reply. "I've only just gotten to know you. Jo and Tobey have had a long time together. Their love had time to grow."

Melissa reached out and caressed his cheek. "I hope you'll give me that time."

He leaned toward her, kissed her on the lips, and whispered, "We have all the time in the world."

DAY 16

Bernice hitched the team and pulled the lorry to the side of the mine, then unhitched the oxen and led them back to the stable. The crates now sat on the ground. Together, the four of them retrieved tools from under the wagon seat and began to dismantle the crates, prying off the tops, separating the sides, and stowing wooden squares in the back of the rig.

What remained were two large balls of rubberized cloth encased in lightweight cargo netting. Each box contained eight wooden poles that were actually hollowed-out tubes, nine centimeters in diameter, fitted into a threaded metal sleeve on one end.

Fallon used one pole to draw two rough outlines into the ground. They showed where they would position the stretched-out balloons, placing the suspended seat rigging closest to the hose cubby. Fallon marveled at the lightness of the balloon as he and Addie moved one balloon into position and Mary and Bernice positioned the other.

It was time to see if this whole crazy idea would work. Fallon opened the cubby, unspooled the hose, and inserted it into the open cloth funnel at the bottom of one balloon. He slowly pulled back on the lever until it was fully open. They could see the funnel ripple slightly, but the gas appeared to be venting back out the opening.

Fallon shoved the nozzle farther up the funnel. Then he removed his wide leather teamster's belt, wrapped it around the funnel at the location of the nozzle, and cinched it tight.

They placed themselves around the perimeter of the balloon and watched with fascination as the funnel tube slowly rippled with the flow of gas that was being channeled into the balloon.

"This may take a while," commented Bernice.

As the balloon inflated, they had to make continual adjustments to keep it from getting tangled. When it was half full, the leather strap that ran around the circumference of the balloon became exposed. Fallon began to screw the hollow tubes into the evenly spaced brass phalanges bolted onto the leather strap.

When the tubes bent to the ground under their own weight, he became worried. Would the pressure in the balloon be sufficient to force the tubes perpendicular to the balloon? "We have to stop," he said, shaking his head. "I need two short pieces of wood and a clamp."

Before Fallon could move, Bernice was rummaging though the equipment bin bolted to the side of the wagon. She handed a hammer and a saw to Mary, who knew exactly what to do.

Mary banged and pried the crate lid into its individual components, then sawed one of the thin planks into short pieces.

Bernice, clamp in hand, took the pieces and returned to the balloon. "Reckon you're going to pinch off the tube and start filling the other balloon."

Fallon was preparing to remove the belt from around the nozzle. "Eventually. As soon as I un-cinch the belt, put your foot on the funnel just above the nozzle."

Fallon removed the belt.

Bernice stepped.

Fallon withdrew the hose and closed the nozzle, took the slats and clamp from Bernice, and sealed the funnel.

"Perfect! Now help me position the balloon so the center band is on the ground, with the balloon making a dome above it. I want the poles to be flat on the ground, pointing out from the balloon like they should. We'll need a drill and lots of lashing cord."

The dome was sagging so they fed in more gas until it was taut. Mary and Bernice drilled a set of holes in the side of each tube, about twenty centimeters from the end farthest from the balloon. Fallon and Addie, each now outfitted with an all-purpose teamster's knife at their waist, fed a length of lashing cord through the holes. Addie tied one end to the netting halfway up the inflated dome and directly above the tube to its left, then Fallon tied the other above the tube to its right. This formed a V-shaped rigging that would hold the tubes in the required position.

Fallon stepped back, slipped his knife into its sheath, and inspected their handiwork. "That should do." He wiped sweat—or was it just mist?—from his brow. "I hope we didn't add too much weight."

"We'll find out soon enough," said Addie, hands on her hips, stretching out her sore back. "You didn't tell me it was going to be this much work."

"I didn't know—I've never done this before. Besides, be happy Bernice and Mary offered to come along to help." He took two deep breaths and said, "Ready for the next one?"

This time they knew what to do. They snugged the second balloon tight against the first so two tubes from each balloon would crisscross. Then they inflated it halfway. They tied the V-shaped rigging to stabilize the tubes on the second balloon, lashed the crisscrossed tubes together, and "sewed" the two nets together with cord as best they could.

From that point, it became a tedious process of switching the hose from balloon to balloon to inflate them evenly.

When both balloons were about two-thirds full, Mary walked up to Fallon, who was standing with Addie and Bernice, and nonchalantly asked, "How are you going to keep this thing from taking off without you?"

After a pause, Bernice offered a solution. "Don't 'spose these could lift an ox, do you?"

"No, of course not," said Fallon.

"Then how 'bout we put the harnesses on the oxen and we tie it down to them with cord? You and Addie can finish filling the balloons from your perches, clamp them off, and drop the hose back down to us. We can close the panels without your help, can't we?"

"Yes, you can."

"Then you two get your bums moving and prepare yourselves while Mary and I hitch the oxen up to the balloons."

• • •

FALLON and Addie stood on the wicker disks suspended below each balloon, holding tightly to the rope rigging. They wore their sturdy teamster pants, shirts, and canvas jackets with the wide collars folded up against their heads to shield them from the wind Fallon expected to encounter. They had knives on their hips, hats snuggly on their heads, goggles hanging from their necks, and a bag of food and water slung from their shoulders.

The nozzle of the hose was secured in the middle of a length of lash line tied to the under-rigging of each balloon. This allowed Addie and Fallon to pass the hose between them as they struggled with the constant clamping and unclamping required for the final inflation.

Addie's side lurched upward and her disk cleared the ground. She had to clutch the rigging to keep from falling off, but Mary and Bernice quickly stabilized her. "This is going to be a problem," she said.

"Shut off the gas," said Fallon. He sat on his disk and considered the situation. "Okay, I think I have an idea."

"You *think* you have an idea," said Addie, "or you actually *have* an idea?"

"It's an idea. We'll need some of the spare harness supplies and a few empty feedbags…"

The first order of business was to securely attach four empty feedbags to the disk rigging at Addie's feet. "Now, fill the feedbags with dirt until Addie's side is level with mine," said Fallon.

While Bernice and Mary worked at leveling the craft, Fallon called to Addie, "Watch and do what I do." He removed his belt and rethreaded it through a steel harness ring so that one ring extended from each hip. He then used an extra set of reins to fashion leather straps that went through one hip ring and looped around several of the rigging ropes. This allowed them to stand or sit—while keeping them centered on the disk.

Satisfied, Fallon said, "Mary, please turn the gas back on."

An hour later the lift of the balloon and the buffeting breeze made the oxen hard to control.

"I think this is it," Fallon shouted to Addie, who nodded her agreement. "Okay, cut your hose cord, then I'll cut mine."

The hose fell free and Fallon lowered it as far as he could before flinging it clear of the oxen. The balloon tugged against the tethers.

Fallon surveyed the area around the balloon and studied the swirling wind—he didn't want to be anywhere near the spire when it erupted. He yelled to Bernice and Mary, "Can you tow us away from the mine?"

The oxen struggled to move them against the wind, but they eventually gave the craft enough room to clear the mine structure. Fallon signaled the women to stop.

His heart pounded in anticipation. He looked over at Addie and saw the excitement on her face. No fear there!

"Ready?" he asked. He pulled the knife from his belt and knelt on the disk.

"Ready," she replied, mirroring his moves.

"I want to time this when the wind is swirling away from the mine, okay?"

She nodded, positioning her blade against the tether rope.

"On three. One… two… three!"

Fallon tried to time his cut with Addie's but was a second too soon. His side of the craft shot into the air, tipping the balloons to a precarious angle, the crisscrossed poles creaking under the strain. Fallon hung on tight as his disk swung into the lower rigging of Addie's balloon.

The sudden tilt sent Addie toppling headfirst over the edge of the disk and sent her hat and knife plummeting to the ground. Only the improvised harness saved her.

The sudden strain of the added lift snapped the remaining strands of the tether rope and the balloon was propelled into the mist at a steep angle and a terrifying speed. But the bulky craft slowed abruptly in the thick air and eventually settled into a level flight.

"Addie!" Fallon felt helpless as he watched Addie struggle to pull herself into a sitting position on the disk. Once seated, she clutched the lower end of the funnel for security.

Fallon sat cross-legged, holding onto the side ropes. He felt queasy, like his stomach was falling. He leaned forward over the edge of the disk and vomited into the clouds.

There was no way to tell how fast they were rising because all they could see was an unbroken field of grey, which rapidly lightened to white before they broke through the upper limit of the cloud bank.

They were facing east toward a wall of storm clouds. Fallon looked over his shoulder to see the jagged Rift wall looming just behind them. He shouted to Addie, "The good news is we seem to be slowing down. The bad news is we're going to crash into the cliff. So brace yourself!"

Fallon's balloon struck first and the poles did their job well. They flexed without breaking and pushed the balloon away from the rock face, sending the craft into a spin that made Addie's balloon strike all the harder. The tubes strained under the blow, but they held. The craft rebounded away from the cliff and slowly spun 180 degrees—so they now faced the impregnable stone wall.

Another crash was imminent. "Brace yourself!" Fallon yelled. He heard Addie scream as the craft struck broadside this time.

Again, the tubes flexed and pushed the craft back.

Yet another gust spun Fallon's side cliff-ward. A single tube made contact with the unyielding rock and groaned as it flexed until it reached its breaking point. With a horrifying *crack!* it snapped in two. Its lead end, guided by the cording strung through the two holes, shot back toward the balloon. The thin cloth of the balloon was no match for the jagged projectile, which easily pierced the balloon's skin.

As Fallon's sphere lost gas, Addie's continued to rise, reversing the situation they'd encountered at launch. Fallon angled below Addie as her balloon impacted the wall. Her balloon absorbed the impact and rebounded, propelling the crippled craft clear of the rocks for a few more moments.

Then Fallon saw the impossible—the lip of the Rift! All they needed was one more gust to push them over solid ground. But Fallon's balloon had lost too much gas and they began to sink. They were below the lip when the next gust slammed them into the cliff. Addie screamed as her balloon collapsed under the fatal impact.

"Addie!" he cried.

Fallon's rigging swung him hard into the rocks, knocking the wind out of him. Still, he managed to pull out his knife and desperately began to extricate himself from the tangle of rigging before the ruined craft sent them both plunging to the ground.

But the netting must have caught on the rocks.

"Addie!" yelled Fallon. He heard a groan from above. He frantically sliced through the last of his restraints and sheathed his knife. Looking down, he saw storm clouds crashing against the cliffs. Then he looked up and strained to get a handhold on the netting just above. The net gave a certain sense of security—plenty of foot- and handholds. He crawled over the wreckage, the deflated balloons between him and the sharp rocks.

"Addie!"

Another moan seemed a little above and to his right.

"Hang on, I'm almost there!"

"I'm trapped," came Addie's voice.

"I'm trying to find you. Can you push out with your hand?"

Fallon spotted some movement and felt Addie's hand beneath a layer of balloon and netting.

"Okay, I'm here. Now just hold your hand still. I'm going to use my knife."

Fallon locked his left leg through the netting, retrieved the knife from its sheath, and carefully cut a slit in the cloth a few centimeters from Addie's hand. As soon as he withdrew his knife, Addie's fingers poked through the slit, ripping the cloth and widening the opening. Soon, her head appeared through the hole. She blinked a few times and shook her head groggily. Then she looked Fallon in the eyes and smiled. "Some ride!" she said.

They both erupted with laughter, the kind of laughter that's too loud, and too long, and turns into weeping. As they clung there on the side of a sheer stone precipice, nearly two kilometers above the surface of Neworld, the challenges of their situation began to overpower their raw emotions. They felt fatigued and found it hard to breathe.

"Addie, are you able to move? Can you climb?"

"Yeah. A few bruises, nothing broken. How about you?"

"The same." He held out the knife so Addie could see it. "Stay back. I'm going to make a hole in the net, just big enough for you slip through, then we'll climb up the netting and see how close that gets us to the top."

Three slices were enough for Addie to worm her way free. Carefully, they began crawling up the netting. Progress was slow but they were rewarded with one bit of good luck—the top of Addie's balloon had cleared the lip and was snagged on a boulder.

Using the netting, they pulled themselves well away from the edge before they helped each other to their feet. With SolMajor at their backs, they stood in daylight and watched the shadow of night creep eastward along the top of the storm clouds.

x~2.18

Eagle's Nest

2.19.1

FALLON pointed down and to his left. "Somewhere down there, below that storm, Tobey and Sean and a handful of teams…" He stopped to take a deep breath. "…are spreading across Neworld to find the remaining Green Jackets and… administer the anti-dote. And Frank and Danny Bianchi are heading home."

"If everything… went well," Addie cautioned.

With a slight lift of the shoulders, Fallon acknowledged the possibility that not everything had gone according to plan.

For the first time, Fallon turned westward and surveyed their surroundings. The top of the Rift was a dry, lifeless landscape of dark, barren rock. He looked back at the storm below. The tops of the clouds were hundreds of yards below the rim of the Rift.

Fallon eased himself to the ground. "I need to catch my breath."

Addie sat beside him and rummaged through her supply bag. "At least… I didn't lose this," she said, pulling out a canteen of water. "Looks like… we're going to need it."

"Good idea," said Fallon, opening his own bag. "But we'd better ration… no telling… how long before we… find water."

They sat silently with the steady westerly breeze in their face and sipped at their canteens, then shared an apple. SolMajor was setting and the temperature was beginning to drop when Fallon struggled to his feet and went to inspect the collapsed balloon. He tugged and probed until he was satisfied that the wreckage was securely snagged. Then he lifted an edge of the flattened balloon and looked under it. "We can take shelter… under here for the night." He folded a section of the balloon onto itself, revealing a wedge of space created by the taut balloon, ground, and the large rock on which it had caught.

Addie crawled to the balloon on hands and knees, then climbed through the opening. Fallon followed her in. The simple clearing away of loose stones exhausted them.

They lay down facing the opening, snuggled together for warmth, and fell asleep.

. . .

FALLON found it a bit easier to breathe in the morning. When he and Addie crawled from under the balloon, SolMajor was just peeking over the far eastern horizon. They were standing in daylight while the land below them was still in night.

"Where to now?" asked Addie.

"It's hard to tell, since I don't know exactly where we are. If we rose straight up, Eagle's Nest should be a short distance that way." Fallon pointed north. "Or it could a long ways off if we were blown south."

As SolMajor rose, they discovered the storm clouds had dissipated.

"There… see that silver line?" Fallon pointed down toward Neworld and to his left. "That's the Riftwater. Eagle's Nest is south of the falls."

They were several hours into their trek when Fallon extended an arm and balled his hand into a fist with the thumb sticking up. He closed one eye and sighted down his arm with the other. "That's it!"

"Where? Show me."

"The captain said to look for a thumb of rock pointing to the sky—said I couldn't miss it. That must be it—up there a kilometer or so, a little to the west."

Addie leaned her head against his arm and looked past his thumb. "I don't see..." Fallon lowered his arm and she saw the landmark poking above the horizon.

"An hour's walk, tops," said Fallon.

Step by step, they watched the thumb rise higher above the horizon. Four hours later they realized exactly how tall it was. It was actually a peak at the end of a long, 150-meter-tall ridge of rock that angled toward the northwest. They could hear the sound of rushing water in the distance.

The thumb rose another sixty or seventy meters above the ridgeline. The east-facing base of the thumb and the top of the Rift met at an unnatural 90-degree angle. The east face was hewn into a flat wall forty meters tall. In the center of the wall was a door identical in size to the one that opened onto the Basin from the aviary. A wide span of windows was inset to the right of the door about two stories above the ground. Fallon was sure they'd find a small entrance near the door, just as in the aviary.

Addie gave in to the excitement and broke into a run. Fallon kept pace behind her, letting her reach the gleaming metal hatch first. There was no spinning wheel locking mechanism so Addie searched the frame for the telltale sign of a sliding panel, found it, opened it, and looked expectantly to Fallon.

He knew what she wanted, so he told her the code, letting her unlock the door and be the first human in more than two hundred annums to set foot into Eagle's Nest.

Addie punched in the code and watched the door swing inward.

2.19.2

ADDIE stepped through—into a darkened cavern.

Fallon braced his hands on the sides of the hatchway and leaned in. The air was still and stale. "Do you see a light control?"

Addie felt along the wall on the inside of the hatchway, located the familiar glass pad, and powered up the ceiling illumination.

"Wanna bet they have a generator plant under the Rift Falls?" asked Fallon as he stepped inside. He stood behind Addie and wrapped his arms around her.

"I've seen this somewhere before," said Addie. "How about you?"

The layout was identical to the aviary. To their immediate right was an administrative area with a hydroponics farm, no doubt, beyond it. On the far wall they saw a line of occupied vehicle bays and a long tunnel that led to what would be the Eagle's Nest version of the Commons cavern.

And to their right, where two large bays stood empty in their own aviary, sat two large, flat-bottomed white craft—each more than a hundred meters long. The tail end was eighty or ninety meters wide and tapered into somewhat of a beak in the front. Fallon imagined looking down on the craft from above and decided that it was roughly wedge-shaped.

The underbelly was flat, and the upper line of the craft formed what Fallon could only describe as a lazy W. It had a bulbous body with short, upturned wings.

The couple walked toward the nearest craft. It rested on three sets of wheels that must have been inflated like their balloon at one time. There was enough room to walk under most of the craft but, at what must have been its front, a windowed cabin, tapered to the line of the overall craft in front and flat in the back, extended almost to the floor. Windows and a door were built into the rear wall of the cabin.

Fallon wandered to the back of the craft and saw reels of hoses mounted to the bay wall. They looked like the hose down at the gas mine, but the nozzle had a different style and looked as if it were designed to lock into place.

He returned to the flat underbelly of the craft. Like much of the Builders' work, it appeared seamless. But to Fallon's now-trained eye, subtle outlines of panels were visible. He pressed up on one and, as expected, it popped open and slid to the side. Inside was a fitting that seemed to be a mate for the hose nozzle.

"It's a balloon!" shouted Fallon. He turned to see that Addie had already opened the cabin door and entered. He started toward the front of the craft when the entire thing disappeared. He stopped and tried to figure out what had happened. He extended a hand above his head and his fingers struck a solid surface. Then it hit him—the bottom of the craft had lit up, just like the ceiling in the quarters—it was projecting an image of the ceiling of the aviary. At that moment, the image disappeared and he was once again looking at the plain white underbelly.

"It's a balloon," Addie shouted from the door of the cabin. She waved excitedly to Fallon. "Come see!"

It was two steps up to the cabin's spacious deck. Immediately inside was comfortable seating that could accommodate a dozen passengers. At the front, a smooth, curved control panel extended inward from the seamless window. Addie was standing in front of the panel, talking with Anika Bystrom, the blond engineering avatar.

"This is Anika," said Addie. "Sort of…"

"Sort of?"

"She doesn't know who I am. She asked for a palm print but wouldn't accept mine."

Fallon walked up to the panel and greeted Anika, "Hello Anika, I'm Fallon."

Anika blinked and replied, "Please identify yourself."

Fallon pressed his palm against an outline of a hand that appeared on a panel next to the hologram.

The hologram flickered and faded from view. When Anika returned she was the person they had grown to know down in the quarters. *Person.* It was a concept not wasted on Fallon. All the avatars were as real to him as any living being—particularly the captain.

Anika spoke with some urgency. "Aidan. Fallon. You made it to Eagle's Nest! There is so much for you to learn, but Captain Maczynski needs to talk with you as soon as possible. He says to contact him from the armory."

"Thanks, Anika. Tell the captain that I'll be right there." Fallon took Addie's hand and pulled her to the door, saying, "Come on."

They trotted across the aviary, toward the administrative complex. Fallon became aware that he was breathing easily now that they were inside Eagle's Nest.

"What's the armory?"

"It's the place I disappeared to when… you know. Randall and I are the only two who knew about it, and I was the only person authorized with a palm print to enter it. You're going to see it now, so I might as well prepare you for what you'll find there."

They were inside the office complex and Fallon knew he could find the room blindfolded, even here in the Eagle's Nest. He stopped in front of an unmarked, anonymous door.

"Is this it?"

"Yeah." Fallon faced Addie and put his hands on her shoulders. "Before I take you in, I want to tell you that an armory is where the Builders stored their weapons. You remember the video about war, right? You saw what weapons can do. When Randall showed me the armory in the quarters, it fell on me to decide what to do with the weapons. I was tormented by the decision. Well, I destroyed all the weapons in the quarters. I wanted to protect us from even the idea of them. Now I have to face the dilemma again."

"I'll be here to support you this time." Addie stood on her toes and kissed him.

Fallon pressed his palm against the reader and the door unlatched. He pushed it open and was stunned by what he saw. The room was empty, just like in the quarters. On the lighted tabletop stood Captain Maczynski and, next to him, a holographic version of Missus Grier sat at the table in the archive.

"Grandmother!?"

"Addie! Fallon!" said the Missus. "Are you okay?"

"Yes, yes. We're fine. We'll have quite a story for Jo."

The captain held up his hands, cutting off the conversation. "There will be time for that later. We need to update you on what's happening topside. We have nearly five hundred people heading upriver and I fear many will die."

Fallon was shocked by the news. "What? Tell me what's going on."

"Our breakout and the capture of the Green Jackets' headquarters went almost as planned—some injuries on both sides, but no deaths. The young men we saved are starting to recover their memories and the teamsters are preparing to return them all to their homes when they're up to traveling."

"Then the antidote worked," said Fallon.

"Perfectly," said the captain.

"Make sure Frank and Danny get home first," said Addie. "We owe them that."

Missus Grier's reply caught in her throat. "Danny has died, my dear."

The shock was too much for Addie, who broke into tears and was overcome with grief. Fallon guided her to a stool at the table, where she laid her head into her folded arms and sobbed.

Fallon rubbed her shoulders as he fought back tears himself. Once again, he felt the urge to personally kill the chancellor. "Where are the guns, captain?"

The Missus looked confused by Fallon's question, but the captain answered without hesitation.

"We took them with us—long ago. It's best they're not there, son. Your method worked in Primacitta but I fear it will have poorer results on Big Island."

"Why?" asked Fallon. "I'd think that five hundred people should be able to handle—what, another 150 or so Green Jackets, most of them trainees?"

"Things didn't go well on Capitol Island," said the Missus. "We found bodies. More than thirty members of the chancellor's serving staff with their throats slit."

"Tell me you captured the bastard."

Fallon knew the answer by the hesitation in the old woman's answer. "The chancellor and his men had fled more than a week before."

"Why...? How...?"

"One of the new Council members, Helen Hobbs, betrayed us and warned him," said the Missus.

"They fled upriver," said the captain. "Most assuredly to the stronghold we believe the chancellor's constructed on Big Island. That's where your people are headed. Two-thirds of the island is perpetually hidden in mist from the Rift Falls and the only information we have on the island is more than two hundred years out of date. It's native, son—the only place on the surface of Neworld the Builders didn't touch."

"Our people have no idea what they're headed into, Fallon." He could hear the concern in the old woman's voice.

"Listen, son. I don't know if you've made it to Eagle's Nest in time, but if you have, there's a way the two of you can help. You'll have to wait a bit longer for your answers 'cause we need to take action right now."

x~2.19

2.20

Big Island

2.20.1

WHILE FALLON and Addie slept under the wreckage of their balloon...

Peculiar things had been happening in Westport recently, like the collection of cruisers that sailed west in the middle of the night a week or so ago and never returned. Then there was the influx of teamsters filling the local inns.

So the dockmaster wasn't too surprised to see another private craft approaching in the midst of the storm. She half-expected it to disappear into Rift Lake with the others. However, when she noticed it was slowing down, she put on her rain gear, stepped outside the dockmaster's office, and rang the brass bell mounted next to the door. Lights came on in the dockworkers' dorm.

Westport had only one dock for passenger boats. The real business was done at the logging docks a bit farther downriver, below the bridge, and at the fishing wharves inside the mouth of the lake.

The master was a slender, middle-aged woman with stooped shoulders and salt-and-pepper hair. She began barking orders as soon as the first of the six night hands joined her on the dock.

The split stern wheels on the private packet churned in opposite directions, angling the boat's nose toward the shore. The dockworkers spaced themselves along the length of the dock and prepared to receive the docking lines. Fifteen minutes later, the cruiser was moored and the gangway extended.

Only three people disembarked—two men and a woman. Like the dockmaster, they were outfitted in rain gear. The hoods, sputtering gas lights, and heavy rain made it impossible to make out their features as they strode briskly down the ramp.

The man in the lead said, "Can we talk?" and walked right past her in the direction of her office, as if he knew the place. It wasn't so much a question as an order. The master took offense to the treatment and was going to tell the man so.

She followed the three into her office and closed the door behind her. The wind rattled the windows and the rain drummed loudly on the roof. The visitors' backs were still turned to her when she started to complain. Then the lead man lowered his hood and turned to face her, a grave expression on his face. The dockmaster was struck dumb.

"Mister Conrad!" She had met the head of the guild many times when he made his semi-cycle visits upriver. She didn't recognize the dark-skinned young woman and man with the start of a grizzled beard.

"Grace, isn't it?" said Conrad, extending his hand. "Sorry for being gruff, but these are trying times."

"No problem, sir," said Grace, shaking her boss's hand.

"And this is Jim and Lenore Bedford."

Graced nodded to each before saying, "You weren't due upriver for another three months, sir."

"I know, I know. Now, here's the thing…"

Grace sagged into a chair as Henry Conrad told her of the recent events in Primacitta. She had heard stories of unrest in the capital and young men gone missing but she had hoped they were just rumors.

"Yes," she said in reply to a question. "They came through without stopping seven, maybe eight, days ago." She got up and walked to her desk. "I noted it in the log…"

The dark-skinned man, Jim, spoke for the first time. His voice was deep and commanding. "No need to show us, Grace. We believe you. We're in a hurry. There's a flotilla of packets a few hours behind us and they should start to arrive toward dawn. We think the chancellor has taken refuge on Big Island, that he has a stronghold there."

"Could be," said Grace, her head bobbing. "For the last four or five cycles, the fishermen have talked about lights crossing the lake just inside the veil."

"The veil?" said the young woman, Lenore.

"You see, the far end of the lake is enshrouded in a permanent fog. The farther west you sail, the more humid it gets. A light fog is to be expected, but the veil comes up on you like a wall."

Her visitors hung on her every word.

"Best guess is that it stretches some thirty kilometers from the Rift. The fishermen never go near it—too many rocks and the water gets turbulent because of the falls."

Jim looked at Conrad. "It's possible that the chancellor's men use the cover of the veil to move between the island and the shore."

Conrad nodded. "Makes sense. So, Grace, what can you tell us about Big Island?"

"Not much. Only the end of it extends beyond the veil."

"Any structures?" asked Lenore. "Anyplace to put ashore?"

"None that have been reported. The isle is thick with trees and undergrowth and the shoreline is treacherous."

Jim stroked his stubbly chin. "Our people will be useless if we can't get them ashore."

Conrad said, "Here's as far as we were able to plan, Grace. We're going to steam into the mouth of the lake and anchor. The rest of the flotilla will form up around us. I'd like you to get Jim and Lenore up to the fishing wharves before dawn so they can talk to the fishermen before they leave port. Can you do that?"

Grace assured Conrad she'd do as he asked. Then Conrad explained what he had in mind.

2.20.2

THE RAIN had stopped and the wind had died down to a breeze by the time Bedford and Lenore reached the wharves. It was still dark but the docks were alive with boat crews preparing for the day's work: mending nets, maintaining equipment, and stowing empty crates on deck.

Bedford was aware of the onlookers' stares as the dockmaster led them quickly along the wharf. He could smell the aroma of breakfast cooking and was happy that Grace seemed to be leading in its direction.

"The cantina is the best place for you to meet the people you need," said Grace. "Everyone stops in for at least a cup of warm coffee before they head out."

Grace made introductions while Bedford and Lenore spread the news and questioned the fishermen about Big Island. They also arranged for five swift launches to help shuttle people from the assembling flotilla back to the wharf for a meeting.

By HighNoon Conrad was calling the meeting to order. More than one hundred Movement leaders, citizen volunteers, and fishermen gathered on the cantina's veranda.

Bedford and Conrad stood atop a table so everyone could see them. The guildsman deferred to Bedford, whose booming voice carried over the crowd.

"Friends of Westport… You've all heard the news by now so you know why we're here. We think that Chancellor Brennan…"

"The skreel!" shouted someone in the crowd, setting off a general clamor.

Bedford held up his hands in a plea for silence. "Please, please. Time is of the essence… Brennan has fled to Big Island and we intend to bring him to justice."

The men and women crowding the wharf cheered. Bedford was slower to stop their interruption this time.

"Now, we think he has a stronghold somewhere on the island but we don't know shite about the place. We might as well be working blindfolded out there so we need to be cautious. Here's what we're going to do: First, we're going to take up positions just within sight of the island.

"The fishing fleet will accompany us and take the lead in the next phase of the operation. They'll probe the veil for clear passage, then guide one of our boats to a safe place to anchor. Our objective is to carefully pierce the veil and cut off any traffic to and from the island. By the time that's done, we hope to find a way to land a small scouting party. Henry Conrad's cruiser will anchor due east of the island and serve as the center of the line. Get your position assignment from Lenore before you head back to your boats. That's all for now. See you all on the water!"

Bedford spotted Tobey in the crowd. "Find Sean," he called over the general din of excitement. "Then meet me inside as quickly as possible."

Bedford and Conrad climbed down from the table and retreated into the cantina. Before they could sit at a table, Tobey and Sean were at their sides.

"Scouting party?" asked Sean, displaying his usual grin.

"You lads pick four others and get yourselves to Conrad's boat before we take up positions by the island."

"See you there," said Tobey, heading out with his arm draped over Sean's shoulder.

"They seem like close friends," said Conrad.

"Brothers, actually."

"Good men?"

"The best."

2.20.3

BEDFORD stood on the observation deck of Conrad's cruiser, filled with awe. The trees on Big Island weren't quite the size of the behemoths they'd found in the Basin but they appeared to be of the same family, rising more than fifty meters into the air with leaves more than a meter in length.

Sean quipped, "Been there, done that."

Tobey nodded in agreement.

On the lake, the air was clear, but the day was gloomy with much of SolMajor's light filtered out by the mist as it set toward the rim of the Rift. Rift Falls sounded like the distant roll of continuous thunder.

Lenore made her way through the group and confronted her father. "There's no way in Below I'm not going with them."

Bedford smiled as he touched his daughter's cheek. "Never said you weren't."

He turned his attention back toward the island. Two fishing boats sailed close to the shoreline and others were entering the veil on the right side of the island. A fishing boat was already guiding a packet into the veil on the left.

"Nothing to do but wait," said Bedford. "Henry's given you the staterooms for the night. So go down to the dining room, have a good meal, and get some rest. Be ready to go ashore at dawn."

●　●　●

THE NEXT MORNING the scouting party clambered over the side of the cruiser and into a narrow launch. After they were all in and their supplies stowed, the pilot pulled away and set course for the right side of the island. The surface of the lake was as smooth as glass.

"Can't get you into shore," shouted the pilot over the noise of the engine, "but we found a narrow gap between some rocks that this old boat should be able to wedge into. If it doesn't break up before we stop, you should be able to get out and hop across the rocks to shore."

Sean put his mouth near Tobey's ear and said, "Did he just say, 'if we don't break up?'"

"I believe so," answered Tobey.

"Well, that's okay, then," said Sean.

He looked across at Melissa. He thought Tobey was lucky to have someone like Jo, but Melissa!

"Tell me," he shouted to the pilot, "Is the lake always this calm?"

"Out here? In the morning? With no storm? Yeah, I guess it is. We're a good fifty kilometers from the falls out here, and the lake is deep."

"How deep?"

"Deep, deep."

Sean grinned at that answer and patted the pilot on the back. *Good guy*, he thought. "We need to share a drink or two when this is over."

"Be happy to," said the pilot. He slowed the launch as he neared the rocks and proceeded parallel to the shoreline. "Be ready to jump if we run aground. I'm easing her in."

The man expertly threaded the needle, then idled the engine so they'd glide the rest of the way in. "You two in the front, use your hands to keep us from scraping if you can. Easy now... Pull us forward slowly... That's it."

Jerry and Roddy were the first onto the rocks, followed by Percy, Lenore, Melissa, and Tobey. Sean thanked the pilot, stepped to the front of the boat and accepted Melissa's hand up.

"I'll be here, but only till SolMajor sets," said the pilot. "So don't be late."

Sean was pleased to find the rocks had large, flat tops that made it easy to hop from one to the other. Soon they were on shore and Sean was leading the group through dense pockets of fog that drifted through the trees.

. . .

AN HOUR later, they entered the veil and the roar of Rift Falls grew steadily louder. The landscape uncannily resembled that in the Basin. As they walked on the thick bed of damp, rotting leaves, Sean kept a wary eye out for toadsnares and other plants and beasties he had encountered on their descent to Below.

He turned and said, "Keep close," to Roddy, who was a couple of paces behind. Roddy passed the advice down the line.

They hiked for two more hours and were deep into the veil when Sean heard a *snap* in the distance. He held up his hand and everyone stopped in their tracks. Sean slowly advanced another fifteen meters.

Another *snap*. It was closer this time. Sean pressed his back against a tree and signaled the others to spread out and take cover. He wondered how he was able to hear something as soft as a snap. Then it finally registered. The roar of the falls had faded away and the woods were eerily quiet.

Snap!

Sean peeked around the tree trunk and saw a single Green Jacket materialize through the mist. He ducked his head back behind the tree and waited. He felt for the carton of capsules in his pocket and fished one out.

When the Green Jacket came alongside, Sean quickly stepped behind him and threw his left arm around the patrolman's chest. The man started to call out a warning, but Sean muffled the Green Jacket's cry with his right hand and, at the same time, administered the antidote.

The guard struggled in his arms. Sean winced in pain as the man finally sagged to the ground. He saw the others coming toward him. He had to warn them.

As Tobey came closer, Sean pressed his left hand against his lower right abdomen and felt the flow of blood.

"They have knives," he said, collapsing to the ground.

. . .

TOBEY grabbed Melissa and clamped a hand over her mouth to stifle her scream, then pulled her behind a tree as the others rushed to help his brother.

"Can you stay quiet?" he whispered. "We don't want to call any more Green Jackets down on us. She nodded and he removed his hand, then rushed to kneel at Sean's side.

Lenore had Sean's shirt and jacket open and was pressing a blood-soaked cloth—Roddy's shirt—against the wound.

"Didn't see that coming," said Sean, grimacing.

"Quiet, brother," said Tobey.

"Everything's gone quiet."

"I'll not hear any of that, Sean. Hang in there, you hear?"

"What are you talking about, you twit?" said Sean. "Listen! Everything's gone quiet."

Jerry cocked his head and looked puzzled. "The falls…" he said cryptically.

"He's right," said Sandra. "I don't hear the falls."

Tobey was confounded. "How can that be?"

"Okay, I made my point," said Sean. "I'm dying here. And I want it to be a slow death. Say, sixty to seventy annums. Get me to the boat, for crying out loud!"

"Yeah," said Jerry. "Let's get the B out of here!"

2.20.4

EARLIER…

Addie was working in a control room high in Eagle's Nest—a room that had no analogue in the quarters. It looked over a large canyon to the north of Eagle's Nest. At its bottom was a river, the source of the great Rift Falls. Compared to the Riftwater, it really wasn't much of a river, but falling some two kilometers over the side of a cliff did give its flow some punch.

"Well, did it work?"

"The gates are closing," replied Anika. "Eagle's Nest will go on reserve power in two hours when the gates are fully closed."

"Will we be able to open them again?"

"If you return within four months, there should be sufficient power. The captain says to remind you that Fallon needs you in the aviary as soon as possible. There's much more to be done."

2.20.5

THE LAUNCH PILOT left his boat and stood on a rock, looking back at the island. He knew something was wrong. It was never this quiet on the lake. He was frightened and was just about to take off early when he saw the team coming through the last of the trees.

He counted only six, in two columns of three. All were in their shirtsleeves except for one man who was shirtless. And they were carrying something, some*one*, between them. As they got closer, the pilot realized it was the shorter guy with the beard who'd wanted to share a drink.

He jumped across the rocks and rushed to give them a hand but they waved him off, not wanting to stop for him to relieve any of them. He made his way back to the boat and fired up the engine so they could pull out as soon as everyone was aboard.

The scouts had used their jackets and a layer of broad leaves to fabricate a crude litter. But when they reached the rocky shore, the litter was problematic. So they set it on the ground and the big fellow hoisted the limp body of the man in his arms and carried it to the boat.

The others climbed into the craft and set the makeshift litter in its bottom. Then the big man lowered the body down to them and they laid it on the litter. The big man got in and gave the launch a mighty push away from the rocks.

The pilot nosed the boat toward open water and set the throttle to full.

When he saw the shocked look on his passengers' faces as they, in unison, looked back at the island, the pilot glanced over his shoulder and was aghast at what he saw.

The veil was collapsing, disappearing, evaporating, or whatever you'd like to call it.

Pointing at the collapsing veil, one of the women said, "Maybe we shouldn't have left the Green Jacket behind."

"I'm sure he's in better shape than Sean," snapped the big fellow.

One by one, the packets that had been guided into positions down the length of the island came into view and then the Rift revealed itself in its awesome glory. The falls had disappeared.

• • •

BEDFORD decided it would be best for the launch to take Sean directly back to the wharf so he could get medical attention. Tobey and Melissa accompanied him to shore.

In the distance Bedford saw several launches headed his way from the line of packets on either side of the island. He immediately told a deckhand to send the visitors up to the observation deck when they arrived.

Conrad was shaking his head when Bedford and Lenore reached the observation deck. "I just can't take it all in," said the guildsman. "It's like our whole world has been turned upside down."

"It has," said Bedford.

x~2.20

2.21

The Eagle

2.21.1

BEDFORD rubbed his chin nervously as he listened to the messengers give their reports. They had learned three things:

1. The collapse of the veil revealed stretches of sandy beach on either side of Big Island.
2. The south side of the island had a small dock, to which a single, flat-bottomed transport barge was moored.
3. Two more transports and the chancellor's cruisers were docked at a large wharf on the north side.

"Obviously, if we can see *them*, they can see *us*." Conrad anxiously massaged his knee. "We know for sure that the chancellor is on the island. So what do we do now?"

Lenore took exception to Conrad's statement. "We *think* he's on the island. All we know for sure is that his boats are there. Brennan himself could have gone ashore anywhere along the river."

"Of course, you're right, Lenore," said Bedford. "But it seems to me that we have to act as if he is on the island. If he isn't, then we'll cross that bridge when we come to it. The first thing we *must* do is cut off their means of escape, and the sooner the better."

"I agree," said Conrad, voicing the sentiment of the group.

"Good," said Bedford. "Do boats carry any flammable liquids on board, Henry?"

"Well, most boats would have cans of turpentine in the maintenance room, I suppose."

"That's good... that's good," said Bedford. "Now I'll need your two fastest launches for a nighttime raid."

All the pilots claimed their launch was the fastest, so Conrad picked two at random.

Bedford explained his plan. "Percy, you take the south dock. Lenore, you take the north. Scavenge turpentine from as many of our boats as you can... You get the idea. Now I don't want you going ashore—it's just going to be you and your pilots, so only get close enough to the chancellor's barges and boats to set them ablaze."

"We should put the turpentine into jars or bottles," said Percy. "Something we can throw... that'll break when it hits the boat."

Lenore added, "And we can toss lanterns to ignite the stuff."

Bedford stood and said, "So what are you waiting for?"

He and Conrad shook hands with Lenore and Percy and wished them luck as they left.

"Now, for the rest of us..." Bedford sat down again, put his hands on his knees, and leaned forward. "Our assault starts at the dawn of SolMajor..."

    • • •

THE SKIES were clear and SolMinor was dipping toward the Rift.

Percy was the first to reach his objective. He could see four GreenJackets standing on the dock and several more on the deck of the barge. They looked agitated and were gesturing toward the black void to the west and the line of lights out on the lake.

The patrolmen pulled out their knives and took defensive positions as Percy's launch, brightly lit with a half-dozen lanterns, approached the end of the dock and slowed. Percy noticed that the GreenJackets backed away as the launch got closer. *Drugged or not,* he thought, *they must be rattled to their bones by this eerie silence and the sudden loss of their cover. Maybe their fear is more powerful than the drug... Maybe I can reason with them.*

"Take me to the end of the dock," said Percy.

The pilot hesitated, then inched the craft forward.

When the launch neared the dock, Percy stood up, moved to the bow of the craft, and used his hands to stop its momentum. His shoulders and head were above dock level.

The men on the dock retreated a few steps and were joined by their comrades from the barge.

They really are skittish, thought Percy.

"Hi, guys," he said with a smile. "Whatcha doin'? Pretty strange, isn't it? Bet you're nervous."

He took a carton of capsules from his jacket pocket, opened it, and held a capsule between his thumb and forefinger. "I've got something here for you that'll help you relax. It's better than juice. Look…"

He pretended to put the capsule in his mouth and chew it. "Mmm, that's good. Tastes like strawberries. Here, you can have these."

When he held out the carton, the patrolman in front lunged forward a step and made threatening gestures with his knife.

"Okay. Okay." Percy put the carton in his pocket and signaled the pilot to back away.

"Got some business to do, then we'll be on our way. You might want to get up on the beach a ways."

The pilot steered the launch to the outside of the barge and guided it slowly down its length. The Green Jackets ran onto the barge, trying to see what people in the launch were up to.

Then, when the launch was in range of the barge, Percy shouted, "Stand back!" and tossed two jars of turpentine that smashed satisfactorily on the wooden deck. Next, he threw one of the lanterns into the spreading pool of combustible fluid. A low flame spread across the deck.

The Green Jackets, looking confused and disoriented, fled the barge and ran inland.

Percy started three more blazes before he and the pilot turned back and cruised out to open water.

· · ·

LENORE also modified her father's plan. She recruited three additional launches to help her at the north wharf. Each launch held four people in addition to the pilot.

SolMinor had set; if they didn't light their lanterns until the last moment, her strike team would be practically invisible from the shore.

The launches motored toward the wharf as quietly as possible. Then, a hundred yards out, they went full throttle and the team started yelling and banging on the sides of the launches. The startled patrolmen scanned the water, desperately trying to locate the incoming boats. Twenty meters from the wharf, the team lit their lanterns. As they sped past the barges and cruisers moored at the wharf, three people in each boat hurled jars of turpentine while the fourth flung lanterns.

The panicked guards fled toward the shore and sought shelter among a row of low buildings that serviced the wharf.

Lenore whooped in triumph as her launch completed its run. The cheers of the men and women of the flotilla reverberated across the water as the pier was consumed in fire.

· · ·

BETWEEN the half-sunken hulks of the destroyed boat and the charred planking of the dock, the wharf was no longer a viable point of debarkation for the invading force. Even before dawn broke, the packets took turns drawing close to a sandy stretch of shoreline and a veritable fleet of fishing boats ferried the warriors and their citizen partners to shore. From east and west, the fighters streamed toward the wharf.

As she passed from boat to boat, gathering turpentine and lanterns, Lenore had spread the word about Sean and warned everyone that the Green Jackets were equipped with knives. She suggested that the trained warriors tie towels, cloth sacks, strips of canvas, or spare clothing around their forearms for protection. She herself had fashioned leather armbands from the tops of a spare pair of boots.

Those on her boat who could find boots to cannibalize followed her lead and called themselves the boot-guards. Some made their guards of leather; others used the tough, rubberized material from the all-weather boots most deckhands wore during storms.

The boot-guards landed on the small beaches immediately adjacent to the wharf and stormed nearby buildings, with their citizen partners keeping a safe distance behind. They found more than twenty Green Jackets defensively massed in the corner of the largest building, which appeared to be a supply depot.

Lenore came to the same conclusion as Percy—fear must be conflicting with the Green Jackets' conditioning. She could only imagine what must have gone through their minds when they saw the sheer number of boats on the lake and the size of the force that was coming ashore.

"Don't be afraid," said Lenore as the boot-guards closed ranks around the patrolmen. "We don't want to hurt you." She held her hand up, palms forward, to show her good intentions. She still had hopes for a peaceful resolution.

But the combined effects of the drug and the conditioning kicked in when a patrolman in the middle of the pack started screaming, inciting the others to attack. The Green Jackets, knives drawn, charged toward the cordon of warriors. The warriors spread out, giving themselves room in which to perform the martial arts moves that now came to them reflexively. The boot-guards' training trumped the patrolmen's brute force and unskilled use of lethal weapons. The makeshift arm guards prevented more than one serious injury.

As a Green Jacket was disarmed and fell, a volunteer dashed forward, knelt on his chest, and administered the antidote.

The first skirmish in the Battle of Big Island was over in fifteen minutes.

. . .

ON THE south side, Percy's group made unfettered progress toward the interior of the island. Members of his group had the idea to strap pot and kettle lids to their defensive forearms.

When Percy saw them, he banded them together and, with this "tin-pan patrol" in the lead, his force marched inland.

They were the first to arrive at the broad clearing in the middle of the island. It was too generous to call it a clearing; it was dotted with huge stumps of trees that rose a good meter above the ground. In the center of the clearing stood a massive fortress with ten-meter-tall walls constructed of tree trunks that were sharpened and sunk into the ground with their pointed ends poking skyward.

Percy held the main force well back in the tree line as he surveyed the area. He was at the southeast corner of the structure. No gates, doors, or openings of any sort were visible in the south and east walls. Odds were, the only entrance faced to the north, toward the larger of the docks.

An unbroken barrier of crisscrossed sharpened poles slanting toward the woods surrounded the fortress. Percy was sure that, if they moved carefully, his force could wend their way through the barrier without getting hurt. So, if it wasn't meant to stop them, what was its purpose? The answer was obvious—to slow them down. He studied the top of the wall. There! Movement between the pointed ends of the tree trunks.

Percy put the pieces together. The men on the wall must be planning to attack the Movement's people as they worked their way through the barrier. He decided to test his theory. He turned to the tin-pan patrol and found the largest shield available—which, as it turned out, wasn't tin or metal of any sort. It was the wooden top of a pickle barrel.

"May I borrow that?" he asked.

The woman untied the strips of cloth that held it to her arm and handed it over to Percy.

He asked the woman to tie the barrel cover to his left forearm. "If I'm right, I'll have this back to you shortly. If I'm not, thanks and good luck."

With a nod of appreciation, he turned and strode into the clearing, his left arm held tight across his body. His appearance elicited more movement along the top of the wall but he walked steadily toward the barrier. As he neared it, he saw a flash of movement and instinctively raised his arm. Some sort of projecttile knocked him on his backside. He quickly pulled himself into a crouch and began to retreat. He suffered another hit, fell, and recovered. Then it was over.

He carefully peeked over the shield and saw two rocks land a couple meters short of his position. He stood, defiantly lowered his shield, and made a rude gesture to the men on the wall. Before him was a scattering of rocks about the size of apples and several pointed poles that had pierced the ground closer to the barrier.

What was that Earth adage Jo had mentioned? Something about sticks and stones. He turned on his heel and walked back into the trees, laughing out loud.

When the tin-pan patrol rallied around him, he said, "Did you see that? They can't touch us if we stay five meters this side of the barrier. I want to make them shite in their pants, so here's what I want you to do…" He explained his idea and then asked for a volunteer who was fleet afoot.

"You heard my instructions?" he asked the young man who stepped forward. "Good. Now head over to the north side and intercept the others. Find Lenore Bedford and tell her the plan. Tell her it's Percy Williams's plan."

The young man started to run along the tree line. "Cut across," shouted Percy. "It's faster."

. . .

LENORE'S force was marching down a muddy road that cut inland from the wharf. She raised her hand and halted the advance when she saw the runner splashing down the road through muddy puddles.

"I need to find Lenore Bradford," he panted.

"That'd be me," said Lenore, not bothering to correct the fellow.

"I have a message from Percy Williams..." He gasped for air. "We're on the south side of the wall..."

"Wall?"

"Yeah... about half a kilometer ahead. He sent me to tell you his plan."

Lenore listened carefully to what the runner said. She was still unsure about the wall he mentioned, but she'd find out soon enough. She singled out Jerry and told him to bring the main body of the force along on a march. She then rallied the boot-guards and led them down the road on the run.

It was more than a wall, but the runner's story made sense when Lenore and the boot-guards reached the clearing. She heard a commotion from atop the fortress wall and, out of the corner of her eye, she caught movement in the trees to her left. A line of people was advancing out of the trees—a line that stretched out of sight around the far side of the fortress. It was Percy's unit.

Percy's plan was to give a show of force... to encircle the fortress, just out of the chancellor's reach. Lenore explained the plan to her people and they spread out to either side of their leader, who marched them straight down the center of the road. She halted the line five meters from the barrier.

As the northern force emerged from the trees, the warriors passed orders and they spread out until their line met the line of the southern force.

Lenore faced the gate, which had a roofed balcony across the top with guard towers at each end. The dirt in front of the gate looked freshly upturned from the hasty extension of the barrier across the road.

Percy Williams came running along the line with several of his tin-pan patrol and took up a position with Lenore.

"Good plan!" said Lenore.

"Thanks," he said.

"What now?" she asked.

He flashed her a wry smile and said, "Thought you'd know."

Lenore clenched her hands in frustration and then shook her fists at the sky and let out a primal scream. Someone must have taken this as part of the plan, for echoing screams and raised fists erupted to her right, then to her left, and soon the whole line was bellowing at the sky.

The ridiculousness of this whole situation struck Lenore and she began laughing. "Earth people used to go to war over the littlest thing. They had to be out of their minds! Out of their bloody minds."

"And here we are, trying to kill each other with sticks and stones. You know, I found it exciting. I was looking forward to the battle, hoping to be the one to bring down Brennan. Hoping to kill the skreel. But killing's senseless."

She scanned the scene and her heart ached. "I swear, Percy, we can never let this happen to Neworld again, never again."

There was movement above the gate. A line of Dark Men spread out along the balcony. Behind them came a tall, red-haired man wearing a black formal coat and shirt and red gloves.

"Chancellor Brennan," called Lenore. "Nice of you to show yourself."

"And who might you be?" he called back.

"Lenore Bedford. I've met you a couple of times."

"Hmm... Bedford? Bedford? Oh, you're James Bedford's cur."

"Yeah, that's exactly who I am."

"What can I do for you?"

"How about jumping down from that wall and killing yourself? It would save us all a lot of trouble."

"Now don't be nasty."

Lenore stepped forward a few paces. "Look. We don't want anyone else to get hurt—not even you, believe it or not. So give yourself up. You've already done enough damage to Neworld."

"I am the chancellor." Brennan spread his arms to take in all before him. "I *am* Neworld."

"We don't want you as chancellor anymore."

"It doesn't matter what you want, I just *am*."

"You won't *be* forever, you know. How old are you anyway? Seventy-two? Seventy-three? Your daughter will be chancellor soon." Lenore was on the verge of an epiphany. "Where is she, chancellor? Where is your daughter?"

"I have no daughter."

"But you have a grand..." Then the realization hit her and made Lenore sick to her stomach. "You evil old man," she spat. "That's why you burned down the Grier estate. You were trying to kill your only living heir. Your own granddaughter."

The warriors within earshot began to shout angrily, and additional voices joined the chorus as the word was spread up and down the line.

The chancellor didn't respond for a long moment. Then he leaned forward on the rail of the balcony and shouted, "How many of you are willing to die today? My men will die for me without question or pause."

"They don't have to die for you," Lenore retorted.

She was struck by the man's disconnection from reality. What were the Earth words Jo had used? Egomaniac. Delusional. Earth history was filled with individuals whose personal delusions of grandeur had led entire nations to ruin.

Lenore changed tactics and addressed the Green Jackets directly. "You don't have to die for this man. He's nothing. You're everything. Forget your numbers and dig deep into your minds. You're normal people just like us. You have families! You were abducted... drugged..."

She saw the startled look on Brennan's face. "Yes, Brennan. We know about the drug." She pulled a carton from her jacket and held it up. Then she looked to her right and her left, silently telling the citizens of Neworld to follow her lead. Instead of howls of anger, the people demonstrated the power of their quiet resolve and held out the antidote in outstretched hands.

"Do you hear me?" called Lenore. Do you see what we offer? Your life back. A return home to your families!"

Lenore stepped to the barrier and the chancellor roared in anger while his men sent a stream of projectiles hurtling toward her. A rock struck her head, knocking her to the ground, and a sharpened stick pierced her shoulder before the tin-pan patrol could shield her and drag her back out of range. Percy pulled the stick from her shoulder and several citizens rushed up to tend to her.

As she lay there on her back, the sky seemed to ripple and warp—she must have been on the verge of passing out.

Lenore feared that the warriors' blood had been riled and they were about to make what would be a bloody charge. She had to stop them before she passed out. "Percy! Stop them before..."

But it was too late—they had already begun to rush the barrier.

"*Stop! Fall back!*" came a commanding voice from the sky. "*Do as I say.*"

The people of Neworld halted and began to retreat, fearful of the voice from above.

"*Farther. Into the woods,*" it commanded.

Percy and his patrol carried Lenore back down the road, With some help, Lenore managed to sit up and study the sky over the fortress. There! She saw it again—a disturbance, a rippling in an otherwise even field of blue.

Fear and confusion overwhelmed the men on the walls as well. The chancellor leaned over the railing as far as he dared and looked up. Then he raced to the inside rail and searched the sky again.

"Who are you?" he screamed.

"*I am the Eagle. The Lord of Kons. The Master of Below. The Conqueror of the Rift.*"

Lenore's eyes widened and she and Percy exchanged knowing looks. "Fallon!" said Lenore.

"Bloody B," said Percy. "It is."

"*Surrender yourself, Angus Brennan. You are no longer the chancellor of Neworld.*"

Brennan snatched a sharpened stick from a Dark Man and hurled it futilely into the sky. "I will not surrender! Neworld is mine!"

"*Accept my judgment. All of you. Sit down, where you are. I warn you, sit down or you will suffer harm!*"

All the movement between the pointed tree trunks stopped, save the Dark Men on the balcony who rallied around Brennan.

Then a trail of fog fell from the sky. Lenore could see that it was emanating from the center of the disturbance. It was deliberately circling the fortress wall.

* * *

BRENNAN watched helplessly as the fog enveloped the west wall, then the south wall, and the east, his men dropping to the walkway in its wake. Then it moved toward him. He leaned over the railing and shook his fist defiantly at the approaching shroud. He was engulfed momentarily as the fog drifted over him and he could hear the Dark Men, his most loyal guards, striking the floor behind him.

Brennan was still leaning over the rail when the fog faded away. But he could no longer shake his fist. He felt so tired, he couldn't even raise his arm. He struggled to pull himself upright. His left hand slipped, he fell forward, and he tumbled over the railing.

* * *

SCREAMS erupted along the line when the chancellor's limp body plummeted from the wall and crashed onto the muddy stretch of road in front of the gate.

Lenore tried to make sense of what had just happened. Then she remembered something an avatar had once told her. When was it? Seemed like ages ago. Something about the builders having to sedate and relocate large herds of native animals. Relocate? Everyone in the fortress was asleep—everyone except the chancellor.

Lenore looked to the sky, smiled, and muttered, "That'll do."

The voice continued. *"You have four days to sort this out. At noon on the fifth day, the falls will mark the restoration of order to Neworld."*

. . .

LENORE and Percy set about the task of "sorting things out."

Percy organized his force into scouting teams to find and disarm any Green Jackets who might be wandering about or gone into hiding and take them to the nearest dock for retrieval.

Lenore's people set about dismantling the barrier in front of the gates. She assigned Jerry, Roddy, and Sandra the task of discreetly removing the chancellor's broken and muddy body and unceremoniously burying it under the damp soil and rotting leaves on the west end of the island, close to the falls—"Where," as Lenore put it, "the water and the skreel can do their work."

The gate was finally breached under the red glow of SolMinor. The people of Neworld worked tirelessly through the night, retrieving the sleeping men within the fortress. They carried each Green Jacket through the gate, gave him the antidote, and laid him on top of a wide stump to rest until he could be carted to the north wharf.

No women were found on the island: neither Aidan's mother nor Helen Hobbs. Most likely, their bones lay at the bottom of the ocean in the Below.

The Dark Men were bound and marched to the shore. They were the last to be ferried off the island.

At LowNoon on the second day, the people of Neworld left Big Island.

x~2.21

Epilogue

2.22.1

THE FLOTILLA was still at anchor in the mouth of Rift Lake—awaiting the "fifth day event," as were the more than two thousand people who lined the shore along the fisherman's wharf.

"It's almost time," said Melissa.

She and Tobey helped Sean up from the chair and supported him as he took his place at the railing of the observation deck on Conrad's cruiser. They were all there: Conrad, Bedford, Lenore, Percy, Tobey, and Sean.

As promised by the "The Eagle," the falls blossomed from the side of the Rift at noon on the fifth day. Cheers erupted from the flotilla and the shore.

Sean began to cry. "Well done, little brother. Well done."

• • •

CONRAD'S cruiser was the first to head downriver. He and his passengers had a litany of tasks to accomplish when they returned. A lot of responsibility had fallen upon their shoulders.

Bernice and Mary made it to Westport in time to see the renewal of the falls. They had come to help their fellow teamsters in Westport with the tasks Fallon had assigned them. Some of the drivers transported warrior/citizen teams to the far corners of Neworld, where they sought out the last of the Green Jackets and rounded up Dark Men. Other drivers divided the recovering young men among them and delivered them to their homes. These would be the most important deliveries any of them had ever made.

• • •

A WEEK later the new Council convened on Capitol Island to discuss what to do with the captured Dark Men, decide who would fill the seventh Council seat, and pick a new chancellor. Lenore and the entire leadership from the quarters also attended.

"The chancellor has always been a Brennan," said Averill Harper. "He has a granddaughter, does he not?"

"Yes, Aidan Brennan," said the Missus. "She happens to be my granddaughter as well. And I feel confident in declining the position for her."

"Then who?" asked Harper.

Henry Conrad said, "I think James Bedford should take up the mantle."

Bedford immediately protested. "No, no! I refuse. I'm honored, but I'm much too old."

"Can I say something?" asked Percy timidly.

"Please do," said Jean Connelly.

Percy recounted the words Lenore had spoken at the fortress gates. "She said, 'We can never let this happen again! Never again.'" Those are the words I want the new chancellor to live by. I think Lenore Bedford is the person you want."

After much discussion and some arm-twisting by her father, Lenore agreed to accept the position.

Sarah Fleming congratulated the newly chosen Chancellor Bedford and asked her what their top priority should be.

With only a moment's hesitation, Lenore said, "The truth. We must agree on a new truth that will keep us united for another two hundred years."

* * *

WORK WENT on in the quarters and plans were made to build a Basin Research Center on the ruins of the old manor house.

Almost a month after the events on Big Island, Bedford summoned the sixty remaining members of the Movement to the aviary. Even Chancellor Bedford was in attendance.

They all milled around, reminiscing about their shared experiences over the last cycle, when an alarm suddenly sounded.

EERRT! EERRT!

"Aviary door is opening."

EERRT! EERRT!

"Aviary door is opening."

A red light flashed as the door slid open, revealing a clear blue sky over the white blanket of clouds that covered the Basin. The door stopped moving and the alert silenced.

Then something large, and curved, and white rose from the clouds and glided through the door. It was practically silent. The window on its front looked black.

Finally, it came to rest. Everyone watched expectantly. Fallon and Aidan emerged from underneath the craft, and the team swarmed around them. So many hugs, tears, and questions!

Naturally, the celebration moved to the Commons courtyard. The projection of the Earth's moon was directly overhead when the old team—plus Melissa—was finally able to get some time alone. Fallon and Aidan took turns feeling Jo's baby kick and telling Sean, who still couldn't stand up totally straight, how happy they were for him and Melissa.

Fallon looked around to see if anyone else was near before leaning toward the center of the table. He beckoned the others to lean in as well.

Then, in an almost conspiratorial tone, he said, "Addie and I got some answers while we were at Eagle's Nest, and we flew over the western lands. We found where the builders relocated the native wildlife. They're amazing! But we've still got a starship to recover, an ocean to chart, and continents to visit. Who knows what we'll find? So, what do you say? Want to do some exploring?"

$$x \sim 2.22$$

CPSIA information can be obtained
at www.ICGtesting.com
Printed in the USA
LVOW13*2056080818
586372LV00011B/196/P